STAL
THE LEVELS

An addictive crime thriller full of twists

DAVID HODGES

Detective Kate Hamblin Mystery book 9

To Jerry
with Best Wishes
David Hodges

JOFFE
BOOKS

Joffe Books, London
www.joffebooks.com

First published in Great Britain in 2021

ISBN: 978-1-78931-993-4

This book is dedicated to my wife, Elizabeth, for all her love, patience and support over so many wonderful years, and to my late mother and father, whose faith that I would one day achieve my ambition as a writer remained steadfast throughout their lifetime and whose tragic passing has left a hole in my life that will never be filled.

AUTHOR'S NOTE

I served as a police officer, progressing from constable to superintendent, during thirty wonderful years, though not in the Avon and Somerset Police in whose area the action of this novel takes place. The story itself and all the characters in it are entirely fictitious and are not representative of any of the personnel I worked with. At the time of writing, there is no police station in Highbridge. This has been drawn entirely from my imagination to ensure no connection is made between any existing police station or personnel in the force. Some poetic licence has been adopted in relation to the local police structure and specific operational police procedures solely to meet the requirements of the plot. But the novel is primarily a crime thriller and does not profess to be a detailed police procedural, even though the policing background, as depicted, is broadly in accord with my own recollections of the many years I spent in the force. I trust that these small departures from fact will not spoil the reading enjoyment of any serving or retired police officers for whom I have the utmost respect.

David Hodges

BEFORE THE FACT

She left home, as usual, just after the sun had come up, driving from Marloes village to the National Trust car park at Marloes Sands. There she started her run, taking the familiar track which struck off between tall hedges towards the coast, several hundred yards later veering left across gated fields to drop down onto the narrow Pembrokeshire Coastal Path.

Once there she paused a moment, overawed, and not for the first time, by the magnificent spectacle which met her gaze. She gulped down great lungfuls of the sharp, clean morning air and listened to the melodious chorus of birdsong all around her. The frothy whitecaps were piling in from the softly glowing horizon in glorious, never-ending succession and she could taste the rich, salty tang of the sea, hear the muted thunder in the background as it broke against the cliffs. The west coast of Pembrokeshire was beautiful at any time of the year, but particularly now with the hedgerows bursting with colour, and new life emerging everywhere. It was as if the world was being reborn, and she felt privileged to be a witness to it all.

She started off again, though at a much slower pace than before, taking extra care on this stretch of rough, treacherous path which crept uneasily around the ragged cliff edge.

The sun gleamed on her shapely muscled legs and trim, bare midriff and her hair, gathered in a golden ponytail, bobbed up and down behind her, in time with the rhythm of her pounding feet.

As she ran, her mind wandered. She thought about the little island of Skomer, lying just off the coast, and the visit she had made there with her new camera the previous year. She guessed that, along with a multitude of different seabirds, including razorbills, guillemots and kittiwakes — the island would be alive with puffins about now, the pretty little birds nesting in burrows beneath the carpets of bluebells and red campion or dotting the sheltered inlets and coves as they dived for food.

Even here on the mainland, there was plenty of wildlife to capture with a camera — voles, stoats, rabbits and other furry inhabitants scurrying through the low-level vegetation that tumbled down the cliffsides, and magnificent birds of prey, like buzzards and peregrine falcons, soaring overhead or floating on the upward currents of warm air. On calm days like this it was also possible to spot seals on the strips of beach below the cliffs, and dolphins leaping and twisting in one of their legendary acrobatic displays high above the waves before returning like glistening arrows to the depths with scarcely a ripple.

As a freelance photographer living in the village, Jane Tannahill knew she had it all. But after enduring the worst few years of her life following the death of her mother, then her father's terminal cancer diagnosis and recent move to a hospice, it had taken time for the therapeutic influence of West Pembrokeshire to work its magic on her. Now, with this vibrant spring on her doorstep, and the sound of wedding bells in the offing, she had at last begun to recover her sense of purpose. A new beginning was opening up before her and with it, hope for the future.

She thought of Ray then, dark-eyed sensitive Ray, with his quick, darting glances and sharp smile. She had met him at a local art exhibition just ten months ago and had immediately fallen for the quiet landscape artist. They were made for each other, sharing a passion for the arts and classical music, both seeking a future life immersed in the natural environment around them, and both now looking forward to being joined as one in the local church in two months' time.

Her only regret was that there would be no one from her side of her dysfunctional family to share in her happiness. She had always hoped her mother would see her happily married and that her father would be the one to lead her up the aisle. But it was never going to happen now. Cruel fate had seen to that. There was no chance that either of her siblings would be there either. Bad brother Frank was on the run from the police after stabbing someone at a local pub and was believed to be somewhere abroad. As for older sister, Melanie, there was no way she was going to come all the way from London for the big day. They had never really hit it off and Jane had not had any real contact with her since Melanie had moved out, apart from a couple of occasions when she had come back to visit their father in the hospice. All in all, her life had been a bit of a mess up until now and she saw her forthcoming union as her first real opportunity to find happiness.

Then, abruptly, she had to refocus her mind on seeing another runner coming towards her as she rounded a bend in the path. He or she was wearing jeans and a hoodie, so she couldn't tell whether it was a man or a woman. But either way, she was surprised to see a like soul on the coastal path at such an hour. Usually, she had this stretch of it to herself until well after breakfast. This particular runner was certainly not hanging about either.

Slowing even more, as the path was not really wide enough for two abreast, she frowned. The approaching figure did not appear to be slackening pace. They had their head down, maybe to avoid tripping on the path or because they were plugged into some music, and it occurred to her that they probably hadn't even seen her.

Finally, she stopped altogether and seeing that the oncoming figure was hugging the fence and grassy bank on her left, she politely moved to the outward side of the path to wait for them to pass, throwing a quick uneasy glance at the sea below as she did so. The drop was almost sheer at this point, the slate-grey cliff face completely exposed, all the way down to a litter of fallen rock, and for some unaccountable reason, she shivered.

Then, looking back up at the path, she saw to her consternation that the oncoming runner was just feet away now and was still showing no sign of slowing down.

'Watch out!' she shouted in alarm. 'Look where you're going.'

But they didn't, and those were the last words Jane Tannahill ever uttered. At the last minute, the figure did raise their head, so must have seen her. But instead of taking evasive action, they seemed to deliberately veer even further over to her side of the path, slamming into her and knocking her completely off balance. In one brief second, she was gone, propelled right over the edge of the cliff, her hands desperately clutching at empty air and her screams merging with the high-pitched cries of the wheeling gulls, before she hit the rocks below with sickening force, her dream of a new life shattered along with almost every bone in her body.

* * *

With the assistance of the coastguard, the local police recovered Jane's broken body from the rocks below the cliff late that afternoon after it was spotted by a couple of passing walkers.

'Who was she?' the coastguard queried as her body was taken away.

Huw Roberts, the local police sergeant, grunted. 'Jane Tannahill,' he replied and peered over the cliff edge. 'Used to run along here most mornings. Knew her well. Usually waved if she saw me about. Lived in the village. Local photographer. Looks like the poor kid must have slipped.'

The other man sighed. 'Easily done on these paths. One wrong step and—' he shrugged — '*finito.*'

The policeman grunted again. 'Was getting married in a couple of months. I'll have to break the news to her fiancé and get him to ID the body. Lives over in Dale apparently.'

The coastguard made a face. 'You coppers get all the good jobs, don't you?' he said drily, adding, 'No other relatives locally then?'

The policeman rubbed his chin. 'Her dad's in a hospice down the road on the way out with cancer, and her mum passed away a while back. She has a brother, Frank, but he won't show his face around here. He's on the run, with a warrant out on him for GBH. As for the older sister, Melanie, they say she lives somewhere in London. Comes back to the area on the odd occasion but just to see her dad, and that's about it.'

'Poor kid hasn't had the best of things in her life then, has she?'

'Well, you know what we say in this job, "life's a bitch and then you die."'

'Some earlier than others, it seems.' The coastguard hesitated, then looked directly at the policeman. 'I suppose it *was* an accident? Couldn't have been anything else, could it?'

The other frowned. 'Now don't you go complicating things, Wynn Davis. Poor kid had an accident, that's all, and she won't be the last one on these cliffs neither. Tripped and fell, nothing more.'

Davis gave a rueful smile. 'I 'spect you're right.'

'I'm always right. Now, how's about a crafty pint down the local before I pop over to Dale?'

CHAPTER 1

Tamara Callaghan sat back in her padded swivel chair and swung it from side to side. For a few minutes she just sat there contemplating, without seeing a fly on her computer screen, her finely chiselled features puckered in concentration as she reviewed what she had just typed.

Finally, she released her breath in a snort of irritation and swept the fly off the screen with a flick of her beautifully manicured fingers.

'Bollocks!' she said with emphasis. 'Absolute bollocks!'

Who said the life of a professional crime novelist was easy? Sitting at a bloody computer hour after hour, trying to turn a first draft of drivel into something resembling a proper manuscript could be torture. Yet she had been doing it for quite a few years now and the rewards had been well worth the eyestrain, headaches and frayed nerves that seemed to afflict her on a permanent basis.

The undeniable fact was that murder sold books. The reading public could not get enough of it, and as a bestselling crime novelist, it had given her a lifestyle many would have — and she chuckled as she selected a cigarette from a walnut box on her desk — died for. Now, on her eighth Detective Inspector Rupert Dixon investigation, the only problem she faced, in common with most writers of series crime fiction, was coming up with something new and not lapsing into predictable formular writing.

With a resigned sigh, she ran both hands through her shoulder-length black hair, the rich glossy colour courtesy of Lucienne's Beauty Parlour in Taunton. And it had cost enough, hadn't it? As had the two-hour massage, facial and visit to the nail bar. She smiled. Well, a girl had to keep up appearances, didn't she? Especially one in her position. And having just turned forty-three, she needed to take extra care of herself.

Finishing the glass of expensive red wine standing to one side of her laptop, she stood up, glanced at her watch and frowned. Better return Spencer's phone call before it got too late. She couldn't put it off any longer or he would go into a sulk. Spencer Little was a damned good agent, though she seldom let him know it. He had secured some brilliant contracts for her, but the would-be Don Juan of Somerset could be a pain at times. She knew the suave, smooth-talking ladies' man, with his lazy blue eyes and silky blond hair, fancied her, and he would use any excuse to drop in, ostensibly to "see how the manuscript is going". But though keeping him sweet might be the sensible thing to do, there was no way this charismatic gigolo was going to get into her knickers.

'Darling,' she breathed into the receiver. 'Sorry I'm a bit late. So busy with the new book, you know.'

There was a discernible note of irritation in Little's voice when he answered. He didn't like being kept waiting. It bruised his ego.

'It was just a courtesy call, old love,' he said. 'Wondered how the manuscript was coming along. Happy to pop over and take a look at it if you like. No bother.'

She feigned a yawn. 'Oh, can we leave it tonight, Spence? I've a bloody awful headache and I thought I'd turn in early.'

'Got a nice bottle of bubbly here if you're interested? Good for headaches, that is.'

She made a face. 'No, honestly, darling. Take a rain check on that if it's all the same to you. Sweet of you though.'

'We do have a few things to discuss, Tam. I've had Dick Grey from the publishers on to me again asking when he can expect to see the first draft of the MS, and he's getting a bit twitchy about the delay. Then there's the book-signing talk at Highbridge Library coming up. We need to make sure we've got everything covered there.'

'You worry too much, Spence. The talk will be fine. But maybe we should get together tomorrow for a chat about the new novel.'

'Tomorrow? What time?'

'Give me a ring about ten and we'll fix something up—' She broke off. 'Oh, no, I almost forgot. I'm seeing my shrink at eleven.'

'Your *shrink*?'

''Fraid so. It's the fashion now, darling, from across the pond. Everyone has a psychiatrist these days. Listen, I'll ring you sometime over the weekend and we'll get together then. Ciao.'

Before he could protest any further, she rang off.

Smiling, she selected a cigarette from a walnut box on her desk, lit up and left her study, walking barefoot along the hallway to the living room. Her feet sank into the thick pile carpet as she crossed the room to the glass doors leading onto the patio and slid one open.

The moon had just emerged in a vault of glittering jewels. The low stone walls of the patio blazed pure white beneath its cold, enigmatic stare and the woodland encircling the big house cast long shadows out across the lawn and driveway.

It was a warm night, but clad in just a short, silk nightdress, she shivered slightly, sensing a slight, underlying chill in the air. A rabbit raced across the grass and disappeared among the trees, and she glimpsed a dark winged shape float past her like a ghost. Probably an owl. The marshy wilderness around the property, with its patches of wet woodland and peat bogs, criss-crossed by a latticework of ditches — or rhynes, as they were called in this part of the world — was noted for its wildlife, particularly birds. Tamara wasn't that interested in either flora or fauna. The truth was, she found flowers a bore and all the furry, feathered things that inhabited the woods, fields or riverbanks quite creepy. But living in this remote part of the Somerset Levels, it was to be expected, and it was a small price to pay for the privacy she demanded as an absolute priority.

She hated publicity and although she was happy to do book signings, she rarely gave interviews, except on the radio, and she refused to have her picture or personal details posted on the jackets of her books or in review material. 'I want my books to do the talking,' she'd always told Spencer. 'Who I am and where I live is totally irrelevant and I regard that sort of publicity as an intrusion.'

Despite protesting that self-promotion was vital in achieving the best sales as a writer, he had got nowhere, but he'd secretly admired what seemed to him to be a complete lack of ego on her part and that made him desire her even more. Not that, unbeknown to him, he was ever likely to get anywhere in that quarter.

Drawing on her cigarette, she turned to go back inside, and it was as she did so that she saw the figure. At first it was just a shadow on the edge of the treeline, but then it took shape and became a man — a man who stepped out brazenly into the full glare of the moonlight. His sudden appearance on her property was shock enough, but what made it even worse was the fact that he was wearing some kind of black hood, which covered his head and face, and he was otherwise totally naked.

With a gasp, she dropped her cigarette and fled back into the living room, slamming and locking the patio door behind her. And she was only just in time. The next instant he was on the patio, pressing his white, hairless body up against the door, his dark eyes studying her fixedly through slits in the hood.

* * *

9

Detective Sergeant Kate Lewis was driving back from a CID meeting in Bridgwater when she got the call on her radio. As usual, the meeting had ended in a "three-line whip" get-together with colleagues in the police club and also as usual, things had gone on for far too long. Kate had only had a couple of glasses of red wine but following a full shift at Highbridge police station before the meeting, she was looking forward to a night crashed in front of the TV with her detective constable husband, Hayden.

But it was not to be. Twenty minutes after the radio call, she met up with a couple of uniformed patrol officers at the big, ivy-clad house in an isolated part of the Somerset Levels, bearing the curious name of "*Scribbler's Halt*" on a plaque outside. The pair were waiting for her beside a grey Volvo XC90 parked by a lighted front porch. There was no one else in evidence, although a warm yellow light penetrated curtains drawn across double glass doors a few yards beyond, partially illuminating a stone-flagged patio. Someone was at home.

'So, what have we got, Les?' she asked testily, smoothing her long auburn hair back off her face. She stared around her at the heavily wooded grounds. 'Control said an intruder.'

Sergeant Les Honeywell rubbed his chin. 'Sounds more like a flasher to me, Kate,' he said, nodding towards the house, which was lit up from end to end. 'Complainant says a naked bloke wearing some sort of hood came out of the woods when she was standing on the patio and chased her indoors.'

'And she's actually *complaining*,' his colleague added with a laugh.

Kate's sharp blue eyes fastened on him coldly and the laugh abruptly died. 'What time was this?'

'About nine apparently. As you can see, it's a full moon tonight, so she could see him quite clearly.'

'And I assume you didn't clock anyone as you arrived?'

The sergeant shook his head. 'We had a look around as best we could, but he was obviously long gone.'

'Did you call for a dog?'

'Yeah, but there's only one dog mobile on tonight and he's at a robbery scene near Wells.'

'Any thoughts?'

He shrugged. 'Not really. Pervs are everywhere nowadays, aren't they? But we've had a spate of this kind of thing over the past month, as you probably know already.'

She nodded. 'Couple at Woolavington, two in the Wedmore area and another one at Meare. If it's the same guy, he certainly gets about a bit.'

'Sounds like the same one. From what I've heard, in all the cases he's been wearing this black hood. Don't know what he gets out of doing something like that, I must say.'

She smiled grimly. 'Probably gets some sort of a kick out of scaring his victims half to death, rather than just exposing himself to them.'

Honeywell sighed. 'Whatever turns you on, I suppose. He certainly put the wind up this lady and that's a fact.'

'Not surprising under the circumstances, is it? Where is she now?'

'Having a stiff drink inside. I said you'd be having a word with her. But don't expect much cooperation. She refuses to make a statement and wants her name kept out of it all. Says she can't afford the publicity.'

'Who is she then? Someone special?'

'You'll know when I mention her name.'

'Oh?'

'Tamara Callaghan.'

Kate shook her head. 'So?'

Honeywell looked dumbfounded. 'Surely you've heard of her. She's that bestselling crime novelist.'

Kate grunted. 'Sorry, Les, I don't read many crime novels. I'm too busy dealing with the real thing.'

* * *

Kate found Tamara Callaghan sitting on a large settee in the living room, a glass of red wine in one hand and a cigarette

11

in the other. Her face was very pale and the hand holding the cigarette was trembling slightly.

She forced a smile, but her eyes seemed hooded and reflective.

'Ah, you are the detective sergeant I was told about,' she said, more as a statement than a question. 'Do have a seat, Miss, er—'

Kate perched herself on an armchair opposite. 'Kate Lewis, Miss Callaghan. Highbridge CID.'

Callaghan nodded and Kate could feel her eyes boring into her, sizing her up — no longer reflective but sharp and perceptive.

'Well, Kate Lewis,' she went on, 'this was a rum do and no mistake.'

It was a strange choice of words and Kate raised an eyebrow.

'Not a very nice experience, I'm sure,' she said. 'Can you tell me what happened?'

Callaghan shrugged and drew on her cigarette. 'Not that much to tell. I was standing on my patio when this naked man, wearing a sort of black hood, appeared on the lawn and chased me indoors. I managed to lock the patio door behind me, so he couldn't get in. Then he proceeded to press up against the glass, obviously enjoying every minute of his exhibition — dirty little sod. I rang the police but by the time they arrived, he had gone.'

Kate hesitated. 'Nothing you can remember about him that might help us to find him?' She realized after she'd asked the question how stupid it must have sounded under the circumstances.

Callaghan laughed, a noticeable glint in her eyes. 'Well, he wasn't very well endowed, I can tell you that. If I were him, I wouldn't bother trying to flash my privates at anyone.'

Kate reddened. 'Sorry. Silly question.'

'Yes,' Callaghan said, 'it was rather, wasn't it? But never mind. It cheered me up anyway.' She stubbed out her cigarette in an ashtray and took a sip of her red wine. 'Would you like a drink, Sergeant? It's an excellent vintage.'

Kate shook her head. 'Thank you, but not on duty, I'm afraid,' adding, 'I gather from my colleagues that you are reluctant to make a statement about the incident.'

'Not reluctant, Sergeant, I absolutely refuse. I will not be prepared to attend an ID parade or go to court either if you catch this horrible little pervert.'

'Can I at least arrange for one of our scenes of crime officers to pop over here to do a forensic examination of the patio area? The offender may have left fingerprints on the glass or traces of his, er, DNA in the vicinity.'

'DNA traces? Elegantly put, Sergeant, though I don't blush easily, so you need have no worries on that score. But again, the answer is absolutely not. I am quite sure this creature didn't get to the orgasmic stage you are suggesting in the time he was here.'

Kate was blunt. 'So, why did you call us in the first place, if you don't mind my asking?'

Callaghan's eyes narrowed and she gave a frosty smile.

'I always thought the police were here to protect the public against criminals, Sergeant. Perhaps I was wrong.'

The barb hit home. Kate made a grimace, and she inwardly rebuked herself for allowing her irritation over Callaghan's uncooperative stance to show itself so markedly. What was it she had been told by her tutor constable during her probation all those years ago? Oh yes, "engage brain before operating mouth." Pity she hadn't remembered that advice in time.

'No, you're not wrong, Miss Callaghan, and you can be assured that we will do all we can to catch this offender. But to convict anyone we need evidence. If a witness is not prepared to substantiate an allegation in writing or to agree to support a prosecution, and we have no access to forensic material, our hands are somewhat tied.'

Callaghan laughed, a rich, husky sound. 'Touché, Sergeant. But I'm afraid that's the way it is. You must understand that as a writer of hard-nosed crime fiction, I would end up as an absolute laughing stock if it were to become known that I had become the target of — of a flasher.'

Kate shrugged and stood up. 'Okay, Miss Callaghan. I have to respect your wishes and I will, of course, arrange for police patrols to give your house passing attention, but beyond that, I'm afraid there's not a lot we can do.'

Callaghan nodded and held out a hand. 'Fully appreciate that, Sergeant, and I hope we haven't got off on the wrong foot. Thanks for coming anyway.'

Kate shook her hand. 'No problem.' On the way out, she half turned. 'Maybe I should read one of your novels now I've met you. Can you suggest one for me to try?'

Callaghan's eyes sparkled. 'I'll do better than that, Sergeant. I am holding a talk and book-signing event tomorrow at Highbridge Library. My agent wants me to cash in on the fact that my books are set in this locality — might sell a few more, apparently. Why don't you come along? Seven-thirty start.'

Kate smiled and took the small invitation card the other had picked up off her coffee table. 'I might just do that.' She glanced at the card, adding with a chuckle, 'I've always wondered what it takes to become a writer.'

'You'd be surprised,' Callaghan retorted. 'Very surprised indeed.'

CHAPTER 2

The little thatched cottage on the edge of the village of Burtle where Kate lived with detective husband, Hayden, was in virtual darkness when she got home at just after nine. But the bright porch light and the suffused glow issuing through the thick curtains drawn across the living room window was welcome enough, and she smiled as she put her key in the door and went in.

Hayden was not a pretty sight. His large overweight figure was sprawled across the settee, one arm over the edge, almost touching an overturned wine glass and his mouth sagging open in a long, drawn-out snore. The congealed remains of what looked like some sort of takeaway meal leered from the coffee table and the bottle of red wine beside it appeared to be almost empty.

Shaking her head in resignation, Kate dumped her anorak and mobile in an armchair and stood there for a few moments studying the love of her life, noting that his trousers were undone to allow his ample stomach more freedom to expand and that there was a large red stain down his shirt front, which suggested he had either been stabbed or, more likely, that he had spilled some of the wine down himself before the rest went over the carpet when he knocked his glass over.

'What *do* I do with you?' she murmured and shook her head again.

She had no illusions about the man she had married and sometimes she just couldn't fathom what she saw in him. The complete antithesis of the popular perception of a police officer, he was, as the present state of him suggested, neither the muscular tough guy able to take on all-comers, nor the suave ladies' man radiating wicked charm and sex appeal that many women went for. Clever, yes, possessed of a high IQ and first-class honours degrees in history and philosophy, with a keen analytical mind that had aided her in solving several criminal cases. But he was so laid-back that he was virtually horizontal — a complete waste of a brain as one of his colleagues had once put it — and although he liked to describe himself as an eccentric free spirit, Kate preferred instead to call him a lazy, untidy, overweight bum. On top of this, he could be extremely obstinate when the mood took him and he came across as infuriatingly pompous at times, reflecting his insular public-school background, typified by his plum-in-the-mouth way of speaking.

Yet it was also true to say that he was intensely loyal, good-natured and kind to the vulnerable and those he considered to have been unfairly treated, exhibiting the sort of old-fashioned, moral values that were regarded by much of modern society as well past their sell-by date, including an indignant aversion to the use of foul language, especially by women. His absolute St Bernard-like devotion to Kate was plain for all to see and for her part, although at times her comments to him could be quite brusque, even caustic, her love for her "big lump" or "fat man", as she often called him, had remained undiminished since the day they tied the knot.

Now, kicking off her trainers, she crept over to her husband, a mischievous grin on her freckled face, and bent close to his ear. 'Fire!' she shouted, then jumped back with a shriek of laughter as he erupted from the settee in a panic, kicking the wine glass across the room and shouting wildly and incoherently as he stared around him in a state of total confusion, the fingers of one hand buried in his unruly thatch of blond hair.

'I say,' he protested, his vision finally adjusting and fastening on his other half standing a few feet away. 'I could have had a heart attack!'

'After the amount you seem to have drunk, I'm surprised you were able to wake up at all,' she retorted.

'The bottle was only half full to start with,' he countered defensively, 'and I've had a busy day.'

She dropped onto the settee he had so quickly vacated. 'Oh you poor little man,' she mocked. 'I thought you'd enjoy interviewing all those young bits of stuff.'

He frowned. 'It was highly embarrassing actually,' he said. 'Going into intimate details about all that happened was quite unpleasant.'

'Didn't you have DC Purewal with you, as I instructed?'

He nodded. 'Yes, Indrani was there, and she was a big help, but it was still embarrassing.'

She sighed. 'It's true what poor old DI Roscoe said at his farewell do, isn't it, Hayd? You'll never make a copper as long as you've got a hole in your arse.'

He bristled angrily. 'Will you not be so crude, Kate. You know how I hate that sort of thing coming from you.'

She chuckled, unabashed. 'As long as all that intimate stuff didn't give you any naughty ideas of your own. Now, how about getting me a glass of red and we'll swap notes. Fresh bottle, please.'

He returned, still scowling, as she was clearing the remains of his meal from the coffee table, and she handed him the dirty crockery in exchange for the full glass of wine.

'Right,' she said from the corner of the settee when he came back again. 'What have we got?'

He perched on the edge of the armchair opposite, sweeping her anorak and mobile out of the way. 'Do we have to go into all this now? We're off duty, for heaven's sake.'

She sipped some wine and set her glass down on the coffee table.

'For your information,' she said, 'I was called to another flasher job on the way home from the CID meeting. Some local author, name of Tamara Callaghan—'

'What, the crime novelist?'

Kate raised an eyebrow. 'You've heard of her then?'

'Of course. She's a bestselling author. Written seven or eight novels. Very good too. They feature a Detective Inspector Rupert Dixon.'

'Seems I've led a sheltered life. I'd never heard of her until tonight.'

He looked smug. 'Well, you don't read much fiction, do you? And I met her once when she came to the nick for some police procedural info. It was ages ago. Must have been four or five years now, just after she arrived here.'

'Where from?'

He shrugged. 'Haven't the faintest. I hear she's a very private person.'

'You can say that again. She wasn't prepared to make a statement or support any prosecution.'

'Not surprised. It was the same with a couple of the women Indrani and I interviewed today, though I suspect their reason was mainly fear of a reprisal.'

'So, you got nothing?'

He shook his head. 'Not nothing. Two of the women gave statements and descriptions, but as the flasher was naked at the time and wearing a black hood, there was not a lot to describe.'

Another chuckle from Kate. 'Oh, I don't know. There must have been *some* distinctive feature they could have come up with?'

He scowled again, ignoring the innuendo. 'Can we just leave all this tonight? We are going to have to brief the DI in the morning anyway.'

Kate grinned again. 'You're probably right. So, what shall we do for the rest of the evening?'

He threw her a quick glance, then looked away again. 'Well, there's a good late-night film on in an hour. We could watch that and finish the bottle of wine.'

She drained her glass and studied him through half-closed eyes. 'Oh, I've got a much better idea, Hayd,' she said. 'Unless you happen to have a headache?'

* * *

Jason Spindler came home just after eleven. His father was waiting for him.

'Where the hell have you been at this time of night?' Hector demanded, having emerged from the living room in a couple of strides when he heard the key turn in the lock on the front door. 'Up to your usual dirty tricks, were you?'

Jason stood there quietly, head down as usual, studying the hall carpet with a faint smirk on his thin, pasty face. He had hoped to creep in and up to his room without being noticed, but this time he had been well and truly caught out.

'Well?' the big, red-faced farmer snarled. 'Answer the bloody question.'

Jason threw him a quick glance, then looked down once more, as he always did. 'Went for a walk,' he muttered. 'No law against it, is there?'

The meathook of a hand struck him across the side of the head, almost knocking him off balance.

'Don't give me that, you dirty little pervert!' Hector shouted. 'I've about had it with you. I'm just glad your mother is no longer alive to see how you turned out.'

Jason tried to hold back the tears and treated him to another furtive glance. 'So am I,' he mumbled.

'Look at me,' his father shouted. 'Why can't you act like a man instead of behaving like some girlie wimp?'

There was no answer. Hector ran a despairing hand across his bald, freckled scalp. 'What is it with you? Didn't you get enough of clink before? If the police catch you a third time, me lad, it won't be six months you'll get but real time inside with all the other perverts.'

'I — I said I went for a walk, that's all,' Jason repeated stubbornly. 'I needed some fresh air.'

'A walk? Where?'

'Just around.'

'Around where? At it again, were you? Peering through windows and exposing yourself to some unfortunate woman?'

'I wasn't *at* anything. I was just walking.'

'Yeah, and I'm the Archbishop of Canterbury.'

There was no answer. Hector looked his son up and down for a few seconds, contempt written into his expression.

'You're a total disgrace,' he grated. 'I'm a God-fearing man and I've worked hard all my life. To think that a worthless creep like you is all I've got to show for it.'

'Can I go up now?' Jason asked. 'I want to go to bed.'

Hector snorted. 'What? To drool over those dirty mags I found in your drawer today, eh? Well, for your information, they're not there anymore. I burned them.'

Jason flushed angrily. 'You've no right—'

Hector thrust his face close to his. 'No right?' he yelled. 'I've got every right. And I'm telling you now, if you end up in trouble again, you can find somewhere else to live. I wash my hands of you.'

Then he turned on his heel and stomped off down the hallway, kicking out at a black cat which appeared suddenly through the kitchen doorway.

Up in his small bedroom, Jason locked the door, pulled the curtains across and checked the drawer of the corner chest. It was empty. So, the old bastard *had* taken his mags then. Jason swore under his breath. Friggin' liberty! Then he smirked again and bent down to lift the mattress on the single bed. His other collection of pornographic magazines was still there. 'Up yours, you old fart,' he murmured with a sneer. Letting the mattress fall back into place, he threw himself onto the bed and lay there with his hands behind his head, staring up at the ceiling.

He knew there was something wrong with him, that he was weird. He didn't need a shrink to tell him that. His father had called him a sick freak enough times already, and it was certainly true that he was not much to look at. In fact, he was a bit of an insipid, non-person really — thin, pasty-faced, with pointed features, hardly any chin and sparse, black hair, just like bloody Pinocchio. Small wonder that, with his looks and introverted personality, he had always found relationships difficult — especially where girls were concerned.

Sex in particular was a non-starter, even with the ugliest cow in town, which was hardly surprising when he couldn't even pluck up the courage to ask a woman out, let alone try kissing or fondling one. But that didn't mean he wasn't plagued by the same thoughts and urges as every other young, hot-blooded male. He just couldn't satisfy those urges in the normal way, so he was reduced to secretly watching the women and fantasizing — particularly when they were in the bedroom or taking a shower — then openly abusing himself in front of them as a sort of compensation for the real thing. The hood had been necessary to hide his identity, of course, but it served another purpose too. Frightening his victims enhanced the experience. When they screamed or ran away, it gave him a sense of power and stimulated his libido.

He tugged the hood out of his pocket and spread it out on one knee, sticking his fingers through the eyeholes and gloating over it.

That last woman had been one of the best. He'd seen her before, though she hadn't seen him then. She'd been walking about the house stark naked with all the lights on and the curtains not even pulled back. She must have thought she couldn't be seen by anyone from the road in that big house with its wooded grounds. How wrong she was. That had really got him going and encouraged him to make his return visit. Okay, so she must have been in her forties, but she was in very good nick and obviously looked after herself. He'd heard locally that she was a writer. Well, she could write him up any time she liked.

Then he frowned. He knew he would have to go back — he couldn't help himself — but he would have to be careful. He'd seen the coppers arrive as he'd sneaked away. The thought of getting caught and doing more time terrified him, but he just couldn't stop doing what he did. It was a sort of compulsion. Still, maybe he should give that particular woman a miss for a while, just in case. After all, there were plenty of others about, weren't there?

Rolling off the bed, he lifted the mattress again and pulled out one of his magazines. Then he lay back on the bed and went through it cover to cover, thinking and imagining . . .

CHAPTER 3

Kate and Hayden were late arriving at Highbridge police station the following morning. Kate saw that the dapper head of CID, Acting Detective Inspector Des Percival, was already ensconced behind his desk in the glass-panelled office at the end of the room. He was on the telephone and didn't look too pleased when Kate walked in after a peremptory knock on the half-closed door. Irritably, he waved her to a chair opposite. 'Understood, guv,' he murmured in a mark- edly conciliatory tone. 'Of course, whatever it takes.' Then, replacing the receiver, he stared at Kate with unconcealed hostility.

Percival had been given temporary promotion to depart- mental DI until a substantive replacement could be found, and although deep down Kate still resented his appointment after he had pipped her at the post for the same job, she quite liked this athletic, charismatic flier, with his silky, blond hair, neatly trimmed moustache and immaculate appearance. In short, as she had once said of him to colleagues, 'What is there not to like?' Percival may have been destined for much higher rank, but he lacked the arrogance of his contemporar- ies. He was a gentleman and as a rule, very easy to work with, which was a pleasant change from the previous old-school incumbent, the late Ted Roscoe, who had been about as basic as it was possible to be. But the new DI was still very much finding his feet and he could become quite testy at times when under stress, which was evidently the case now.

'So, what do you call this, Kate?' he snapped, his blue eyes hard and angry. He consulted his gold watch. 'It's half-past nine. Having a lie-in, were you?'

Kate threw a scathing glance at Hayden through the glass partition as he dropped guiltily onto a plastic chair in front of his desk. 'Sorry, Des,' she said tightly. 'It won't happen again.'

He grunted, plainly still far from happy but driven by the need to move on. 'For your information, that was the DCI on the blower, and he was not in the best of moods. The super has torn into him over our failure to catch this bloody flasher.'

Kate nodded. Toby Ricketts didn't take criticism easily. A career policeman with his gaze set on the next rank, everything he did was calculated to improve his standing with the top brass, and he was not someone who could be relied upon to shoulder the blame if anything went wrong, especially if he saw it as sullying his own reputation. She could well imagine the icy blast that had come down the line to the unfortunate Percival, and she was glad he was in the firing line rather than herself.

'The perv might be just a minor offender in the scheme of things,' Percival continued, 'and ordinarily, we would have left the whole business to uniform to deal with, but he's become a real pain in the arse. I make it five instances of indecent exposure so far, and the press are having a field day.'

He pushed a folded newspaper across the table towards her and sat there for a moment, waiting for a reaction.

She disappointed him by ignoring the paper altogether. 'If that's the local rag, they need to catch up,' she said. 'It's six now. I was called to another complaint last night. Local crime novelist, Tamara Callaghan.'

'What, *the* Tamara Callaghan?' he exclaimed. 'Detective Inspector Rupert Dixon and all that?'

Kate scowled. Was she the only person in the force who hadn't heard of the bloody woman? Maybe she moved in the wrong circles.

'The same,' she replied tartly.

He grimaced. 'Just the news I didn't want,' he said, then waved a hand wearily in her direction. 'Okay, I suppose you'd better tell me all about it.'

When Kate had finished, he slumped back in his chair, slipping both hands down inside the back of his trousers in the characteristic, though curious, mannerism he adopted in moments of stress.

'Persistent pervert, isn't he?' he observed drily. 'What do we know about him?'

Kate frowned. 'Not that much actually. All the complainants are agreed that he is a white male, possibly in the twenty to twenty-five age group, of very thin build — one said almost skeletal, with a prominent ribcage — and very agile. He wears a black hood, completely covering his head and face, and is totally naked, apart from black-and-white trainers.'

'What about his MO? Is he just a flasher or is there more to it?'

'It varies. He has so far exposed himself to both young and middle-aged women through the windows of their homes, either after dark or just before, and once to a woman walking her dog in woodland. Four of the victims have said he masturbated in front of them, but the others say he simply exposed himself, then ran off.'

'Have we examined any of the scenes forensically? If he abused himself, he is likely to have left traces of semen or other DNA behind.'

'The first cases were handled by uniform before we took the investigation over and they didn't think of calling out SOCO for such minor offences. Of the others, heavy rain after the incidents put paid to that consideration, and the complainant I interviewed last night — the novelist — absolutely refused to cooperate.'

'Brilliant! I sometimes wonder why we bother to try and help people. So, what is the geographical reach of our nasty little perv?'

'As far as we know, he has stuck to a limited part of the Levels, encompassing the villages of Wedmore, Bason Bridge, Woolavington and Westhay, which suggests that he is a local man. But at the same time, it also means he probably knows his territory well — including all the droves, byways and back lanes — so, feeling his collar is not going to be easy.'

'Surely, he must have transport of some sort, though — maybe a car or a motorbike. It isn't a massive area, but it would be difficult for him to get around it on foot and safely back home before running into a police patrol.'

She shrugged. 'He could do it all on a bicycle — especially as the offences have been spread out over several weeks, which means he isn't pushed for time in getting from one place to another. Maybe he just wanders about the area and picks somewhere at random when he feels the urge and there's no real planning behind his activities.'

'But with all the press coverage he has received, surely someone must know or suspect who he is? I mean, the communities around here are quite tight, aren't they?'

'If someone *is* wise to his ID, they haven't come forward yet, and the fact that he is currently in all the papers, and everyone must know he is out there and be watching for him doesn't seem to deter him in the slightest. Maybe he just can't help himself.'

'You say it's likely our man is local. So, what about PNC and local records? Have we done a trawl to see if it turns up any likely merchants with pre-cons for indecency?'

She nodded. 'All in hand. Hayd and I will be looking at a few possible faces this morning.'

He sighed and straightened up in the chair, jerking his hands out of the back of his trousers.

'Right, well I'd better let you get on with that, hadn't I? Just keep me in the picture, will you?'

'And what about all the other jobs piling up in my tray? They won't just disappear.'

He made a face. 'Have to fit them in when you can, I'm afraid. It seems naked flashers have priority.'

* * *

'So, what did he say?' Hayden asked when Kate left Percival's office and strode over to her desk.

Kate treated him to a critical glance. 'He wasn't best pleased that we were late in.'

He hesitated. 'What did you tell him?'

Kate pulled a bulky A4 envelope out of her tray and peered at the contents for a second.

'I told him the lazy sod I share a bed with wouldn't get up,' she lied.

He gaped. 'You said that to him? I say, that was a bit strong.'

She raised an eyebrow. 'Maybe, but it was true, wasn't it? You *are* a lazy sod, and you *didn't* get up when you were supposed to. Which is precisely why we were late. End of.'

'You never seem to understand,' he protested. 'I need my rest. It's an inherited thing. Runs in the family — and anyway, it was your fault. You, er, kept me up late, not the other way about. It deprived me of at least two hours of my normal eight hours' sleep.'

'You didn't enjoy our little romp then?'

He threw a quick glance around him. 'Don't talk like that. Someone might hear you.'

Kate chuckled. 'They have no idea what a wicked ram you are, do they, Hayd? Perhaps I should tell them, eh? Give them the full SP on your sexual proclivities?'

He stepped away from her, darting more apprehensive glances about the room. 'Just stop it, will you?' he hissed through his teeth. 'You're embarrassing me.'

A couple of the other detectives looked up from their desks, curious as to what had so upset Hayden.

Kate laughed again and slapped him across the chest with the bulky A4 envelope.

'Calm down, fat man,' she said. 'I won't tell them if you don't. Now come on, we've got work to do.'

Twenty minutes later they were sitting with steaming coffees at a desk in a vacant interview room downstairs. The papers from the A4 envelope were spread out on the table in front of them and Hayden had been restored to happiness with an extra-large Chelsea bun, now on a plate beside him.

'Dave Gort,' Kate said, referring to the station's local intelligence officer, or LIO, 'has spent quite a bit of time pulling these D/Fs off PNC.' She tapped one of the descriptive files in front of her. 'They're all CROs living in our area with pre-cons for indecency. We need to go through them and see if anyone fits the bill for our flasher. We're looking for a thin male, twenty to twenty-five years, living east of the M5 and to ensure we don't miss any possibles, within an area bounded by the A38, A39, and A371, though I reckon he will actually be living somewhere much closer to the crime scenes. Disregard anyone who doesn't fall within these criteria. I'll take one pile and you the other — but do try not to get your Chelsea bun over any of the pages, eh?'

He frowned at her. 'What a poor opinion you seem to have of me, old girl.'

She grinned. 'Joke, Hayd, just a joke — and if it's any consolation to you, you'll always be my man of the moment and I can't think of anyone else I would rather be with than good old Hayd — even though he's a lazy, untidy, pompous arsehole.'

He frowned. 'Was that supposed to be some kind of compliment?'

Her grin broadened. 'Sort of, fat man. Now eat your bun.'

An hour later, the two piles of computer printouts had been whittled right down and they were left with just three possibles between them. Kate went through all three a second time, then handed them to Hayden. 'What do you think?' she asked.

A few minutes later, they were both agreed on two suspects.

'Lunch first,' Kate announced to Hayden's obvious delight, 'and then I think we'll go a-visiting.'

* * *

The old, grey bungalow stood on a small plot of rotting vegetables and scrub just outside Westhay. Hayden threw Kate a dubious look as they came to a halt beside the open gateway, and she switched off the engine of the CID car.

'The residence of one Douglas Moore,' he said, referring to the D/F on his lap. 'Currently on licence from stir, following release after serving ten years for rape and GBH. Long history of indecent exposure, indecent assault and circulation of child pornography prior to his rape conviction. Not a nice man at all.'

Kate grunted. 'Are any of them?'

He frowned. 'Not a very prepossessing place either, is it? I doubt that we'll receive much of a welcome.'

'He's on licence, Hayd,' Kate reminded him, throwing open the driver's door. 'If he steps out of line with us, he'll be back inside, and he knows it.'

'Maybe he's not at home,' Hayden said hopefully.

But he was.

'What do you want?' a deep voice growled from the gloom when Kate knocked on the half-open door of the bungalow.

There was movement inside and a tall, thin figure with lank ginger hair materialized in the doorway. Pale blue eyes studied the two detectives and a sneer spread across the pock-marked, stubbled chin.

'So, it's the cops come visitin', is it?'

'How did you know who we were?' Hayden asked.

The man emitted a hard, unamused laugh and spat on the ground, narrowly missing Kate's foot. 'Smell you lot a mile off.'

'We'd like to have a quick chat with you,' Kate said.

'What about?'

'Can we come in?'

'No. Anythin' you got to say, you say out there.'

'Are you Douglas Moore?' Kate continued.

'What if I am?'

'I understand you were released from prison on licence eighteen months ago.'

'So?'

'Well, it might be advisable for you to be a bit more cooperative in that case.'

'Is that right? Well, I don't give a shit, missie, 'cause there ain't nothin' more you pigs can do to me.'

He stepped out of the doorway with difficulty and stood there for a moment leaning on a wooden crutch they hadn't noticed before.

'What on earth happened to you?' Hayden exclaimed, staring at the stump where a leg had once been.

'Thanks to you lot,' he snarled, 'I got worked over inside for bein' a nonce. The leg never set properly and six months ago the hospital took it off, didn't they?'

Kate grimaced. One thing was evident. Moore was definitely not their man, and his days of flashing were long gone.

'Sorry about that,' she said, annoyed that Moore's file had not been updated and embarrassed to find herself in such an uncomfortable situation.

'So, what do you want?' he went on. 'Come to check on me welfare, have yer? Like hell you have.' He laughed harshly. 'I bet I know what you're here for. Been in all the papers, ain't it, about this bleedin' flasher? Come to see if I was up to me old tricks again, did yer?' He tapped the thigh of his missing leg with his other hand. 'Bit hard trying to toss yourself off on one leg, don't you reckon. Now, both of you, piss off!'

Then he turned awkwardly to disappear back into the gloom. Seconds later, the front door slammed in their faces.

'How crude,' Hayden murmured as they returned to their car. 'The man has no shame.'

Kate nodded, then abruptly burst into laughter. 'Yes,' she gurgled, 'but you have to admit, a one-legged tosser is a novel concept.'

He shook his head and climbed into the car. 'Trust you to crown it. And that remark was in very poor taste. I'm surprised at you. The man has lost a leg, for goodness' sake, whether he's a criminal or not.'

But Kate couldn't help herself and she was still laughing when she practically fell into the driving seat beside him. 'I mean,' she chortled, 'can you imagine it? Hobbling round on one leg as he tries to flash his privates, then falling flat on his back with his stick in the air.'

He huffed. 'Do you have to be so obscene?'

She almost choked. 'Hayd, I said *stick*, not *dick*.'

He glared at her. 'For goodness' sake, Kate, you really are disgusting.'

But for all his apparent disapproval, there was more than the suggestion of a smirk on his face as they drove away.

CHAPTER 4

Jason Spindler lived at Short-Oak Farm, which nestled in a fold of the Polden Hills a couple of miles or so from Shapwick village. A long driveway, bordered by ploughed fields, led off a narrow back lane to a jumble of barns and other outbuildings gathered around a poorly maintained concrete hard-standing. The farmhouse was an austere, grey stone place, which looked as though it had managed to withstand the insidious wet and windy conditions of the Somerset Levels for a couple of hundred years.

'Let's hope this suspect proves to be more promising,' Kate breathed, having now overcome her fit of misplaced humour.

An old doddery collie dog greeted them with a half-hearted bark as they approached the open front door, then turned and disappeared back into the house, as if off to tell someone they were there.

As it was, the rough, inquiring voice spoke from behind them in a strong Somerset accent. 'Help you, me ducks?'

They turned quickly to find a large, red-faced man in his late fifties or early sixties, dressed in blue overalls and cloth cap, standing there with a shovel in one hand. They guessed he must have come out of one of the barns when he'd heard the car pull up. Despite the shovel, there was no animosity in his expression and his calloused hands rested lightly on the shovel while his brown eyes studied them curiously.

'Mr Spindler?' Kate asked with a smile, holding up her warrant card and introducing Hayden and herself.

'That's me,' he confirmed. 'Hector Spindler. Problem, is there?'

Kate smiled again. 'Is your son, Jason, about?'

She saw his eyes narrow.

'Why, what's he done now?'

Kate avoided a direct answer. 'We just want a quick chat with him.'

He thought about that for a second, then released his breath in a heavy, resigned sigh and nodded. 'In his bedroom, I shouldn't wonder. Spends half his time up there.'

He turned. 'If you come inside, I'll call him down.'

The floor of the big farmhouse kitchen was paved in slate and had an old-fashioned range cooker set against one wall, with oak units on each side. A long oak table and chairs occupied the centre of the room and iron hooks, from which rabbits and game would no doubt have once hung, reached down from the smoke-stained ceiling like eagles' talons.

Leaving them there, Hector Spindler strode along the hallway towards the stairs, and they heard him yell, 'Jason? Come down here. Folk to see you.'

There was no response and they heard him climbing the stairs, muttering irritably to himself.

Thunderous knocking on an apparently closed door followed, and Kate heard a muffled conversation before there were further footsteps on the stairs and Hector reappeared in the doorway, pushing a young man in front of him.

Kate studied the new arrival with interest.

Dressed in tight blue jeans and a white, long-sleeved T-shirt, he was tall and thin, with sparse black hair, a pale unhealthy-looking complexion and pointed features that lacked a proper chin. At first sight, he seemed something of an oddity, with what Kate suspected from his head-down demeanour to be a withdrawn, introverted personality.

'Hi, Jason,' she said, manufacturing another smile. 'Could we have a few words with you?'

He said nothing, simply shrugging his thin shoulders and staring at the slate floor. She noticed that his thin lips wore what seemed to be a faint smirk.

'Well, answer the detective,' Hector boomed and slapped him none too lightly across the shoulder.

'If you like,' he said, still staring at the floor.

Kate looked directly at his father. 'Could we speak to Jason alone, sir?' she asked. 'He's twenty-four, I believe, and an adult, so there's no need for a chaperone.'

Hector hesitated. 'He's not good with people. Maybe I should stay?'

'He'll be okay with us, sir. It's only a chat. He's not in any trouble.'

For a few moments, the big man thought about it. Then, with a scowl of grudging acceptance, he turned on his heel and left the room, shutting the door behind him.

'Shall we sit down, Jason?' Kate suggested quietly.

Another shrug and the boy's dark eyes flicked upwards for a second, the smirk still hovering over his lips. 'If you want.'

Pulling out a couple of chairs, the two detectives sat and watched him choose a chair opposite and slump into it. Kate noticed that the sleeves of his T-shirt were over-long and that he curled his fingers around the cuffs in the way an immature girl of ten or eleven might do.

'I understand you've been in a bit of trouble, Jason,' Kate began.

He nodded but didn't raise his head. Kate saw that the smirk was still there and guessed it was a self-conscious affliction.

'Last year,' he said. 'Went to prison for six months.'

'And why was that?'

Yet another shrug. 'Indecent exposure.'

'Who to?'

'Some girls coming out of school.'

'Why did you do that?'

'I didn't. It was a mistake. I was going for a pee.'

'But you did it again, to other girls, on two more occasions, didn't you?'

He nodded.

'And one of them was so scared she tried to run away and got hit by a car and was seriously injured, wasn't she? And all because of what you did. That's why you were put away — to teach you a lesson and get you some help for your problem.'

No answer.

'Have you *had* any help?'

A quick upward flick of the eyes again. 'I see this doctor every two weeks. But I don't do that flashing thing anymore.'

'Are you sure about that?'

The smirk was even more pronounced. 'Yeah, I'm okay now.'

'Do you have a girlfriend?'

He shook his head. 'Don't get on well with girls. They laugh at me.'

'Why do they do that?'

'They think I'm weird.'

'Are you? Weird, I mean.'

'Don't think so — just quiet.'

'Do you know about the person who's been going around flashing his private parts at women?'

'I heard about it, yes.'

'Is that person you?'

He looked up, then looked away again, apparently focusing on the window.

'No, that's not me.'

'Are you working?'

'No. Can't get a job.'

'But according to your record, you are very clever. Four A Levels, two of which were A*, even.'

'No one wants to take on a convicted flasher, do they? 'Sides, I can't drive.'

'So, what do you do all day?'

'This and that. Walking, cycling, birdwatching.'

'You sure that's all?'

'Sometimes I help my dad on the farm.'

The mouth seemed to curl in an unpleasant sneer. He's laughing at us, Kate realized. The little jerk is laughing at us.

'Okay, Jason,' she said. Thanks for talking to us. Would you ask your dad to come in here, please?'

Kate watched the thin figure leave and threw a quick glance at Hayden. He raised both hands in a gesture of resignation. They had nothing on the boy and Jason knew it.

'You wanted to speak to me?'

Hector came into the kitchen and closed the door. Above their heads they heard a heavy metal band start up.

'We're making inquiries into a series of complaints of indecent exposure in surrounding villages,' Kate explained.

Hector nodded. 'I realized that when you arrived. Jason's got form, so you were bound to come here sooner or later.'

'How's he doing now?'

He shrugged. 'How should I know? I rarely see him. He's always out riding that damned pushbike of his, and he hardly speaks to me anymore.'

'Do you think he may have reverted to his old ways?'

'Of course, I think that every time I see a report in the papers, but he's a cunning little sod and I've given up trying to help him.'

He paused a second, then went on in a rush. 'Look, I'm doing my best to run a farm here, with a good head of beef cattle to look after, and most of the time I have to do that on my own. I lost my wife five years ago, so it's been difficult trying to bring my lad up as well. I've been very strict with him, but in the end, it's made no difference at all, and he's turned out to be a proper wastrel. On top of that, everybody round here knows me, so can you imagine how it feels to have a son who's been put away for indecent exposure? It's nearly destroyed my life.'

He sank onto one of the chairs they had pulled out, panting heavily, his face even redder than before.

'Do you think you may have been too strict with him?' Hayden asked. 'Sometimes that can have the opposite effect.'

He glared at him. 'Too strict? No, I flaming well don't. Spare the rod and spoil the child, that's what my old dad always used to say, and he was right. Anyway, being strict with a kid doesn't make him a bloody pervert, does it?'

He mopped his head with a handkerchief and Kate poured some water into a glass on the nearby draining board and handed it to him.

'You okay?' she said.

He gulped a mouthful and nodded. 'So, what happens now? Are you running him in again?'

Hayden shook his head. 'We can't prove he's done anything wrong, sir. These local incidents may have nothing to do with him and if they have, all we can hope for is that our visit here today will act as a deterrent and put a stop to any future offences.'

'I understand he is currently receiving some psychiatric help after his time in prison?' Kate resumed.

Hector nodded. 'A Dr Wyn Hayward over in Bridgwater. He goes there on the bus every two weeks. But I don't think it will straighten him out. He's an arrogant little bugger, you see, and clever with it. He'll play the game as long as he needs to and then do exactly what he wants afterwards.'

Kate dropped a business card on the corner of the table beside him. 'Okay, Mr Spindler, we'll be off. I'll leave my card in case you feel you need to talk to someone later. Let's just hope things turn out better for you and Jason in the future.'

'Some hope of that,' Hayden muttered, glancing over his shoulder at an upstairs window of the house as they climbed back into the CID car. 'The nasty little pervert is only waving goodbye to us from his bedroom.'

'You think he's our man then?' Kate said, following the direction of his gaze and seeing the figure at the window.

'I'd bet my Mark II Jag on it,' he said.

* * *

37

Percival was cock-a-hoop when Kate returned to the station and gave him her report.

'Bloody brilliant, Kate,' he said. 'I knew I could rely on you. Half a day and you've virtually cracked the case.'

Kate made a face. 'It's only a suspicion, Des. All we're saying is that this Jason Spindler fits the profile and from the look of him seems to be a likely candidate. But we've got no proof and if he is the perp, short of catching him in the act, we're not likely to get it. He may be young and he's certainly weird, but he's also smart and I suspect he always makes sure he covers his tracks well.'

The optimistic gleam faded from Percival's eyes. 'So, what do you suggest we do? Put some sort of surveillance on him for when he does it again? After all, we know he always carries out his antics between just before dusk and eleven in the evening, so we'd only have to set something up for a four-hour period.'

She looked dubious. 'I can't see that working very well. He rides a pushbike, and it would be next to impossible to keep tabs on him even in a plain car. All he has to do is stick to the droves and bridleways and we're snookered—'

He cut her off with a theatrical snap of his fingers. 'Problem solved. We have our own answer to that in this very department — *Ben*!'

His shout brought the young man sitting at a desk just outside the small inner sanctum to his feet in a rush.

'Yes, guv?' he said, poking his head through the open doorway.

Just twenty-five and seconded from uniform as a TDC — or temporary detective constable — Ben Holloway was an ex-university graduate, as keen as they come and desperately anxious to become a substantive detective constable. One of six children whose parents originally hailed from Barbados, he had a lean, wiry build, and the most sincere, disarming smile Kate had ever seen. Immensely popular with everyone, he had been unofficially adopted as the departmental favourite, and he endured constant ribbing about his legendary following of adoring female colleagues. But he put up with all the banter with a grin and the occasional witty quip in response that often had his tormentors in fits.

'Ben,' Percival said sternly. 'You're a keen cyclist, are you not?'

Holloway stared at him a little uncertainly, plainly wondering what was coming next.

'Well, yes, guv. I like to keep fit.'

Percival grinned suddenly and made a sweeping gesture towards him with one hand.

'There you are, Kate,' he said triumphantly. 'He's made for the job.'

Kate still looked less than convinced. 'I'm not sure it would achieve anything. After all, Ben would have to keep our man in sight all the time on otherwise deserted byways, without being spotted.'

Holloway looked at each of them in turn, obviously baffled by what was going on.

'Then it's settled,' Percival continued. 'Ben, I have a very important job for you this evening.'

'Job, guv?' Holloway echoed.

Percival nodded and began shuffling some papers about on his desk. 'Yes. Detective Sergeant Lewis will tell you all about it — er, won't you, Kate?'

CHAPTER 5

'It's daft.' Hayden shook his head repeatedly, even less impressed with Percival's plan than Kate, and he shook his head several times to emphasize his disapproval of the whole thing. 'What's he supposed to do? Sit around there all night after doing nearly a full shift already, in the hope that this weirdo will decide to ride out on another flashing expedition? It's like something out of *Monty Python*. And how long is he supposed to keep it up? A couple of days? A week? A month? Talk about hit-and-miss. Spindler might not show at all.'

Kate shrugged, pushing her empty cup away from her. It grated on the patches of spilled sugar left stuck to the tabletop. So much for canteen hygiene.

'I don't think Ben Holloway was too keen on the idea either when I briefed him,' she said. She smiled benignly at Hayden. 'Still, he'll have some backup at the scene, just in case Jason is compromised and tries to do a bunk.'

Hayden didn't twig at once. 'Oh, who's doing that then? Bum job, if you ask me. Especially if it goes on a bit.'

'The same dedicated officer who is taking him out there in the Trannie this evening,' she said.

His jaw dropped. He'd finally got the message. 'Oh, come on, old girl, that's not fair. It's hardly a job for an experienced detective like me.'

Kate chuckled. 'Experienced? I think you're just the man for it, Hayd. You know the area as well as anyone and you're good at sitting in one spot for hours on end without doing anything. You also like completing crosswords, which you should have plenty of time to do while you're keeping an ear on the radio.'

He snorted in indignation. 'And what will you be doing while I'm out there, risking life and limb?'

She produced a small card and twirled it between her fingers.

'*I* have an invitation to attend an author's talk with Tamara Callaghan,' she said. 'Seven thirty. Should be very interesting, I think — especially as I've always wanted to write a novel. Not jealous, are you?'

* * *

Dr Wyn Hayward rose from his chair with a puzzled frown when Kate walked into his consulting room.

'Good of you to squeeze me in at the last minute, Doctor,' Kate said with a smile. She dropped into the chair he had indicated with a wave of his freckled hand.

Hayward sat down opposite. A small man, with thinning ginger hair and large tortoiseshell glasses, he wore a slightly crumpled grey suit and from the extra-thick sole of one his black ankle boots, Kate guessed he had some form of foot deformity.

'My secretary said it was a pressing matter to do with one of my clients,' he said, 'and fortunately I have a reasonably light afternoon, so I was able to accommodate you.'

Kate smiled again and crossed her legs in her short black skirt, but quickly uncrossed them when she saw his gaze dropping briefly to her knees, hoping he hadn't read something into her body language. Then it occurred to her that perhaps he was not carrying out some form of impromptu psychoanalysis but was just a dirty old man.

'So, how can I help you?' he said, his eyes big and owl-like behind the glasses.

'Jason Spindler. He's one of your patients, I believe.'

'Ordinarily, I wouldn't be able to confirm or deny that, due to client confidentiality, but in his case I can, as he is subject to an order of the court. But that is all I can tell you, I'm afraid.'

Kate nodded. 'I understand that, but the reason he has been referred to you is, I think, beyond doubt, since he recently served six months in prison for indecent exposure.'

He shrugged, saying nothing.

'We are currently investigating a number of complaints of indecent exposure on the Somerset Levels, and he fits the description of the offender.'

He grimaced. 'I'm sorry to hear that.'

'How long has Jason been with you?'

'I'm sorry, I can't go into that.'

She tried to choose her words carefully. 'Are you able to say whether you feel he is responding to the professional help he is receiving, or whether there is a possibility he could have regressed?'

As soon as she came out with the question, she realized how clumsy it must have sounded and she wasn't surprised to see the flicker of irritation in his expression.

'You know I cannot tell you that,' he snapped.

Kate nodded and tried a different approach. 'We are concerned that the offender in this case may ultimately go beyond simply exposing himself and resort to actual physical assault. Do you think there is a risk here?'

A tic developed in his cheek. 'Are we talking hypothetically or about my client personally? If the latter, my answer must remain the same: I can't discuss it.'

Kate sighed. 'Okay then, Doctor, leaving your client out of it, can you tell me *hypothetically* whether someone who is prone to exposing themselves to women is likely to become violent and commit a more serious sexual crime later?'

He smiled faintly. 'Speaking solely hypothetically then, Sergeant, although there is a divergence of opinion among professionals in my specific field, I would say that, while it is not impossible, the occurrence is rare. Men who commit acts of indecent exposure tend to be inadequate, introverted individuals, lacking in communication skills or the ability to engage effectively with the opposite sex. Often, they have either suffered abuse themselves or are dominated by another person, such as a parent or guardian. As a result, they have little sense of self-worth. But by exposing and abusing themselves in front of their victims, they create fear and embarrassment, which not only enables them to achieve the sexual fulfilment they crave, but the sense of power they are ordinarily denied. Does that answer your question?'

Kate took a deep breath as she tried to digest the wooden, apparently textbook answer he had provided. 'It goes a long way towards it, sir,' she said. 'So, if someone like Jason — and I say *like Jason* since this is purely hypothetical — had an overbearing father who for much of his life had resorted to physical punishment as a means of ensuring compliance with his wishes, it could have had an adverse effect on the boy's transition to manhood and could account for his present deviant behaviour?'

He beamed. 'Couldn't have put it better myself, Sergeant, though rather than saying "account" for his present behaviour, I would prefer to say "contribute" to it, as there are often many other factors involved.'

He glanced at his watch and stood up. Kate got the message. The interview was over.

'So how is your inquiry going, Sergeant?' he said after they had shaken hands and he was showing Kate to the door. 'Any real progress?'

Kate treated him to her best smile. 'Oh, I'm afraid I cannot discuss that with you, Doctor. Strictly confidential, you see . . .'

* * *

43

The Levels Community Library was already filling up when Kate arrived for Tamara Callaghan's talk. She saw the author standing behind a large table before a phalanx of plastic chairs, talking to a middle-aged woman in tweeds, plus a short, blond man dressed in fawn trousers and a light green shirt, complete with cravat. A neat stack of hardcover books occupied one side of the table, a jug of water and a glass tumbler occupying the other.

'Ah, Sergeant,' Callaghan exclaimed, spotting her hovering by the door, and walking over. 'I'm so glad you decided to come. I hope you won't be bored.'

Kate smiled. 'I'm looking forward to your talk. Maybe I'll pick up some tips in case I decide to try my hand at writing a novel myself when I retire.'

Callaghan frowned disapprovingly. 'When you retire? Nonsense, you shouldn't wait that long. Get weaving now.'

Kate laughed. 'Oh, I don't think my boss would approve of that while I'm a serving officer.'

At which point the blond man joined them. The author turned slightly, one eyebrow raised inquiringly.

'Ah, Spencer,' she purred. 'This is my detective sergeant friend, Kate Lewis. Kate, Spencer Little, my agent.'

'Pleased to meet you, Sergeant,' he said, with a flash of perfect, white teeth. He lowered his voice and glanced around him conspiratorially. 'Haven't caught that dirty bugger of a flasher yet, I suppose?'

Kate saw Callaghan raise her eyes heavenwards. 'Oh, you know about that then?'

'Yes, Tam told me.'

'Well, there's no news yet, I'm afraid.'

He grunted. 'Chaps like that need to be put down, you know — no good to anyone.'

For a moment, Kate was taken aback by the venom in his tone, but before she could think of a suitable reply, Callaghan cut in quickly.

'Don't mind Spencer, Sergeant,' she drawled. 'He's about as credible a fascist as he is an author's agent.'

Little's smile seemed to freeze and his laugh emerged forced and unconvincing. Kate saw his eyes harden as her barbed comment struck home and just for a second, he looked thrown. Oh dear, Kate mused, there is something going on behind the scenes here all right. A tiny drop of acid had just been introduced into the conversation and there was no telling what its ultimate effect would be.

As it was, the awkwardness of the situation was unwittingly resolved by the middle-aged woman in tweeds — the library assistant and president of the local writers' circle, who had evidently set up the talk. Her discreet cough focused the attention of both Callaghan and Little on the audience, most of whom had now taken up their seats and were waiting with evident impatience for the talk to get underway.

Kate found a vacant seat at the back next to a very large woman with an equally large floral hat and a musty-smelling woollen wrap.

'Are you a writer too?' she asked in a loud, high-pitched voice as the president started to introduce Callaghan.

'No, just a guest,' Kate replied in just above a whisper.

An elderly man sitting in front of them turned and hissed, 'Ssh!' glaring at Kate as if she had started the conversation.

Great, Kate thought, this promises to be a real fun evening. Maybe she would have been better off going on surveillance duty with Hayden. Yet, as it turned out, she was pleasantly surprised.

The talk itself was delivered with polish and good humour, and although some of the questions thrown at the author afterwards were a lot less inspiring, they were nevertheless entertaining — some in a cringeworthy sort of way. The large woman beside Kate who, predictably, started the ball rolling, didn't so much as ask a question, but made a statement bemoaning the fact that she was an aspiring writer who, despite friends and relatives telling her how good her work was, could never seem to find a publisher for it. Then there was the elderly clergyman who asked why it was necessary for modern writers like Callaghan to use foul language in their books, and the middle-aged man with a tan and a thick mop of greying hair and matching beard further along the row in front of Kate, who asked if she believed that all murderers should receive the death penalty.

To give Callaghan her due, she answered all the questions put to her in a non-judgemental tactful way, skilfully avoiding committing herself on sensitive, emotive issues like the death penalty. Kate couldn't help admiring her for the way she handled things.

Following the question-and-answer session, Kate was left seated as the audience rose en masse and surged towards Callaghan like a tidal wave in their eagerness to obtain a signed copy of her book. Refusing to join the crush and conscious of a hollow feeling in her stomach that reminded her how hungry she was, she got up to leave, slipping the long strap of her handbag off the back of her chair and threading her way between the chairs in the direction of the door.

But her escape was not to be so easily accomplished. She found her way blocked by the middle-aged man who had been sitting in the row in front of her.

'My apologies,' he said with an engaging smile, 'but I couldn't help hearing you being introduced by the author earlier. You're a police officer, then, are you?'

Kate nodded, studying the man and thinking how much he resembled the late footballer, George Best, in his final years. He was dressed casually in dark green chinos and a thick brown sweater and carried a spiral-bound notebook. He looked to be in his fifties and had the sort of rugged, lived-in face and dark brown eyes that many women would have died for. 'For my sins, I'm afraid so,' she said and made to step past him. But he held out his hand. 'Ed Templar.'

Left with no real option, Kate shook it. 'Kate Lewis. Enjoy the talk, did you?'

He nodded, propping his behind on the back of one of the chairs. 'Very illuminating. She obviously knows her craft.'

'Are you a writer?' Kate went on, just for something to say.

'I try.' He laughed, and his brown eyes looked almost whimsical.

'So, what do you write — novels?'

He shook his head. 'No, I'm a freelance journalist.'

Kate's eyes narrowed, her inbuilt antenna quivering in warning.

'Writing about what?' she said more brusquely than she had intended.

'I'm researching life as a novelist for a new book I'm currently working on, though sadly—' and he looked peeved — 'Tamara Callaghan refuses to give me the time of day, I'm afraid. A very private lady, I think. Can I ask you something?'

'I can't promise I'll answer it.'

He laughed. 'Well, let me give it a try.' His expression became more serious. 'Do you believe that murderers should face the death penalty?'

Kate shook her head firmly. 'It's not something I am prepared to go into, I'm afraid. Why do you ask?'

He shrugged. 'Just something I'm working on. You know, professional versus private views and all that. It would have been useful to have had the perspective of a police officer as well as a crime writer. Only Tamara Callaghan rather avoided the question just now.'

'And so shall I. Sorry.'

He laughed again. 'Ah well, I did try.' He hesitated. 'Can I ask you something else?'

Kate sighed. 'Look, I'm off duty and I really need to go home and get something to eat.'

'I'll buy you dinner if you like.'

Kate stared at him. 'That would hardly be appropriate. I don't even know you.'

'Strictly business.'

'Goodnight.'

He held up his hands defensively. 'Okay, so I'm not handling this situation very well. Just let me ask my question and then I'll leave you alone.'

She waited, her eyebrows raised inquiringly.

'When you were talking to Tamara Callaghan earlier, I happened to overhear the blond gentleman asking you if you had caught the flasher yet. Is that how she came to know you — because she was a victim of indecent exposure?'

Kate compressed her lips into a tight line. 'I think you should stop listening in on other people's conversations and drawing your own conclusions.'

He winced. 'Ouch! That hurt.'

'Goodnight, Mr Templar,' she said again, conscious of his eyes following her as she walked out through the door. Despite the anger she felt towards him for his impertinence, she couldn't help thinking guiltily, 'Wow! What a dishy fella!'

CHAPTER 6

'What, you mean, like the Saint?' Hayden asked Kate as he climbed into bed beside her.

'Who?'

'Well, you said this journalist fellow was called Templar.'

Seeing his explanation had no effect, he sighed. 'You know, Simon Templar, the fictional sleuth in Leslie Charteris's books. He was nicknamed *the Saint*. You must have heard of him.'

She tossed her head irritably. 'I've told you before, Hayd, I don't read detective fiction, so how am I supposed to know about characters like your *Saint*?'

He stared at her in amazement. 'But it's literature, old girl, the bread of life.'

'It's bollocks if you ask me.'

He scowled. 'There you go again, debasing everything with foul language.'

'Never mind my language, Hayd, just tell me how you and Ben Holloway got on tonight. In the absence of any dramatic announcements from you, I gather nothing much happened.'

He snorted, wrapping his half of the duvet around himself and managing to take part of her half with him into the bargain.

'Complete waste of time. I told you it would be. I sat in that blessed car for four hours, bored to tears, while poor old Ben crouched with his bike among the trees at the front of Spindler's farm, and neither of us saw or heard a solitary thing. I am exhausted—'

'You're what? You weren't doing anything.'

'Well, er, sitting somewhere, doing nothing, can be very tiring, and . . . and Ben got half bitten to death by midges.'

Kate shook her head, yanked half the duvet back off him and turned over to go to sleep.

'Tosser!' she muttered.

* * *

Eighteen-year-old Julie Morey had heard the sharp crack of the branch breaking shortly after turning off the lane and onto the footpath. She froze, staring about her in the gathering gloom but saw nothing. The footpath was a bridleway which cut through a strip of woodland at the back of a line of houses and bungalows fronting the busy B3139. It was her usual route to Mark village centre and enabled her to avoid dicing with death on the main Wedmore Road, which lacked both pavements and street lighting. But the muddy, pot-holed track, constantly churned up by the hooves of cantering horse-riders, was also more than a bit creepy, with dense undergrowth on each side complemented by overhanging trees, which rustled and creaked in the low breeze like the dry voices of old men. Now, having heard the branch breaking, she hesitated, wondering if, as her father had told her so many times before, she should have taken the main road instead.

She frowned, peering at her wristwatch. Damn it! She was already late and knowing the crowd she was due to meet at the local pub, she was quite sure they wouldn't be keen on waiting too long for her. They would be in full party mood, no doubt already well-oiled or high on weed and ready for the off. The prospect of walking from Mark to the birthday bash at Wedmore was not something that appealed to her.

She swore under her breath. Sod it, she had no choice. It was too late to turn back now. She was too far along the path. At least she had come prepared. She was wearing her leather boots — her "heels" were in her bag — and although the sun had dipped and the light was gradually fading, it was still bright enough for her to see her way, so she didn't think it would be a problem.

After a few more yards, however, the gloom started to press in on her again and the last of the season's flies feeding off patches of recently deposited horse manure buzzed angrily around her as she picked her way through. A bird erupted in a panic from the tangle of undergrowth as she was passing, making her jump, but she relaxed again when it flew off after a shrill cry of alarm. Otherwise, a heavy stillness seemed to have settled over everything, broken only by the distant murmur of traffic on the main road and the sound of a motor mower starting up in one of the gardens backing on to the footpath. A late-autumn cut, it seemed.

She reached a bend and glimpsed a wider patch of shrubbery just beyond and was pleased to see the trees thinning out for a short distance, once more allowing some light to reach the track. A large flock of birds — starlings, she thought — swept overhead, no doubt en route to their nests for the night, and a stray cat crossed the track in front of her, stopped briefly to stare at her, then vanished into the undergrowth opposite.

The comforting sound of the mower ceased, and she heard a distant car horn. Ordinary, familiar noises that were strangely reassuring and put her at her ease.

And then, suddenly, he was there! Seemingly erupting from nowhere, a naked, male figure in full, obscene arousal, wearing nothing but a sinister black hood and trainers. He had his arms extended so as to bar her way.

With a wild scream, she stumbled, tripped and fell flat on her back, her bag tumbling into the undergrowth. And as she squirmed away from him, using the heels of her boots to propel herself backwards, he laughed and followed her, plainly revelling in the situation.

How things would have ended did not require too much imagination, but as it was, a big white Labrador saved the day. Whether the animal sensed the man was up to no good or he just wanted to play was not clear, but when he bounded into view around the bend, barking his head off, the outcome was predictable. Uttering a loud oath, the would-be assailant sprang across the track into the bushes and disappeared.

But the dog was not about to give up so easily and started after him. Only a loud whistle stopped him in his tracks.

'Ben! Here, boy!' A man dressed in a floppy sweater and jeans arrived on the scene, flourishing a stout cane.

'Good heavens,' he exclaimed, bending down to help the sobbing girl back onto her feet. 'Whatever's happened?'

'A — a man,' she choked. 'He had no clothes on and — and—'

He frowned and peered at the undergrowth into which the man had disappeared. 'Well, he's gone now, me duck. Ben soon saw him off. He won't be back, you can bet on it. Let's hope he did himself a mischief running away, eh?'

Crouched in the bushes a hundred yards from them, the hooded figure retrieved the clothes he had left in a hollow tree and tried to stem the flow of blood from a nasty gash on his leg caused by the barbs on a low-level, broken-down fence. Sod bloody Labradors, he muttered through tightly clenched teeth, carefully tying his handkerchief around the wound.

* * *

A bearded man in an old army camouflage jacket sat at the window of the small room, smoking a cigarette and sipping from the tumbler of cheap whisky in his hand. It was pitch black outside and just as dark in the room, but content to sit there in the darkness, he made no attempt to light the paraffin lamp behind him. He had learned from bitter experience the folly of sitting in front of a lighted window, where you couldn't see out but someone else could see in and decide when to put a bullet in your head. That had happened to a mate of his in the mob, and he well remembered the wet, sticky feeling of the other's brains on the side of his face after his head had exploded.

Okay, so he wasn't in Beirut anymore but sleepy old Somerset, and the desolate Levels were hardly likely to harbour a ruthless sniper. But old habits die hard, and he wasn't about to change them any time soon. So, he continued to sit there in the dark, smoking, drinking, and thinking, as he nursed the long-festering hatred in his heart. It would, he knew, only be satisfied when he had finally achieved what he had come to this godforsaken part of the country to do.

It had taken him a long time to track her down — if indeed it was her, of course, and he still wasn't a hundred percent sure about that yet. She was a lot older now and had filled out a bit. But most people changed as they got older, didn't they? People he had mixed with in the past would almost certainly think the same about him — probably even more so if they had been able to see some of the evidence of what had happened to him in the course of his life. The crescent-shaped scar across his right pectoral from the slash of the bowie knife, the old, badly stitched "railway line" down his right side from the bayonet and the wound in his left thigh made by that jagged piece of shrapnel.

He had earned a lot of money as a mercenary, but there had been a cost to it, and six years in a stinking Lebanese jail had aged him well beyond his forty-five years. He'd realized after the breakout that it was time to quit the mercenary business for good, before it killed him. All he wanted now was to settle down somewhere quiet and live out his days in blissful seclusion, fishing, drinking beer and whisky and maybe getting a dog. But before that could happen, he had this one thing to do, and that meant first making sure she was the right one and that she still had what was rightfully his.

Unconsciously, his grip tightened on the tumbler as he visualized the confrontation that would eventually come, mentally relishing the moment and how it was going to end, and there was a loud crack when the glass fragmented, burying multiple shards in his hand. Cursing, he lurched to his feet and strode to the derelict bathroom, following the beam of his torch. There, he gingerly pulled out the jagged pieces of glass as blood, mixed with spilled whisky, streamed down his wrist. Pouring water over his hand from the two-litre plastic bottle he'd left on the windowsill in the absence of mains water, he poured some disinfectant over it from the first-aid box he always carried with him and carefully wound a bandage around the deep cuts, securing it with a safety pin. Then he stared at his bearded face in the cracked bathroom mirror and smiled as another thought occurred to him. Maybe he could draw the bitch out? Rattle her cage somehow, see how she reacted. That would give him some indication that she was who he thought, and it would wind her up as well. Pile on the fear and the agony. Let her know that after all this time, he was coming for her and for what she owed him. He smiled. Yeah, that sounded ace, and now he knew just what to do.

* * *

Jason Spindler managed to get indoors without his father spotting him. Hector was obviously out somewhere on the farm, maybe checking his herd of cattle, which could not have been better as far as Jason was concerned. The wound in his leg was giving him real gyp and he couldn't wait to check it out. Grabbing some disinfectant, a wad of lint and some plasters from the bathroom, he sank onto his bed and slipped off his jeans.

The gash in his leg was not a pretty sight and it was still bleeding. Having to flex his leg muscles to cycle back home hadn't helped matters and the inside of his trousers seemed to be saturated with blood. He gritted his teeth and tried to clean himself up with the disinfectant. He applied the plasters and opened the bedroom window to release some of its distinctive smell. The last thing he needed was for Hector to smell disinfectant when he came in and start asking questions.

Feeling sick and woozy, he pulled on some old tracksuit bottoms and lay back on his bed as the room swam around him and he tried to get his thoughts together. That bloody dog! It had ruined everything. Okay, so he had got away without anyone recognizing him, but he was sure the police would have been called. What if his wound had leaked all over the place? He had read somewhere that a person's DNA could be extracted from spilled blood and matched to that of someone whose DNA was held on the police database. What if the police were already doing that? He had no idea how long the process would take them, which meant they could already be on their way to the farm. He had to get away, find somewhere to lie low until he worked out what to do next.

Groggily, he climbed to his feet and pulled his rucksack from the top of the wardrobe, then began going through his chest of drawers and packing some clothes into it. There was a place he could go to out on the marsh — an old, ruined barn on the edge of the farm. He had retreated there many times before to get away from the old man and read his porn mags. All he needed now was a torch, some food and a couple of cans of pop from the kitchen and he was out of there.

Ten minutes later, wearing a woolly hat and a heavy, waterproof coat, he was wheeling his bicycle round the back to the partially overgrown footpath he always used to avoid being seen leaving the house via the main driveway, and even as his father stomped back indoors, he was pedalling off into the night.

CHAPTER 7

Des Percival was not a happy man, though to be honest, he hadn't really been happy ever since taking on the job of Acting DI, and he was beginning to wonder whether all the hassle was worth it. Life had been a lot simpler as a DS on the National Crime Squad. Okay, so it had been risky dealing with dangerous criminals who had often been armed, but you knew what you had to do, and you just got on with things, coupled with which, there had been the heart-thumping, adrenalin rush that went with nearly every operation. Sitting in a cramped office in his present role, trying to balance internal politics with operational necessity, ploughing through innumerable crime statistics and case files submitted by the detectives under him, managing a departmental budget, plus staff overtime and sickness, and all the while doing his level best to keep the DCI at arm's length, was not what he had joined the police force for. Then there were the difficult decisions that had to be made — not whether simply to arrest someone or not, which was part and parcel of the job, but how to avoid possible criticism from the top for authorizing or not authorizing a course of action that could result in something going pear-shaped. 'The buck stops with you,' the superintendent had warned him when appointing him to Acting DI — and didn't he know it after just a short time in the office.

Now, slumped in his chair, he glowered at Kate sitting opposite, the report on the previous evening's indecent exposure incident on the desk in front of him.

'How the hell did Hayden and Ben manage to miss the little turd?' he said heavily. 'I just can't believe it. While Holloway was sitting on his arse at the front of the farm, the perv must have somehow slipped out the back. This poor girl was traumatized by the incident. The guvnor will have kittens.'

Kate grimaced and nodded. 'I'm just surprised no one belled me about it. I didn't even know it had happened until I walked in here this morning. Who attended?'

He shoved the incident report away from him. 'Not one of ours anyway. We were short-staffed last night. A DS from Bridgwater was in the area and went to the scene for us. Said not to bother to ring you as he had it covered. Bloody good job he did too, but he wouldn't have had to if our "star players" hadn't managed to cock things up to start with.'

'So, where were Indrani Purewal and Danny Ferris? I thought they were covering the late turn on a twelve-hour shift?' she said.

'Dealing with a violent domestic out at Meare,' he retorted. 'They didn't finish until after this flasher incident was over.'

'Well, we can't blame Hayden or Ben for what happened. They did what was asked of them. If Spindler *was* the flasher, he must have got out of the farm another way, and Ben couldn't have been expected to cover every drove or footpath he might have used. And with respect, it was your idea to set up this madcap surveillance duty in the first place. It never had any real chance of success.'

'Oh, thanks very much. So, have you got a better idea, *Miss Marple*?'

She shook her head ruefully. 'No, not at the moment, I must admit. But I just think it is too hit-and-miss to be worth continuing.'

He sank back in his chair, hands once more down the back of his trousers. 'Do you? Well, something has to be done. Give it another night and get Ben a bit closer to the farm. He might then be in a better position to spot Spindler leaving.'

She shrugged. 'Your call. So, who was the DS from Bridgwater?'

He frowned. 'Someone called Charlie Woo? Who the hell has a name like that?'

Kate looked a little surprised that Percival hadn't heard of Woo, even in the short time he had been on the police area. 'He's Chinese — ex-Hong Kong Police.'

'Oh, you know him then?'

'Very well. He's a good detective and has helped me on at least a couple of cases in the past. But what's the full SP on this incident?'

He retrieved the report and scanned it again, gradually cooling down as Kate's query forced him to consider the facts of the case instead. 'Not a lot yet. As you know, incident reports only give us the bare bones. All this one says is that an eighteen-year-old girl called Julie Morey was indecently exposed to by a naked, hooded man on a footpath near Mark village at about 1900 hours last night. Offender apparently ran off when a walker approached with his dog.' He pushed the printout across the desk to her. 'Here, you can have it. I gather your Charlie Woo got another couple of jobs after this one and finished very late, so he's sending the full details through when he comes on duty sometime this morning.'

She nodded. 'I'll give him a bell.'

'You do that and after you've done it, maybe you could come up with some brilliant strategy for catching the perverted arsehole who's currently running rings around us.'

* * *

Kate didn't need to ring Charlie Woo. While she had been closeted with Percival, the short, dapper detective had turned up in the office and was sitting on a corner of her desk.

She smiled when she saw him. 'Charlie, my man. It seems we owe you a favour.'

He grinned back. 'It will be collected, Kate, don't worry.' He waved a plastic sleeve containing some papers, in front of her. 'A present for you.'

She took it from him, conscious of his gaze studying her as she flicked through the papers. Then she stared at him, a gleam in her eyes. 'Blood?'

He nodded. 'I missed it at first, as it was getting dark, but then I spotted the traces on the leaves of some of the bushes concealing the broken strands of a barbed wire fence close to where he'd run off.'

'But that's brilliant.'

He shrugged modestly. 'Thank the CSI who attended — after a bit of hemming and hawing, I have to say. She did a thorough job, though. The barbs on that fence must have cut up our perv something rotten going by the amount of splatter that was present.'

'Let's just hope the samples that were captured will prove to be good enough for analysis and not have been compromised by the delay in securing them.'

He shrugged. 'Luck of the draw, I'm afraid. Fortunately, I got to the scene within minutes and the SOCO team were quite quick off the mark too — once they were finally given the green light. It was also a dry evening and some of the blood traces were on the underside of leaves, so were protected to an extent.'

'But nothing else was found, I suppose? No traces of semen or anything?'

He shook his head. ''Fraid not. It seems he was interrupted by the arrival of a dog, so he didn't have time for self-abuse — and from what the victim said, he seemed to be more interested in frightening her to death than satisfying his sexual urges.'

She thought of what Dr Wyn Hayward had told her. 'The power thing.'

'The what?'

'Oh, something someone told me recently. Anyway, at least we've got the chance of this latest development leading somewhere and we'll just have to wait until the samples have been analyzed and NDNAD — the National DNA Database — comes back to us to say if they've got a match with the profile of the suspect we've got in mind.'

He nodded. 'They're very efficient, but the whole process could take a while. They must have a lot more serious cases to deal with than a minor indecent exposure. I just hope you've got the right suspect in the frame.'

'You and me both,' she said heavily. 'There's a lot riding on it, especially for poor old Des Percival's mental wellbeing.'

'Just tell him this new development will be like looking forward to Christmas.'

She made a face. 'Yeah, and he's likely to throw all his toys out of the pram if in the end he doesn't get his bloody present.'

He straightened up with a chuckle. 'Well, you know what they always say?' She joined him in intoning the familiar police maxim: "If you can't take a joke, you shouldn't have joined."'

Then, as their laughter subsided, he added, 'Anyway, that's my good deed done for the week. Now you can lead me down to your excellent canteen and buy me a cup of coffee and a nice cream bun. I think I've earned it.'

* * *

Jacob Williamson had really enjoyed Tamara Callaghan's talk and was particularly pleased with himself for having had the foresight to order fifty of her books well before the event. There had been quite a bit of advance publicity in the local newspapers, and the follow-ups, including at least three book reviews recommending the novel, promised to earn him a nice little return for his flagging business, especially as the author had given his shop a plug at the end of her talk. Readers liked crime stories set in their own local areas and he was quite sure that, although she had personally sold quite a few signed copies on the night, word would get around and customers would soon be flocking to his shop. As a further inducement, he had put up a poster-sized photograph of the book cover on an easel in his window. It took up half the window space, together with some copies of the book arranged beside it, and he was confident that the prominent display would stimulate the necessary footfall when he opened up the following morning.

What he did not expect was to find the front door standing open, with evidence of the lock having been forced, and the words "*Your Sins Will Find You Out, Bitch*" scrawled in big red letters across the poster in the front window, and the books which had been put out on display ripped apart and dumped in a pile of ugly debris beside it.

He headed straight for his safe in the back room, his heart thudding wildly at the thought of losing the meagre takings of the last month, plus the large float he had put together in readiness for the sale of Tamara Callaghan's novel. But he need not have worried on that score. The safe was intact. But any sense of relief was short-lived. The cardboard box holding his main stock of Callaghan's novel had been ripped open and the books strewn everywhere. Some, like those in the window, had been ripped apart, and others seemingly stabbed with a knife or some other sharp object, defacing the covers and rendering them completely unsaleable. It was a scene of total devastation, as if a madman had run amok in the room in an orgy of wanton, senseless destruction. Shaking fitfully, he picked up the telephone and dialled 999.

* * *

Kate was perched precariously on the edge of a very unstable, plastic seat in the ladies' toilet, cursing someone's failure to replace the broken hinge, when the tannoy blasted her name twice, instructing her to contact the CID office.

Jamie Foster waved a piece of paper in the air from his desk when she walked in. 'Uniform are attending a break-in and criminal damage at the Reading Room bookshop down the road,' he said. 'They're asking for CID.'

Kate scowled. 'So? Are your legs broken or something?'

He grinned. 'Some guy there—' he peered at the piece of paper — 'a Mr Little? Asked for you personally.'

'Did he now? Well, just for that, smart-arse, you can come with me.'

There were several people standing outside the shop when Kate and Jamie Foster arrived, pulling up behind a marked police patrol car. One, a young woman with pink, spiky hair and dressed in blue denims, homed in on the detectives even as they climbed out of their car. She looked very much like a punk rocker, but Kate knew she was nothing of the sort. She had run up against this irritating woman several times before on crime investigations and knew she was from the local newspaper and a proper pain.

'Debbie Moreton,' spiky hair blurted. 'I'm from—'

'I know who you are,' Kate cut in, brushing past her. 'But as I've only just arrived, I don't know any more than you.'

'Tamara Callaghan is a bestselling author, isn't she?' Moreton said, trotting after her.

'So I believe.'

'Any idea why—?'

'Not a clue,' Kate snapped over her shoulder and left her standing there.

Tamara Callaghan's smooth-talking agent, Spencer Little, was standing on the edge of the pavement opposite the door of the shop, looking smart but slightly effeminate in a brown leather coat, the familiar fawn trousers, and a cream shirt with a bright yellow cravat. Smoke trailed from a cigar in his hand, and he seemed to be engaged in a worried conversation with a tall, thin man, dressed in blue flannels and a blazer — a man Kate immediately recognized as the so-called freelance journalist, Ed Templar, whom she had met at Tamara Callaghan's book-signing event at the library.

'Well, if it isn't Mr Templar,' she said, breaking into the conversation. 'This is rather a coincidence, isn't it?'

Templar treated her to a warm smile.

'Detective Sergeant Lewis,' he said, extending a hand, which Kate ignored. 'Good to see you again. Unfortunately, as a result of buttonholing you at the talk, I missed out on a signed book, so I trotted along here today to get a copy from the shop. It seems I was a bit too late.'

Looking past him, Kate saw the defaced poster in the window with the offensive words scrawled across the photograph of Tamara Callaghan's novel, and beside it the dismembered pile of books.

Little half turned, noting the direction of her gaze, and sighed heavily. 'That's not the worst of it, Sergeant. You'd better come inside.'

An elderly, balding man, dressed in an open-necked, grey shirt and matching corduroy trousers was sitting behind the shop counter, his head in his hands. He looked up as they all filed in. Kate introduced herself and Foster.

'Jacob Williamson,' he replied gloomily. 'Came in this morning, found the front door had been forced open and . . . and . . . Who would do something like this? And I'll still have to pay for around fifty books.'

'There are more then?' Kate asked.

A uniformed policeman emerged from a back room as she spoke. 'PC Walker, skip,' he said, and indicated the door behind him. 'You might want to look in there.'

Kate followed him back inside and stared in astonishment at the carnage. A large cardboard box had been ripped open, with the books which had obviously been inside pulled out, torn apart or otherwise defaced, like those in the window, and strewn everywhere.

'I've heard of someone criticizing a writer's work,' she said drily, 'but this strikes me as a bit extreme.'

Little, crowding in behind them, shook his head. 'I only called by this morning to make sure Jacob had got all the books he'd ordered from the distributers. Tamara will be really upset about this. Local sales are important with a new novel — especially when the plot is set in the area and the author also lives in the locality.'

Kate wandered back out of the shop and found Ed Templar still there, studying the poster.

'Why would someone write something like that?' he said as they reappeared. 'They must have a screw loose.'

'There's some strange people about, Mr Templar,' Kate replied, lowering her voice when she spotted the reporter still hovering in the background, 'and believe me, I've dealt with quite a few of them in my career.'

'No doubt you have,' he said, glancing over his shoulder and taking her cue by also lowering his voice, 'and I don't envy you your job trying to nail this one.'

'Oh, we'll get there in the end.'

He nodded. 'I'm sure you will. No ideas, I suppose, on who it could have been? Someone certainly doesn't appear to like Miss Callaghan.'

She shrugged. 'Maybe another failed writer?'

'Or someone with a personal grudge. I mean, the message appears to be very personally directed. I wonder what sins she is thought to have committed?'

'Your guess is as good as mine.'

'Another mystery?' he said.

'Seems like it.'

'I'll leave you to it then.'

At which point, with a cheery wave, he sauntered off along the street with his hands thrust into his pockets.

'Friend of yours?' Foster asked at Kate's elbow.

Kate stared after the disappearing figure thoughtfully. 'Hardly. But he did have a point. Whoever did this has to be off their trolley.'

She turned as Little came back out of the shop. 'Any idea who might have done this, Mr Little?'

He shook his head. 'Not a clue. Nothing like it has ever happened before. It's most disturbing.'

'Has Miss Callaghan ever received any hate mail or nasty phone calls?'

'Not as far as I know.'

'What about rivals in the writing world — someone who might be jealous of her success?'

'No one springs to mind. It's just weird.'

'It *is* weird,' Kate agreed. 'Weird enough to cause me some concern about Miss Callaghan's safety. Have you spoken to her today?'

Little's eyes widened as he realized what Kate was implying.

'Good Lord, no. I . . . I was going to head over there after calling in here.'

'Give her a ring to see if she's okay, will you?' Kate asked. 'Just to be sure.'

Taking Foster to one side, while Little dialled the number on his mobile, she said, 'Can you sort things here? We'll need a statement off Williamson, and we'd better get SOCO out to give the scene the once-over.'

Before he could reply, Little butted in. He looked worried. 'There's no answer from Tamara's number.'

Kate digested the information. 'Probably nothing. She could have gone out.'

Little shook his head vehemently. 'No way. I was due to meet her there—' he glanced at his watch — 'five minutes ago. I'm surprised she hasn't phoned to ask where I am.'

Kate's eyes narrowed. 'Then we'd better get over there pdq.' Her stomach churning, she turned back towards the parked police cars.

'Something up, Sergeant?' the reporter with the hair called excitedly.

'Yes,' Kate retorted. 'I'm late for lunch.'

CHAPTER 8

Leaving the keys to the CID car with Foster, Kate went over to Callaghan's house with Walker in his patrol car. They arrived just seconds before Little.

Kate noticed the same Volvo parked on the hardstanding by the front door but could see no sign of life. The front door was locked and there was no response to several presses on the old-fashioned bellpush.

'I'll see if I can get in around the back,' Walker offered.

'No need,' Little snapped, clearly in a state of agitation. 'I know where she keeps the key.'

He left the porch and bent down a few feet to one side of it. There was a broken pipe protruding from the wall, and he slipped his hand inside and returned to the porch with a Yale key.

He was not so eager to be first in the house, however, and was happy to let them lead the way.

'Hello?' Kate called, advancing along the hallway. 'Miss Callaghan? Are you there? It's DS Lewis.'

There was no reply and Walker threw Kate a worried look.

'Tam? It's Spencer!' he shouted. 'You okay?'

Still nothing. Kate pushed a door open on her left and entered a small study littered with books on bulging shelves and piled up in corners, and boasting a large, old-fashioned desk and padded bosun's chair. There was a laptop on the desk, which was still illuminated, displaying a screen of double-spaced text. A half-full coffee mug stood beside it, which Kate checked and found to be cold, plus an ashtray piled high with dogends. The room itself was empty.

Little walked past her and stared at the screen. He shook his head. 'Not her usual standard of prose,' he said. 'I hope she can do better than that for the next book.'

Kate treated him to a scathing glance. 'I think we have more to concern ourselves with than her use of prose.'

Little flinched. 'Yes, yes, of course.' He went back to the door to shout again. 'Tam? Where are you?'

The answering voice was not that of Tamara Callaghan but Walker. He had evidently left Kate to check the study and moved on to the next room. 'In here!' he shouted.

Kate found herself back in the living room where she had interviewed the writer before, Callaghan was lying sprawled out on the settee, one hand hanging over the edge. Her eyes were closed, and a red stain had spread across the front of her cream blouse.

'Good grief, is that blood?' Little gasped, his face suddenly ashen. 'Is she . . . ? Is she dead?'

Kate bent down to pick up a miraculously unbroken wine glass lying beside the settee. 'No, it's not blood, and she's not dead — just pissed!'

'Pissed?' he echoed. 'On red wine.'

Kate raised an eyebrow. 'You might make a good detective one day, Mr Little. Meanwhile, we'll leave you to sober her up. Maybe if you tell her what happened to her books that will do the trick — especially when she hears that the incident will be in the local newspapers tomorrow.'

* * *

'So, our burglar was not a member of Tamara Callaghan's fan club then?' Percival commented after Kate had briefed him on the afternoon's shenanigans.

Kate frowned. 'Clearly not. But for someone to go to those lengths to express his or her feelings does bother me. It suggests she could become a target for more serious attention later.'

'Could the perp be our flasher, do you think? Maybe he already had an axe to grind against her or he's taken exception to her reporting things to us.'

She shook her head. 'If Jason Spindler *is* our flasher, I can't see him going that far. It wouldn't be his style, and anyway, why would he pick on Callaghan for punishment any more than one of his other victims?'

'You're probably right,' he said, and he was grinning for some reason, 'but at least we have the blood samples from the last incident and hopefully, they will ultimately give us all the evidence we need.'

Kate stared at him for a moment. It was funny how the discovery of the blood had led to a complete change in his attitude. He was suddenly surprisingly upbeat and good-humoured — as if he had received double his daily dose of happy pills.

'Fingers crossed,' she replied. 'There are no guarantees. But what about the surveillance you asked to be set up? There hardly seems much point to it now — until we get the results from NDNAD.'

He grinned again. 'Oh, I think we might as well carry on with it for the time being. After all, it gives Ben the chance to improve his fitness and poor old Hayden the opportunity for a kip and a Mars bar.'

For some reason Kate bit on the last remark. 'That's not fair, Des. Hayden is one of your team and he doesn't deserve that sort of derogatory comment behind his back.'

His jaw dropped and his grin seemed to freeze. 'Okay, okay,' he replied hastily, holding his hands up in an apologetic gesture. 'I was only joking, Kate. After all, you yourself have a go at him regularly, calling him "fat man" and such like.'

Kate stood up. 'That's different. It's only in fun, and anyway he's my husband, so I have the right to take the mickey out of him if I wish. As his DI, you don't, especially not to someone else.'

Then she turned on her heel and walked out of his office, her "wild" well and truly up.

It was only when she got back to her desk and had sat there for a few minutes that she cooled down and thought about what had just happened. Des *had* only been joking and her outburst had been uncalled for. What was the matter with her? Maybe the fact that he was sitting in the chair she thought should have been hers was still getting to her, eating away at her insides and turning her into a resentful, envious bitch.

Abruptly, she stood up and marched back to his office. 'I owe you an apology, Des,' she said. 'I was totally out of order and I'm sorry.'

To her surprise, he smiled at her. 'No problem, Kate. Come in and close the door, would you?'

She complied, frowning in puzzlement, and dropped back into the plastic chair she had just vacated. 'I know you must be wondering why I'm so full of it this afternoon,' he said. 'Actually, it has nothing to do with this indecent exposure case. It's something entirely unconnected — and by the way, what I'm about to say is in the strictest confidence.'

He hesitated and reaching in his pocket, produced a single piece of paper. Kate recognized it as a report form and glimpsed the headquarters banner at the top. 'The super had me upstairs earlier,' he said. He flashed the form and then Kate understood. 'He told me I'm being promoted to DI at the "big house" — Professional Standards.'

Kate gaped. 'Complaints and Discipline?'

He nodded. 'As we all used to call it, yes, but things have moved on since those days.'

She whistled. 'Well, congratulations. How do you feel about being a "rubber heel"?'

He shrugged. 'It's a DI's job and anyway, I won't be doing much investigatory work, I'll be mainly bag carrying for one of the supers or DCIs.'

It was her turn to hesitate. 'When?'

'Well, it seems it's a bit of a rush job, due to a retirement. They want me in post in five weeks' time.'

'Five weeks?' Kate echoed. 'Talk about due notice. So, who will be replacing you?'

He studied her fixedly. 'That has still to be sorted, but it seems that, whoever it is, they can't start until at least a couple of months' time, and I am told I must use up all my leave before taking up the post, which amounts to around two weeks, so it will have to be an acting job for someone in the interim . . .'

Kate swallowed hard and he sighed sympathetically. 'Sorry, Kate, but I have no idea who will be appointed. I know how much this means to you after missing out last time, but I haven't been told anything.'

Kate nodded and stood up, feeling suddenly light-headed. 'Congratulations anyway, Des. I'll miss you.'

He half-closed one eye. 'Even if I do take the piss out of poor old hubby? Strict confidence, though, okay? Not a word to anyone.'

Kate got the call fifteen minutes after returning to her desk. Superintendent Rutherford smiled at her when she entered his office, his bald head gleaming in the sunlight streaming in through the window behind him and his brown eyes studying her over the top of his spectacles.

'Sit down, Sarge,' he said. 'I've got some good news for you.'

* * *

The man in the camouflage jacket sat behind the wheel of his Land Rover, which was parked in a gateway opposite the house a short distance past the front entrance. He was drinking from a can of coke and watching the comings and goings with keen interest. There had been a few too. First a Royal Mail van delivering the post and then, maybe half an hour later, a marked cop car and an old-fashioned MG sports job — possibly nineteen-fifties vintage — with the hood down and a blond-haired man driving. Neither the cop car nor the MG were hanging about either, so something was obviously up.

He smiled grimly. It seemed very likely that the visit had been prompted by what had happened at the bookshop — at least, that's what he hoped — and he allowed himself to sink lower in the seat in a more comfortable, relaxed posture to await developments, crushing the empty coke can in one hand and tossing it out of the window.

Breaking into the shop and destroying the books had been pretty satisfying. It had given him the opportunity to let out some of the anger and frustration that had built up inside him over the years. And more importantly, it had sent her a warning signal — that he was out there somewhere, watching, waiting for the right moment to finish things. Not that that would happen yet. Oh no, he wanted to play first. Get her really wound up, so she was an emotional wreck before he materialized to administer the *coup de grâce*. He thought of the message he had scrawled across the poster, wondering if it would strike the intended chord and whether that would generate the panic he wanted so much to create. She might not twig things at first — possibly she'd think some nutter who didn't like her books was behind the destruction at the shop. But he would ensure that she didn't labour under a false premise for long. The beauty of it all was that when the truth dawned on her, she wouldn't even be able to enlist the help of the police because she would have to tell them everything else as well, and that was right out of the question.

He yawned and glanced at his watch, then started as the cop car suddenly emerged again and drove off at a more leisurely pace. Well, they weren't in there long, were they? Not long enough for a heart to heart anyway. He frowned, wishing he could have been a fly on the wall. Maybe they hadn't called about the bookshop. But in that case, why would they have gone there at all?

Then he remembered the woman detective he'd seen at the talk and book-signing. From his seat right at the back of the room, he had heard her being introduced to the blond character he'd gathered was some sort of publisher's agent. Could be that the cop was a personal friend, or perhaps someone giving the author some background info on police procedure for one of her books. He had formed the impression that there had been a woman in the passenger seat of the cop car, so it could have been her. But no, the police would hardly have raced there at speed, two up in a marked car, just to give her that sort of info. There had to be another reason and the job at the shop was the most likely. But why hadn't the guy in the MG reappeared? His face creased into a sneer as his thoughts hit a more basic level. Maybe he was shagging her? Well, he'd better make the most of it, because she wouldn't be around that long.

* * *

In fact, Spencer Little was doing nothing of the sort — chance would have been a fine thing. Instead, he was sitting beside the now wide-awake crime novelist, watching her down the mug of black coffee he had just brewed for her after delivering the shock news about the break-in at the shop.

'I can't understand why anyone would do that, Tam,' he said as gently as he could. 'Poor old Jacob is beside himself.'

Callaghan stared at him for a moment over the rim of her mug, her eyes narrowed, her thoughts seemingly miles away.

'What did the vandal mean by the vicious slur he scrawled across the poster? Do you think that flasher could have been responsible?'

Her eyes refocused on him and she shook her head. 'Hardly, Spence. He was just an over-sexed pervert. Different sort of thing. This one's probably just some would-be writer who can't get anything published themselves.'

Little looked dubious. 'I think you ought to be careful, though, he could be dangerous.' He brightened. 'If you like I could stay here with you for a while, to make sure you're okay. I expect you have a spare room?'

'How sweet of you, Spence,' she said drily, secretly thinking quite the opposite, 'but really, I'll be fine.'

She stood up. 'Now, I really must have a shower and get changed. So, if you don't mind . . .'

Reluctantly, he allowed himself to be ushered back to the front door. But climbing into his MGC, he called out, 'Ring me any time of the day or night if you need to, I really wouldn't mind.'

'I'm sure you wouldn't,' she murmured as she watched him drive away. Then, walking quickly back into her living room, she collected a lead-crystal glass from an ornate drinks cabinet and poured herself a double scotch.

As she put down the half-finished bottle, she stared at her white face in the mirror on the wall. 'Shit!' she said slowly and distinctly. 'Double shit!'

Draining the glass in one gulp, she hurled it across the room against the far wall.

Outside the house, on the main road, the gateway was now empty.

CHAPTER 9

Kate left Rutherford's office on cloud nine. It had happened. Finally, after all this time, she had got what she wanted, and in just three weeks' time, she would be sitting in Des Percival's chair. Okay, for the first couple of weeks her new role would be unofficial, since Des would only be using up his leave, but at the end of that period the appointment would be made official, and she would be Acting DI. It was not a permanent promotion — it would only last until a substantive DI was appointed to the position — but it would be her chance to prove she could hold down the rank and it could eventually lead to a full promotion when a vacancy became available somewhere in the force.

She ran into Jamie Foster as she headed back to the CID office and treated him to an extravagant wink as they passed each other, knowing full well from what Rutherford had told her that Jamie was about to be offered the Acting Sergeant position to replace her.

She could hardly wait to tell Hayden when he came on duty for his support role in Ben Holloway's surveillance of Jason Spindler's home, and after giving Percival her news and receiving his hearty congratulations, she returned to her desk, her head still spinning. But as she tried, without much success, to focus on the mountain of paperwork in her tray, while at the same time trying to keep an eye on the office door to catch Hayden's arrival, the buzz of her mobile telephone brought her abruptly back to the real world.

'Detective Sergeant Lewis? It's Hector Spindler here. Can you come and see me? Jason has gone missing.'

* * *

The red-faced farmer met Kate in the yard when she pulled up outside the farmhouse. He looked tense and worried.

'He didn't come home last night,' he said. 'At least, I didn't see him. His bed's not been slept in and there's food missing from the fridge.'

Kate nodded, staring about her. 'Then he must have come home last night.'

'His bike's gone too,' Spindler said.

'You've no idea where he might have gone? No friends he might be staying with?'

'He hasn't got any friends as far as I know. Always been a loner. I just hope he's not going to do something stupid.'

'Like what?'

He shrugged. 'Dunno. You know, like something stupid — top himself and that. This has only happened since you came here and spoke to him.'

'Well, he'd hardly take his bike and nick some food if he were going to take his own life, would he?'

'I dunno. He's a mixed-up kid. He might do anything, 'specially if he thinks he might be going back inside. I'm worried in case he tries to hurt himself.'

Kate said nothing about the previous night's incident and the discovery of the blood found at the scene of the indecent exposure.

'Can I take a look around?'

'Be my guest, but you won't find him. I've already done the rounds.'

He was right too. Kate checked all the barns and outhouses, but there was no sign of anyone.

'Can I have a look in his room?'

Spindler nodded. 'I'll show you where it is.'

It wasn't difficult searching Jason's bedroom. It was very small and there was just the bed, a single wardrobe and a chest of drawers to look through. Kate noticed the pile of clothes on top of the wardrobe, however, and the fact that they seemed to have been disturbed, with half of them hanging over the edge.

'Looks like there was something up there,' she said to Spindler, who was watching anxiously from the doorway.

'His rucksack probably,' he said. 'He kept it up there.'

'Well, it's not there anymore.'

'So, he must be hiding out somewhere?'

She nodded. 'Looks very much like it. All we can do is put out an alert and see if one of our patrols spots him.'

'What then?'

It was Kate's turn to shrug. 'He's an adult. So, unless we can prove he did anything wrong, he's free to do what he likes.'

He made a face and jerked some magazines out of his coat pocket. 'I found these up here. I told him I'd burned them, but I'd just stuck them in the dustbin.'

Kate glanced at the picture of the naked woman on the cover of the uppermost magazine and smiled sadly. 'Obviously, he's still got a problem. But looking at dirty magazines is no offence. You'd be surprised how many men do — and many of them are married and the height of respectability.'

'I can't understand why anyone would want to look at that filth.'

'Each to their own,' she said. 'Looking at dirty magazines is one thing but acting out some perverted fantasy is quite another.'

'What if he's been doing that again around here?'

'Then he becomes *our* problem,' she said. 'Let me know if he turns up, will you?'

* * *

76

The pile of dirty, wet sacks provided little comfort and even with his coat spread over them, Jason found the wet creeping through. The barn was in a poor state of repair, and it was apparent that it had been abandoned long ago. The corrugated iron roof had several large holes in it and the bales of straw in the corner had long since decomposed into a glutinous mess, populated by rats.

He had already eaten the food he had stuffed into his rucksack and drained his second can of coke, and he could feel the pangs of hunger already beginning to start again. Furthermore, after a cold sleepless night, during which the wound in his leg felt as if it were on fire, he now also found that it was leaking through the plasters he had put on, and he was left with no choice but to remove them and affix the fresh ones he'd brought with him. Then, on top of everything, he was still no further forward in coming up with a game plan. With little money in his pocket, going back home seemed to be the only option, but what then? Wait for the police to call, and cart him off to the cells like before?

More for something to do than anything else, he flicked through the half-dozen porn magazines he had taken from under his mattress and felt the powerful urges begin to start all over again. Why did he do it? Why did he keep winding himself up by looking at the things? He threw them across the barn into the rotting straw and tried to concentrate on his perilous situation instead.

So, what if the police did call to see him about that last business — the girl on the footpath? They had nothing on him. He'd been wearing a hood at the time, so neither she nor the old man with the dog could describe him. Okay, there was the risk that he had left some blood behind when he tore his leg on the barbed wire, but that had happened well into the undergrowth, so there was every chance the police hadn't spotted it. Even if they had, the blood would probably have dried out before they'd found it, and from what he'd read about DNA, it would not have been much use if that was the case.

What a fool he was. He had panicked unnecessarily. He should pack it all in and go back home. At least there was a nice, warm bed waiting for him there, and he'd be out of this dirty, wet barn. He knew he couldn't stomach another night in the place. Even the inevitable interrogation by his father was better than pneumonia, or sepsis from the wound in his leg.

His mind finally made up, he picked up his bike and headed back along the track towards home. But he never got there.

He kept thinking about the woman in the big house — the one he had chased inside from the patio. He had previously seen her walking about the place naked, and that last time, the shortie nightdress she had been wearing had been so transparent that it had left very little to the imagination. Okay, so she had to be around forty, but she was still something to look at, and for some reason, she excited him more than any of the other, younger women he had preyed on.

Already aroused by the raunchy pictures in the porn magazines he had been looking at in the barn, he knew he had to go back to that house before he went anywhere else, regardless of his injured leg. Whether he headed home now or later would make no difference to anything — his old man would still interrogate him — and at least the later he went back, the more chance he had of making it to his room unnoticed. Then he could attend to his leg again.

Slipping a hand into his pocket, he felt the rough fabric of the hood and his excitement mounted. Reaching a fork in the track, he swung left instead of right, bypassing the farm and pedalling straight for the main road.

* * *

'Acting DI, you say?' Hayden gaped at Kate across the table.

Kate hissed at him and cast a glance around the police canteen. 'Not so loud, you dipstick. I don't want half the nick to know about it before it's officially announced.'

He stuffed the last piece of lardy cake into his mouth. 'But Acting DI? Honestly, however did you manage to land that?'

She snorted. 'Well, thanks for the vote of confidence.'

He swallowed the cake in a gulp and shook his head quickly. 'Sorry, I didn't mean it like that but Gordon Bennett, this is a turn-up for the books, isn't it? And — and Jamie Foster as Acting DS. Phew! I never saw that coming either. Er, congratulations, though, of course.'

'Well at least you remembered to say it in the end,' she said sarcastically.

But the rebuke went right over his head. 'And when is all this supposed to happen?'

'In four days, apparently. Des has some leave to take, so I'll be covering his absence unofficially for a couple of weeks, then I'll take over properly after that.'

'Till when?'

She studied the anxiety written into his face and smirked mischievously. 'Could be a couple of months, might be a lot longer—'

'A lot longer?' he echoed, his dismay evident.

'Depends on when a substantive DI can be appointed,' she said, keeping a straight face.

'Lordy!' he breathed, staring down at his empty plate as he fully digested her bombshell, and for a few moments there was an awkward silence between them, during which Kate finished drinking her coffee and he picked at the crumbs on his plate. Another thought occurred to him, and a frown developed on his flushed face. He looked up.

'Er — I won't have to call you ma'am, will I?'

She stared at him levelly. 'I would expect nothing less.'

His jaw tightened and he straightened in his chair. 'Then I'm applying for a transfer. I mean, it's humiliating enough having to call my wife "Sergeant", but DI . . . ? I don't think I could stomach calling you ma'am.'

She grinned and rested a hand on his arm. 'When have you ever heard a DI called ma'am, Hayd? For heaven's sake,

I'm joking, you pillock. Having you on, okay?' Then, seeing him relax, she couldn't resist adding, 'I would be a bit put out, though, if you continued to call me "old girl", as you frequently do now, but boss or guv would be fine.'

'Boss?'

Again, she laughed. 'Oh, Hayden, you're so easy to wind up, you really are.'

He clambered to his feet, plainly not amused. 'Am I indeed? Well, I'm sorry to have to spoil your fun, but I have a job to do with Ben Holloway.'

'Not anymore you don't,' she said, 'so sit down again, you daft bugger. The surveillance is off for now.'

'What?'

She nodded. 'Jason Spindler has gone walkies and we don't know where to yet. I've briefed Des and he agrees that there is little point in Ben sitting outside the farm when the little perv you're supposed to be watching isn't there. That's what I needed to tell you before you went out to start the surveillance.'

He sniffed. 'I thought you brought me down here just to impress me with the news of your elevation to the dizzy heights of DI.'

Kate winced, knowing she had asked for that. 'Well, it was certainly part of it. As your wife, I didn't want you to find out about it from someone else, once the grapevine got to work, and I could hardly tell you upstairs in the office with all the flapping ears, could I? But the change of plan for tonight was also a priority.'

'And this change of plan is what?'

'Well, instead of sitting parked up in the Trannie, bored to tears, waiting for a shout from Ben, you're to grab the keys to one of the plain cars and collect him from the CID office. Des thinks it would be a good idea for the pair of you to cruise the immediate area to see if you can locate our runaway. Check a few derelicts or outbuildings, that sort of thing.'

'What would be the purpose in that? He's an adult after all.'

'Ostensibly, it is to find him and see if he is okay. His father is worried about his mental state and what he might do to himself, so he has become a person at risk. We have already circulated the fact that he is missing to all patrols so we can be seen to be going through the motions just in case he does do something stupid to himself, and as far as anyone else is concerned, this is an extension of that.'

'And if we find him, what then?'

'Obviously check that he's okay, but also try to pinpoint where he's gone to ground, so we know where to find him if the blood lab tests turn out to be a positive match from the samples taken at the Mark crime scene. We can't arrest him yet, because we have no evidence linking him to any offence, but we do need to try and keep tabs on him. You never know, if you're careful, you might actually catch him at it somewhere.'

He looked wary. 'And how long are we to do this point-less driving around? The original obs job was only for four hours.'

'To give you a clue, you can tell me all about it when you get home in the morning.'

'The *morning*? We're expected to be driving around all night?'

She chuckled. 'It'll make a nice change for you, Hayd. Proper police work and all that. I've ordered some coffee and sandwiches for you both from the canteen, and you'll be able to tuck into it out on the road. Think of it as a sort of nocturnal picnic. Oh, and I've ordered your favourite sarnies — cheese and ham, plus a big slice of juicy fruit cake.'

* * *

Jason Spindler left his bicycle half buried in the hedge at the front of the property, noting for the first time the sign on one of the gate pillars, bearing the name "*Scribblers Halt*". He had been sitting among the trees on the other side of the road for a long time, waiting for dusk. Now it had come, and he could feel his heart thudding with excitement as he crept through the gateway, then slipped into the belt of woodland which bordered the driveway on his left and hid the house from the road.

As he made his way through the trees something scurried among the fallen leaves in front of him, startling him for a moment, and although it was a warm night, he couldn't repress a shiver. The woods were full of tiny rodents and large eight-legged creepy-crawlies that spun their silken webs between the trees. He didn't like spiders at the best of times and these fat, mottled autumn monsters really freaked him out. He remembered on the farm getting one stuck up his nose as a child and running around screaming in a panic — 'like some bloody girl,' his father had later said, relating the incident to a crowd of friends and making no secret of how much he despised his only son.

His childhood had been like that all the way through. Constantly humiliated by his father and everyone else. Friendless and bullied at school for being different. Ostracized by the local village where they called him a weirdo. The only person who had understood and tried to protect him was his mother, and she had died just before his nineteenth birthday. Since then he had been totally alone, retreating into himself and his perverse, fantasy world, where he held the power and could instil fear into the young women he revealed himself to and terrorized. And now he was going to do it all over again to the sexy bitch in the big house.

He soon found the oak tree — *his* tree — with the convenient hole in its trunk. It was where he had left his clothes the last time he was here. But he did not start to undress immediately. Instead, he pushed through the undergrowth to the edge of the woodland until he could see into the house. As before, the curtains downstairs had not been pulled and he could see the woman, sitting facing one of the downstairs windows. A lamp to one side of her, she had her head down, as if she was looking at something. Straining his eyes, he could just make out something sticking up above the window and recognized it as the back of a laptop. She was either typing or reading something off the screen. He smirked, his excitement mounting. He would soon put a stop to that. She had another shock in store.

Making his way back through the trees, he stopped again by the oak, slipped off his coat and started to unbutton his shirt. Then he froze, peering about him nervously. He had heard a noise — the sound of a branch breaking in the gloom close by. His mouth began to dry up and his excitement turned to fear. Was there someone else lurking among the trees? Someone who had seen him arrive and was watching him? But what would they be doing in the wood? It couldn't be the police, surely? They wouldn't have known he was coming back here. Then who? He listened intently, but the sound wasn't repeated.

An owl hooted some distance away and all at once the moon emerged, sending a host of pale, ghostly beams through the branches of the surrounding trees, tingeing the leaves of the evergreen bushes carpeting the ground with bluish fire. Another loud crack, behind him this time, and he spun round. He was able to see more clearly now, and his legs began to shake. Something was creeping stealthily towards him from among the trees — a dense shape, with eyes that seemed to blaze in the moonlight with an eerie luminescence.

Uttering a terrified whimper, he shrank back against the oak tree, but as his legs started to give way beneath him, the muntjac deer — for such it was — jerked to a stop and with a snort of alarm, swung away from him, barking noisily as it careered off back into the shadows.

Laughing at his own stupidity, he leaned back against the comforting bark of the old oak, sucking in great gulps of the cool night air. But his relief was premature. At that very moment, a pair of black-gloved hands reached around from behind the tree, gripping his throat in an unbreakable stranglehold and cutting off his oxygen supply. Despite his frantic struggles, his vital senses shut down within seconds and Jason Spindler was plunged into oblivion.

CHAPTER 10

The man in the camouflage jacket had no difficulty carrying
the body through the woods to his Land Rover. The corpse
had little weight to it, and he had carried a lot heavier loads
over his shoulder back in the day. He was parked on a narrow
track just down from the house and was able to get to it the
same way he had got into the grounds, through a gap in the
perimeter hedge.

The unexpected arrival of the kid had put paid to his
original idea of getting closer to the house to carry out a recce
for when he finally decided to come back to finish things. He
needed to have as much information on the layout as possible
— ways in, exits, cameras, that sort of detail — just in case
things went pear-shaped on the big day. That wasn't going
to happen tonight. At first it had puzzled him as to what
the youngster had been doing in the woods, but he made a
habit of reading the local newspapers and finding the black
hood in the lad's pocket had explained everything. Dirty little
moron! Well, he wouldn't be doing any more flashing, that
was for sure.

He had not enjoyed killing him, but it had been necessary. He couldn't be sure the kid hadn't already caught sight
of him creeping about among the trees. If he had, he might

have told someone, like the police, about it later — especially if he was nicked and saw the chance of striking a deal on a quid pro quo basis. It would have been a lot more concerning to the killer had he known that this was Jason Spindler's third visit and that the police were already out looking for him. *Had* he been privy to that information, things might have ended a lot differently, but then as he would no doubt have put it, 'Shit happens.'

As it was, he stuck his victim in the back of the 'Drover and re-joined the main road, heading out onto the moonlit Levels. Carting a body about in a car at night was a risky undertaking, particularly if it attracted the attention of a bored police patrol, but there was no way he could have simply left the kid's corpse in the woods to be found by a groundsman or an inquisitive dog, especially as he had snapped his neck after rendering him insensible — a useful technique he had learned in his days as a mercenary. Finding corpses with broken necks tended to make the "Bill" a mite suspicious. Burying was an option, of course, but even that was risky. He knew from his time overseas that buried bodies had a nasty habit of rising to the surface, dug up by foraging animals or whatever. He'd heard that there were plenty of deep peat bogs on the Levels but he didn't know exactly where they were, and he couldn't be sure that even the deepest bog wouldn't eventually give up what was dropped into it.

No, the best plan was to conceal the murder in plain sight. Rig up a nice suicide to explain the broken neck and with a bit of luck, that's exactly what the police would think it was. And he knew just the place for his debut enactment. A little spot, far enough away from the scene and right next door to the route of his regular morning run . . .

* * *

Hayden was tired and irritable. It was years since he had done a full night turn — not since his days on the beat as a uniformed plod — and he resented having to do one now.

After devouring his sandwiches and cake within half an hour of leaving the police station, much against Ben Holloway's advice, he was hungry again. Glancing at the dashboard clock, he looked across at Holloway in the front passenger seat and cleared his throat. 'Pedro's Diner should still be open,' he said, 'if you feel like a snack?'

Holloway chuckled. 'No need, mate. I haven't eaten my sarnies yet.'

Hayden frowned. 'I might just schlep over there. It's the sort of place young Jason Spindler might pop into if he's hungry. Worth a check.'

But Holloway was wise to him. 'Could be awkward if we were spotted. It's only just past the nick and if we were seen, questions might be asked as to what we were doing there. We're supposed to be out checking derelicts and outbuildings.'

Hayden's frown became a scowl. 'Darned stupid driving around the marshes in the middle of the night anyway. Spindler could be anywhere. We're detectives, after all, not woodentops.'

'Hey, steady on,' his companion censured. 'As a TDC, I'm still technically a woodentop. I could be back on the beat anytime.'

Hayden grimaced. 'Sorry, nothing meant. I'm just so hungry.'

The sandwich appeared as if by magic in front of his nose and the car swerved slightly as he grabbed it. 'You sure?' he said, sinking his teeth into it without giving Holloway time to change his mind.

'I don't eat at night,' the other replied, shaking his head as he watched half his meal vanish with incredible speed. 'You retain more calories at night — which leads to fat.'

The dig was lost on Hayden, who instead threw him another quick glance. 'Then you won't be eating the other half?'

Holloway shook his head, still grinning. 'Not even the fruit cake,' he said, and suddenly Hayden was happy again.

* * *

Josh Carrick felt good. The all-night party he had set up at his parents' home while they were abroad on holiday had got off to a great start, with over forty of his friends and room-mates from university turning up so far. There was plenty of booze, and the distinctive odour of cannabis was already heavily present. He just hoped no one would bring in any of the hard stuff, like crack cocaine or PCP. His father was a barrister and a police drugs bust in the big, detached house would definitely not be appreciated by the old man — especially as he didn't know anything about the party in the first place.

But Josh was not the sort of person to let worries like that prey on his mind. It was the end of four years' hard graft at uni, and he was determined to let his hair down and enjoy himself. He hadn't expected to score straightaway — that usually came after a few drinks — but to his delight, the girl with the raven hair and enigmatic smile had come on to him within minutes of her arrival. She said her name was Denise Lawson and she was on holiday from the north and staying with her aunt in Glastonbury. She had a willowy figure and large brown eyes that seemed to sparkle in the light of the candles dotted around the living room. Carrick fell for her immediately, and it wasn't long before they were dancing to the deafening beat produced by the powerful sound system before retiring to a dark corner, where several shared joints had the effect of releasing her inhibitions and led to a heavy petting session.

Emboldened by her response and now fully aroused, Carrick was determined to go the whole way and satisfy his almost uncontrollable urges. She agreed to go upstairs to his bedroom with him, but after twenty minutes of constant interruptions when other partygoers burst in with the same idea in mind, he pulled her off the bed with an exasperated sigh and suggested they took a walk.

It was mild outside and there was a full moon as he led his "prize" along the narrow track from the back of the house to the old barn his father had renovated at the end of the property, which adjoined one of the marshland droves.

She giggled expectantly as he pulled the door open and reached for the electric light switch. The glare hurt their eyes for a moment, reflecting off the sleek Mercedes car and mini tractor parked inside.

'Whatever are you up to, Josh Carrick?' she said, feigning innocence. 'I'm a good girl, you know.'

He grinned. 'Let's find out exactly how good you are then,' he suggested and led her past the car towards a shadowy corner beneath what looked like an old hayloft, supported by wooden pillars.

It was her unexpected choking gasp and the sudden tightness of her grip on his arm as she came to an abrupt stop that drew his attention to the grisly sight in front of them. In an instant his grin vanished, and his lust took an immediate nose-dive.

The young man was dangling from a length of rope attached to a roof beam a few feet away, his arms hanging limply by his sides. The big knot in the noose behind his neck had forced his head forward, so that he seemed to be staring down at the aluminium stepladder which was lying on the floor beneath his feet. The single word scrawled in black six- or seven-inch block capital letters on the cracked concrete in front of it said simply, "Sorry".

* * *

Hayden and Ben were checking an old Second World War bunker when the call came through from the Control Room, and within twenty minutes they were pulling up outside the house where the party was being held. There was a marked police patrol car and an empty emergency ambulance already parked beside the kerb, both empty and still with their blue lights flashing.

The ambulance crew — a man and a woman — were leaving as they pushed through the front gate. The woman paused for a moment to shake her head grimly.

'Nothing for us, I'm afraid,' she said. 'Casualty is deceased. Doc's on his way, we understand, so we'll leave you with it.' She smiled without humour. 'Have a nice night.'

The detectives found a small crowd of youngsters, many of them bevvied up or spaced out on cannabis, jostling for a place inside the barn, anxious to get the best view of the corpse, which had been cut down from the beam and was lying on the floor under a tarpaulin protected by a length of police tape strung between a mini tractor and an oil drum. Josh Carrick and a young, uniformed police constable stood between the makeshift barrier and the noisy crowd, desperately trying to get all the oglers to leave. They might as well have tried talking to the wall.

Most of the partygoers did drift away when the two detectives arrived, but in every situation there are always those who just will not cooperate. In this case, a dozen of them stood their ground, shouting about citizen's rights, swearing at the policemen and making threats. The situation dramatically changed when, in response to Hayden's radio call, a second police patrol car arrived and two rather large, uniformed officers materialized. That was the signal for a rapid departure and within seconds Hayden and Ben had the scene to themselves.

'Who is he, do you think?' Holloway asked, as Hayden lifted a corner of the tarpaulin to peer at the corpse, conscious of the white face of Carrick hovering in the background.

'Oh, I know who he is,' Hayden replied grimly. 'His name is Jason Spindler — the very man we've both been searching for tonight.'

Holloway looked up at the single strand of rope that had been left hanging from the beam. 'Looks like he decided to end it all then.'

Hayden nodded and stared at the word "Sorry" scrawled on the floor below it. 'So it would appear,' he replied. But his frown suggested otherwise.

Then someone coughed at his elbow. He turned and found the young policeman who had been trying to disperse the crowd of partygoers standing there.

'PC Jukes,' the officer said, and stepped to one side to reveal Carrick hovering in the background. 'This guy lives here.'

Hayden studied the blond, tousle-haired youth in the tight fawn jeans and open-necked flowery shirt.

'And you are?'

'Joss Carrick. My parents own the place.'

'And where are they now?'

'Away on holiday.'

'Let me guess, they know nothing about the party that you were obviously having here tonight.'

Carrick made a sheepish grimace. 'No,' he admitted, and sighed heavily. 'My dad will kill me when he finds out.'

'So, tell me what happened.'

'Well, I came into the barn about half an hour ago and found this guy hanging from the beam up there. I cut him down with a pruning knife I found on the workbench in the corner and called for the ambulance and police. But it was obvious he was already dead.'

'Do you know him?' Hayden asked.

'Never seen him before.'

'Any idea why he would do something like this in your dad's barn?'

'Not a clue.'

'So, what made you come into the barn in the first place when I assume your party was in full swing?'

Carrick cleared his throat, looking uncomfortable. 'I, er, I met this girl at the party and offered to show her my dad's new Merc.'

Hayden couldn't repress a soft, unamused chuckle. 'Yes, right. Well, it makes a change from "would you like to see my etchings", I suppose.'

Carrick reddened, catching his drift, and stared down at his feet.

'Where's this girl now?' Hayden asked.

'She freaked out when we found the body and drove off home.'

'Okay, well we shall want her full name and address and the names and addresses of as many of your partygoers as you can remember.' Hayden nodded towards Jukes, who had been first on the scene and had just come back into the barn. 'In the meantime, the constable here will return to the house with you and take down the details of any of your guests who are still there. Got that?'

Carrick nodded resignedly and followed the uniformed officer out of the door, with his shoulders bent as if he was carrying the weight of the world on them.

'So, what now?' Holloway asked, staring back at the corpse.

Hayden jerked his radio out of his pocket. 'I think perhaps under the circumstances we should get the duty DS out here while we are waiting for the doctor to arrive.'

'Good idea. Who's on call tonight?'

Hayden chuckled, a vengeful gleam in his blue eyes. 'Do you know,' he said, 'I do believe it's my very own Sergeant Lewis, bless her cotton socks.'

* * *

Kate was slightly less sour-faced when she turned up at the barn than Des Percival who joined her a few moments later. The divisional surgeon had already been and gone after carrying out the formal certification of death, though without stating a cause. He had declared that while it seemed to be a case of suicide, there would have to be a post-mortem, and the coroner would be the one to determine the cause after hearing all the facts at the resultant inquest.

'Tell us what we don't already know,' Kate commented drily when Hayden gave them the message on their arrival before briefing them on his interview with Carrick.

'You are sure the stiff *is* Spindler, though?' Percival muttered when he had finished.

Hayden shrugged and indicated the corpse with a wave of his hand. 'Be my guest, guv.'

91

Kate grinned but went over with him to check. 'It's Spindler all right,' she confirmed, studying the greying, ghost-like face. She looked at the word "Sorry" scrawled on the concrete and added, 'Thoughtful of him to apologize to us for killing himself, though.'

Percival's eyes narrowed. 'What are you saying?'

She grimaced. 'Nothing really. It just seems a bit too clear-cut.'

'Isn't that what we want? It makes things a lot easier, surely?'

'True, but I can't help feeling there's something not quite right here. I mean, leaving a one-word message like that is a bit theatrical, isn't it? Almost as if to remove any doubt that he committed suicide. You know — "I'm sorry, folks, for being such a pervert and I've decided to make amends by hanging myself from this beam."'

'You're reading an awful lot into one word.'

'Maybe I am, but I met and interviewed Spindler. He came across to me as a weak, seriously introverted character, not the sort of person with the emotional strength — if you can call it that — to string himself up, or to take the trouble to hint at why he'd done it by leaving an intriguing one-word message like that.'

'I agree with Kate,' Hayden cut in. 'And why do the job here in the first place? It must be three miles at least from his home. Also, where is his bike?'

Percival shrugged. 'He could have dumped that in a hedge or a rhyne somewhere close by.'

'Point taken, and we can get the troops to do a search for it in the morning. But why bother to dump it anywhere? Why not just leave it in the barn?'

'Yes,' Kate put in, warming to things. 'And what about the rope? Where did he get that from? Did he bring it with him or was it here already? And if it was here, how would he have known that in advance or that there would be a nice ladder for him to stand on?'

'Could be his decision to kill himself was a spur of the moment thing.'

'Okay but think about it. Are we actually saying he came here to doss, saw the rope, and thought, "Oh, I think I'll kill myself today," helpfully scrawling the word "Sorry" on the floor with what looks like some sort of black crayon, which he conveniently had with him? That he then calmly sat down to prepare the noose, chucked it over the beam, which has to be at least twelve feet off the ground, tied it off — presumably standing on that stepladder which just happened to be there — and did the business with his leap into oblivion without a second's thought? I don't buy it.'

'Neither do I,' Hayden agreed.

Percival sighed. 'So, you're suggesting someone could have done the job for him and made it look as though he killed himself out of remorse for what he had done?'

'I'm just saying the whole thing seems more than a bit iffy.'

'But if someone *did* do the business and rigged it up to look like suicide, what would be the motive?'

Kate emitted a short cynical laugh. 'After what he's been up to, I would think half the local population would have one and according to his father, most of the locals knew he had just done time for indecent exposure. It must be common knowledge that a young girl was seriously injured running away from him after one of his previous escapades, so it's possible someone drew their own conclusions after the latest spate of incidents.'

Percival thought about that for a few seconds, then nodded. 'Okay, then I'd better get the forensic pathologist out here to take a look, and I'll also give SOCO a call — not that there is likely to be much for them to find after the world and his wife have been trampling all over the scene. But we'll have to go through the motions. There's bound to be an inquest eventually and I don't want the coroner asking awkward questions we can't answer.'

'Spindler's father will also need to be told about his son's death pdq,' Kate said.

'You can leave that with me. I'll get the early turn inspector to send one of his bods round there first thing in the morning and liaise with the coroner's officer to arrange formal ID.'

She studied him suspiciously. 'And if I were to hazard a guess, I'd say you're about to Foxtrot Oscar. Which means you'll be wanting me to stay on here to wrap things up?'

He grinned. 'You're very perceptive, Kate. But it's not worth you going back to bed now anyway. Think of it as a foretaste of what's to come when you take up your new post as Acting DI, eh? Keep me informed.'

Then he was through the door of the barn and striding purposefully back towards the main road.

CHAPTER 11

Kate had known Dr Lydia Summers for several years and had worked with her on numerous crime investigations, where her technical skills had been invaluable in solving many a complicated case. Kate had always regarded the witty, sharp-tongued forensic pathologist as quite conservative in her appearance and when Summers stepped into the barn about two hours or so later as the police photographer was finishing up, it was a shock to see that her hair had been cut short and dyed blonde with pink highlights.

'Nice hairstyle,' Kate observed.

Summers treated her to a waspish smile.

'Glad you like it, Kate,' she said. 'I thought I would change my persona a bit. You should try it sometime. Frees your inner self. So, what have we got here? A nice hanging, your DI told me on the phone.'

'I can think of a better description for it,' Kate replied grimly. 'But it is rather a curious case.' And she quickly briefed her on the circumstances and Spindler's history.

While they were speaking, the pathologist's gaze roved around the barn, noting the body, the rope hanging from the beam, the ladder on its side underneath and the word that had been scrawled on the concrete floor. From past experience, Kate knew she was listening intently to her but that her gaze would have missed nothing.

The subsequent examination she carried out was thorough and protracted, and when she finally stood up from the body, her first observation had nothing to do with Spindler's death.

'Well, to start with, your young man here has a very nasty wound to his lower left leg, possibly from contact with something very sharp, like a barbed wire fence, which tends to support your suspicion that he may be the culprit in your indecent exposure case. The wound has dried now, but it looks as though it might have been leaking heavily and could be infected. I note that some plasters are trapped in his sock, which appears to be saturated with what may be blood.'

'We found blood at the scene which is currently being analyzed,' Kate said.

She nodded. 'I would think the wound is deep enough to have required a stitch or two and without that, would have continued seeping, despite the plasters. There are also some minor scrapes on the back of his right hand, which could have been caused by contact with a wall or, more likely going by what he was evidently up to, a tree or thorny bush of some sort, but they don't seem to be significant.'

She raised an inquiring eyebrow. 'So, what are your own thoughts on the cause of death here, Sergeant?'

'I don't buy suicide,' Kate said. 'I think the whole thing was set up as an elaborate con.'

'Why do you think that?'

So Kate told her, repeating much of what she and Hayden had said to Percival.

Summers nodded. 'Interesting analysis, and I have to admit that my examination so far leads me to suspect that you could well be right, although I cannot be specific until I have conducted the pm.'

'I'm all ears.'

Another waspish smile and she said, 'Okay, obvious things first. Do you remember the case of the woman who was found hanged in her barn at her home a while back? I believe it was near the village of Lower Godney.'

'Roberts,' Kate breathed, adding, 'The woman was called Jennifer Roberts.'

'You have almost as good a memory as me. But I wonder if you can recall one of the things that persuaded me her death was murder rather than suicide.'

Kate frowned, thinking hard. 'Something to do with rope marks, wasn't it?'

'Good girl,' Summers patronized. 'Exactly that. There were other signs too, but the rope marks — or lack of them — was an early visible indicator, and it is the same here. I would estimate that your young man died around six to seven hours ago, and rigor mortis is already beginning to take effect. Yet signs of ecchymoses — the inflamed red line around the neck where the rope has ruptured the blood vessels, and which would normally have begun to appear by this time — are completely non-existent. Blood vessels don't rupture after death, and it therefore suggests to me that he was dead before he was hung from the beam.'

'So, it *is* murder then?'

'A reasonable assumption, but let's not jump the gun. Anomalies can occur and it is possible that signs of ecchymoses will appear later, which could alter my opinion.'

Summers beamed and, knowing how the pathologist just loved to lead the police on, Kate sighed.

'Come on, Doc, there's more, isn't there?'

The pathologist chuckled. 'Of course there's more. You know I always like to save the best until last. The fact is that, following my preliminary examination, I am of the opinion that the actual cause of death in this case may well have been a broken neck.'

'A broken neck? But couldn't that have been due to the hanging?'

'That is not beyond the realm of possibility, but it would be most unusual for this to happen in a straightforward hanging, where asphyxia would be the normal cause of death.

Furthermore, the additional tell-tale signs I would expect to be present in such circumstances as well as the ecchymoses are still absent. So, in my professional opinion, that is a non-starter.'

'But if, as you seem to be inferring, he was strung up by someone *after* he had been stiffed, and yet his death was due to a broken neck, which was not caused by the rope, where the hell does that leave us?'

'In something of a quandary, Sergeant,' she replied. 'We shall just have to wait and see what the pm tells us, but I am confident that what I have said will prove to be correct.'

'Which would mean Spindler either had an unfortunate accident caused by someone who set up the suicide to conceal the fact, or that that same someone deliberately killed him by manually snapping his neck — which is usually a technique favoured by the military.'

Summers smiled again. 'Yes, I know. Interesting, isn't it?' Then she nodded to one of the SOCO officers, collected her briefcase and turned for the door.

'Happy hunting, Sergeant,' she called back over her shoulder, leaving Kate staring after her in a semi-daze. 'Be in touch.'

Kate's night of revelations was not yet over either. The SOCO team leader in her white nylon overalls walked over to her the moment Summers left. 'Thought you might like to see this before we bag it, skipper,' she said. 'Found in deceased's pocket. Looks like he was a very naughty boy.'

Kate stared at the black hood with its sinister eyelets dangling from her gloved hand and took a deep breath. 'He was a naughty boy, all right,'

she said grimly, 'but it seems someone else was a whole lot naughtier. Don't suppose you found a black crayon too, did you?'

The other grinned. 'This, you mean?' she said, holding up a plastic bag. 'The lad certainly came equipped.'

Kate nodded. 'Well, someone certainly did.'

* * *

Dale Harris was the sort of youngster the County Lines drugs network would have been very interested in. Ten years old, street smart but with an angelic face and long blond hair, he was the last kid anyone would have suspected of being mixed up in a sordid criminal enterprise like that — unless they knew him. The fact that he wasn't didn't mean that one day he wouldn't be. It was just that he hadn't been spotted by any of the gangs' recruiters yet, though he was certainly well known to the police in other respects. A petty criminal even at that tender age, with a string of misdemeanours behind him already, mainly for thieving, two things had stopped him being locked up or put into care. One was the plain fact that he was below the age of criminal responsibility, and the other, that no one had actually been able to prove he had done anything wrong — he was too careful to avoid leaving any incriminating evidence behind.

At just ten, he should not have been allowed to wander the streets at night. He should have been safely tucked up in bed like other ten-year-olds. But Dale came from what was commonly called a broken home. His mother, Linda, was an alcoholic, who drifted from one stupor to the next, and in Dale's short life, she had had so many boyfriends — on occasions two at the same time — that it was a mystery who his real father was. Anyway, none of her "casuals" had lasted longer than a couple of months before moving out. Dale's older sister was "on the game", supplementing Linda's state benefits with a proportion of the money she got from her clients, and his two older brothers were currently inside, doing three and five-year stretches. All this meant that Dale was free to roam and do as he pleased, even in the middle of the night when he did most of his opportunist thieving. Although his family circumstances had come to the notice of Social Services and he was now on the "at risk" register, so far that had amounted to nothing more than a mention of him at joint case conferences and the occasional visit from his overworked case social worker.

For obvious reasons, Dale didn't like the police and he would have laughed out loud if any of his delinquent cronies had ever suggested that one day, he would be helping them with their inquiries. But that is exactly what happened when, on the night of Jason Spindler's death, his nocturnal wanderings took him along the main road past the home of Tamara Callaghan. He saw something glinting on the opposite verge as he drew level with the main entrance and swung his old, rusted bicycle round to investigate.

Someone had left the newish-looking mountain bike propped up against a tall privet hedge and it had gradually sunk further into the hedge, partially concealing it from view. But one handlebar protruding from the foliage had caught the moonlight.

Dale emitted a soft whistle. It was as if Christmas had come early for him. He didn't care why the bicycle had been left there or whether or not it had been stolen. As far as he was concerned, it was a case of finders keepers. Pulling the machine out of the hedge, he wheeled it across the verge to the road, leaving his own bicycle behind in its place and after some difficulty getting himself up onto the higher saddle, he rode off back the way he had come, wobbling a little as he went.

It was just his bad luck that the police patrol car chose that moment to appear from a side road and that its powerful headlights caught him in their beam as they turned in his direction. Whether it was the wobble of his mount or his obvious age, or both, that attracted their attention was never explained, but before Dale could separate his slender frame from the over-sized bicycle and take to his heels, they had swung across the road in front of him and one of the two officers in the car had jumped out and taken hold of the handlebars. Dale's next bit of bad luck was that the second officer knew him.

'Well, hello, Dale,' she said with a chuckle. 'And what are you doing out here at this time of night?'

'More importantly,' the male police officer said, 'where on earth did you get that bike?'

Dale scowled. 'It's me bro's.'

'Your bro's, is it? Why are you riding it then?'

'He's inside, doin' porridge.'

The woman officer examined the bicycle in the beam of her torch. 'What's your brother's name then, Dale?'

'You know his bloody name.'

'Well, I do know you have two brothers — George and Mike.'

'So?'

'Funny that there's a nice metal tab attached to the bike which says "*Jason Spindler*" then, isn't it?'

* * *

Kate and Hayden were both in a deep sleep when the telephone rang on Kate's side of the bed. It took her several seconds to focus on the sound and recognize it for what it was. Hauling herself up against the headboard, she saw that sunlight was streaming through a gap in the curtains. True to form, Hayden hadn't stirred a muscle and was still snoring away.

Peering, bleary-eyed at the clock on the bedside table, she saw that they had only been asleep for just over four hours since handing the death scene over to Jamie Foster and returning home.

'Yes, what is it?' she snapped, conscious of the fact that she was slurring her words.

'Didn't wake you up, did I?' Des Percival asked breezily.

She muttered an expletive. 'What do *you* think?'

Percival chuckled. 'Sorry about that, but I thought you should know that uniform found Jason Spindler's bike last night.'

Now Kate was wide awake. 'They did? Where?'

'A plod patrol clocked a young local lad — a little toe-rag by all accounts, called Dale Harris — riding it. Says he found it.'

'How do we know it's Jason's bike?'

'There was a metal strip attached with his name on it.'

'Is Harris still in custody?'

'No, we had to release him. He's only ten and there was no reason to keep him in. His mother refused to attend the nick, so he was handed over to Social Services.'

'Damn!'

'But he was interviewed by Indrani Purewal, and it will be of interest to you to hear that he says he found the bike leaning against the hedge of a certain property owned by Tamara Callaghan.'

'What?'

'Exactly. The plot thickens, as they say. I was going to send Indrani round to see the good lady but thought you might wish to do that visit yourself, though if you're too tired . . . ?'

'Hold everything,' Kate exclaimed. 'I'll be right over.'

Then she looked at Hayden and gave him a hard kick.

CHAPTER 12

Kate gave up trying to wake Hayden. It was a lost cause. As a rule, he became virtually comatose when he went to sleep. And as on this occasion he had had just a few short hours in the land of nod, he was even more comatose than usual. Short of causing him serious pain, she had to accept that she was not going to rouse her other half any time soon. Anyway, had she been able to, he would have been of no real use to her in the foul mood he would have been in — and to be fair, under police regulations he was entitled to a full eight hours off between shifts, and he had previously completed over twelve hours' continuous duty already. So, she got washed and dressed, gave him a big sloppy kiss that went completely unnoticed and headed for Highbridge police station on her own.

The bicycle was in the property store, and she examined it carefully before doing anything else, noting the metal plate with Spindler's name on it affixed securely to the machine and the non-engaged cable-lock hanging from the seat post under the saddle.

'So why didn't you use the cycle lock, Jason?' she murmured to herself. 'Were you interrupted or was it because you needed to be able to make a quick getaway if things went wrong?'

One thing was for sure. She would never know now.

Calling into the CID office next, she found Percival's inner sanctum empty and just Detective Constable Indrani Purewal sitting at her desk, her protracted yawn suggesting she had been up for quite a while.

Kate grinned. 'Hi, Indi,' she said. 'Not tired already, are you?'

Purewal's brown eyes treated Kate to an old-fashioned look, and she took her time adjusting the bun containing her glossy, black hair. 'Not a bit of it, skip. I enjoy being brought in at five thirty in the morning to interview some mini version of *Al Capone* for nicking a bike!'

Kate laughed. 'Well, it's your lucky day, Indi. You're now about to pay a visit to a famous crime novelist. I'll brief you on everything on the way.'

Purewal sighed. 'Is that before or after breakfast?'

* * *

There were two cars parked close to Tamara Callaghan's front door, her own big Volvo and Spencer Little's MGC sports car.

Little answered her ring on Callaghan's behalf. He looked even paler than usual and was plainly agitated.

There was a heavy atmosphere present when Little showed the two detectives into the living room and Callaghan looked flushed and angry. Kate suspected that differences of opinion had just been aired over something and that Little had come off worst.

Nevertheless, Callaghan put on her usual smiling face, though her eyes remained cold and hard.

'Ah, Sergeant Lewis,' she exclaimed, rising briefly from the settee to shake Kate's hand. 'How nice to see you again.'

'This is my colleague, Detective Constable Indrani Purewal,' Kate said. 'We would like to speak to you about a development.'

Callaghan nodded to Purewal and said, 'So where is the Boris Johnson look-alike today?'

Kate couldn't hold back a smirk. It wasn't the first time Hayden had been likened to the Conservative Prime Minister and it always annoyed him because it had been made plain that it was not because of the politician's undoubted intellect, which Hayden would have welcomed, but his somewhat rumpled appearance and mop of unruly blond hair.

'He's, er, on another inquiry,' she said, thinking of her husband lying flat out in their big double bed.

Callaghan smiled again. 'Ah, I see. No peace for the wicked, as they say — but please, do sit down, both of you. I won't offer you a drink as I know you are both on duty and would only refuse. Now, what is this development you mentioned? I am intrigued.'

As they settled into adjacent armchairs, Kate couldn't help but notice Little's eyes focused intently on Purewal's knees in her short skirt and she wasn't sure whether to feel relieved or jealous that his attention was not on her. She cast him an icy glance as she responded to Callaghan's question, and saw his face colour up.

'I wondered whether you'd had any further visits from your prowler, Miss Callaghan?'

The writer chuckled. 'Oh, the flasher, you mean. No, he hasn't been back. Perhaps he has latched on to someone else.'

Kate shook her head. 'I'm afraid we have reason to believe he is dead. The body of a man we think may have been him was found in a barn a few miles from here.'

'Good Lord,' Little exclaimed, tearing his gaze away from Purewal's knees. 'How on earth did that happen?'

'I'm afraid we can't go into the details, Mr Little,' Kate said. 'Suffice to say that the death is currently being investigated.'

'How awfully tragic,' Callaghan murmured, though her tone lacked sincerity, and Kate felt she was just saying what she felt was the appropriate thing under the circumstances. 'If it was my prowler, he seemed so young.'

'Were you at home last night?' Purewal asked quietly.

Callaghan frowned. 'But yes, all night. I was working on a critical stage of my next novel.' And she threw a venomous glance at Little, adding, 'Not that everyone would believe I'm writing anything.'

'And you didn't catch sight of anyone in the grounds or hear any suspicious noises?'

'Not a thing, no. But what is all this about?'

'Would you mind us taking a look around outside?' Kate asked, without answering her question.

Callaghan's frown deepened. 'No, of course not, but I would really like to know why that is necessary.'

Kate hesitated. 'We suspect that the dead man may have been on your property a short time before he died.'

'Heavens! But how do you know that?'

Kate shook her head. 'We don't. It is one of our avenues of inquiry. We are trying to trace his movements before his death.'

Callaghan spread her hands. 'Then by all means wander at will, Sergeant, though I'm not sure what you expect to find.'

The woods were very still, apart from a slight breeze rustling the fallen leaves. Even the cawing of the rooks was absent, almost as if they were holding their breath, and a strong autumnal smell of decaying vegetation greeted the two detectives as they pushed through the trees.

'What exactly are we looking for, skipper?' Purewal asked after they had gone a few yards.

Kate shrugged. 'I'm not really sure. Anything, I suppose. Spindler would not have dumped his bike against the hedge of the property unless he was in here—'

'It could have been dumped there by someone else after his death — an assailant, for example.'

Kate faced her colleague. 'So, why would an assailant leave it outside this house in particular — especially as it was one of the places Spindler had previously visited to flash his assets? Bit of a coincidence that.'

'They could have been trying to send a message.'

'Why bother? If, as is highly possible, Spindler *was* stiffed, why go to all the trouble of making his death look like suicide then advertise the fact that he had been murdered?

And why cart his bike all the way from the death scene to here just to do that? It doesn't make sense. No, I think he was killed here, and his body driven to the barn where he was strung up. But his killer either forgot about his bicycle or didn't know he'd ridden here on it.'

'That's if he *was* murdered and we're not all barking up the wrong tree because of one or two peculiarities at the scene.'

Kate shrugged again. 'I don't think so, and the pathologist seemed mightily suspicious too, but we'll just have to wait for the pm before we can consider sending the balloon up. The important thing for us now is to gather as much evidence as we can, so that if a murder investigation is subsequently launched, we will already have done much of the basic spadework.'

'Provided there *is* anything to find.'

Kate raised an eyebrow. 'Have you somewhere else to be? What could be more therapeutic for the soul than a nice stroll through the woods in the fresh air?'

Whether she was right, and it was therapeutic, it nevertheless turned out to be worth the effort, and ironically, it was Purewal who made the discovery. Shortly after they split up, her shout sent Kate stumbling through the undergrowth in the direction of her voice.

Purewal was standing a few feet from a large oak tree and even as Kate approached, she could see what the detective had spotted. The ground around the base of the tree was badly churned up, with several ragged furrows in the carpet of leaves. Stopping beside her, she noticed a distinct shoeprint in the soft earth and more significantly, some dark stains on the base of the tree itself and the leaves immediately around it, with a trail of similar stains leading off through the woods on the other side of the tree.

'Looks like blood,' Purewal breathed.

Kate nodded grimly. 'And almost certainly signs of a struggle,' she said. 'We'd better preserve the scene and get SOCO here.'

'But you told me Spindler was found hanged. So, where would the blood have come from? There are a lot more than a few splashes.'

'Remember I told you on the way over that we believe he gashed his leg badly when he indecently exposed himself to Julie Morey near Mark? Well, there was evidence of a nasty wound to his left leg when he was found dead in the barn. That wound probably hadn't healed sufficiently since the indecent exposure incident and it's possible it opened up again when he was prowling around these woods.'

'If it *is* blood, of course, and provided that it's Spindler's. Could be a fox made a kill here. We'd look pretty stupid if we called out SOCO on just this basis and the blood turned out to be from a pheasant.'

'Rather a lot of it for a pheasant, though, don't you think? And anyway, that impression in the ground over there looks like it was made by the sole of a trainer. As far as I know, foxes don't wear shoes of any sort, and they certainly don't wear coats.'

'Coats?'

Kate pointed. 'If I'm not very much mistaken, that looks like a leather button lying there, and when I saw Spindler's corpse, he was wearing a coat with leather buttons. What's the betting one is missing?'

* * *

'So, you *do* think that flasher was on my property again?' Callaghan exclaimed. 'Well, if he was, he didn't show himself this time.'

'We only suspect he may have been here,' Kate said. 'We need to preserve the wooded area for forensic examination. It may turn out to be nothing, but we cannot afford to take the chance. I have left my colleague to secure a particular area and I have called for our forensic specialists to attend. I'm sorry, but I'm afraid I must ask you both not to enter the woodland until the team have completed their task.'

Little stared at her. 'But if the flasher is dead, why would you bother to check whether he was here? Are you thinking he may have been murdered in the woods?'

'I'm not saying anything of the sort, Mr Little, and I'm afraid I cannot go into it any further. As I explained when we first arrived, we are simply trying to trace his movements before his death. It's purely routine.'

'But you've obviously found something,' Little persisted, his excitement apparent, 'otherwise you wouldn't be calling in a forensics team.'

'I'm sorry, Mr Little, I can't tell you anything more, and it would be wrong for you to jump to conclusions just because of the action that is being taken.'

Kate knew she was wasting her time trying to lower the temperature. Neither Little nor Callaghan were stupid, and Little's curiosity was obviously now fully aroused.

Callaghan revealed another concern, however, one that seemed to have suddenly occurred to her.

'I trust this business won't be leaked to the press?' she snapped. 'I don't want half of Fleet Street invading my privacy with their bloody cameras.'

Little had taken a gulp of what looked like whisky from his leaded crystal glass, and he choked when it went down the wrong way.

'But if this is a murder investigation, think of the publicity, Tam,' he wheezed finally. 'It is just what we need to promote your new book. The media will love it. I can just see the headlines: "*Murder At Home of Bestselling Author.*" It would be a golden opportunity for you — pictures, interviews on television, the whole works—'

'No!' Callaghan rapped, cutting him off. 'There will be nothing of the sort. It was enough to see my name splashed all over the newspapers after that business at the bookshop without stirring up more aggravation. I've already had to send two reporters packing from here and you know how I value my privacy. This business stays with us. Is that clear?'

'Strewth, Tam,' the agent protested. 'As your agent, I really must insist—'

'Insist?' she exclaimed. 'Another word, Spencer, and I'll be looking for another agent.'

'I'm afraid I share Miss Callaghan's views regarding the press, Mr Little,' Kate put in hastily, trying to cool things down. 'The last thing we need is to attract further interest from the media. They would be all over the place like a rash and could well destroy any evidence that may be here.'

'Evidence?' Little went on, his excitement mounting. 'Then you *do* suspect murder? Why else would you be looking for evidence?'

Kate was spared the effort of trying to think up a suitable reply.

'Get out, Spencer!' Callaghan grated, her tone low and menacing. 'And if any of this does get into the newspapers, you can look for another client. Now get into that stupid toy car of yours and piss off.'

The agent was white-faced and trembling when he stood up. 'Come on, Tam. There's no need for this.'

Callaghan surprised even Kate by springing to her feet, her eyes blazing and her face twisted into a venomous mask.

'I said out, you despicable little wanker,' she snarled, seizing a wine bottle off the coffee table. 'Before I brain you with this.'

Kate tensed, anticipating that she would have to intervene at any second, but the agent was not brave enough to stand his ground. Holding up both hands in surrender, he scuttled from the room without further argument. Moments later, Kate heard a door bang, followed by the throaty roar of a sporty engine starting up. Crisis over.

Callaghan took a deep breath, put the wine bottle back on the coffee table and sat down again.

'Sorry about that, Sergeant,' she said heavily. 'But sometimes Spencer can be an insufferable jerk.'

Kate nodded. 'Like so many men,' she said. 'Now, before I go to see whether my team have arrived, I must say how sorry I am about what happened at the bookshop. I have been meaning to come back to you regarding the incident. Unfortunately, I got rather hijacked by other events.'

Callaghan poured herself another glass of red wine from the bottle she had threatened Little with and shrugged. 'No problem, Sergeant. Some nutter ran amok in a local bookshop and destroyed all the books of mine they had for sale. Not much else to say, is there?'

'The incident must have come as a bit of a shock to you.'

'Not really. These things can happen, I'm afraid, even though this one was a bit extreme. Some readers become obsessed with an author. Others take an intense dislike to them. It goes with the territory. That's partly why I shy away from publicity about myself. I prefer my novels to do the talking.'

'But this was quite a determined, targeted attack. Has it ever happened before?'

'Not to my knowledge, no. I expect someone just got carried away.'

'I assume Mr Little told you what was written across the poster on display in the shop window?'

She nodded and Kate saw her eyes narrow. 'I believe it was, "*Your Sins Will Find You Out, Bitch.*" Not very nice, I agree — especially the last word. But there you are. That's the reading public for you.'

'Why would someone write something like that, though?'

'I haven't the faintest idea. It takes all types and as far as I know, I haven't committed any sins.' She gave a short laugh. 'Not unless you count a couple of tickets for speeding. Spencer seemed to think it could have been my flasher on one of his nights off.'

'I wouldn't think it was his style. Flashing and vandalism don't generally go together — which brings me to my main question. Is it possible someone could be stalking you?' Kate studied her intently, looking for a reaction, but the false smile was in place.

'What a strange question. But no, not as far as I know.'

'SOCO found nothing of value at the scene, I gather, which means the offender must have taken great care to ensure they didn't leave any forensic traces behind. That is not the behaviour of someone in a one-off moment of spontaneous fury. It was as though it was calculated. Someone who has it in for you over some imagined slight or grievance and means to do you harm.'

'And why on earth would someone want to do that? Are you suggesting I've got some deep, dark secret tucked away in my past? You know—' and she assumed a hard, slit-eyed expression — 'I poisoned Number 10 Downing Street's cat?' She laughed again. 'No, Sergeant, I'm sorry to disappoint you, but there aren't any skeletons in my cupboard. I'm sure this was just some nutter on the rampage. I think you're reading too much into it.'

Kate stood up. 'I do hope so. But I would advise you to stay vigilant. Lock your doors, secure your windows and let us know if you see or hear anything suspicious.'

Callaghan held up the three main fingers of her right hand. 'Guides honour, Sergeant,' she said with mock solemnity.

CHAPTER 13

'So, it's looking more and more likely that we could be dealing with a murder,' Percival said after Kate had briefed him on developments.

She crossed her legs in the uncomfortable plastic chair and made a face. 'There are certainly enough anomalies in the case to suggest that Spindler's death may not have been a straightforward suicide. But we have no precise evidence to say yea or nay yet — just some professional hypothesizing and a load of unanswered questions. We'll be in a much better position to make a judgement once we have the result of the pm — plus, of course, the forensic analysis of the suspected trace material found at Callaghan's home.'

'But you reckon there is every possibility that Spindler was stiffed and that it happened at Scribbler's Halt?'

'It's what I suspect, yes, but suspicion is all I have at present and that's the frustrating bit.' She changed tack. 'So, how did Spindler's father take his son's death?'

Percival frowned. 'Not the way you'd expect a father to react on hearing such devastating news. He just shook his head and said that "the bloody fool" had brought it on himself. Then he simply pushed past me, claiming he had work to do on the farm, and cluttered off into one of the barns.'

'People deal with grief in different ways, I suppose.'

'Hopefully, it's not more than that.'

Kate shook her head, picking up his meaning immediately. 'I can't see Hector having anything to do with Jason's death. That really *is* stretching things a bit far.'

'Stranger things have happened.'

'Maybe they have. But say, for argument's sake, that you're right, let's try and visualize a scenario. The pair have a row at the farm, maybe at the top of some steps or in a hayloft, and in a fit of rage the old man goes for the kid. Jason loses his balance and falls, breaking his neck. So, to cover himself, Hector rigs up a suicide. Feasible? Of course it is, but then why would the old man bother to cart his body all the way across the Levels to the barn where he was found just to stage his hanging? He could quite easily have strung him up in one of his own barns or simply buried him somewhere on his land, never to be found. In addition, how is it that Jason's bike was left against the hedge of Scribbler's Halt? How did that get there if not ridden to the spot by Jason? The whole thing doesn't compute.'

Percival nodded a little sheepishly and sighed. 'Yeah, well, it was only a thought. I was just taken aback by the fact that the old man didn't seem in the least bit upset by his son's death. There were no tears, no discernible shock, not even an expression of regret.'

'That doesn't surprise me. It was obvious when I went to the farm originally that the pair didn't get on because of what the kid was. Hector despised him for it. He was more concerned with the effect Jason's behaviour was having on his own reputation than anything else. Perhaps what you interpreted as a lack of grief was relief at the fact that his son was no longer going to be a problem for him.'

He grunted. 'A nice Christian attitude, that. What is it they say, "There's naught so queer as folk."'

'Naught so deep either.'

He raised an inquiring eyebrow. 'Oh? How's that?'

'It's Tamara Callaghan. I can't help thinking she is hiding something.'

'In what way?'

'I don't know. I can't put my finger on it yet. She seems far too dismissive of everything — the indecent exposure she suffered, the break-in at the shop and now the fact that Indi and I found what could turn out to be a crime scene in the woods at her place. She nearly bit her agent's head off when he suggested that Spindler could have been stiffed on her property.'

Percival's hands were thrust down the back of his trousers again and his brows puckered in thought. 'So, you think she may know what happened to Spindler?'

'That has occurred to me, obviously, but I'm not sure it's what's bugging me. She certainly has another side to her character that is very different from the relaxed, easy-going woman of the world she tries to portray. I witnessed it very briefly today when her agent stepped out of line. Her reaction was like that of a she-cat, and I think that if I hadn't been there, she might well have resorted to physical violence.'

'So, is it possible she could have caught Spindler on her property again, lost her cool and attacked him? I gather that Scribbler's Halt is a big house, so it must have rooms on the upper floor. Maybe she disturbed him in one of those rooms and he fell or was pushed trying to escape. You told me that the pathologist suspects the cause of Spindler's death to have been a broken neck and falling two storeys would certainly do that.'

Despite initially setting the hare running, Kate looked dubious. 'There *is* a balcony upstairs, but—'

'There you are then. A more likely scenario than the previous one.'

She shook her head. 'As you yourself must have spotted when you visited the death scene, Spindler didn't appear to have any injuries consistent with a fall and the pathologist certainly didn't refer to any. Furthermore, Spindler had a nasty wound to his leg, which we believe was leaking, and there are those blood traces we came across in the woods at Scribbler's Halt—'

'Which have yet to be subjected to forensic analysis, so cannot be taken as definitely blood or blood from Spindler—'

'True, but I'm fairly sure it will turn out to *be* blood and that it *was* from Spindler, which would then confirm that he *was* in those woods. There's also other potentially supportive material, including a stray button lying on the ground and the imprint of a trainer in the soft earth, which I am convinced will be linked to Spindler.'

'That still doesn't mean he died there. His body could have been dumped in the woods temporarily before being taken out to the barn where he was found, and that could put your author right back in the frame.'

'I just don't see Callaghan as being capable of setting all this up —lugging his body from the scene, dumping it in the boot of her car, driving it all the way to the barn, then stringing the body up from the beam. She looks fairly fit, but not to that extent.'

'Maybe she had help — a male friend, for example?'

'Well, I've never clocked anyone else at the house and I can't see it being her agent. Spencer Little is hardly the strong, athletic type and anyway, he was obviously shocked by our discovery in the woods and was pushing Callaghan to capitalize on the prospect of it being a murder scene for publicity purposes. He'd hardly want that if he was complicit in it all. And anyway, why would Callaghan need to resort to all these shenanigans? Like Hector Spindler, all she would have had to do was bury the corpse somewhere in the grounds and forget about it.'

He sighed. 'So, if this isn't a runner, there's no real point in continuing with it and wasting time looking for skeletons in Callaghan's cupboard. It would be more sensible just to focus on the case itself.'

'Maybe, but my gut feeling tells me that something's not quite right with Callaghan. The words scrawled across the poster at the shop suggest someone has a grudge against her for whatever reason, and it's possible that if Spindler *was* stiffed by someone, he wasn't the intended victim but was in the wrong place at the wrong time and suffered the consequences.'

He looked unconvinced. 'Gut feelings can be notoriously unreliable. As I've indicated, it makes more sense to stick to known facts and the core investigation. The airhead who caused the damage at the shop may just be some disgruntled reader who flipped after hearing her talk at the library and has now gone on their merry way.'

Kate shrugged. 'Point taken, but it won't hurt to make a few inquiries on both Callaghan and Little to see what we can dig up.'

'On PNC you mean?'

'As a start, yes, but I was thinking of a more wide-ranging inquiry. See what we can find out about their background and history, particularly Callaghan's. When did she start writing novels? Is she from Somerset or from somewhere else? Has she ever been married? Is Callaghan her maiden name or is it a nom de plume? Has she come to our notice down here before? That sort of thing.'

He frowned. 'I'd advise you to tread very carefully there, Kate. After what you've just said, it's clear that neither Little nor Callaghan are legitimate suspects in a criminal investigation. At this stage, one is merely a victim and the other a witness. If it was to get out that we were probing the personal backgrounds of two innocent citizens without good reason, we could find ourselves in some very hot water indeed — in particular, with regard to privacy and Data Protection laws.'

'I will be discreet.'

He laughed outright. 'You? Discreet? That would be a first. Just be careful, eh?'

He jerked a hand out of his waistband to snap his fingers at her as she rose to her feet. 'And, Kate. I don't want to know about what you are up to with Callaghan or Little, okay?'

* * *

Hayden was sitting behind his desk when Kate left Percival's office and he did not look at all happy. He scowled at her as she approached.

'Oh, so you've finally decided to come in then, have you?' she said sarcastically, winking at Jamie Foster seated opposite him. 'When I left, you looked as if you were dead. I nearly called for the hearse.'

'Very funny,' Hayden said. 'As you well know, I had been up for over twelve hours. I was absolutely worn out.'

'Oh, you poor boy. Having to work a full twelve hours must have been a real strain.' She patted him on the arm. 'Come on, I'll take you downstairs and buy you a coffee and a bun to help you recover.'

Seated at a corner table in the canteen, she brought him up to speed on all that had happened while he tucked into a massive lardy cake.

'Seems to me that Percival was right,' he commented when she had finished and was sipping her coffee. 'You could land yourself in a lot of trouble by doing what you propose. Callaghan appears to guard her privacy jealously and if she were to find out you were poking your nose into her personal life for no good reason, you could end up with lawyers crawling all over you.'

Kate made a face. 'You mean over *us*, don't you, Hayd? I thought we were in this together. After all, we are partners, aren't we?'

His face froze in mid-chew. 'Oh no you don't,' he protested, a piece of lardy cake escaping from his mouth and dropping onto his plate. 'I'm not risking my neck in yet another of your madcap hunches, so you can forget it.'

Smiling, she stroked his knee under the table. 'You don't really mean that, do you, my precious?'

He pulled his leg away. 'Absolutely. That's my final answer.'

'And I respect your feelings, honestly. Now, here's what I want you to do. Get on the net and see if you can find out anything about our author — age, place of birth, previous places of residence, career history . . . anything that might help us build up a picture of her or give us a link to someone or something for a follow-up.'

'Is that all?' he said warily. 'Nothing else?'

'Not quite. I also need you to have the name Tamara Callaghan checked out on PNC to see if anything comes up — pre-cons, that sort of thing. Then get the LIO to check his box to see if she has ever come to our notice locally.'

She slid a piece of paper across the table to him. 'Also, you might as well have her car run through the system just in case that turns up anything. Best to be thorough. That's the reg number.'

He swallowed the last of the lardy cake in a half-strangled gulp, his worst fears realized. 'Gordon Bennett, I knew it! And what reason would I give for interrogating PNC if I'm asked?'

She shrugged. 'Checking on a suspect?'

'Oh, come on. She's no more a suspect than I am.'

'Everyone targeted by Spindler must be regarded as a possible suspect for the time being, and don't forget it is very likely that the lad met his death in the grounds of her house. She would have had the means, the motive and the opportunity to take him out.'

He snorted. 'Talk about walking on thin ice. You can't be sure yet that he *was* stiffed on her property, and the rest of it is a load of old hooey, as you well know.'

She stood up, brushing crumbs off the front of her coat, and feigned a pout. 'Sometimes you say the most hurtful things, Hayd. You really must learn to be a lot more trusting. Oh, and by the way, you might as well include Spencer Little in your checks too, though I don't have his car number . . .'

* * *

There was a white Audi convertible parked by the verge close to the front entrance to Scribbler's Halt when Kate arrived, and a figure in a long coat was standing in the gateway. He appeared to be chatting to the uniformed policeman who had been assigned to monitor access to the property while SOCO were examining the incident scene. She recognized Templar immediately and pulling up just inside the gate, walked back to speak to him.

'Well, I do believe it's Mr Templar again,' she said tightly. 'You seem to be popping up everywhere lately.'

He laughed, his eyes twinkling. 'Truth is, I finally found out where Tamara Callaghan was living and came out here to see if I could set up an interview for my new book. Bit cheeky, I know, but you have to keep trying or you don't get.' He peered past her up the driveway. 'I must admit, I was a bit surprised to see the policeman standing here. Is it linked to the bookshop incident by any chance?'

'I can't tell you anything, I'm afraid.'

'That's what your policeman said.'

'Quite right too.'

'Can you not even give me a hint?'

'Not even that.'

He sighed. 'It'd make a good piece for my book. You know, crime writer with a real crime on her doorstep. Brilliant addition.'

'I never said there was a crime here.'

He laughed. 'Well, you'd hardly be securing the scene and attending yourself if there wasn't at least a suspicion of one.'

'You should stop reading so much into things,' she said. 'It could become an obsession.'

He smiled at her. 'Could you not even pass on a little snippet to a struggling writer?'

Kate chuckled. 'Not even to one of those. Now, I must ask you to leave before I start thinking of things like obstructing a police officer in the performance of their duty.'

He held up his hands and assumed a bad American accent. 'Say no more, Sarge. I'm outta here.'

Kate watched him as he walked back to his car and climbed behind the wheel. She was faintly amused by this attractive, personable man but not entirely sure about him. Following the Audi with her eyes until it had driven off and disappeared around a bend in the road, she carefully wrote down the number of the vehicle in her pocketbook.

The SOCO team were just finishing up when Kate finally moved the CID car to the front of the house and went looking for Indrani Purewal. The DC met her at a corner of the taped-off section.

'SOCO have bagged the button you saw,' she said, 'and they've taken a plaster cast of the trainer impression — quite a good one too, they reckon.'

'Anything else?' Kate asked, watching as the team began carrying their equipment back out to their van also parked by the house.

Purewal nodded and pointed. 'They got some nice fibres off that tree trunk and what seemed to be some fragments of skin.'

'Skin?'

'Yes, they reckon Spindler might have caught his hand on the rough bark.'

'The pathologist mentioned that Spindler had some scrape marks on the back of his right hand, but she said she didn't think they were significant,' Kate said.

'Seems she could have been wrong. There are some deep but indistinct marks in the soil behind the tree too, which SOCO think may have been caused by heavy boots or shoes.'

Kate followed her around to the spot and stared at the ground. 'That suggests to me that Spindler's assailant might have reached around the tree from behind, maybe grabbing him in a stranglehold—'

'Which could account for the skin fragments found attached to the bark on the other side,' Purewal finished for her. 'Maybe Spindler's assailant got him in a stranglehold from behind the tree and the kid scraped his hand on the bark as he tried to reach behind him to break the grip.'

Kate's nodded approvingly. 'Good analysis, Indi. I'm sure you've hit the nail right on the head.'

Purewal smiled in satisfaction. 'And there's more,' she said and pointed back at the ground. 'If you look carefully, you can see that there are some dark patches, like more dried blood traces, on the fallen leaves, plus further deep indentations in the soil just over here,' she moved a short distance away, 'and here—'

'Footprints again,' Kate exclaimed.

'Exactly and from the look of them, heading away from the scene. Their depth suggests that the person was carrying a heavy load at the time — possibly Spindler's body. SOCO followed them right through the wood to a gap in the hedge — here, I'll show you.'

Minutes later Kate stood on the rough track adjoining the property, staring at a patch of oil on the broken asphalt surface. 'Where does it lead?' she asked.

'Nowhere really. Just a circular hardstanding and what looks like some sort of old electricity sub-station, it's enclosed within a barbed wire fence.'

Kate got down on her haunches and studied the ground. 'No tyre marks then?'

Purewal shook her head. 'A few impressions, but nothing identifiable because of the hard surface.'

Kate stood up, biting her lip. 'So why take Spindler's body all the way across country to that barn instead of simply stringing him up from one of these trees?'

'Perhaps because his assailant didn't want anyone to know Jason was here at all. He needed him to be found a few miles away.'

Kate's eyes gleamed. 'Which means our man was here because he has a particular interest in this property and Tamara Callaghan,' she murmured, staring through Purewal, thinking. 'The question is, what sort of interest?'

'Maybe we'll never know,' Purewal said. 'So, what's next on our agenda?'

Kate squeezed her arm. 'For you, Indi, nothing. Time to go home, I think. You look knackered and you've already been on duty since the early hours.'

She nodded towards the police patrol car parked by the house. A uniformed policeman was climbing into the driving seat. 'Go back to the nick with the plods. I'll head back myself in the CID car when I've finished here, okay?'

Purewal frowned. 'What's left to finish?'

'Well, I'd better let Callaghan know we're away, and I think a final little chat with her might be in order.'

'You don't want me to be there too?'

Kate shook her head. 'No, she might feel threatened if two of us were questioning her. I think I might get a bit more out of her in a sort of woman-to-woman chat, if you know what I mean.'

CHAPTER 14

He remembered as a child reading Henry James's horror story, *Turn of the Screw*, and he thought of that now as he once more sat in his Land Rover, half hidden in the same open gateway just past the entrance to Scribbler's Halt. Then he mused on what the term meant more generally, and that he was about to do exactly that to the bitch in the house opposite — once the bloody coppers had left. He had been surprised to see the uniformed officer standing in the front entrance when he'd pulled in and had felt a stab of alarm on seeing two police "Scientific Support" vans driving off minutes later.

So, Old Bill had found something, had they? It had to be to do with the kid he had stiffed in the woods. There was unlikely to be any other explanation. Maybe he had left some forensic traces behind, though he couldn't think what. It had been a totally bloodless execution and there had been no witnesses around, so what could possibly have drawn them here in the first place and then aroused their suspicions enough to investigate further?

He considered abandoning his planned visit altogether. After all, he could always come back another day and he couldn't afford to risk being spotted in the grounds by some eagle-eyed bluebottle. But he decided to wait a little longer. It was approaching dusk and from his limited knowledge of police operations, he surmised that they wouldn't be doing much forensic searching in the dark. "Patience," urged the little voice in his brain. "Just wait another half-hour and see what happens."

As it turned out, he didn't have to wait even that long. Around twenty minutes later, the policeman on the gate went back inside and shortly afterwards a marked patrol car, with two uniformed officers in the front and what looked like a woman in civvy clothes — a detective? — in the back, swept out of the entrance and disappeared at speed in the same direction as the two Scientific Support vans. They'd all obviously finished for the day. He waited a further ten minutes to make the half-hour, then climbed out of the Land Rover, crossed the road and stood for a few moments more in the gateway, listening.

Nothing moved and he smiled grimly. Time to give that old screw a final turn. He took a deep breath and slipped through the entrance.

* * *

'Finished now then, Sergeant?' Tamara Callaghan drawled in a slightly slurred tone when she answered the door.

Kate nodded. 'Just about, but before I clock off and go home, I thought we could have a quick chat.'

Raised eyebrows now. 'Another chat? What on earth could this one be about?' Callaghan stepped to one side. 'But come in and if you are about to clock off, as you put it, then maybe this time you'll join me in a glass of wine?'

Kate smiled, thinking that the novelist looked as though she was already well into her cups. 'I might just do that, Miss Callaghan. But just the one.'

Shortly, seated with a glass of red on the green, leather-upholstered chair in Callaghan's study, Kate remembered the last time she had been in the room following the incident at the bookshop. All was the same, except that this time the laptop on the old-fashioned desk under the window seemed to be switched off.

Callaghan sat opposite her in the bosun's chair and swivelled round briefly to open a walnut box on the desk.

'Cigarette?' she asked, producing a filter-tip from the box, and holding it aloft.

Kate took a sip of her wine and shook her head. 'No thanks. I don't smoke, I'm afraid.'

'Oh, don't apologize. Neither should I,' Callaghan said, lighting the cigarette. 'I had a scare a few years back and the hospital doctors advised me to quit. But—' and she drew deeply on the cigarette, exhaling a cloud of smoke — 'writing creates its own comforting vices.'

'Oh, Weston Hospital, was it?' Kate asked, trying to sound casual.

Callaghan's eyes focused on her intently for a second, then looked away She waved the cigarette in her hand airily. 'No, some clinic or other in the Smoke. It was a long time ago. The important thing is that it turned out to be a false alarm, so I just carried on. Need my nicotine fix, you see, to cope with the stress.'

Neatly batted away, despite the booze, Kate thought and said, 'A lot of stress in writing then, is there?'

'You'd better believe it — especially when you're tied into legal contracts, and you have a bloody pain in the arse of an agent on your back the whole time.'

Kate watched her pick up a brim-full glass of wine and drain half the contents in a gulp. 'You wouldn't advise a career in writing then?'

Callaghan laughed and turned back towards the desk to set the glass on the edge. 'Oh, it has its rewards. Why, are you thinking of taking it up?'

'I must admit I've thought about it if ever I decide to pack in the job, but I'm rather curious as to how you got started. Did you just wake up one day and say, "I'm going to write crime thrillers," or what?'

'More or less, yes. I was bored with my life in London when I met Spencer at a party. We got talking and Bob's your uncle. Been with the little toad ever since. Convenient for him, you see. He has an office in Bridgwater as well as ones in Liverpool and Essex Street in the Smoke, but he has now made Bridgwater his main base. That way he can make my life as much of a misery as possible.'

'I'm sure that isn't his intention. You say you met him at a party in London. Must have been a fab life up there in the city. What were you doing before you took up writing?'

The eyes focused on Kate's face again and she blew smoke at the ceiling. 'Oh, this and that. I had a flat in Peckham when I decided to sell up and move to the country, where it's quiet — at least, it *was* quiet before all this nonsense.'

'You don't strike me as a Londoner.'

'I'm not.' The eyes were very sharp now, almost challenging. Kate sensed that Callaghan knew full well what was behind the questions and had absolutely no intention of satisfying her curiosity. A clever cookie, this one, Kate mused, and easily underestimated. But why all the secrecy about herself? What was she hiding?

'I gather you've now had seven novels published. That's quite an achievement.'

'Not really. Agatha Christie had over seventy. There's no way I'll manage that number — half a dozen more at most. Too old, you see, and the old grey matter starts to shrink as the years advance.'

'You don't look much older than me.'

The challenging glint was still there. It was like playing mental chess with a grandmaster who could anticipate and block every move. 'Don't I? You'd be surprised. But there you are . . . Now what about this chat you wanted with me? I'm sure it wasn't about my novels or my age.'

Game over. Kate could see that she wasn't going to get any more out of her and reluctantly gave up trying.

'Obviously not,' she laughed, and took a couple of sips of wine to give her a few seconds' grace. 'It's just that our examination of the patch of woodland in your grounds suggests that the lad who indecently exposed himself to you *did* pay you another visit before he died. And there are indications that a second individual may have been present in the same area at the time.'

'Another individual? Heavens, are you saying someone *did* murder this boy in the woods as Spencer suggested?'

'I'm not saying that at all, but there were other traces that we cannot match to your flasher. You remember I asked you before whether you thought someone could be stalking you after the shop incident? I just wondered if you had given any more thought to the possibility that someone might have a personal grudge against you.'

Callaghan blew smoke rings and when she returned her gaze to Kate, there was irritation in her expression.

'I thought we'd been over all this, Sergeant. I believe I told you previously that, as far as I know, there isn't anyone. This harping on the same subject is becoming a little tiresome.'

Kate nodded. 'My apologies. But I must pursue every avenue of inquiry, I'm sure you understand that, and I would be negligent if I didn't make absolutely sure you're not at risk in some way.'

The false smile was back. 'That's very sweet of you, but you can rest assured that if I had any concerns on that score, I would be on the phone to the constabulary immediately. Now, I see that you've hardly touched your wine. Is it not to your taste? I know some people aren't keen on Rioja.'

Kate glanced quickly at the glass in her hand and finished the remainder. 'No, it was very nice, thank you.'

'Another one then?'

She stood up. 'Better not, thanks, I should be on my way now and I'm sure you'll want to get back to your book.' She hesitated. 'Before I go, though, I couldn't be very cheeky and ask to use your loo, could I? I'm afraid red wine does this to me.'

'But of course. Up the stairs. Second door on the right.'

The stairs were thickly carpeted, likewise the corridor on the next floor, deadening every sound, which suited Kate fine. She was no more in need of the toilet than another glass of wine, but she was curious as to what she might be able to find out about Callaghan from a swift look around a couple of rooms. She knew she would have to be quick, though, or the smart-arse female might smell a rat.

The first room, next to what she could see through the half-open door to be the bathroom and toilet, appeared to be a small second bedroom — sparsely furnished with just a single bed, a wardrobe and a chest of drawers. Kate didn't waste her time on it but checked the next one on the other side of the toilet. Another bedroom, dull and spartan like the first, only bigger, with a double bed.

Crossing to the other side of the corridor, she opened a third door and stared into a large, thickly carpeted room furnished with what looked like a king-sized bed, a chest of drawers, a row of tastefully embellished built-in wardrobes and a beautifully carved dressing table, laden with tidily arranged cosmetics. It was spotless. There was a gilt chandelier suspended from a white-painted ceiling that looked as if it had been moulded in the style of a traditional wedding cake and French doors accessed a balcony overlooking the hardstanding and woodland at the front of the house.

Bingo! This had to be Callaghan's "boudoir".

She checked the wardrobes first, but found just rows of expensive dresses and suits, plus enough shoes and handbags to stock a department store. She heard a creaking sound then and rushed to the door to peer along the passageway, but the corridor was empty. She breathed a sigh of relief. False alarm.

"Hurry it up," a voice urged in her head, and she visualized Callaghan crossing the hallway downstairs to find out what was taking her so long.

Gritting her teeth, she checked the drawers of the dressing table. Nothing but more cosmetics and an assortment of tights and fancy handkerchiefs. A door banged downstairs and she wheeled round in a panic.

It was then that she saw the picture on the wall. For some inexplicable reason it arrested her attention. It was a photograph of a coastal scene, with rugged cliffs curling round towards the centre of the picture from right to left and seagulls sweeping low over a calm blue sea. A woman, maybe in her late twenties or early thirties, stood beside an old man, who was leaning on a stick and apparently looking out towards the far horizon. The picture had obviously been taken a long time ago, but there was nothing on it to say where or by whom. There was a brass plate at the bottom right-hand corner with an inscription on it, but the picture was too high up on the wall to be able to read it. It was just an ordinary photograph, and Kate couldn't for the life of her think why she had been attracted to it.

'Sergeant?' Kate heard the muffled voice calling, apparently from the bottom of the stairs. 'You okay up there?'

Clawing her mobile from her pocket, Kate took a couple of quick snaps of the picture and ran for the door. She got to the head of the stairs to face Callaghan coming up. The novelist stopped and fixed Kate with a hard stare.

'I thought you'd got lost,' she remarked.

'Oh damn,' Kate said. 'Forgot to pull the chain. Sorry.'

Rushing back to the bathroom and toilet, she jerked the door open and pressed the button on the modern low-level cistern, then ran one of the taps before shaking out and replacing a towel on the wall rack to suggest it had been used.

'Really, there was no need,' Callaghan commented frostily when she re-joined her.

Kate smiled again. 'Thanks anyway. Sorry to be a nuisance. I'll be off now.'

Callaghan closed the front door as soon as Kate had stepped through. She sensed the animosity hanging in the air behind her. The writer was certainly no fool, and it had been plain from her stiff demeanour that she had suspected her of having been up to something upstairs. It was only when she was driving away that she suddenly remembered that she had not closed the main bedroom door again. She just hoped Callaghan wouldn't remember it being closed before.

CHAPTER 15

He nearly got caught out. He hadn't expected one of the coppers to be still on the premises. He heard the car start up when he was halfway up the drive and only just managed to spring into the adjacent woodland before it swept by. He could tell it was a cop car by the aerials on the roof and he recognized the woman driver immediately. It was that bloody interfering detective he'd first seen leaving the library after the talk and then again standing outside the bookshop following his destructive handiwork. She was getting to be a real pain.

But there was no way he was going to be deterred from doing what he'd come here to do, and he made his way through the trees in a diagonal approach towards the house. He found the spot the police had been interested in within a couple of minutes. The police tapes still enclosed it, taking in the oak tree where he'd snapped the kid's neck.

He scowled. Although he tried to reassure himself that they could not have found anything of importance, it still worried him that they had shown so much interest in the very spot where he'd stiffed the kid, suggesting that they might have tumbled to the fact that the suicide in the barn had been rigged and he had actually died here in the woods. How they could have worked that out he had no idea, but it could bring on some real heat now, which meant he'd have a lot less time in which to play his twisted game.

He moved more quickly, working his way through the woodland to the lane where he had parked the Land Rover on that previous visit, then cutting through some shrubbery on the boundary towards the back of the house. He crossed the side lawn at a run, then followed the wall along until he found a convenient window. It was half open. He eased the catch, pulled it out to its fullest extent, then grabbed hold of both sides of the window frame to haul himself up onto the ledge. Seconds later, he was in the house.

* * *

Kate was uneasy. She thought she had caught sight of something as she was leaving Callaghan's property — a shadow in the gathering dusk disappearing into the woodland beside the driveway. It had only been a glimpse and could have just been a trick of the fading light, even a deer, or maybe nothing more than the product of an over-fertile imagination. But it had brought her to a halt in the road outside, and she glanced back up the driveway for a moment, undecided.

She was quite sure Callaghan would not welcome another interruption to her day if she knocked her up again, but then, on the other hand, what if there *had* been someone lurking in the driveway? Someone who had heard her car approaching and taken refuge in the woodland just in time? She couldn't afford to take the chance.

Swinging up onto the verge by the long front hedge, she switched off and sat for a moment studying the empty road and tapping the steering wheel with the fingers of one hand. Then she focused on the nose of a green Land Rover Defender poking out of a gateway on the other side of the road a short distance away and frowned. She could see that there was no one in the vehicle, and it was a strange place to be parked as there were no other properties nearby. It could have broken down, of course, or have been parked there by a farmer working in the wooded area on the other side of the hedge, but it was worth a check, nevertheless.

Climbing out of the car, she crossed the road and peered in through the windows. The thing looked quite old and scuffed inside, but remarkably clean. No hessian sacks, plastic sheets, rolls of barbed wire or other stuff that might be carried by a farmer in the back of his or her wagon, just a bare steel floor with what looked like a red petrol or diesel can in one corner, held in place by a leather strap. It seemed to be the same inside the cab. She tried the door and to her surprise, found it to be unlocked. Ducking inside, she checked a couple of cubbyholes and the dashboard tray, but again, they were completely empty of anything — documents, wipes, even sweets. There was not a trace of the usual detritus found in most vehicles — no screwed-up sweet papers, discarded cigarettes, crumpled drink cans and the like. It was as though the interior of the vehicle had been thoroughly valeted.

Climbing out again, she checked the index number and discovered that, according to the plate, it had to be around twenty years old. Yet, while its dented, scratched bodywork and worn tyres were certainly in keeping with its presumed age, the way its interior had been kept so scrupulously clean and tidy struck Kate as more than a little odd. After all, who would normally be so fastidious about the state of the inside when the exterior of the vehicle had been so neglected?

Shaking her head in puzzlement, she peered across the road at the lights of the house, which had only just come on and were showing through the trees. She made a face. Take another look around or head back to the nick? That was the dilemma.

An owl hooted close by, startling her, but it also jolted her into action. She went back to her car and collected a torch. Probably stupid, but it might be best to take a look around, just in case.

The moon came out as she walked slowly up the drive and she pocketed her torch and turned off her radio, straining her ears to catch the faintest unusual sound. The house was lit up on both floors and as she got closer, she could hear the faint sound of music — Beethoven, she thought. It seemed that Tamara Callaghan was anxious to give the place as much life as possible. Maybe Kate's warnings earlier had resonated with her after all.

She paused at the end of the drive to scan the hard-standing in front of her and the woodland curving away to her left from the edge of a wide expanse of lawn. A flock of birds, starlings possibly, flashed in V-shaped formation over the roof of the house and into the woods, but nothing else moved.

Silence. She moved away from the woodland, crossing the driveway to a small patch of lawn on her right, and followed a high perimeter wall towards the house itself. At the end of the lawn, there was a narrow gap between the house and the wall with a shingle path continuing beyond it towards the back. She hesitated, then plunged into the shadows.

She emerged shortly afterwards in a large area of lawn bordered by shrubberies and the continuation of the wall. A gravel path ran the whole length of the house, with a door opening onto it at halfway point. She followed the house wall along, peering into the lighted windows as she went, but saw nothing of interest save empty rooms. There was a big farm-house-style kitchen, a library with shelving crammed with more books, from which access could be gained to the garden via the single back door, and a couple of sparsely furnished bedrooms, which she supposed to be guest rooms, like the one she had seen upstairs earlier. It was certainly a big place and she smiled ruefully when she thought of the tiny cottage she and Hayden lived in at Burtle.

She heard the stealthy noises as she reached the end of the building. Scraping sounds, heavy breathing, followed by a grunt and what sounded like the thud of feet dropping onto a hard surface. Very cautiously, she peered around the corner and was just in time to see a bearded, long-haired figure — almost certainly a powerfully built man — dressed in some sort of camouflage jacket, straighten up in the moonlight beside the open window of an unlit room, then carefully turn as if to close the window again.

It was such a shock to see the intruder standing right there in front of her that for a second Kate froze. Before she could recover, he seemed to sense her presence. Throwing a quick glance in her direction, he took to his heels and with surprising speed for a man of his bulk, disappeared around the opposite corner of the house. She got there just in time to see him streaking across the lawn and into the belt of woodland fronting the property.

Guessing that he was heading for the Land Rover parked in the gateway on the other side of the road, she raced across the hardstanding towards the driveway, intending to cut him off. But he was too fast for her and had too much of a head start. Even as she approached the front entrance, she heard the sudden roar of an engine and the screech of tyres. Stumbling out onto the roadway, she was presented with a fast-disappearing shadow, displaying no lights.

Snatching her radio from her pocket and calling up police Control, she quickly reported the circumstances and passed them the licence plate of the Land Rover, which she had had the presence of mind to jot down in her pocketbook earlier, the torch shaking in her hand under her laboured breathing. Declining the offer of backup, she then headed back up the driveway. She heard the alert being passed out to all units as she approached the house, knowing that the chances of the vehicle being spotted before it lost itself in the immensity of the marshes were almost nil.

Callaghan was already standing on the doorstep, waiting for her, when she got to the front door. The novelist was dressed in blue, boot-leg trousers and a red, silk top and her expression was tight-lipped.

'Well, if it isn't Sergeant Lewis,' she snapped, smoke curling from the cigarette in her hand. 'I saw you run past my study window just now. Mind telling me what the devil's going on?'

Kate nodded, still breathless. 'I thought you might be able to tell me that,' she said. 'I just disturbed a man climbing out of one of your side windows.'

Callaghan stubbed out her cigarette on the doorpost and made a face. 'I suppose I'll have to level with you,' she said. 'Why don't you come in?'

* * *

The glass of whisky was thrust into Kate's hand before she could say no.

She had shown Callaghan the open window from which the intruder had emerged — evidently another bedroom — and having closed and locked it, they had adjourned to the living room, where Kate was waved to a chair.

'The fact is,' Callaghan said slowly, 'I haven't been exactly truthful.'

Now there's a surprise, Kate thought sardonically.

'For some time now, I have been plagued by some erk who seems to have a particular aversion to my novels. I don't know who he or she is, but I've received quite a few nasty letters, which I've simply chosen to ignore.'

'Do you still have those letters?'

'No, I burned them, I'm afraid.'

'Has this person ever physically bothered you before?'

'No, the business at the shop was a first, but it seems he or she is getting bolder. As I said to you before, writers do tend to get a mixed following. You know, the adoring fan who regards them as almost godlike, which can be a real pain in the arse, and the other sort who hates everything about them. It goes with the territory, I'm afraid. It's annoying that this particular character seems to have found out where I live, but—' she shrugged — 'there's a fat lot I can do about it, except, as you told me before, to remain vigilant. The insecure window was negligent of me, but it won't happen again.'

'What does Mr Little say about this stalker of yours?'

'He doesn't know. I've never told him, and I want it to stay that way, understood?'

136

Kate sighed. 'You're not making it very easy for yourself if you don't mind my saying. You should have someone you can turn to in this sort of situation. You're all alone here after all, which makes you rather vulnerable.'

She laughed, a hollow sound. 'Well, I would hardly turn to poor old Spence for protection. He would pass out if a bird hit the window.'

'Unfortunately, we don't have the personnel to provide round the clock protection—'

She cut in quickly. 'I wouldn't want it, Sergeant. Absolutely not. It would be certain to get to the ears of the press and that is something I will not tolerate.'

'Then, might I suggest you have one of our crime-prevention officers round to survey your premises? They would be able to advise you on all aspects of home security, including alarm systems.'

Callaghan stood up, signalling that the conversation was at an end — at the same moment casting a critical glance at Kate's untouched glass of whisky on the arm of her chair.

'I will think about it,' she said. 'Now, I must get back to work. Thank you for your support this evening. I'm only sorry you didn't catch the nasty little erk.'

Kate also stood up. 'Would you like me to have a look around the house before I go? Just to reassure you.'

Another laugh. 'Good Lord, no, Sergeant. You worry too much.'

'And if anything is missing—'

'I will be sure to let you know. Goodnight, Sergeant Lewis.'

Climbing back into her car, Kate sat for a few minutes running through in her mind everything that had happened and coming to one inescapable conclusion: there was a lot more to Tamara Callaghan's intruder than she had said, and she knew it. Not to put too fine a point on it, the woman was lying through her pearly white teeth. The problem was, why?

* * *

Kate would have been even more perplexed had she been privy to the discovery the author made shortly after she had driven away.

Callaghan was not surprised to find that the chandelier in her bedroom was lit when she went upstairs to change into her more comfortable night clothes. She had switched most of the lights on in the house with the arrival of dusk as a kind of reassurance, and she had no intention of turning any of them off until she went to bed. But what she did not expect to find was the ominous message scrawled in what looked like her own red lipstick across the dressing table mirror: "*The Lord Giveth And The Lord Taketh Away.*"

Recovering from her initial shock, she quickly removed the offending words with a couple of wet-wipes and, returning her lipstick to the glass tray on the dressing table, she stood there for a moment, staring at her white face in the mirror. Then abruptly opening one of the drawers with a trembling hand, she carefully withdrew a small Glock 26 pistol from under a pile of underclothes. It fitted comfortably in the palm of her hand and was very light. Checking that the magazine was fully loaded, she slipped it under one of the pillows on her king-sized bed before crossing to the window to stare out into the night. She had never fired the weapon or even bothered to clean it, but she felt confident it would do what was necessary if ever she needed to use it.

'Come whenever you're ready, bro,' she mouthed softly at the face of the moon. 'I'll be waiting right here for you.'

CHAPTER 16

Hayden and Indrani Purewal were the only detectives in the office when Kate got back to the station, and both jumped up from their desks when she walked in.

'You okay?' Hayden asked, concern etched into his expression. 'Control said you had turned up an intruder at the house — a guy in a camouflage jacket.'

Kate nodded and walked straight over to the coffee machine. 'Ran too bloody fast for me,' she said, pouring a black coffee into a plastic cup. She glanced at Purewal. 'I thought you were going home?' she said, perching on the corner of her desk to sip her coffee.

Purewal shrugged. 'I was until you called up,' she said. 'Maybe I shouldn't have come back when I did.'

Kate shook her head. 'We still wouldn't have caught him. He's one fit guy, I can tell you. Never seen anyone leg it so fast in all my life. Anything on the Land Rover?'

Both shook their heads. 'All units are still out looking,' Hayden said, 'but no trace so far. He's probably hunkered down somewhere out on the marshes.'

Purewal handed her a slip of paper. 'Control Room checked the reg on PNC. It's allocated to a Ford Transit, allegedly scrapped six months ago and was subject of a SORN declaration.'

'Which means our man must have got hold of the plates from somewhere.'

'Looks like it. Apparently, the last RO was a farmer from just outside Wells, who sold it to a scrappie near Bridgwater.' She grinned. 'Gypo by the name of Tommy Smith.'

Kate snorted. 'It would be, wouldn't it? Right. Anything else to tell me?'

'Just about the button you clocked in the woods at Scribbler's Halt,' Purewal said. 'SOCO have confirmed that it does match a button missing off the coat Spindler was wearing when he was found.'

Kate's gaze sharpened. 'So, it looks like he *did* pay a visit to the house the night he died?'

'Seems so, yes. As for the plaster cast that they made of the shoe impression, it's being sent to the lab to check against the trainer Spindler was wearing, but they're fairly sure it will prove to be a reasonable match.'

Kate threw Hayden a quizzical look. 'And what about the inquiries you were doing for me on the net?'

He gave her his best smile, glancing briefly at the clock on the far wall. 'Nothing of any real note. Just a couple of things I can tell you later if you like.'

'Sounds like your stomach is calling again, Hayd,' Kate said, winking at Purewal.

Hayden shuffled his feet uncertainly. 'Well, I could do with some vittles, I must admit, but there's no point in hanging on here any longer anyway, is there? We can't see this Smith fella at the scrapyard until tomorrow and as the guvnor's already gone home, why shouldn't we?'

Purewal yawned and turned to retrieve her handbag from her desk. 'He's got a point, skip.'

'My Hayden has always got a point,' Kate said drily, 'at least, where food is concerned.'

* * *

'So, give,' Kate said as, now at home, she and Hayden tucked into a Chinese takeaway. 'What did you find out about Callaghan and Little on the net?'

Hayden washed down a mouthful of chicken chop-suey with a gulp of red wine. 'Not a lot really. But I didn't want to say too much in front of Indrani, as I know that what we're doing is a bit out of order.'

She treated him to a tight smile. 'How very tactful of you, Hayd. It wouldn't also have had something to do with getting to Wang Ho's before they closed, would it?'

He ignored the dig. 'Thing is, the information on the net about Callaghan is rather light. All I could find was a list of her books — seven in all — with the first being *Virtue In Death*, published eight years ago. Her biog merely says she's a bestselling novelist who came to prominence with her crime series set on the Somerset Levels, featuring, and I quote, "the enigmatic Detective Inspector Rupert Dixon." I could find nothing about her past life, including where she was born, or even her interests and although I've scoured the web, I could find no photographs of her anywhere. It's as though she appeared suddenly from nowhere and has no previous existence. She has no website of her own, doesn't seem to belong to any of the usual writers' organizations, like the Society of Authors or the Crime Writers' Association, and all inquiries about her and her books are referred to the Spencer Little Authors' Agency.' He shrugged. 'As for Spencer Little himself, it seems he is a respected authors' agent who has been in business for around twelve years. He has offices in London, Bridgwater and Liverpool, and represents around forty different authors.'

'So, what about PNC?'

'Zilch on Little. But Callaghan is a rather different story . . .'

Kate picked up on the dramatic pause and leaned forward. 'Go on.'

He smirked, savouring the moment. 'Well, as you'll know, her Volvo has personalized number plates, but the vehicle turns out to have been purchased from a London dealer three years ago and according to the DVLA, is registered in the name of one Jennifer Sykes.'

'Sykes? Are you saying someone else owns the motor?'

He shrugged. 'It's one possibility, yes. Or that Callaghan owns it and has not yet notified change of ownership, though I think that is rather unlikely, for she would have had to disclose her details when taxing the car with the DVLA.'

Kate snapped her fingers as a more likely possibility occurred to her. 'She's using a nom de plume! Tamara Callaghan isn't her real name. It's her pseudonym or pen name.'

He bestowed a patronizing smile on her. 'Well, at least you got there in the end, old girl. But it could possibly even be a change of name by deed poll.'

'But a deed poll change would have had to be registered and we can soon check on that.'

He shook his head. 'Not necessarily. Anyone can change their name quite easily in this country through a solicitor and without registering the change. The only problem is that, while you get an official certificate for a registered change, you don't if it is unregistered, and many banks and other organizations won't recognize an unregistered change, which can soon be lost as a record over time.'

'But why would Callaghan want to change her name?'

'Possibly to hide something in her past that she doesn't want anyone else to know about,' he said.

'Such as?'

'Well, as Sykes, she has a nice bit of form on PNC. She was arrested for excess alcohol consumption and dangerous driving on the A40 near Haverfordwest nine years ago, after a nasty accident which left the other driver — a young woman — with serious life-changing injuries. She was driving another car then, I discovered, an old Fiat, which she totalled, and she ended up in A and E overnight. She got off with the dangerous driving but received a heavy fine and twelve months' disqualification for the drink-driving offence.

It wouldn't look good for a crime novelist to be associated with something like that, would it?'

'And where the hell is this Haverfordwest?'

'Pembrokeshire in south-west Wales, I believe.'

'So, what the hell was she doing there?'

He shrugged. 'No idea, but it's a free country. Maybe she was on holiday or out for a drive?'

'Go on. There's more, isn't there?'

'A bit, yes. Fact is, it doesn't appear to have been her only visit to that part of the world. There's another incident recorded against her, which happened the year after that. She apparently lost her rag with a parking warden in Pembroke Dock and slapped his face. Got bound over for that and got hit for costs.'

'Wales again.'

'Yep. Obviously likes the place.'

'Nothing else?'

'What do you want — blood?'

'No, you've done brilliantly, but there are a few more inquiries I'd like you to carry out tomorrow on another character.'

He groaned. 'Then you really *do* want blood, don't you? I'm really chancing my arm with a further dodgy PNC check. Don't tell me it's another of your so-called suspects?'

'Let's just say it's a person of interest — chap by the name of Ed Templar.'

'What, the Leslie Charteris fella you mentioned before?'

'The same. He just keeps popping up everywhere. It's getting to be a bit too much of a coincidence. Says he's doing this book on novelists and is trying to get an interview with Callaghan, but I'm convinced there's more to it than that.'

'So, once again, you're getting me to do your dirty work.'

She gave him a quick peck on the cheek. 'But you do this sort of thing so well, Hayd. Why do you think I chose you to do these checks in the first place?'

He snorted. 'Soft soap will get you nowhere.'

She shook her head, now serious again. 'No, Hayd, I mean it. This is not just an off-load. You have a keen, analytical mind and are commendably thorough. That is where your talents lie. By rights, you should be in Criminal Intelligence.'

He stared at her suspiciously. 'You really think that?'

She nodded. 'We make a good team, you and I, and while you're doing your stuff, I will be looking into one or two loose ends, starting with a certain scrapyard and a Mr Tommy Smith.'

He frowned. 'Be careful. Smith, or whatever he's called, seems to be a villain and I don't want you going off at half-cock as usual, and sticking your head in the fire.'

She grinned. 'I promise I'll be good.'

'I'll believe that when it happens.'

* * *

When he got back, the man in the camouflage jacket removed the registration plates from the old Land Rover, stashed them in a gap under a loose floorboard and replaced them with the correct ones. The obliging, avaricious scrappie who had parted with the fakes — one of a number of duplicates he no doubt kept in a cupboard somewhere on the premises — had charged him an exorbitant seventy-five quid for them and that was after he had knocked him down from a ton. But it had been well worth it.

He had got the plates as a form of backup insurance. True, he had been able to make use of the many tracks and droves that criss-crossed the Levels each time he went to Callaghan's home, which drastically reduced the risk of falling foul of a police stop-check, and anyway an old green Land Rover was unlikely to attract much police interest, since similar vehicles were used by the farming community all over the Levels. But it was sensible to put the bogus plates on during his visits rather than sticking to the real ones, just in case the motor was spotted near Scribbler's Halt and some bright spark noted the number at the worst possible moment.

His main worry was the interfering woman detective who had just disturbed him breaking into Callaghan's house. That had been a really close call. It was true he had got away okay without much chance of being identified later in any line-up and with the lights on the Landy having been switched off, she'd have needed infra-red vision to clock the registration number of the motor. But it was an unwelcome hitch, and he couldn't afford another.

At least the right index plates were on the vehicle now, and if he was pulled over on a police stop-check, he could quickly prove his purchase of the Land Rover from that second-hand car dealership in Bridgwater. All nice and legit, with no possible comebacks.

Furthermore, it would not be long before he concluded his business at Scribbler's Halt altogether. Then he would be able to turn his back on this godforsaken part of the country for good. It was just a three-hour drive down the M4 to Pembroke Dock, and once there, he knew plenty of secluded places close to the port where he'd be able to dump the Land Rover for good and torch it. After that, it would just be a case of boarding the ferry to Ireland as a foot passenger and four hours later, picking up the car he had previously garaged near the Rosslare ferry terminal and disappearing into the wilds of Ireland's West Coast. Couldn't be better. Maybe when he got to his pre-rented cottage in Mayo he'd have a chance to read a few of Tamara Callaghan's books while he sat by the river, fishing, or, even better, to sit quietly in the cottage, knocking back a few drams of Jameson's whiskey while he worked out what he was going to do with all his new-found wealth, courtesy of a certain recently deceased crime novelist.

But that was for later — something to look forward to. Right now, he was looking forward to another visit to Scribbler's Halt, just to turn the screw once more before the delicious moment when he could finish the game and mete out the justice she so richly deserved.

CHAPTER 17

The scrapyard occupied a large piece of land on the outskirts of Bridgwater, bordered by unkempt fields and a rubbish-choked rhyne. The sign above the entrance read "*Tommy's Motor Cemetery*", and as she drove through the open gateway Kate had to smile. At least Mr Smith seemed to have a sense of humour. She hoped it would still be intact when she finally left.

She passed between a variety of abandoned wrecks awaiting disposal and on the far side of the yard, saw a crawler crane hoisting a van of some sort over towards the gaping jaws of the crusher while a couple of men in overalls looked on. She pulled up before a ramshackle part corrugated iron, part concrete building labelled "*Reception*", and went in.

A balding rat of a man dressed in filthy green overalls was bending over a photocopier behind a long document-strewn counter, and he glanced up quickly, then transferred his gaze to the window and her own Mazda MX5 parked outside.

'Bit new for the crusher, ain't it?' he said, flashing a gold-toothed grin.

Kate had deliberately dressed in an over-sized sweater and tatty jeans and had driven there in her own car, wanting to look as little like a police officer as possible. She felt his little piggy eyes giving her the once-over.

146

'Not selling that,' she said, leaning casually on the counter, 'but I might have some other business in mind.'

His grin faded and his eyes narrowed. 'What sort of business?'

Her heart began to race. 'I hear you're good with numbers.'

He stiffened noticeably. 'What sort of numbers would they be then?'

'SORN numbers.'

'Who said so?'

'Jimmy Rowe,' she said, using the name of a well-known local traveller she had arrested several times in the past.

He scowled. 'I heard Jimmy was in stir.'

'So he was. Came out a couple of months ago.'

'How do you know him?'

'Family connections.'

He crossed the office and leaned towards her across the counter.

'What connections? You ain't no traveller.'

'Quite right, but I've done business with Jimmy in the past.'

'What sort of business?'

This character certainly wanted to know the ins and outs of a cow's arse. 'My business.'

'How do I know you're kosher?'

'You don't. Let's just say that Jimmy and my old man were muckers in stir.'

'Your old man? And who would he be?'

Kate sighed heavily. 'You know very well who he is.'

He said nothing in reply, but she could feel his eyes boring into her as he tried to make up his mind.

The man she was referring to was Ronnie Duggan, a serial thug in his day, and Kate had dropped the hint because she knew from the criminal intelligence files she had accessed that Duggan and Jimmy Rowe had done some heavy jobs together. Duggan had to be in his seventies now but was still inside. Kate had chosen him because he was known for his flaming red hair and had a daughter about her age, named Rose, who was on the game. Nevertheless, she was taking a real leap of faith by assuming Smith's criminal enterprises had served the needs of the "Levels Clan", as Rowe's team were called, and she just had to hope that Smith had never met Rose.

'You ask a lot of questions, mister,' she said. 'Are we done now or when I see Jimmy again, do I have to tell him you're not interested in any further business?'

He licked his lips, a shadow passing over his face. The threat had landed where she'd intended, and she knew the fear the name of Rowe engendered among the criminal fraternity.

'What d'you want?' he said finally.

'We need some numbers,' she lied, knowing that her bold pretence was likely to be seen as that of an agent provocateur were Smith's response ever to lead to a criminal prosecution.

'I can let you have one reg,' he said. 'But it'll cost you a ton.'

'No probs. Terry will see you right.'

Smith gave a non-committal grunt and abruptly turning away from her, crossed the room and disappeared through a door into a back office. She went after him almost immediately, just in case he was phoning Jimmy Rowe to check on her bona fides. But instead, as she carefully eased open the door, she saw him crouched in front of a big floor safe with the door already half open.

'Shut it again, Tommy,' she said quietly.

He jerked round so quickly that he fell over. She waited for him to get up again and held out her warrant card in front of her. 'CID, Tommy, and I don't want to see what you've got in there because then I'd probably have to nick you.'

'You bleedin' bitch,' he snarled, his face ashen. Grabbing a monkey wrench from a desk to one side of where he was standing, he started towards her.

'Don't!' she snapped and produced her police radio in her other hand. 'This is equipped with a GPS trace. If I'm not out of here safely in ten minutes, the heavy mob will be all over you. They'll tear this place apart.'

He stopped dead and after a long hesitation while he appeared to chew that over, he dropped the wrench back onto the desk, suddenly deflated. 'What do you want?' he said sullenly.

'A name.'

'What name?'

She pocketed her radio and warrant card and fished out a piece of paper from her pocket, stepping forward to slap it on the desk beside him.

'You sold him that number off a SORN Ford Transit.'

'Dunno. Can't remember.'

'Well, either you tell me, or I'll have to get a warrant and call in the stolen vehicle squad.'

'They won't find nuffin'.'

'Maybe not, but Jimmy Rowe will hear about it and maybe he'll think you talked to the police to get yourself off the hook. He won't like that at all — especially as we think the character you sold the plates to may be linked to a murder investigation.'

His eyes widened. 'Murder? I ain't murdered no one.' His voice was suddenly a lot more high-pitched than before. 'And I wouldn't be part of nuffin' like that anyhow.'

She shrugged. 'Well, if you're holding back on info, what are we supposed to think?'

'Okay, okay,' he muttered hastily. 'Geezer come here about a week or so ago, drivin' an old green Land Rover. Give his name as Tony Cameron, though that obviously weren't legit. Said he had a cottage out on the Levels somewhere and he needed another number for his motor.'

'Did he say why?'

'No, and I don't ask daft questions like that.'

'Business must be slack if you can remember that much about one customer after a week.'

'Yeah, well, there was somefin' about him. He give me the creeps. And when I said I couldn't help him, he got out a bloody great commando knife and started pickin' his fingernails wiv it, so I let him have the reg numbers off the Trannie.'

'He had a commando knife, you say?'

'Yeah. I did time in the mob, so I recognized it.'

'Didn't get the number of his 'Drover, I suppose, did you?'

He scowled, and took out a small, black book from one of his desk drawers. He opened it, turned it around to face her and stabbed a finger at a scribbled entry. Kate peered closely at the book and grabbed a biro off the desk to make a note in her pocketbook.

'I ain't no nark,' he blurted out, 'so it wasn't me what told you, right?'

'Mum's the word, Tommy. Final question, what did this character look like?'

He screwed up his face for a moment. 'About fifty, six feet, plenty of muscle. Er, bearded, wiv black hair down to his shoulders. I reckon he were ex-army — I can tell a squaddie a mile off — and he was wearin' one of them camouflage jackets.'

Kate raised her eyebrows in surprise. 'Camouflage jacket?' she echoed, remembering the intruder at Scribbler's Halt. 'Very good, Tommy. With your eye for detail we could use you in the force.'

'Very funny,' he sneered. 'Well, that's all I've got. Now, can I get on? I've got a scrap business to run.'

Kate smiled. 'Of course, Tommy. Sorry to hold you up. But a word to the wise. Stick to your legit scrap business in future, eh? That way you won't be joining Ronnie Duggan in stir. *Capiche*?'

Then she turned on her heel and walked out the office, feeling his eyes boring into her back and knowing they were following her until she climbed into her car and drove away.

It was only when she was well clear of the yard and heading back across the Levels that she allowed herself to take a deep, trembling breath of relief. It had gone well. Better than she had expected. Now all she had to do was carry out an RO check on the number of the Land Rover Tommy had given her, and that should bring her another step closer to tracing her mystery man in the camouflage jacket.

* * *

It was pure luck that the man in the green Land Rover caught sight of Kate pulling out onto the main Bridgwater road from the lane leading to the scrapyard as he was driving past. He had been to an off-licence in Highbridge to replenish his supply of whisky when he saw her. He recognized her immediately, even though she was driving a Mazda MX5 instead of the usual plain CID car. He braked and pulled into the side of the road, watching her in his rear-view mirror as she disappeared in the opposite direction.

That bloody cop cow again. It was plain she had been visiting the scrapyard. It was the only thing down the lane she had emerged from. So, she had been to see Tommy Smith, had she? That suggested she may have somehow got hold of the bogus number he'd been using on the 'Drover, had matched it to the Trannie and been to the scrapyard to check it out. Maybe it had just been a fishing expedition, but it could mean bad news for him and his plans if Tommy had snitched to her about his visit there. There was only one way to find out and that was to pay Tommy another visit. But that would have to wait until the yard closed for the day and the little arsehole was in his caravan at the back. Meantime, he needed to check things out, just to be sure.

* * *

DWB Autos occupied a small, red-brick building on the outskirts of Bridgwater, maybe a couple of miles or so from Tommy's scrapyard. There was an assortment of second-hand cars and vans on the forecourt in front of the showroom, each one bearing a garish yellow roof sign, with the sale price in red letters.

A slim, dark-suited man with greasy hair creeping over his collar and an insincere smile met Kate as she pushed through the showroom door.

'Jeff Dilly,' he said, stretching out a manicured hand adorned with several gold rings. 'Can I help you?'

'I do hope so,' Kate replied, declining the handshake, producing her warrant card and introducing herself.

At once the smile vanished and the hand dropped as if it had touched a hot stove.

'Police, eh? So, what have we done now?'

The question implied that the firm had done other things in the past which had attracted the unwelcome attention of the authorities. Kate guessed from the look of the place and the shifty salesman now staring at her with undisguised hostility that it was likely to be for dodgy sales practices, like selling unroadworthy vehicles.

'Just a routine inquiry,' she said lightly so as not to scare him off. 'We're trying to trace a green Land Rover Defender our records tell us you sold to a client recently.'

He feigned puzzlement and ran a hand over his chin. 'Green Land Rover. Can't say I remember ever selling one of those.'

Kate gave him the registration number and he shook his head. 'No, doesn't ring a bell.'

She sighed. 'Mr Dilly, I want you to understand something. First, you aren't in any trouble over the sale. We are only interested in the man you sold the vehicle to. Second, I am cold, tired and short on patience, and if you piss me about, I will arrange for this place to receive a visit from the local authority Trading Standards department to investigate possible breaches of trading practices.'

His face darkened. 'We have nothing to hide.'

She shrugged. 'Then you won't mind if I give them a call?'

Abruptly, his memory returned, and he snapped his fingers. 'Do you know, I remember now, silly me. Getting old, I think. It was an ex-farm vehicle we had on our forecourt after taking it in part exchange for a second-hand Range Rover. Owner was a chap from Wells if I recall. To be honest, we were glad to get rid of it. It looked bad for our business out front.'

She nodded. 'Go on, Mr Dilly.'

He made a face. 'Yes, well, this chap came in and asked us how much we wanted for it and when we quoted him a price, he agreed without hesitation. Said he wanted to use it for off-roading. It was sound body-wise, if rather shabby, and it had a good engine, so we quoted a low price just to get rid of the thing.'

'How did he pay you?'

'In cash. Had quite a bundle on him.'

'Do you know his name?'

'I can find out from our records.'

'Please do — right away.'

Kate could feel hidden eyes on her as she wandered around the showroom giving each of the three cars parked there a cursory glance. Looking up quickly, she saw the venetian blinds blanking out the window of what was obviously an office part slightly then fall back into place.

Dilly returned moments later with a piece of paper in his hand.

'Got all his details for you. Name, address, etcetera. All tickety-boo.'

Kate took the note from him and studied the information written on it in block capitals, noting with a start that the customer had given a Pembrokeshire address. Wales again!

'Tony Cameron?' she said.

He shrugged. 'That's what he said. Told me he was moving into the area from Pembroke Dock and renting a cottage out on the Levels until he could find a more permanent address, so he hadn't yet changed the Pembroke address on his driving licence.'

'Did he give you the address of this cottage?'

'No. He said he was still in the throes of negotiating terms.'

'How very convenient. But you did see his licence and make sure he had insurance?'

He hesitated. 'We have to by law when selling a vehicle to anyone, and we gave him an insurance cover note that we always offer customers from a firm we regularly deal with. This lasts for fifteen days or until the recipient takes out the insurance in full with the company. The Land Rover already had a current MOT.'

'So, to return to my previous question, you did examine his licence then?'

He fidgeted with his tie and looked away from her. 'Well, you have the licence number there, so obviously.'

'You haven't answered my question. Did you examine it yourself?'

'I would have done, yes.'

'And his face matched the photograph on the card?'

More hesitation and Kate jumped straight in. 'I would be very careful how you answer that, Mr Dilly.'

He grimaced. 'Well, if I remember correctly, he said he had mislaid the card part of the licence and he only had the green paper part, which doesn't carry a photograph.'

'The paper part of the driving licence is no longer valid, as you well know, and that has been the case for some time now.'

He shrugged. 'Well, it was all he had. But he said he would bring in the card part for me to see when he found it.'

'And did he?'

'Er, no.'

'But presumably you took a copy of the paper document.'

'Er, no, our photocopier was broken. I had to take down the details by hand.'

Kate's expression hardened. 'How very annoying for you, Mr Dilly. But let's be honest. Everything you've told me so far is a load of balls, isn't it? The fact is, you were so relieved to get the Land Rover off your forecourt that you weren't too bothered about the legal niceties of the sale, were you? I'm quite sure you suspected your purchaser was far from legit, but you were happy to overlook this for a quick sale. That's about it, isn't it?'

He flushed. 'Of course not and I resent your inference.'

'I don't give a damn what you resent. I am dealing with a serious crime inquiry here. Did you even bother to ask for any other proof of identity?'

He shuffled his feet a little. 'Well, seeing as he was paying cash, we didn't think that was really necessary.'

Kate shook her head in disgust. 'I bet you didn't. So, how did this character arrive — in another motor?'

'I don't know. Presumably, he was dropped off by someone. He, er, just appeared in the showroom.'

'Can you describe him?'

He thought about that for a second. 'If I remember correctly, he was late forties to early fifties, of average height, with a heavy build and long black hair to his shoulders. Oh, and he had a full beard.'

'Anything else? Welsh accent? Dress?'

'Well, he wasn't from around here, but I couldn't say he had any sort of distinctive accent, though his voice was quite rough. Dress-wise, he seemed to be wearing something like an army camouflage jacket.'

Kate stiffened. That jacket again.

'Nothing else distinctive? Facial scars, that sort of thing?'

'No, that's about all. What, er, has he done?'

'I can't tell you that, Mr Dilly, but you can rest assured that this isn't the end of the matter as far as your business is concerned.'

She handed him a card. 'In the meantime, if you see this man again, it might help your case if you were to give me a call. My name and number are there.'

'But of . . . of course,' he stammered. 'Always glad to help the local police.'

I bet you are, Kate thought as she left the showroom and drove off. There couldn't be a more public-spirited citizen than Mr Jeff Dilly!

* * *

155

The man in the camouflage jacket had caught up with Kate and had followed her from Tommy's scrapyard almost to the door of DWB Autos. He glimpsed her turning onto the forecourt and, keeping a safe distance, pulled up behind a parked lorry a hundred yards or so before the garage.

He stayed there until she came out again and drove off but made no attempt to follow her. He had seen enough to confirm his suspicions. So, Tommy had grassed him up, had he? There was no other explanation for the copper paying a visit to the garage straight after calling at the yard. It would be interesting to see what the scrawny little rat had to say about that, and he was quite sure Tommy Smith would tell him everything . . . eventually.

CHAPTER 18

Kate got back to Highbridge police station just after lunch and joined Hayden in the canteen for a late snack.

'How did the checks on our Mr Templar go?' she asked.

He sniffed. 'Zilch there. Nothing on PNC and every search I put in for the name Templar took me to either Leslie Charteris or the actors, Roger Moore, Ian Ogilvy or George Sanders. Seems our man is clean — or is using an alias.'

'What about the electoral roll?'

He shook his head. 'Nothing there either. I even rang around the local papers, just in case he was on their staff, but they'd never heard of him.'

'So, I've been talking to a ghost, it would appear. Damn it! This business is getting more and more complicated by the hour.'

He shrugged. 'How about *your* inquiries? Mission accomplished?'

She nodded and filled him in on the morning's events. 'Just done a check on the driving licence that was produced to Jeff Dilly. It seems it was reported stolen from a carry-on bag left unattended on a seat in the Rosslare to Pembroke ferry a couple of weeks ago, together with a wallet, credit cards and car ignition keys. Cameron's car, a Honda CRV, was then also stolen and brazenly driven off the ship when it arrived in Pembroke Dock. It was later found abandoned and burned out in woodland on the Levels near Catcott.'

He pushed his empty plate away from him, burped, apologized and pulled his apple turnover and custard towards him. 'Catcott? So that's how he got here. No idea where he could have gone to ground, I suppose?'

She shook her head. 'He told Jeff Dilly he was renting a cottage somewhere on the Levels but was still negotiating terms.'

'So, we're looking for a man of around fifty, about six feet tall, with a heavy, muscular build, a full beard and shoulder-length black hair, wearing a camouflage jacket, who could be living in a rented cottage somewhere out on the Levels — an area of around 170,000 acres?'

'That's about it, yes.'

He prodded the apple turnover with his fork. 'Then finding him should be a piece of cake, shouldn't it?'

She acknowledged his sarcasm with a faint smile. 'We wouldn't have to cover the whole of the Levels, just a small part of it. Getting around as he has been suggests that, like Jason Spindler, he must be living locally — say within a ten to fifteen mile radius of Catcott where he dumped the Honda. We've no other reports of stolen vehicles in that area, so it is likely he walked from there to where he is living now.'

'Or called for a taxi on his mobile.'

'I can't see him doing that,' she said. 'He wouldn't have wanted to risk being traced later.'

'But how would he have got to Bridgwater to buy the Land Rover later if he had no wheels? It would have been a long walk. He must either have used a bus or hired a taxi at that stage at least, which we could check.'

'True, but that doesn't help us much. The bus option is virtually a non-starter. There aren't that many routes operating in the remote parts of the Levels and how would we go about checking them all? We have a less than adequate description of our man and we have no idea when he would have used any of the available services anyway — which would apply in relation to the taxi option too.'

'Well, since house-to-house inquiries are plainly out of the question, even for the much smaller area you suggest, the process could be short-circuited by concentrating on the cottage you say this character told Smith and Dilly he was renting. A ring around of local rental companies and estate agents might be worth considering?' he said.

'A long shot, but doable, I agree. Good point.'

He grunted and stared into space for a few seconds, seemingly lost in thought, his first mouthful of apple turnover perched on his spoon. Kate waited patiently.

'Penny for them?' she said finally.

He surfaced with a frown. 'It's just that I was thinking about the bogus registration plates Tommy Smith admitted to selling our mystery man.'

'What about them?'

'Well, think on it. Okay, so Tommy Smith runs a scrapyard, and it's obvious he deals with the scrappage of SORN vehicles. But how did our man know that he was in the business of selling dodgy plates? There are only three possibilities. One, that he chanced his arm on the assumption that Tommy might be amenable to a bit of illegal business on the side. That seems highly unlikely since he could have ended up being reported if Tommy had been kosher. Two, that some local villain in the know had recommended that he approach Tommy, which means he might have underworld connections. Or, three, that he knew about Tommy because he is or was himself a local man who had used him before.'

Kate pursed her lips and nodded. 'Which means that maybe Tommy knows a lot more than he admitted to me, and maybe he could even lead us right to our man's doorstep if a little bit more pressure were to be applied?'

'Exactly.'

She glanced at her watch and stood up. 'Bit late now. Maybe it's something we should reserve for first thing tomorrow. Anyway, I've got to brief Percival about the latest developments, so I'll leave you to get stuck in.'

'Stuck in? Stuck into what?'

She beamed at him. 'I thought your idea about ringing around the rental firms and estate agents was a brilliant one, and who better to make a start on that this afternoon before they close than my clever, analytical husband? I should get Indrani to give you a hand if I were you. I'll pop back later to see how you're getting on. But finish your dinner first. I don't want you getting emaciated.'

Then she left him sitting there gaping after her and thinking about his penchant for opening his big mouth at just the wrong moment.

* * *

Percival was in his office when Kate returned to the department before heading out again. He listened intently, without interruption, to her detailed briefing, in which she covered everything that had happened since they had last spoken.

When she had finished he sat back in his chair, slid his hands down the back of his trousers and studied her thoughtfully. 'And we have no idea why this mystery man has travelled all the way from Ireland to Somerset and is now suspected of harassing Tamara Callaghan?'

'None whatsoever, though it seems very much like a grudge thing to me. That's why I believe the same man was responsible for the carnage at the bookshop and that he was the intruder I disturbed climbing out of the window of Scribbler's Halt.'

He looked dubious. 'So, if he means Callaghan harm, why hasn't he done that already? You say he was leaving her house when you spotted him. Yet Callaghan herself was unharmed and by the sound of it, quite blasé about the intrusion.'

'I think he's playing with her. Trying to wind her up. It's like some revenge thing. But I am concerned that when he tires of the game, he will do what he came here to do. I am quite sure he was responsible for the death of Jason Spindler and that he rigged his so-called suicide, which indicates he is totally ruthless and capable of anything.'

'But we're not sure Spindler's suicide *was* rigged. There's no pm result yet and Dr Summers wasn't prepared to say one way or the other.'

Kate released her breath in a sharp, frustrated hiss. 'But it is still a suspicious death, and surely we should have set up a full investigation by now — especially after all that we have uncovered so far?'

He grimaced. 'I have briefed the DCI regularly on the state of play, but he is adamant that not enough positive evidence in relation to Spindler's death has yet been obtained to justify going the whole hog. He feels we should continue investigating the case as thoroughly as we can, so that all the right steps have been taken, both forensically and otherwise, just in case the situation changes, but that, until we have the results of the pm, we should hold fire.'

'And the super, what does he think?'

'He's away on leave until next week.'

Kate shrugged in resignation and stood up. 'I've got a bad feeling about this, Des. I'm just glad I'm not the one who has to make the decision, or who will have to carry the can at the end of it all.'

'You won't enjoy that luxury for much longer once you're occupying this chair,' he said. 'Believe me, I know from bitter experience.'

* * *

He sat in the Land Rover, parked on the road opposite the mouth of the lane leading to the scrapyard. He had decided to wait until Tommy Smith's small band of workers knocked off for the day before he paid Tommy another visit. He saw them all leave a little earlier than he had expected, and quickly made his move, keen to get into the yard before Tommy padlocked the gates.

He was in luck. There was a light still on in the office and the gates were wide open.

Tommy never even heard him enter. He was doing something in the back office, and it was not until he came out again that he saw the figure lounging against the windowsill, studying him with a cold smile.

'Hello, Tommy,' the man in the camouflage jacket said softly. 'I think you and I need a little chat.'

The little man's Adam's apple jerked spasmodically, and his face suddenly lost all its colour.

'What . . . what about?' he said in a cracked voice.

His visitor straightened up and advanced slowly around the edge of the counter towards him, causing Tommy to shrink back through the door of the office.

'Shall we say, business confidentiality?' he drawled. 'Seems to be a relevant topic.'

Tommy found the wall of the far office at his back and froze like a rabbit cornered by a fox. 'I don't know what you mean.'

'Don't you, Tommy? What did you say to the woman copper?'

Tommy licked dry lips. 'I didn't say nuffin' to no one.'

The other continued to advance. The dark eyes trained on him were suddenly hooded. 'Don't waste my time, Tommy. I need to know what you told her.'

Tommy was visibly trembling now. 'I didn't tell her nuffin', honest. She . . . she just wanted to know if anyone had tried to buy any old reg plates off me and I said no.'

'Is that right? So, the fact that she went straight from here to DWB Autos — the very place where I bought my Land Rover — was just a coincidence, was it?'

'I dunno. But I didn't say nuffin' about you. I ain't no nark.'

'Oh, I think you are, Tommy. A proper little nark, and I know you told her all about me. The registration number I obtained from you, what I looked like, what I was wearing — maybe you even threw in my inside leg measurement.'

Tommy shook his head vigorously as his accuser stopped just a couple of feet away and studied him silently. 'On me muvver's grave, I didn't tell her nuffin' about you, you got to believe me. I don't tell Old Bill nuffin' — never.'

The muscular hand moved like lightning, the long fingers gripping him tightly by the throat, cutting off his air supply, and the hard, bearded face was thrust to within inches of his own.

'I'm out of patience, you little toad,' the other grated. 'So give, or I'll choke the life out of you.'

Tommy's eyes were already glazing over, and his struggles had degenerated into a series of feeble twitches when the stranglehold was released. As a rasping gasp erupted from his throat and the light gradually returned to his eyes, his assailant treated him to a grim smile. 'Now, give. All of it.'

'She freatened me,' Tommy whispered. 'Had me done up like a kipper she did. Knew all about the plates already. I just told her what she already knew. But I didn't say nuffin' else.'

The stranglehold was reapplied, and the little man clawed at the muscular wrist, gasping in distress, before the grip was once more relaxed. 'Did you tell her what I looked like and that I was driving a green Land Rover?'

'I had no choice, honest. She had me by the short and curlies.'

The other nodded. 'Very awkward for you, Tommy, I agree,' he said, straightening the collar of the scrap dealer's overalls and patting him gently on the chest. 'But you see, you've caused me a bit of inconvenience, so you'll have to be punished.'

Then, before Tommy realized what was happening, he was spun around to face the wall. In a single swift movement two powerful hands gripped him, one on each side of his head. The double wrench to his neck was accomplished with little difficulty and he probably never even heard the fatal *snap* of his spine.

* * *

Briefing Percival had taken less time than Kate had expected, and impulsive as ever, she changed her mind about saving the return visit to Tommy's scrapyard until the following day. She had over an hour in hand before dark, so she reckoned she could easily make it before the yard closed. After all, what was the point in waiting? Strike while the iron is hot had always been her strategy and it had paid dividends in the past, so why not now?

Grabbing her police radio, just in case of problems, she headed out straightaway, using her own car to attract less attention, reasoning that she might as well use some of her official casual user mileage allowance while she was at it. She got to the yard just as the afternoon light was beginning to fade. The front gates were wide open but the place looked dead, and she saw no sign of activity among the rows of abandoned metal skeletons as she pulled up outside the main office. It seemed Tommy's workers had already gone home. She just hoped he was still here.

He wasn't, but it appeared that someone was still working inside. A single lamp had been left on in the main office and a donkey jacket was draped over the counter, as if in readiness for the off. There was a pile of documents on the desk in the back office, and the laptop was on, displaying a list of vehicle numbers and other information in four neat columns.

She frowned, walked back out again and scanned the yard for any sign of the little man or his workers. But apart from a black-and-white cat, which streaked across the rough ground in front of her and disappeared among the lines of abandoned wrecks, the whole site looked to be deserted. Her frown deepened. From what she had seen of Tommy earlier, she thought it highly unlikely that he'd departed for the day leaving his office unlocked, his computer still on and the main gates of the yard wide open. So, where was he?

At that moment she spotted a sudden movement in one of the aisles of abandoned wrecks and her gaze focused on something that sent an icy chill down her spine. A tall figure had appeared briefly in the gap before disappearing among the cars — a figure with black, shoulder-length hair, dressed in a green-brown camouflage jacket. It was *him*, it had to be — the man both Tommy Smith and Jeff Dilly had described. The man she had disturbed in the grounds of Scribbler's Halt. The man who may have been responsible for the death of Jason Spindler.

Instinctively, she reached for her radio to call for backup, but drew back her hand. What if she had made a mistake and the man in the camouflage jacket was simply a scrapyard worker? Camouflage jackets were not exactly out of the ordinary, after all. They had become almost a fashion accessory among the young. Furthermore, the pattern might not even be camouflage. It was getting towards dusk and her eyes could have been playing tricks on her. She needed to be sure of her facts before summoning the "cavalry", or she could end up making a fool of herself. But she'd have to be careful — bloody careful.

She counted to three and raced across the concrete hardstanding to the car graveyard. There, she leaned against the side of an old Renault van while she got her breath back. Nothing moved in the vicinity and the sound of traffic on the distant main road was little more than a murmur. She eased herself away from the van and peered around the side of its comforting bulk. Nothing, damn it! Where had he gone? Trying to find anyone among these aisles of wrecks would be like trying to find a needle in a haystack unless he made a sound. She got to thinking that maybe he had spotted her and was lying in wait somewhere or creeping up on her — indulging in a little game of cat and mouse. She shuddered and threw a keen glance into the gathering gloom behind her but saw only a line of metal skeletons destined for the crusher.

She clenched her teeth and slid around the front of the Renault into another narrow passage. She reached the crawler crane she had seen earlier, noting with a shiver the giant claw suspended from the motionless hydraulic arm above a

Peugeot saloon car which had no doubt been given a temporary reprieve until the workers were back in the morning.

She saw the green Land Rover seconds later. It was parked just beyond the Peugeot, close to the side of the massive crusher. Even from several yards away, she could see the registration number clearly. It matched the number she had been given by both Jeff Dilly and Tommy Smith. She stopped again, warning bells sounding in her head. So the Land Rover was there, but where was its owner?

Even as the thought occurred to her, a powerful hand closed over her mouth and nose from behind, shutting off the air, and seconds later total blackness enveloped her.

CHAPTER 19

Consciousness brought no relief from the darkness. Kate knew her eyes were open, but she couldn't see a thing and she could feel a constant, irritating trickle down her forehead, which suggested that she had sustained some sort of head injury and was bleeding. She was lying on her side, crammed into a restrictive, box-like space, with her legs bent at an acute angle that she was unable to straighten. A rag or something had been stuffed in her mouth as a gag, held in place by some sort of sticky tape. Her wrists and ankles were tightly bound, and her hands and feet felt cold and dead from the reduced circulation. She tried to sit up, but even after several attempts, only succeeded in slamming the side of her head against something hard a foot or so above her. There was a faint petroleum smell all around her, mixed with another foul, sweet odour that she couldn't identify and wriggling to one side, the back of her hand brushed against something soft and yielding, wrapped in a rough cloth, like a sack of loose compost.

Where the hell was she? She remembered the hand closing over her face and cursed her stupidity for allowing herself to be ambushed so easily. But what had her assailant done with her while she had been unconscious? And why had he simply put her out and tied her up instead of killing her while he had the chance?

For a few moments she desperately tried to pull her hands free of what was securing her wrists behind her back but got nowhere. Then it dawned on her what had been used to confine them. Her own rigid handcuffs, which had been attached to her belt in their black leather holder. The swine had used her own kit on her. But why?

Feeling the panic well up inside her, she raised her head and tried to call out, but could only manage a strangled gasp and fell back on what her questing fingers told her was a rubber mat of some sort, which seemed to be strangely wet.

She was about to try to sit up again when there was a loud "crack", and a shaft of pale light from an early risen moon flooded what was now revealed as the boot of a car — no doubt the Peugeot. The bearded face that stared down at her was partially masked in shadow, but she caught the glint of the eyes boring into her.

'Well, copper,' he said in a rough, sneering voice, 'hope you enjoyed Tommy's company.'

Suddenly tumbling to the truth, Kate jerked her head sideways. It wasn't a sack of loose compost that was crammed into the boot behind her, but the body of a man in overalls. A man she instantly recognized. A man whose parchment white face was turned in her direction, his unseeing eyes wide and staring in the shocked realization of death.

'Sorry it's a bit wet in there,' her captor commented, 'but it seems the dirty little bugger pissed himself when I snapped his neck. I could have snapped yours too, but I thought we'd have a little chat first.'

A big hairy hand reached down and ripped the tape from her mouth, enabling her to spit out the gag.

'Scream and you'll join old Tommy in his scrapyard in the sky,' he warned.

'I never scream,' she retorted, cultivating as much outward defiance as her thudding heart would allow.

'Bully for you. So, tell me how you cottoned on to me in the first place. I need to know, you see, as it could affect my plans.'

'Why should I tell you anything?'

'Because if you don't, I'll wring that pretty little neck of yours.'

'You're going to do that anyway.'

There was a harsh, mirthless chuckle. 'Plucky bitch, aren't you? What if I said that if you tell me what I want to know, I won't lay a hand on you?'

'I wouldn't believe you.'

'Not even if I swore Scout's honour?'

'Get stuffed.'

The moonlight caught the sudden scowl on his face. 'Rude little bitch too. Well, I reckon you've not got much on me anyway, otherwise your lot would have come a-calling long before now.'

'There'll be on their way here at this very moment.'

'I doubt that, girlie. I bet no one even knows you're here. You see, from what I've seen of you over the last couple of days, I reckon you're a bit of a lone wolf. You act on impulse, don't you?'

Kate thought about that and felt sick. He was certainly right there. Not even Hayden knew she had come to the yard. She was completely on her own and it didn't bode well for her survival.

'So, what's it to be?' he went on. 'Come clean or join Tommy?'

Kate's mind was racing. She had to keep him talking while she tried to think of a way out. Delay was her only hope.

'What do you want to know?'

He stepped back a couple of paces and folded his arms. 'Now, that's better. First, how did you suss that the perv's death wasn't suicide? I went to a lot of trouble to set the thing up.'

She met his stare as boldly as she could, even though her insides were quaking. 'You forgot about his bike, which he'd left against the hedge outside Scribbler's Halt. It indicated he'd been there the night he died, and then we found traces of blood in the grounds where you stiffed him.'

'Blood? I broke his neck, so how come there were blood traces?'

'He had a recent wound to his leg, which must have opened up in your struggle with him. That threw doubt on his death being suicide, especially as he was found strung up several miles away.'

All the time she had been talking, Kate had been working at the handcuffs on her wrists. She had quite small hands and there was just a chance she could squeeze one of them even tighter and pull it through the steel loop.

He whistled. 'Big mistake I made there then, wasn't it? I shall have to be more careful in future. So, how did you connect me to it all?'

'That old Land Rover was a dead giveaway,' she said, still tugging at the handcuffs behind her back and praying he hadn't twigged what she was up to. 'The night you broke into Scribbler's Halt, I was just leaving when I saw it parked in the gateway opposite. I checked it out before I went back into the grounds and caught you climbing out of the window. So when you drove off without lights, I already had the index number, which turned out to be off a SORN Ford Transit. That led me to this scrapyard and then to the garage where you bought the motor.'

He grunted. 'Then Tommy gave you more of the SP on me than he admitted, eh? So he got what was coming to him right enough.'

'He told me a lot, yes, but the important thing is that half the force now knows about you and the Land Rover, which means you won't get far even when you leave here.'

'You're talking bollocks again,' he retorted. 'If you had known so much about me before, you wouldn't have needed to come back here to see Tommy again. And as for your

170

mates in blue, I'm willing to bet they have no idea who I am or where I live.'

'I wouldn't be too sure about that.'

'Okay, so what's my name and where do I live?'

She said nothing and he snorted his contempt. 'You don't know, do you? You haven't got a clue. It's all bullshit.'

He stepped forward a pace and seemed to peer more closely at her. She ceased working on the cuffs and carried on talking to keep him occupied.

'We know a lot more about you than you think. The fact that you have it in for Tamara Callaghan for a start. Resent the success of her novels, do you?'

'Her novels?' The derision in his tone was evident. 'Is that what you think? Listen, girlie, I don't give a toss about her crappy novels. You don't know her. She's an evil, scheming cow, who owes me, and I just felt like playing with her for the sheer hell of it before I evened up the score, that's all. It's taken me a long time to find her and now that I have, the fancy name she's given herself won't save her. She's going to get exactly what she deserves very soon. You can bet on it.'

Kate had resumed her struggle with the cuffs, despite the pain in her hand and the fact that her knuckles felt raw and slippery with the blood she could feel trickling through her fingers. But it was fast dawning on her that she had set herself an impossible task. She just couldn't get more than a quarter of her hand through the steel loop, no matter how hard she pulled and tugged at it behind her back. Then he dropped his bombshell.

'No joy with the handcuffs then? I know you've been doing your best to get out of them, but you've been wasting your time. You won't slip out of those babies — your lot make 'em too well. Anyway, I've run out of questions for you now, so I reckon we'll call it a night, eh?'

Producing another ball of rag, he stuffed it into her mouth and applied a fresh strip of tape.

Then he studied her for a few seconds and shook his head slowly. 'You're a pretty little thing, I'll give you that.

Pity you had to stick your nose into things, but that's life, I suppose.'

Choking on the gag and gripped by absolute panic as he bent over her, Kate made one last desperate effort to free her wrist from the handcuffs' cruel grip. But it was pointless and as she turned her head, first one way and then the other, in a futile attempt to prevent those big, muscular hands from closing round her neck, he simply stood there watching her with the patient amusement of a cat playing with a mouse.

But then, when she finally gave up on her struggles and succumbed to inevitable exhaustion, instead of reaching for her to finish what he had started, he straightened up. 'Thing is, I always keep my promises,' he said. 'I told you I wouldn't lay a hand on you if you cooperated, and I won't.' He released a sneering laugh. 'I'll just leave that to Tommy's workers when they come on in the morning and start up the crusher. This car's next in line by the look of it, and I'm willing to bet those Neanderthals won't think of checking the boot before they get started. Being compressed into a steel cube should be a novel experience for you, even if it is your last. Enjoy the ride, won't you?'

Then he slammed the boot lid shut and Kate was once more plunged into impenetrable blackness.

* * *

Kate had known fear many times in her life before and as a police officer, had faced death on more than one occasion. But she had never before been gripped by such absolute terror. She lay there totally helpless in the foul-smelling darkness, anticipating the eventual reverberating crash and screech of tortured metal as the giant claw of the nearby crane seized the roof of the car in its steel talons and hoisted it high in the air before swinging it around towards the gaping jaws of the crusher.

Would death be instantaneous, she wondered, or would she feel everything that happened to her? Would she still be alive when the metal shards that would ultimately be compressed into a single steel cube ripped her body to shreds, pulverizing bone and sinew and crushing her dismembered remains into an unidentifiable pulp? Would the inevitable haemorrhage leak through it all to pool on the ground afterwards or would no trace of her be left behind? She had no idea what happened to car bodies when they left the scrapyard or what processes were involved in recovering the steel. Maybe bits of her would be found when her cube coffin was transported to the foundry, or would her remains just end up being cremated in some raging furnace, obliterated completely by the flames?

Would anyone ever find out what had happened to her? Hayden and her colleagues were bound to initiate a full-scale search when she failed to return to the station, but that would not happen immediately and as no one was even aware of the fact that she had come to the scrapyard, it was hardly likely to be the first place they would look for her. Even if they eventually did decide to check the place out, by the time they got here, found her car parked outside the office and began a search of the scrapyard, it was likely to be too late for her anyway. She would already be history. And in any event, where would they start looking? There were scores of dumped vehicles on the site, plus a whole stack of cubes waiting to be transported. Checking all the vehicles could be achieved over time, but it would be impossible to unravel each of the cubes to find out what was inside.

Okay, so when Tommy's workmen came on in the morning and found he was not there, they might wonder about that, but they would probably assume he had overslept and just carry on with their allotted tasks, including operating the crusher, while they waited for him to turn up. It was unlikely they would think that anything was untoward for several hours, unless they were due to be paid. As for her Mazda car, it was not a new one and had several knocks and scratches, so they would probably assume it was just another vehicle that had been dropped off for disposal and pay little attention to it.

There was no way out. After so many scrapes in the past, this time it looked like she was facing the final chapter in her life — and in the grisliest way imaginable. In a last-ditch attempt to save herself, she forced herself over onto her back and used the heels of her trainers dug into the rubber mat to push her body backwards, bending her neck and partially wedging her head in a corner. She then attempted lifting her legs to try to hammer her feet against the boot lid and spring it open. But there was little available space and in her crouched position, with her hands behind her back, she found it impossible to raise her legs sufficiently for the task. After that, she tried levering her body upwards, so that she could get her head and shoulders under the lid to exert as much pressure as possible to achieve the same result. But the lid didn't even budge, and she was reduced to banging her head on the underside of it in a desperate attempt to attract attention — though who she expected to hear the dull thuds in this vehicle graveyard at such a time of night, she had no idea.

Finally exhausted again, and conscious of increased trickling down her forehead and face and severe lancing pains in her head, which she had effectively been using as a sort of battering ram, she sank back down, once more wedged into a tight space between the underside of the boot lid and the car's wing, lacking the physical ability or even the will to extract herself from her doubled-up position. She was becoming confused and losing her grip on reality. Shock, coupled with insufficient oxygen, had begun to dull her senses, even blotting out the pain in her head and inducing a sense of total lethargy, like that of a drowning victim, steering her towards an abyss of comforting blackness, where she could find peace and security.

At first, she wasn't aware of the succession of heavy thuds on the boot. She didn't even try to blurt out anything through the tape stuck across her mouth, but she was jerked back to horrific reality with the shaking of the car and the screech of tortured metal. The workmen! They had arrived.

She was about to be loaded into the crusher. Her muffled screams were louder in her own head than in reality, and panic lent a new strength to her sinews as she slammed her head upwards into the underside of the boot lid again and again.

Then she was temporarily blinded by brilliant white moonlight as the boot lid flew open and strong hands reached into the cavity to slide under her legs and behind her back to lift her out. A tall figure in a dark woollen coat bent down beside her on the gravel and she heard him breathe a sigh of relief. 'Thank God,' Ed Templar said. 'I got here just in time.'

CHAPTER 20

'Have you been following me?' Kate said in a faint, cracked voice as Templar laid her on a worn leather couch in Tommy's reception office and gently removed the tape from her mouth, enabling her to spit out the evil-tasting gag. Every part of her seemed to hurt, especially her head, which was sticky with blood and felt as if it had been attacked by a road drill, and she was nauseous and giddy.

He slipped a cushion under her neck. 'Let's just say I've been keeping you under observation,' he said, cutting the thin twine binding her ankles with a clasp knife. 'Good job I did too. Looks like you have an "admirer" who was keen to demonstrate the crush he has on you.'

Kate failed to appreciate the joke and tried to sit up, wincing at the sudden pain in her legs produced by the returning circulation. But she was too weak to manage it and fell back again.

'How did you know I was in the boot?' she said in a much stronger voice and turned over onto her side, rattling the handcuffs. 'Can you get these off me? If that swine took the keys, there should be a spare on a ring in the inner pocket of my trousers.'

He hesitated, then slipped a hand into the pocket of the thigh raised towards him. 'I saw you drive into the yard and waited for you to come out,' he explained. 'When you didn't, I decided to investigate. The bloody Land Rover drove me off the road in the lane just before I got to the entrance. Took me a few minutes to reverse my car out of the hedge. By that time, he was long gone. Then I spotted your Mazda outside the office and had a look around for you. Lucky you started banging on that boot lid, or I probably wouldn't have found you.'

'But why were you following me? What's your interest in my investigation? And don't tell me any more fibs about writing a book.'

He found her spare key after some awkward fumbling and threw her a quick glance as he bent over her to insert it in the lock of one of the cuffs.

'Just a healthy curiosity. I am a journalist, after all.'

She carefully released her injured hand from the cuff and flexed her fingers experimentally, wincing again as stabbing pains shot through her bloodied wrist. 'Not around here, you're not.'

Another quick glance at her as he turned his attention to the other cuff. 'Aha, you checked me out.'

'Of course.'

'And what did you find?'

'Nothing. According to the records we interrogated, you don't exist.'

He straightened up. 'I must be a ghost then. Best to leave it that way, eh?'

'I could arrest you.'

He gave a short laugh and shook his head. 'I doubt it. You can hardly stand up at the moment and anyway, what for? I haven't broken any laws — unless saving you from the crusher was an offence.'

She tried again to ease herself up against one end of the couch but failed a second time.

'So, what do you know about the arsehole who waylaid me?'

'Quite a bit, actually. Any idea where he might have gone to ground?'

'I wish I knew, believe me.'

'What about the number of the Land Rover he was using? You were sniffing around a garage down the road, I believe. Is that where he bought it?'

'You're very well informed. But why do you want to know about the Land Rover?'

'Because I need to find him. It's taken me long enough to get this far. So, what can you tell me?'

Despite her pain, she treated him to a keen stare. 'More importantly, what can *you* tell *me*?'

There was a spark of irritation in his eyes now. 'Do you always answer a question with a question?'

'Listen, that swine nearly killed me,' she retorted, 'and you have a moral duty to tell me what you know about him before he harms someone else.'

He shook his head. 'Moral duty, is it? Sorry, no can do. Mine is a private matter. But I will say one thing about him. He's a very dangerous individual — a competent, professional killing machine — and you'd be well advised to stay clear of him from now on.'

'So, why is he plaguing Tamara Callaghan?'

'You'd better ask her that question. Let's just say I believe there is a lot of bad Welsh blood between them.'

She finally managed to haul herself up against the end of the couch. 'You've got to come clean. I'm sure he means her harm.'

'That's her problem, and I really don't much care. She seems to be a nasty bit of work anyway.'

'What makes you say that?'

'Call it intuition. Now I must be off.'

'You're just going to leave me here like this?'

'Oh, I reckon you'll survive. Your colleagues won't be long in turning up once you give them a call.'

'And how do you propose I do that? I don't have my radio anymore.'

'No, I know. I'm afraid your attacker smashed it. I found it in bits by the car. But presumably you have your mobile?'

'Not on me. I left it in the Mazda.'

'Good job you did, or he would have totalled that as well.'

'Can you get it for me? I have my car keys here.'

He smiled knowingly. It was patently obvious that she was trying to delay his departure for as long as possible so she could quiz him further. He answered her by collecting the telephone from the nearby desk and placing it in her lap.

'I'm sure that one will work just as well,' he said.

She stared at the phone with a sour expression. 'I'll come looking for you. You know that, don't you?'

'I expect you will, but you won't find me. So, I'll bid you au revoir.'

Then he turned and was gone, a shadow briefly outlined against the moonlight in the doorway before he disappeared into the night.

* * *

As the man in the camouflage jacket left the scene at speed, it occurred to him that he might have made a big mistake. Dumping the woman copper in the boot of the car could end up working against him in the short term. When she didn't call in, the filth would be all over the area like a rash, and being out and about in a motor that must already have been circulated to every patrol would be just asking for trouble.

But whether sticking the copper in the boot was wise or not, what else could he have done? The nosy cow had clocked his Land Rover in the yard and would almost certainly have radioed the information into the Control Room if he hadn't acted when he did. So, even if he had simply belted her and driven off, the place would have been knee-deep in coppers before he'd got halfway across the Levels.

At least this way, he'd built in enough time to get back to his doss before everything went ballistic. And as for the bitch herself, she would be out of his hair for good now. He had no regrets, felt no sense of guilt at leaving her to face the horrific end he had reserved for her in just a few hours. Okay, so he could simply have snapped her neck like he had Tommy's, but she had been a real pain in the arse over the past few days and to his twisted mind, the abject terror she would be suffering as she lay there in the darkness beside Tommy's corpse, waiting for the sound of the crusher starting up in the morning, was a much more fitting punishment.

The car he had almost rammed as he'd left the site was concerning, though. Who the hell would have been driving into the yard at that time of night? Not a prospective customer, surely? It could have been a workman who had forgotten something when he'd left for the day, of course, but equally, it could also have been someone else, like a police colleague who'd arranged to meet the woman cop there. True, if it had been another copper, the wanker wouldn't know where to look for her, but nevertheless, to be on the safe side, it was advisable to get back to his place and lie low there for a while until things cooled down.

That meant he would have to give his final planned visit to Scribbler's Halt a miss this time, which was a real bummer, but dropping in on Madam another night gave him something he could really look forward to, just like savouring a twelve-year-old malt whisky.

* * *

White, crackly sheets, a strange disinfectant smell and a feeling of disorientation. Kate awoke suddenly and stared around the small, softly lit room and at the steel trolley beside her bed laden with what looked like electronic equipment. She closed her eyes tightly for a second, then opened them again.

'Ah, you're awake.'

The voice spoke from the other side of the bed, and she turned to look. The nurse smiled at her. 'How do you feel? The doctor thinks you'll be okay to go home a bit later. Just shock and a bit of mild concussion, he thinks.'

Kate frowned. 'I'm in *hospital*?' she exclaimed incredulously. 'How the hell . . . ?'

'You passed out as we were leading you back to the car, old thing,' a more familiar voice said.

Hayden was standing at the foot of the bed, arms folded and a look of relief on his face. 'Nice to see you back with us,' he said, nodding his thanks to the nurse as she discreetly left the room. 'But going to that scrapyard on your own was a really daft thing to do. Save for your phone call, we wouldn't have known where you were.'

Gingerly, Kate eased herself up into a sitting position against the pillows, wincing at the sudden flash of light before her eyes and the sharp, stabbing pain in her head. 'You wouldn't have found me anyway,' she said. 'I was in a car boot.'

'So you told us when we picked you up,' he said. 'Good job your knight in shining armour was on hand to rescue you.'

She grimaced. 'It seems he's been following me around all the time, though I can't fathom what his interest in all this is. He seemed to know who my attacker was but refused to tell me anything about him. I got the impression he has been using me to try to track down the arsehole.'

'Maybe your man is your rescuer's long lost relative?' Hayden said flippantly. 'Or he's from the National Lottery and wants to tell him he's won a million?'

She ignored the quip and cut the discussion short with an irritable wave of her hand as she swung one leg over the edge of the bed. 'Just get me my clothes, will you, Hayd? I can't just lie here.'

He stepped forward and placed a firm hand on her shoulder. 'You can and you will,' he said sternly. 'They gave you a sedative, and the doc says it will take a while for the effects to wear off.'

'A sedative? How long have I been here?'

'All night.'

'All *night*? So, what time is it now?'

'Just after two thirty in the afternoon. Doc's due to see you shortly to approve your discharge. Then it's home for a total rest. There's nothing more you can do today anyway.'

Kate stared at him. 'But you don't understand. Tamara Callaghan is in real danger. We have to warn her.'

He nodded. 'You said that last night. So we sent a couple of uniforms around to her place. But she was fine. Spencer Little is with her now. He called at the house as the lads were leaving this morning and said he would stay on for a bit.'

Kate grimaced. 'Fine bodyguard he is likely to be.' But she settled back against the pillows, suddenly too tired to argue.

He perched on the edge of the bed. 'Sorry, Kate, but you need to look after yourself. You look a proper mess at the moment.'

'A mess? What do you mean?'

He reached across and pulled her handbag out of the bedside cupboard. Rummaging around in it, he produced her compact mirror, which he held up in front of her.

The haunted white face, with its patchwork of cuts and bruises and the array of lacerations across the forehead, looked nothing like her.

'I don't know how you got those marks on your head,' he said, 'but I gather there are more like them under your hair.'

She didn't bother looking further but handed the mirror back to him. 'He must have smacked my head against the boot when he put me in it,' she said, 'and then I tried to force the thing open from the inside.'

'What, with your head?' He raised an eyebrow. 'Not a good strategy.'

'It is when you are faced with ending up in a crusher.'

He grinned. 'Good point. Anyway, forget that now. I have some news for you. We got the results of the pm on Spindler this morning. Doc Summers has confirmed what we suspected all along.'

'Murder?'

He nodded. 'A major incident room is being set up at the nick as we speak.'

'So, the DCI has finally made a decision, has he? What did Summers find?'

He shrugged. 'Among other things, evidence of substantial trauma, and a complete absence of the sort of rope mark you'd expect to find around the neck in a hanging—'

'Ecchymoses? Yes, she mentioned that to me at the scene.'

'Whatever — plus the fact that she says the sort of spinal fracture that killed Spindler could not have been caused by being hung from that beam. Something to do with the way the spinal cord itself was snapped and the presence of tell-tale bruising under the chin, which emerged later and which in her opinion was caused by compression of the neck in some sort of brief stranglehold. Apparently, that would have caused hypoxia and temporary shutdown. She believes he was first rendered unconscious and that his spine was probably snapped by a violent twist of the neck after he had passed out.'

She thought about that for a second, then frowned. 'My attacker must have used the same stranglehold on me to put me out when he grabbed me from behind. So, it's obviously the same man, and overall, the chokehold, the manner in which he snapped Spindler's spine and the fact that he likes to wear a camouflage jacket, all smack of military combat training, as I've said before.'

'You can buy camouflage jackets easily these days.'

'Agreed, but putting everything together, the signs all point the same way. Army — maybe even Special Forces. Did you get anything from your checks on the letting agents?'

He shook his head. 'Nothing on the name we had. Indrani is trying to widen the criteria, checking on lets taken out within the last three weeks by someone matching our man's description, but it's a work in progress.'

'Stymied at every juncture, it seems.'

He brightened a little. 'Not quite. There is some positive news. We've had confirmation from the lab that the blood traces found at the scene of both the indecent exposure at Mark village and the woods at Scribbler's Halt were indeed from Jason Spindler, though there's nothing back yet on the plaster cast of the footprint.'

He stood up and stretched. 'At least, with the pathologist's forensic evidence, everything begins to tie in. All we need now is the collar for the murder.'

'And not just the one murder either.' Abruptly, she stiffened and grabbed his arm. 'Tommy Smith! He was in the boot of that bloody car with me. The thing was due to be crushed this morning—'

He patted her hand reassuringly. 'Simmer down, old girl. We got the car and the poor old scrappie's remains after you told us what happened last night. You probably don't remember all that.'

She made a face and sank back against the pillow again, totally drained. 'Only bits of it, but it's all gradually coming back.'

He studied her, concern apparent on his face. 'What you need is a good rest. There's nothing more you can do today. Just leave it to the major investigation team until you're feeling better.'

'You know I can't do that.'

'You've got no choice. I've told the nurse to hide your clothes, so unless you want to walk out of here in that rather fetching hospital gown, you're confined to bed.'

'You shitbag.'

'Thanks, but I'm a very clever one too.'

'What do you mean?'

He looked smug. 'It occurred to me when we picked you up from the scrapyard that we had been provided with a possible boost to our inquiry.'

'How so?'

'Your handcuffs, old girl. You see, both your assailant and rescuer handled them — one to immobilize you and the other to free you.'

'Fingerprints!' she exclaimed.

'Precisely. And I've already set things in motion for a PNC database check. It may be a long shot, but there's every chance that either or both of our men have form and that their prints are on record.'

She stared at him in admiration. 'I have to agree with you, DC Lewis. You're not just a shitbag but a very clever shitbag!'

He frowned. 'I'll take that as a compliment, shall I? Oh, Percival said to tell you not to worry about the smashed police radio. He said you can pay for it in instalments.'

CHAPTER 21

The light was beginning to fade by the time Kate and Hayden left the hospital. Kate felt a lot more like her old self. The aches and pains were still there, but much reduced. Consequently, she was more than a bit put out when Hayden insisted on driving her to the police station in the CID car to pick up her own vehicle, which he had earlier collected from the scrapyard, rather than letting her drive herself. 'You've had a sedative, old girl, so you shouldn't be driving anything until tomorrow.'

Once at the station, however, she defied him and instead of allowing him to take her straight home, she insisted on calling into CID to check on things first. It was a big mistake.

The main office was as quiet as the grave. It turned out later that Percival and most of her colleagues were at a major incident briefing in the Incident Room upstairs. The mobile telephone left on Indrani Purewal's desk rang as Kate finished checking the messages in her own in-tray, watched from across the room by a disgruntled Hayden. She ignored the first three or four rings, but then with an irritable grimace, crossed to the desk to pick it up.

The voice at the other end was low and breathless. 'Who's that?'

'DS Lewis.'

There was a brief pause and then the speaker burst out with, 'Listen, this is Richard Tomlinson, Dean's Letting Agency. DC Indrani Purewal rang me this afternoon to ask if some guy in a camouflage jacket had been in at any point in the past three weeks to rent one of our properties. She told me he was dodgy.'

Kate's heart began to beat faster, and she waved Hayden to silence when he stood up and seemed about to ask her who the caller was.

'Go on,' she said.

'Well, I told the officer no one like that had been in. But I've just come out to a derelict cottage we're trying to sell, after a local farmer who uses it for cattle feed storage told me he thinks someone is sleeping rough there, and I've seen a light in the place. There's also a green Land Rover parked in one of the old sheds outside.'

'Where are you now, Mr Tomlinson?' she snapped.

'On the drove which passes the cottage.'

'And where is that exactly?'

She scribbled down the details. 'Right, now listen to me carefully. We're coming straight out. Give me somewhere we could meet up away from the cottage.'

She noted the details, immediately recognizing the location. 'Got that. Now, on no account go onto the property. If it is the man we're looking for, he is very dangerous. So, just get the hell out of there—' She broke off. 'Mr Tomlinson, did you hear me? Mr Tomlinson, are you still there?'

She slammed down the phone. 'Blast! Cut off.'

Racing across the office, she grabbed a police radio from the office charger and snatched a key to one of the CID cars from the keyboard opposite.

'What the devil are you doing?' Hayden exclaimed.

'Guy from a letting agency,' she threw back over her shoulder as she headed for the door. 'Says someone with a green Land Rover is in a derelict cottage behind the old, disused Pritchard and Bowers peat works near Shapwick. Come on. It could be our man.'

He gaped and stumbled after her. 'Then just ring the Control Room. You're in no fit state—'

'Bollocks, I'm fine,' she snapped back, charging through the office doors into the corridor and taking the stairs two at a time. 'We can call them on the way.'

She was behind the wheel of the CID car and heading for the exit even before Hayden had time to close his door.

* * *

Richard Tomlinson's insides were on the move. He crouched behind the corrugated iron shed housing the Land Rover and peered cautiously around the corner at the partly roofed stone cottage a few yards away.

The flickering light he had noticed on arrival was issuing from a window to one side of the building. It had a dim, fuzzy quality, suggesting that something like a blanket or a piece of sacking had been fitted across it. There was no electricity connected to the cottage now, so the light had to be from a kerosene or paraffin lamp.

He moistened dry lips, conscious of the rapid thudding of his heart, remembering that the police detective had told him to get out of there straightaway. Richard Tomlinson, though, was a man habitually motivated by an intense curiosity which demanded to be satisfied, and in the last ten years of his very ordinary, mundane existence, there had been little excitement to brighten his day, apart from a road accident outside his premises and a visit from a troublesome, drunken woman looking for somewhere to doss. The possibility that one of his properties was being used as a squat by a dangerous, wanted criminal was just the stimulus he needed to revitalize his boring life, and he was desperate to get a closer look at the man before heading back to his car parked outside the old peat works where he had arranged to meet the police.

He had left the brand-new Mercedes Convertible there when he had first arrived and had chosen to walk along the drove to the cottage on foot, to avoid risking damage to the car on the stony, pot-holed surface. He felt confident, therefore, that whoever was in the cottage wouldn't have heard him approach. But after what the police had told him, he was more than a little nervous and he stayed where he was for several minutes before he was able to pluck up the courage to move closer.

Then, after a count of three — or maybe it was six in the end — he crept down the side of the shed to pause briefly at the front to look and listen. When nothing stirred, he sprinted across the muddy ground to one side of the cottage's lighted front window. His senses were so sharpened by fear now that he could even hear the cattle in the adjacent field tugging at the grass, and once he jumped as an owl materialized through one of the holes in the tiled roof and passed directly overhead with the faint rush of air produced by the silent rise and fall of its wings.

Pressing his face close to a lower corner of the cracked windowpane, he squinted through a gap between what looked like a couple of sacks pinned together over the wooden frame. He saw that the light in the room was provided by a paraffin lamp standing on a wooden table, which had been left behind by the last resident. There were a couple of bottles of Famous Grouse whisky, one empty and one half full, beside the lamp, together with a litter of takeaway cartons. An old, torn upholstered chair stood to one side of the table and a rumpled sleeping bag was lying on the floor against the far wall.

He frowned. Clear indications that someone was dossing there, but no sign of the actual occupant. Where had he gone? The prickly sensation at the back of his neck gave him the answer. He turned slowly to stare at the tall figure standing behind him, then shrank back against the wall.

'Hi there,' the other said quietly. 'Looking for me by any chance?'

* * *

The man in the camouflage jacket left nothing to chance. Every trace of him had to go. Knocking back some of the whisky, he emptied the rest of it over his rolled up sleeping bag and dumped them in a corner of the room. He followed that up by slopping the entire contents of the large, three-quarters full plastic bottle of paraffin oil he'd purchased for his lamp over the floor and up the plastered walls of the cottage. Then it was a simple matter of retreating outside, smashing the single window and tossing a burning rag soaked in paraffin into the room. The place ignited with a dull "whoop", sending fiery tongues up through the holes in the ceiling into the loft, which caught on whatever combustible material had been left there over the years. Almost immediately, the flames spread to the rooms below, where someone had stacked bales of hay for winter cattle feed. Within minutes, the whole cottage was a blazing inferno, which devoured everything in its path — including any DNA he might have inadvertently left behind.

He was nearly too late. He had heard the slow-running engine approaching along the drove just before he'd set the cottage alight and as the flames now roared skywards, the vehicle, which had been stealthily approaching without lights, turned its main beam on in response. He made it to the Land Rover in the nick of time, erupting from the shed to career off along the drove in the opposite direction, seconds before the dark hatchback raced into view and slammed to a stop well back from the blazing building.

* * *

'Buggered again!' Kate shouted over her shoulder as she jumped out of the car. 'The bastard's cut and run.'

'You don't know that,' Hayden shouted back, joining her just in front of the car as she radioed Control with the information, feeling the heat of the burning building on his face even from where they were standing. 'It may not have been him in the first place.'

'So, who d'you think started the fire?'

'Could have been anyone.'

They had waited apprehensively for almost fifteen minutes behind the blue Mercedes Convertible — obviously Tomlinson's car — which they had found parked right outside the padlocked main gates of the disused peat works, but the letting agent had not materialized. Finally, fearing the worst, a jittery Kate had refused to wait any longer. Tomlinson had told her that the cottage was on the drove leading off the main road a few yards from the peat works and they had been in the process of creeping towards it along the track with their lights out when the fire had erupted from behind some trees up ahead, leaving them with no option but to abandon any further attempt at subterfuge. But despite their best efforts, they were too late.

'It wasn't just anyone, Hayd,' she retorted bitterly. 'It was *him*.' She glanced wildly about her in the ruddy glow cast by the flames. 'But where the hell's Tomlinson?'

Hayden had left her side to check out the corrugated iron shed a few yards away and her heart sank when she heard his sharp, 'Gordon Bennett!'

Stumbling across the muddy, pot-holed ground to join her husband, she saw the body gruesomely illuminated in the pool of light cast by his torch. The thirty-something-year-old man with the blond hair was dressed in a dark anorak and he had been dumped in a corner of the shed, his head resting in a pool of oil and twisted round at an unnatural angle.

'Broken neck again by the look of it,' Hayden commented grimly, straightening up from his examination. 'Looks like our killer's usual signature.'

Kate turned away with a muttered expletive. 'I told him to get out of the place and wait for us at the rendezvous point. Why the hell didn't he listen?'

Stomping out of the shed just ahead of Hayden, she was greeted by the powerful headlights and the full blues and twos of the first of the backup units they had called for on the way to the rendezvous.

'So much for the silent approach we requested,' she commented, glaring at the flashing roof strobe as the driver shut down the engine and walked over to her. 'That murdering swine will certainly know we're here now.'

Hayden shrugged. 'Whether he does or not is irrelevant. He'll be miles away by now.'

She shook her head grimly. 'I don't think he'll go far,' she said, pulling her radio out of her pocket again. 'He's still got unfinished business with Tamara Callaghan, and he'll be desperate and a lot more dangerous than ever now. We'd better get someone over to Scribbler's Halt pronto. We can't afford to be caught out again.'

* * *

He cursed volubly as he drove. How the hell had they managed to find him? He had been so careful. The only plus side to it all was that at least any DNA traces he might have left in the cottage would have been destroyed by the fire, so the Bill wouldn't be able to identify him that way. Trouble was, the Land Rover would now have to be dumped. It was too hot to use for very much longer.

He was still thinking that when all of a sudden, he ran out of road. He hadn't seen the sharp bend ahead, hidden from the moonlight under a pair of mature willow trees until the very last minute and he was going much too fast to be able to take avoiding action. Before he knew it, the front of the Land Rover was in the rhyne, burying its nose in about three feet of water. Fortunately for him, he was wearing a seat belt, otherwise he would have fared a lot worse, but even so, the force of the collision slammed him first into the back of his seat and then forwards to the limits of the belt, bringing his head into contact with the upper sill of his door.

Shocked, dazed, but still conscious, he managed to open his door and scramble out, sinking up to his waist in icy water. Beneath his feet, he could feel the mud at the bottom of the rhyne sucking him down still further. In a panic, he clutched at some broken bushes lining the bank and bit by bit succeeded in hauling himself out.

Holding his head with one hand and feeling the blood running in between his fingers, he stared back the way he had come. The flames of the burning cottage were now just a ruddy orange glow way out across the fields. There were no blue flashing lights in sight yet on the track behind him, but he knew they would come soon. He turned back to the crippled Land Rover and swore. It was going to be Shanks's pony from now on — a bit earlier than planned and certainly not how he had intended. The wound to his head, which was bleeding even more, was racked by sharp, stabbing pains, and there was a rapidly emerging pain in his chest from the bruising caused by the seatbelt. He felt sick and not a little woozy. But there was no time to think about any of that.

First, he had to attend to the Land Rover. He couldn't just abandon it. Though he had always been careful to wear gloves while driving as well as making sure he didn't use the ashtray or drop anything on the floor that could carry traces of his DNA, he couldn't risk some switched-on police forensic team finding something he had missed.

Getting the rear door open was not easy, as the vehicle was nose-down in the rhyne with the back end still up on the bank, but after a great deal of effort, he finally managed it, wedging the door open with a branch he found on the ground while he grabbed his haversack and a can of petrol from inside.

Unscrewing the can, he breathed a sigh of relief that the Defender was a petrol version. At least petrol burned a lot more intensely than diesel fuel.

Pulling out a handkerchief from his pocket, he soaked it in the petrol and leaned against the vehicle to open the filler cap and stuff it inside. Then, sloshing the petrol over as much of the body as he could reach, he tossed the can into the back and wasted no time in using his lighter.

He stepped back quickly as, like an angry beast, the fuel ignited with a roar. He stood at a distance for a few moments, watching as the vehicle was engulfed in tongues of red and orange fire, which reached out hungrily towards him.

He caught a glimpse of the flashing blue lights across the fields at the same moment. Just in time, he mused grimly. Hugging his bruised chest and pausing only briefly to wipe the blood from his eyes, he pushed through the line of trees behind him and headed at a limping run across a field of stubble to a wood on the other side. He disappeared among the trees even as the police patrol car pulled up a few yards from the burning Land Rover — just in time to see the fuel tank explode.

* * *

Kate had only just requested Control to send a patrol car to Scribbler's Halt as a precaution against the killer turning up there when Percival arrived at the scene with Jamie Foster.

'What the devil are you doing here?' Percival rapped at Kate. 'I thought you were supposed to have gone home to recover from your ordeal.'

'On my way there when this came up, Des,' she said, 'and I'm afraid we've got another stiff. He's in the shed.'

'Another one? Bloody Nora, Kate, are you collecting them?'

She gave a wan smile. 'Sadly, it seems that way.'

Quickly briefing him on the circumstances, she waved a hand vaguely at the darkness hemming them in on all sides. 'And the killer's on his toes out there somewhere. I've just circulated his Land Rover again to Control and a unit has already left here in pursuit, but it will be an almost impossible job running him to ground in the dark with miles of field and marsh to cover.'

She swayed slightly, conscious of sudden nausea and a strange light-headed feeling.

'You okay?' he queried, peering at her in the light of the still-burning cottage.

She gritted her teeth. 'I'm fine.'

'No, you're not. You should never have come out here after what you've been through. You've just had concussion and that can recur.' He turned to Hayden. 'Take her home, Hayden. Jamie and I can sort things out here.'

'But really, Des,' she protested. 'I'm okay.'

He shook his head. 'You're nothing of the sort. So, home, young lady, and straight to bed. I don't want to see you back in the nick until I am satisfied you are fully recovered.'

'But I will be needed at the briefing.'

'I think we can manage without you, and anyway, Hayden can give us all the SP on your behalf.'

She would have argued further, but at that point her legs buckled under her. Hayden was just in time to grab her as she passed out.

CHAPTER 22

He kept going through most of the night, trying to put as much distance as possible between himself and what would by now be the very burned-out remains of the Land Rover. He was forced to take cover from passing police patrol cars on several nail-biting occasions, and once he almost walked into a two-man roadblock, which had been set up at a junction, but he spotted it just in time and managed to go around it. They obviously thought he might have nicked another car and he grinned fiercely in the darkness. Chance would be a fine thing. Maybe later, guys.

He stumbled on the bird hide about two hours later. It was in some sort of wildlife reserve, according to the green sign nearby, and had been constructed on the edge of a lake. Unfastening his haversack, he propped himself in a corner of the long, bare shed and for the first time was able to clean the wound to his head with some antiseptic — which, like all good "soldiers" he carried with him — and to affix some plasters. His ribcage was still very sore and the pain in his head had only eased slightly, despite the four paracetamol he had taken earlier, but he felt more relaxed now that he had found somewhere under cover to doss for the rest of the night.

He had no real idea where he was. But studying the compass and the local map he had in his pocket by the light of his torch, he was able to work it out. It wasn't good. He had to be quite a few miles from where he wanted to be, but that could be remedied later when some of the fuss had died down. At least he was way off the area where Old Bill would expect him to be, so the only thing he had to worry about for the moment was a nocturnal game warden or an adventurous twitcher, both of which seemed unlikely at this time of the night.

He had to admit that he had suffered a major setback, and he could not help feeling acute frustration that his carefully laid plans had gone awry. He should already have been closing in on Callaghan, but now that would have to wait for a bit. Still, he had an abundance of patience — he had picked that up in the military — so he would make his move when he was good and ready and not before. After all, it was often said that "all things come to those who wait", and after the months it had taken him to track down his quarry, he could certainly afford to wait a little longer.

* * *

'Ready for breakfast?'

Kate opened her eyes and stared at Hayden's smiling face for a moment, uncomprehending. He was carrying a tray bearing a mug of tea, a boiled egg in an egg cup and a plate of buttered toast cut up into soldiers.

Very slowly, she lifted herself up in bed on her elbows and sank back against the pillows, blinking in the sunlight streaming into the room through a gap in the curtains.

'What a nice surprise, Hayd. Thank you. What time is it?'

He set the tray on her lap, removing the mug of tea, and placing it on the bedside table.

'Just after nine,' he said. 'Feeling better?'

'Nine?' she exclaimed, sliding the tray off her lap so that the boiled egg fell out of its cup and rolled into a corner. 'You should have woken me.'

Her leg was already half out from under the sheets when he pushed it back in again. He returned the egg to its cup and placed the tray back on her lap. 'You needed your sleep. And anyway, you're not going anywhere today. You've been signed off on a couple of days' sick leave until you're fully recovered.'

'I've what? In the middle of a murder inquiry?'

He shrugged. 'No one is indispensable, old thing.'

'Well, I'm not having it. I'm not being taken off the inquiry at this stage.'

'You have no choice,' he said, 'and if you go in, you'll be sent straight back home again. Now, eat your egg before it solidifies.'

She snatched a finger of toast and rammed it into the decapitated egg with unnecessary force, her face like thunder.

He sighed and sat at the end of the bed. 'You must leave this investigation to the major crime team now. You have to get well. I had a word with the hospital, and they say shock, coupled with the suspected concussion you suffered, could be a recurring problem if you're not careful. They say you need to take things slowly and have a complete rest—'

'Bollocks!' she grated through a mouthful of egg. 'I'm perfectly okay. Who's the SIO?'

'An old friend of yours — Deidrie Hennessey. She's been made up to detective super.'

Kate nodded approvingly. 'Well, that's one bit of good news,' she said, calming down a little as she pictured in her mind's eye the shrewd, no-nonsense woman from Northern Ireland with her short, blonde hair and neat, tailored trouser suit. She had worked with Hennessey on a number of occasions, and she had a great deal of respect for her. 'At least the inquiry will be run by someone who knows what they're doing. Any trace of our man yet?'

He shook his head. 'They found the Land Rover burned out with its nose buried in a rhyne. He obviously lost it on a bend. The dog unit tracked his scent back to the road but lost it soon afterwards. There's a full area search underway with more dogs, and they've asked for the force chopper.'

'What about my handcuffs? Any decent dabs on them that might help us ID the arsehole?'

'Not done yet, and we'll need to check out your prints for elimination purposes at some stage. I'll let you know as soon as I hear anything.'

He had relaxed a little, encouraged by her questions, which suggested that she had finally accepted the state of play. But his relief was short-lived when she suddenly pushed the tray off her lap, threw back the bedclothes and swung her legs over the edge of the bed.

'No need for you to do that,' she said, stripping off her nightdress and bending down to pull out clothes from the chest of drawers. 'I'll be at the nick myself. I'm sure Deidrie Hennessey will overrule Percival's sick leave instruction when she knows it's about me.'

Hayden shook his head wearily. Dealing with his beloved other half could sometimes be like trying to remonstrate with a recalcitrant teenager.

'She won't,' he said quietly, as he watched Kate pull on trousers and a thick polo-necked sweater. 'She was the one who issued the instruction.'

Kate stared at him. 'Who, Hennessey? Then Des Percival must have put her up to it.' She stared at him suspiciously. 'Or you.'

He looked hurt. 'It had absolutely nothing to do with me, Kate. I'm just the messenger — and it's for your own good anyway, so just accept it.'

'Accept nothing,' she snapped. 'I'm going to the nick to have this out with Hennessey.'

He held up a set of ignition keys. 'Then it will be a long walk for you. I've got the keys to the Mazda, plus the spare.'

'You deceitful sod.'

He grinned. 'Thanks for that. Now, I have to go in for the major incident briefing, so, please just sit and watch the telly or read a book or something. I'll pop back in a couple of hours to see how you're doing.'

Then, planting a kiss on her cheek, he left the bedroom and thumped down the stairs. Shortly afterwards she heard the powerful rumble of his Mk II Jaguar driving away.

* * *

'Watch bloody telly? Read a book?' Kate snarled into the mirror as she dried herself after her shower. 'Hayden has to have been joking.'

The face looking back at her through the dissipating steam resembled that of a female boxer who had just finished six rounds in the ring, and she winced as she tugged a length of wet plaster off her forehead. In her panic to get out of that car boot, she had certainly done herself some mischief and no mistake, and there was a nasty lump on the back of her head where she must have struck the ground when the killer had initially put her out.

'So, what now, girl?' she murmured to herself after she had dressed and was sitting at the breakfast bar in the kitchen, sipping a strong, black coffee. She had to do something. She could not just sit on her arse at home while everything was going on outside.

More for something to do than anything else, she checked her mobile, and by mistake pressed the wrong button. The next instant, she was staring at her own face on the screen. She had hit "photo" by mistake. She was on the point of returning to the main screen when she remembered something and stopped short, finger still poised. The picture on the wall at Scribbler's Halt. She had photographed it when she had surreptitiously checked out Tamara Callaghan's bedroom after stumbling upon the suspected crime scene in the woods. She had forgotten all about it.

She found the photo and stared at it, zooming in on the two faces. Immediately she jumped, almost knocking the mug of coffee over. Close-up, the face of the woman in the photograph was a bit fuzzy, but it was still familiar. The hairstyle may have changed and the woman herself had obviously been much younger when her picture was taken, but without a doubt, she bore an uncanny resemblance to a youthful version of Tamara Callaghan — or, as the PNC record stated, Jennifer Sykes.

Now even more curious, Kate tried to zoom in on the brass plate at the bottom of the photograph. It took several minutes zooming in and out to be able to pick out anything, and when she finally succeeded, she sat back on the bar stool, more confused than ever. The inscription read "*Vista from the Marloes*".

Where the hell were the Marloes? And what did the photograph mean to Callaghan? Obviously, she treasured it, as it was up on her wall. But was it just a fond memory of somewhere she had been — on holiday perhaps — or did it have some other significance?

Switching to the web, she typed in "Marloes" and waited. After a pause, a whole list of options came up. She read that it was a village and parish on the Marloes Peninsula on the west coast of Pembrokeshire in Wales, and part of the Pembrokeshire National Park. She went to Google Maps and pinpointed the area, which she found to be a short drive from Haverfordwest.

Haverfordwest? The link to Wales again. She remembered Hayden's PNC checks on Jennifer Sykes and the precons he had found. One of those had been for a drink-driving offence near Haverfordwest and the other an assault on a parking warden in Pembroke town itself.

Other remembrances tumbled out of her subconscious. First, the reference by the killer to the "fancy name" Callaghan had given herself, suggesting that she had indeed changed her birth name. That went some way towards reinforcing the view of both Hayden and Kate that she had previously been called Sykes. In which case, the personal connection between the author and Wales — and Pembrokeshire in particular — seemed beyond doubt, a connection borne out by Templar's comment that there was a lot of "bad *Welsh* blood" between her and the killer.

But even if Callaghan's real name *was* Sykes and she did have a personal connection to Wales, why should that be of any relevance to the current crime investigation? If asked, Kate would have been hard put to come up with a definitive answer to that question. But her gut instinct told her that Callaghan's past was in some way key to all that had been happening, and she suspected that that past had a murky, hidden dimension few people were aware of.

Hints of unsavoury things had been made by the killer himself when, after dumping Kate into the boot of the car, he had referred to the author as "an evil, scheming cow" and then, following Kate's rescue, there had been Ed Templar's comment that Callaghan herself seemed to be "a nasty bit of work".

So, precisely what had Callaghan done to offend? And what had it to do with Wales? There was only one way to find out and this time Kate was determined to get an answer from the evasive writer herself by dropping in on her again.

Grabbing her coat, she rummaged through a kitchen drawer until she found the ignition key and pocketed it. Poor old Hayden had forgotten that she'd had a third key cut a year or so ago when she had temporarily mislaid one of the two originals.

So, they thought they had put her on sick leave, did they? Well, she had news for them.

Moments later, she was behind the wheel of the Mazda and pulling out of the driveway.

CHAPTER 23

A police community support officer was lounging against a big stone urn near the front door of Scribbler's Halt when Kate drove in. So that was the nick's idea of a police "presence", was it? Some use he would be, she thought grimly, if the killer decided to pay Tamara Callaghan another visit. He only looked about sixteen. Then she rebuked herself. She knew the station was short of regular personnel, and with the new major crime inquiry, resources were no doubt even more severely stretched than usual. A PCSO was better than nothing and anyway, the killer was less likely to try anything during the daytime. Furthermore, the lad did have a radio to call for assistance if needed.

The PCSO straightened up when she drove in, nodding respectfully when she produced her warrant card.

'Sorry, Sergeant,' he mumbled. 'I didn't know who you were. All okay here so far.'

She forced a smile. 'You call up straightaway if you see anything even remotely suspicious,' she said. 'Remember, the man we're dealing with is extremely dangerous.'

She rang the house bell several times before anyone came to the door and then she was surprised to see Spencer Little standing there, pale, dishevelled and twitchy. He was unshaven, his hair awry and his white trousers and green shirt — for once without a cravat — were badly creased, as if he had been sleeping in them.

'Ah, Sergeant,' he said. 'Am I glad to see you. I can't stay much longer. I've been here all night and I've got to get back to the office to do some work.'

'Thanks for staying on anyway,' she said, then stepping inside, raised an inquiring eyebrow. 'Miss Callaghan about, is she?'

He made a face. 'In a manner of speaking, yes. But she's been on the bottle again.'

She followed him down the hallway to the living room and he nodded towards a figure lying prone on the settee. One hand hung over the edge and Kate saw what looked like an empty bottle of vodka on the floor beside a broken glass. Her loud snores were clearly audible even from the hallway.

'Totally pissed,' Little said bitterly. 'Paralytic would be a better description.'

Kate approached the settee and stared down at the novelist. 'Miss Callaghan?' she said sharply. 'It's Detective Sergeant Lewis.'

There was no response, and the snoring continued unabated.

'How long has she been like this?' Kate snapped.

Little shrugged. 'I left her with the bottle late last night when I went to lie down in the spare bedroom,' he said. 'I only stayed over because I was told she was in danger.'

'Very good of you,' Kate said, adding, 'Could we have a short chat?'

He nodded again. 'Best next door.'

He led the way back along the hall to the study. There, dropping into the bosun's chair at Callaghan's desk, he briefly flipped through the sheaf of papers beside the laptop computer, which was switched off.

'I don't know why she's gone to pieces like this,' he said gloomily. 'She seems to have abandoned all pretence of writing and we've still got a publisher's contract to fulfil. I despair.'

Grabbing another chair, Kate sat down opposite him. 'Miss Callaghan told me that you two first met at a party in London. Is that right?'

He swung around to face her. 'Yes, one of those off-the-wall bashes at the flat of a friend of mine in Pimlico. We both got totally stoned.'

Drink or drugs, I wonder, Kate thought to herself.

'She had been invited by a friend of hers and we got chatting about writing. As a result, she wrote her first crime novel. She contacted me a few months later, I tried it on the market and it was an instant success. Everything went from there.'

'How long ago was that?'

He frowned. 'Must be all of eight years.'

'Interesting. Do you know where Miss Callaghan came from originally? I thought it was somewhere in Wales.'

'Yes, I believe her family once lived in Pembrokeshire.'

Kate tensed, sat up straighter, but he didn't appear to notice.

'Is Callaghan her real name then?'

His gaze sharpened. 'Why do you ask?'

She shrugged. 'Well, I know many writers use pseudonyms instead of their real names and I wondered whether she has done the same thing. After all, Callaghan doesn't sound very Welsh, does it?'

'Well, I don't think she is Welsh. I seem to remember her saying once that her family moved there from Somerset when she was a child.'

'She has come back to her home county then. Any idea exactly where she used to live?'

'Not the slightest. She never said.'

'But presumably Callaghan isn't her birth name and she's using a pseudonym?'

He hesitated and looked away from her. 'I really can't say.'

'Why is that then?'

He grimaced. 'Tamara has always insisted that her proper name is never revealed. She fiercely guards her privacy.'

'I can understand that, but I can't see why she would object to my knowing. After all, I am trying to protect her and I'm not going to pass the information on to anyone else.'

He shook his head. 'I'm sorry. I can't tell you.'

Kate tried to control her rising frustration. Then she had an idea.

'Okay, so if I were to hazard a guess at it, would you be able to signify with a nod as to whether I am on the right track? That way, you won't have told me anything.'

He thought about that for a second, gnawing his bottom lip. Then with a weary sigh, he nodded.

'Sykes?' Kate said, studying his expression. 'Jennifer Sykes?'

She saw the flicker of surprise in his eyes. After a brief pause, he swallowed and nodded.

'Thank you, Mr Little. You've been a great help.'

He stood up, looking even more twitchy than he had when Kate arrived.

'I have to be off,' he mumbled. 'Work to do at the office.'

She nodded. 'No problem. You go. There's a police officer outside to ensure Miss Callaghan's safety.'

'You — you're not going too then?'

'Not quite yet. I thought I would hang on for a little while longer to see if Miss Callaghan comes round. Make sure she's all right.'

'Of course. Of course. Thank you.'

She couldn't wait to see him leave and she made sure she saw him drive away before she quietly shut the front door and headed for the stairs.

The ticking of a clock on the chest of drawers sounded very loud when she gently pushed open the door to the bedroom and walked in.

The bed had not been made and a dirty mug and plate stood on the bedside table. The curtains had only been partially pulled back and she saw several make-up pots and stained tissues on the little dressing table in a corner. Discarded slippers lay in the middle of the floor and one of the wardrobe doors was open with a pile of clothes dumped in front of it. No wonder Little was worried about his client. She seemed to have really let herself go since Kate had last interviewed her.

Going straight to the picture, Kate reached up to carefully unhook it from the wall. Apart from the inscription on the brass plate she had seen when she first examined it, there was nothing else printed on the frame, and the photograph itself carried little of interest, apart from reaffirming Kate's belief that the woman with the old man was indeed Callaghan.

It was only when she turned it over that she saw that there was more information on the back. The printed label was much like many others Kate had seen on the backs of picture frames, giving the name of the photographer. This time it was just a business name — "*Little Puffin Studios.*" But of equal importance was the address, which read, "*Marloes, West Pembrokeshire,*" with a postal code and a telephone number.

Kate's hands were shaking as she replaced the picture on the wall, and she nearly dropped it in her excitement. Marloes, the same name as on the inscription on the front. It all seemed to tie in with what she had long suspected and what Spencer Little had also told her. Tamara Callaghan *was* Jennifer Sykes and there was a definite Welsh connection — and not just with Wales, but more specifically with the west coast of Pembrokeshire. Kate could feel it in her gut. Somehow that was where the key to everything lay.

Checking Callaghan to make sure she was still breathing, she left the house and headed home, her head crammed full of disjointed thoughts, unresolved questions, and incomplete hypotheses.

Pulling into a layby en route, she tried the telephone number of the photographic studio she had noted from the picture. But it came up as a ceased line. Not really surprising, as the photograph had obviously been taken years before and the business had probably closed down by now.

Arriving home, she sat for several minutes in the living room, going through everything in her mind and making notes of all she had discovered so far.

So, Tamara Callaghan was in fact Jennifer Sykes, a Somerset girl, who had once lived in West Pembrokeshire and had moved to London about eight years ago, where she had met Spencer Little at a party and taken up fiction writing. She had later moved back to Somerset and bought the house on the Levels she had chosen to call Scribbler's Halt. As Jennifer Sykes, she had two criminal convictions — one for drink driving and another for assaulting a parking warden. Both offences would have been committed in Pembrokeshire after she had moved to London, if Spencer Little's recollections were accurate, which indicated that she had been back to her old stomping ground at least twice since moving out. The picture on her bedroom wall was a photograph apparently taken from the clifftops of West Pembrokeshire on the Marloes Peninsula, which suggested that she had a soft spot for the place — indeed, may even have lived there at one time.

Okay, so her Welsh connection was substantiated, but that was all. There was nothing to explain why she was being targeted by the killer. When he had dumped Kate in the boot of the car, he had denied that it was anything to do with her novels, and although he had virtually admitted that it was he who'd trashed the bookshop and had broken into her house, it seemed his actions were intended solely to send her a message and frighten the wits out of her. That he ultimately intended to do her real physical harm after he had tired of his game was beyond doubt, but why? And if that was the case, why hadn't he attacked her when he had broken into her house instead of just quietly leaving? Had he left another message inside the place, or had he been looking for something?

And where did Ed Templar — if that was his real name, which was doubtful — fit into all this? Plainly he had been following Kate hoping she'd lead him to the killer, and when he had rescued her, he had been adamant that he wasn't in the least bit interested in Callaghan, only in the man who was stalking her. So, what was "The Saint's" namesake up to and where had he come from? Was he perhaps linked to Wales as well?

Finally, in respect of Callaghan herself, if she knew she was in such grave danger, why was she not coming clean on what was behind it all — or was it because she couldn't for some reason?

Kate put her pen down and sat back with a hiss of exasperation. So near and yet so far. It was no good approaching Percival or Detective Superintendent Hennessey about any of it because their sole focus would now be on catching the killer, and her inquiries would be regarded as irrelevant and a complete waste of time.

Even as she came to that conclusion, she heard the roar of an engine and the clatter of rotor blades. Running to the front door and peering out, she saw the helicopter pass low overhead. She recognized it straightaway as the police chopper. So, they had called in some air support for the manhunt, had they? Not before time either. Almost certainly there would be dogs out on the Levels too, checking every barn and outhouse for the fugitive. He was certainly being squeezed.

She stamped her foot and swore. It wasn't fair. She had been the one investigating this business from the start, the one who had managed to uncover much of the evidence, the one who should have been in at the kill, and yet she was being callously excluded from it all — treated as surplus to requirements.

'Sick leave, my arse,' she grated, and there and then made up her mind. If she couldn't be part of the chase, then she would do her own investigating and pursue the part of the inquiry that was being overlooked. And as she was on sick leave, she wasn't tied to the major crime investigation protocols. She was off duty and could do what she wanted and go where she liked.

Returning to the kitchen, she fired up her laptop again and indulged in some necessary research on the web, which led to phone calls to Dyfed-Powys police headquarters, then Haverfordwest and Pembroke Dock police stations. Eventually, after some patient digging and the use of her official police status, she was put through to a cheerful civilian station duty officer, called Huw Roberts. Shortly after that, she packed an overnight bag and left the house in the Mazda, leaving just a brief note for Hayden, telling him she was going for a long drive to clear her head. He would have been most put out if he had known just how long that drive was going to be. She herself would have been equally annoyed had she been aware of the fact that from the moment she left home, she had acquired a tail.

The man who called himself Ed Templar had been aware of her every move since the night he had rescued her from the car boot at the scrapyard, the device fixed to the dashboard of his car enabling him to keep tabs on her through the powerful GPS signal emitted by the tiny magnetic box he had attached to the underside of her Mazda. Recognizing her type and the stubborn, single-minded determination that drove her, he had realized soon after meeting her that she was his best chance of tracing the man he had pursued for so long, and the electronic tracker he had quietly attached to her car had enabled him to keep tabs on her far more easily than simply relying on time-consuming surveillance.

Unfortunately, he had got to the scene of the cottage fire and Tomlinson's murder much too late, and the killer had already made good his escape. After that, he had kept his mobile tracker close by him and switched on all the time, and he was right on the ball when she left home that morning. He stayed with her all the way to the M5, and then on to the M49 and M4, heading west.

'Where are you off to now, my love?' he said aloud. 'I do hope you aren't leading me on a wild goose chase.'

CHAPTER 24

Kate's mobile rang a couple of hours after she had left home and was pulling into the M4 Services for petrol at Sarn Park.

'Kate?' Hayden's excited voice shouted. 'Just seen your note. Where the devil are you?'

'M4 Motorway, heading west,' she said, pulling into a parking bay in the car park. She didn't notice Templar's car stopping in the far corner.

'M4?' he exclaimed, his voice suddenly shrill. 'What on earth are you doing there, and where did you get that other car key?'

'I had another spare.'

'I don't understand. Your note said you were going for a drive.'

'So I am — to Pembrokeshire.'

'What? Are you mad?'

'Possibly. But I need to check some things out in relation to Tamara Callaghan, whose real name, incidentally, *is* Jennifer Sykes.'

'What are you talking about?'

So, she told him everything she had found out, conscious of the stunned silence at the other end of the line.

'Sykes — or Callaghan as she calls herself now — is hiding something that is the key to this whole case,' she finished. 'I am convinced it will establish who our killer is and why he is targeting her.'

'You're obsessed, Kate. That concussion thing has skewed your judgement.'

'On the contrary, Hayd, I've never felt so clear-headed and focused as I am now.'

'But — but you can't just take off like this.'

'Can't I? And why not? You said I was on sick leave and going for a drive could not be more therapeutic in that regard.'

She heard some muffled chokes and grinned, visualizing the fury on her husband's red face, and waited patiently for him to recover.

'Kate,' he said in a low, trembling voice, 'you must come back here straightaway.'

'Is that an order, *Constable*?' she mocked, enjoying herself immensely.

'Don't be so stupid,' he snapped back. 'This is a serious matter. Percival will do his crust if he finds out what you're up to.'

'Only if you tell him, Hayd, only if you tell him. By the way, I'll be staying down here overnight but I should be back by tomorrow evening. See you then.'

Before he could say anything else, she cut the call.

Her mobile rang three times after that but she ignored it, and in the end, switched it off altogether. By then Port Talbot was coming up in front of her, smoke billowing from the chimneys of its steelworks, and shortly afterwards the motorway was bypassing Swansea. It was dusk when she finally pulled into the car park of the back-road hotel a few miles from Pembroke town where she had booked a room. After a satisfying dinner with a bottle of red wine, she was in bed and fast asleep before ten. Her last thought was of Hayden, of how big the double bed seemed without him and how much she missed his chubby, good-natured face. 'Night,

Hayd,' she murmured sleepily before drifting off. 'Try not to snore.'

In the car park below, Templar adjusted his seat and prepared for a long uncomfortable night.

* * *

The countryside was crawling with police. He had never seen so many, and he glimpsed one of their cars drive slowly past him as he crouched down behind the hedge. He could almost feel the eyes of the front seat passenger boring into the glossy, evergreen leaves. It looked like they had brought in reinforcements and that the hunt was still on with a vengeance.

His headache was a lot better after a few hours' sleep in the bird hide, but his ribs were still very sore and at times it hurt him to breathe. He had intended dossing there for most of the day and moving off again at night, but the arrival of a couple of twitchers around two in the afternoon had put paid to that idea. The sound of their voices had woken him up and he had only just managed to slip out the door when they appeared around a bend in the path leading to the hide. Whether they saw him leave, he wasn't sure, but he had given them a quick, cheery wave without turning his head as he made his way along the path in the opposite direction, hoping they would assume he was just another birdwatcher.

Cutting back through the woodland when he was out of sight, he re-joined the path further along, then out of the reserve the same way he had come in.

A couple of hours or so later, after trudging across the waterlogged marshes, following the direction indicated by his compass, he was back to the main search area and once more playing hide and seek with Old Bill. The situation reminded him of days spent in warmer climes on the other side of the world trying to dodge men in uniform — but then, instead of a long term of porridge, the penalty for discovery would have been a bayonet in the gut, which was a bit more severe.

Now, crouched behind the hedge, he could still hear the distant sound of dogs barking and guessed that Old Bill's canine trackers were still trying to pick up his scent. But he wasn't unduly worried about them. They were too far away to present any real problem for him, and once it was completely dark, he guessed they would be pulled off the search until the following day. But then he caught the sound of something else — the thud of rotor blades. A bloody chopper. That was all he needed. You could hide from a search party, even if they had dogs, but the eye in the sky was a completely different proposition. Often they could see you before you realized they were there.

He forced himself into a hollow under the hedge and lay there motionless while the flying bug passed low overhead. At first, he thought it had gone and he would have got up again had a sixth sense not warned him to stay where he was. It was wise that he took notice, for it wasn't long before the distinctive thudding sound was back again, and this time the helicopter was hovering over some fields on the other side of the road. Had he left his hiding place, they could not have failed to spot him.

As it was, they continued to sweep the area for another good hour, and by the time they finally flew off and he was able to scramble out again, a comforting autumnal mist was beginning to spread out across the fields and woods, cold, dank and smelling of wet bark and rotting vegetation as it gradually blotted out everything in sight. Now too he could hear the night things beginning to stir around him in the gloom, heralded by strange rustlings at his feet and the soft flapping of fuzzy wings as ghostly apparitions floated through the gathering murk with mournful Banshee cries.

He shivered. He had never liked the countryside. He was by nature a town boy, at home in pubs, clubs and tarmacked streets. But at least the arrival of the mist meant he was invisible to the police and the manhunt would have to be called off for the time being. On the face of it, the swirling white clouds also presented him with a golden opportunity.

He would be able to sneak into the grounds of Scribbler's Halt without the risk of being seen. But there was a downside to such a move too. Old Bill would be expecting him to do exactly that, and they were likely to have a nice reception committee waiting in the wings. Maybe it would be best to wait another night and hit Scribbler's Halt when they were least expecting it. Like in broad daylight.

* * *

Huw Roberts was a big, well-padded man in his mid-fifties, with iron-grey hair and keen blue eyes. Kate found him digging a patch of ground in the back garden of his small cottage in Marloes village. He was dressed in an open-necked — no doubt police issue — white shirt and old, threadbare uniform trousers tucked into gumboots, with red braces hanging down by his sides.

He looked up and nodded when Kate pushed open the wicker gate and stood a little uncertainly on the garden path. Abandoning his fork, he wiped his hands down his thighs and stomped over to her. She produced her warrant card and he glanced at it and nodded.

'Huw Roberts, Detective Sergeant Lewis,' he said in the strong, lilting tones more usually associated with the Welsh valleys, and proffered one large, calloused paw for her to shake.

'Kate, please, Mr Roberts,' she said, more as an acknowledgement than a request.

He peered at her face. 'What on earth have you done to yourself? Accident, was it?'

She gave a tolerant smile. 'Something like that. Argument with a car boot. Anyway, it's very good of you to see me.'

He transferred his hand to her shoulder in a fatherly gesture, steering her round towards the back door. 'As I said to you on the phone, I'm glad to be of help,' he said, 'and I'm on a week's leave from today anyway. Now, come you inside, and I'll pour you a genuine Penderyn whisky.'

215

He led her into the kitchen and indicated one of two chairs set at a small round table.

'I think I'll stick to tea or coffee if you don't mind,' she said apologetically. 'Long drive home.'

He filled the kettle. 'No problem.' He bent down to produce a mug, a glass and a bottle from a cupboard next to the sink. 'But I'll stay with the Penderyn, I think.'

He poured himself a stiff measure of whisky and turned to face her, leaning back against the sink and sipping his drink.

'Lived in the village long, have you?' she asked.

'Much of my life,' he said. 'Came here in my teens with my folks from Rhondda. Got married in my mid-twenties and stayed here ever after.

'And the force?'

'Thirty years, man and boy. Finished up as coroner's officer before I retired three years ago. Wife and I divorced eleven years ago and I was living alone, so I re-joined the force as a civvy, more for something to do than anything else. You?'

'Not as long as you. Twelve years so far. CID for the past seven.'

The kettle boiled and he made the coffee, returning the sugar and milk to the worktop when she shook her head.

'So, still only a sprog, eh?' he mocked gently, then setting her coffee in front of her, abruptly focused on the reason for her visit.

'So, what's all this about? You said on the phone that you were interested in Jennifer Sykes. Why?'

Suspicion was written into his expression and Kate sympathized with his caution. She knew only too well that police hierarchies could be very parochial and protective in their response to inquiries carried out on their patches by other forces. By doing things the way she had instead of applying through the official channels, she was aware that she was well out of order. Obviously, he wanted to be sure he wasn't going to drop himself in it by talking to her off the record. She also knew that if she told him the whole story, he was likely to clam up completely. So, she avoided mentioning the major crime investigation and simply told him that she was carrying out an inquiry into the bona fides of a local woman being targeted by a violent stalker, and that she believed the victim to be hiding something from her past which could have led to the current situation.

He seemed to accept that. 'What do you want to know?' he said, still a little guarded.

'Just a bit about her background and family.'

He grunted, apparently reassured. 'Well, she was married to a chap named Jack Tannahill, an art dealer,' he began. 'Came down here from your part of the world, Somerset, I believe.' He whistled. 'Strewth, must be around thirty-five years ago by now. Time certainly flashes by, doesn't it? Anyway, I was in my teens then. They had two kids, Frank and Melanie. Jack had bought an old semi-derelict cottage just down the road he called "Puffins View", and he renovated and extended it. He wasn't short of a bob or two, I'll say that for him, and some said his art business had already made him a millionaire. Not that he liked spending much of it locally, mind, and according to my dad, he earned a reputation in the local pubs for being as tight as a duck's — er — you know.'

She smiled faintly, and he carried on.

'Both the youngsters were from Jennifer's previous marriage to a Londoner called Bob Sykes, who'd apparently died suddenly, and she insisted on hanging onto the name, even after she got married to Jack.' He shook his head. 'That's the way of things in these modern times, isn't it? Daft, if you ask me, but there you are. Anyway, by all accounts, Jennifer was a flighty bit of goods and spent a lot of time away from home in Cardiff, doing the clubs and such like with different men she'd picked up in bars.'

'How on earth did you find all that out?'

He grinned. 'You can't even sweep your driveway in this village without someone knowing about it,' he said, 'and when I eventually joined the force and became the local live-in copper, I got to hear about most of the scandal, present and past. Anyway, to go back a bit, long before I joined, when I was still a youngster, there was one hell of a row between Jack and Jennifer about her comings and goings, and the police got called to quite a nasty domestic at the cottage. I must admit, being only a kid at the time, I was thrilled to see all the police cars turning up with their blues and twos going, but evidently it was quite a serious confrontation. She had allegedly hit Jack with a bottle, though he refused to level a charge against her.

'Following the incident, I overheard my dad saying that Jennifer had upped and left, dumping the kids on poor old Jack, and the couple later divorced. Gossip had it that Jennifer ended up in Aberdeen, shacked up with some boyo off one of the rigs, but as far as I know, she never came back here. As for Jack, he remained at the cottage on his own with the two kids and for a while was left to bring them up on his own.'

Kate frowned. 'Can I stop you there? If Jennifer and her husband came here around thirty-five years ago as a married couple, Jennifer would be what age now?'

He considered it for a moment. 'Well, from what I understand, she must have been in her early to mid-thirties then, so I would say she'd be at least sixty to seventy by now.'

Kate's disappointment was evident. 'Doesn't sound like the Jennifer I'm interested in,' she commented. 'She would only be in her forties.'

She produced her mobile and showed him the photograph of the picture hanging on Callaghan's bedroom wall.

He raised both eyebrows. 'Well, I don't know how long ago that was taken, but the old man in the photograph is definitely Jack Tannahill and unless I'm very much mistaken, that wouldn't be Jennifer Sykes but Jack's daughter, Melanie Tannahill.'

'Melanie?'

He drained his glass of whisky and nodded towards her mug. 'Your coffee is getting cold. Yes, that *is* Melanie, I'm sure of it. I went to school with her, so I knew her quite well, though if she's calling herself Sykes now, maybe she dropped the surname Tannahill and followed her mother's example. There were only two daughters, Melanie and Jane, and Jane was a blonde — very pretty girl too, and very much a Tannahill.'

Kate tried to conceal her satisfaction that her suspicions had been more or less confirmed. 'And where are the girls now?'

'I'm coming to that. Just a year after Jennifer had left Jack, he went away on one of them cruise holidays with the kids and blow me, when he got back he had another wife in tow — a lovely lady called Beverley. Got married on board ship apparently. They lived here quite happily for a while and Beverley then produced the other little girl, Jane. That photo you have was probably taken by Jane, as she later became a freelance photographer, running her own business from home. Had a studio and everything—'

Kate remembered the name on the back of the picture. 'Little Puffin Studios?'

He nodded. 'You're well informed. But yes, that was her business name. Sadly, Jack's wife, Beverley, died after a long illness some years back, leaving him totally devastated, and his bad luck continued thereafter. His adopted son, Frank, was in his thirties then, but unemployed and still living at home, and he was forever in trouble, thieving and brawling. One night he got into a fight at a party near Pembroke and slashed some kid with a Stanley knife. The kid nearly died, and when Frank tried to get his father to alibi him, the old man finally lost it and threw him out. Frank promptly scarpered and I haven't seen nor heard of him since, which is hardly surprising, as there are three different warrants out for his arrest. I'm told he is overseas somewhere.'

He got up to grab the whisky bottle and poured himself another large measure. 'Well, Jack's luck didn't get any better. Shortly after Frank had scarpered — that was around ten years ago now — the old boy suffered a stroke and later finished up in a hospice with the Big C. Then Jane, who had been just about to get married to a local lad, was out for a run on the cliff path, lost her footing and went over the edge. We found her body on the rocks below. Tragic. She was only twenty-two, I believe, and the old man's favourite child. It finished him. A few months later he simply gave up the ghost altogether.'

'And what happened to Melanie?'

He shrugged. 'Moved on, I gather — to London. She came back once to see the old man in the hospice just before he died, and she stayed on after that just to arrange the sale of the house and to wind up his affairs. But as with Frank, no one has seen or heard of her since.'

Kate was tempted to enlighten him on both counts. Pieces of the jigsaw she had been trying for days to assemble were dropping into place at speed. She was ninety-nine per cent sure she knew where Melanie was now, and she was also confident that she could make an educated guess as to the approximate whereabouts of brother Frank. But although she felt guilty about it, she decided not to complicate matters by sharing her thoughts with Roberts, which would have led to further awkward questions.

Instead, she asked, 'This accident of Jane Tannahill's, was there anything suspicious about it?'

His eyes narrowed slightly, as if his suspicions had returned, and he was weighing up the possible implications behind the question. Kate gripped her hands tightly under the table, fearing that he might clam up if he felt she had a hidden agenda and was there to rake up the whole business again, thereby throwing his own past competence into doubt.

'No evidence of anything like that,' he said slowly, a defensive edge to his tone. 'That west coast path can be quite dangerous if you don't look where you're going and though Jane used it regularly for her runs in the morning, it would have been easy for her to have made a mistake and slipped. The path is narrow and often slippery, and it's a long way down from those cliff tops.'

Kate forced what she intended as a reassuring smile. 'There are always accidents on these coastal paths, aren't there? Whereabouts did it happen?'

Her response seemed to satisfy him, and he stood up and pulled his braces up over his shoulders, throwing a glance out of the kitchen window at the same time. 'I'll show you if you like. Be nice to have a ride in that little job you've got out there. I'll just grab a coat.' He stared at her. 'Don't mind gum boots in your car, do you?'

The difficulty wasn't the gum boots. It was Huw Roberts's size, and it took him some manoeuvring to swing his large frame through the door and into the sports seat of the Mazda. Even then, he seemed to spill over it onto the central console. Kate couldn't help wondering how on earth he was going to get out again when they got to where they were going.

Fortunately, he managed quite well on arrival in the deserted National Trust car park, and after some grunting and heaving, he clambered out. Then, adopting a punishing stride, he led her down a rough, pot-holed strip of tarmac before taking to a track across gated fields towards the sea.

The view from the coastal path took Kate's breath away, and she paused for a moment on the steps down to the path in a futile attempt to take it all in at a glance. The green-clad slopes, which she guessed would be ablaze with spring flowers in a few months' time, dropped away from the edge of the path in front of her and a vast expanse of pristine, blue ocean stretched unchecked to the distant horizon, where it merged with mountainous cumulonimbus clouds. A never-ending succession of white-capped breakers swept in a ragged line towards the shore like an ill-disciplined, invading army, disappearing from sight at the foot of the slope and hurling themselves against the hidden rock face with a rumble of frustration. She could taste the salt on the sharp, fresh air, feel the faint tremble of the ground beneath her feet from the onslaught of the waves and for just a moment was transported to another world.

Abruptly, the spell was broken when she heard Roberts call out from several yards away. She started after him, following a narrow, undulating path which wove snake-like around the ragged edge of the cliffs in both directions as far as the eye could see — momentarily disappearing, then re-emerging invitingly further ahead with the guile of a will-o'-the-wisp. Her late father would have loved it here. She could hear his voice in her head, urging her on, as he had on their many walks in the past, with the words, 'Just around the next corner, love — just a bit further on.'

'This is about it,' she heard Roberts say, and he stopped so suddenly that she slammed into him and had to grab his arm to steady herself.

'Careful, girl,' he admonished. 'You'll have us both over the edge.'

Looking past him, Kate could see that the path here was exceptionally narrow, with a barbed wire fence and a row of bushes on one side and a sheer drop to the sea instead of a slope on the other. Peering down, she saw the surf breaking on a pile of rocks far below and shivered.

'We found her body lying down there,' Roberts went on. 'Most of her bones were shattered from the fall and she must have died instantly, which was a blessing at least. The post-mortem found nothing suspicious, and the coroner recorded a verdict of accidental death.'

Kate watched what she thought was a seal surfacing a short distance out to sea and was conscious of the clamour of gulls directly overhead.

For some reason she began to feel light-headed and nauseous, and her legs started to shake. There was a return of the numbness down one side of her face she had experienced after her concussion, and she found herself beginning to sway. The sound of the gulls seemed to magnify, and she heard a strangely distant voice speaking to her. The next instant strong hands had grabbed her arm and pulled her away from the cliff edge.

'Sit here,' Roberts said, pushing her down onto a grassy bank on the inside of the path. 'Glory be, girl, I thought you were going to pitch over the edge there.'

Kate took a deep breath and swallowed hard. 'Sorry. I'm not good with heights and cliff edges. I'm okay now, though, really.'

He looked doubtful, but after waiting a few more minutes while several walkers edged past them, glancing at her curiously, he helped her back on her feet and they returned to the car park at a much slower pace.

By then, she felt steadier but wedging himself into the passenger seat, he turned his head to stare at her. 'I don't think you're very well, love. You okay to drive?'

She nodded, started the engine and pulled away with her usual churn of gravel. 'I'll be fine now. Sorry to be a pain. Tired, that's all.'

'It's more than that,' he said, glancing at her as she drove. 'Going by those scars on your face, you've had quite a bad thing happen to you. I really don't think you should have driven all the way here.' He patted her knee. 'Take my advice, girl. Book in at a hotel for another night, then go home tomorrow.'

'I will,' she said, 'but before I drop you back, can I ask you something else? What happened to Jane's fiancé? You said she was about to get married when she was killed.'

He sighed. 'Aye, Ray Jordan. He lived over at Dale. I had to break the news to him about her death. It hit him hard, and he upped sticks and left Dale a year later. Living in one of them arty communes up in Scotland I hear. He was a landscape artist, see, and quite a good one, they say. That's why he and Jane got on so well. Shy lad if I remember. Never had much to say. Real pity things had to turn out the way they did.'

Moments later they were back outside his cottage, and he was once more levering himself out of the car.

'Thanks for all your help,' she said. 'It was certainly worth the trip.'

He stretched himself with a grin. 'I've left some genuine Pembrokeshire mud for you on your carpet,' he said. 'You should treasure that. It does wonders for my potatoes.' He inclined his head towards the house. 'Coming in for a bite to eat before you go back?'

She shook her head. 'Thanks for the kind offer, but I'd better get moving.'

'Okay,' he said, walking towards the gate. 'Good luck with your murder investigation,' and as she gaped after him, he turned briefly with a chuckle. 'Stalker inquiry!' he said derisively. 'I'm not as green as I'm cabbage looking, you know. I did my own checks, see.' And he added in Welsh, '*Hwyl fawr* — goodbye for now.'

Then he was through the gate, striding up his garden path and laughing his head off.

Parked a little way up the road, Templar watched Kate drive away before following at a discreet distance.

CHAPTER 25

He had nothing personally against the telecommunications engineer. The guy was only doing his job, bothering no one. But his van was just what the dishevelled figure in the camouflage jacket needed. He had spotted the distinctive, marked Transit purely by chance, just half an hour after leaving the barn where he had spent his second night. It was emblazoned with the company's banner and the promise of "ultra-fast broadband", and it was parked in a layby overhung by trees, directly opposite a couple of isolated semi-detached houses. Maybe the engineer lived in one of the houses, as it was only just light and a bit too early in the morning to be out on a call already. But the reason for its presence on the lonely road was irrelevant. It was enough that it was there, for it settled the dilemma that had been plaguing the fugitive for the past two hours — in short, how he was going to get into Scribbler's Halt without arousing the suspicion of the Old Bill, who he was quite sure would be waiting there for him. A spontaneous plan was not always a good plan, he knew that from experience. But it was all he had, and every minute he remained exposed to curious eyes on this flat, boggy marshland he ran the risk of being clocked by a police patrol or the damned helicopter. So, seizing what looked to be the ideal opportunity of lessening that risk, while at the same time achieving what he had set out to do with a minimal chance of detection, was a no-brainer.

With this in mind, he carefully tested the front doors of the Transit and then the pair at the back but found them to be securely locked. Not surprising, really. He could see the twin racks of tools and electrical equipment inside through the rear windows and guessed that the stuff would be worth a pretty packet to a prowling tea leaf.

There was no point in trying to force one of the doors or attempting to gain entry by smashing a window. The doors were certain to have electronic locks and most modern vehicles like this one were fitted with alarms and anti-theft devices. So, he had no choice but to wait for the engineer to open it up for him. His only worry was that the guy might be having a day off, which meant he would be snookered and have to come up with another plan — but chance was the name of the game.

As it turned out, he need not have worried. The driver of the Transit was not on a day off at all, and he only had to crouch among the trees waiting for him to appear for just under twenty minutes before the front door of one of the semis opened and a figure came out. The figure was dressed in a blue uniform and matching baseball cap, carrying what looked like a lunch box under one arm and a bottle of water in the same hand, and he waved at someone back in the house before walking briskly down the garden path to cross the road to the Transit.

The watcher tensed when he saw the four-way flashers on the van briefly activate, indicating that the doors had been opened remotely, then he quickly darted from hiding and wrenched open the passenger door as the driver climbed behind the wheel. The look of astonishment on the driver's face quickly changed to horror when the long-bladed knife was produced, and it was then that it became apparent that the guy was actually a woman in her thirties, with short dark hair and a gold ring in one side of her nose. Not that her sex made any difference to the fugitive, and he pressed the point of the knife against her side.

'Drive!' he ordered harshly.

The woman's face was parchment white now and her brown eyes registered a mixture of shock and sheer terror.

'Please,' she whispered, 'don't . . . don't hurt me.'

'I said drive!' he snarled, 'or I'll cut you here and now.'

The Transit stalled twice as she made to pull away, hyperventilating, her tears running freely. Then, with a couple of jerky motions, they were out on the road and driving away along a straight tarmacked road.

'What do you want?' she whispered. 'You can just take the van if you like. I . . . I don't care, honestly. Just don't hurt me.'

'Shut it!' he said, studying the road ahead. 'Just drive until I tell you to stop.'

She said nothing after that, but drove on, sobbing quietly and throwing the occasional wide-eyed glance at her abductor, as if she was trying to read what was in his mind. Then, two to three miles further on, he spotted an open gate coming up on the opposite side of the road among some more trees and barked out an instruction.

'Turn in there.'

On the other side of the gate a narrow, rutted track cut through the trees, then abruptly petered out in a clearing among stacks of cut logs.

'Turn off the engine,' he said, 'then get out — and if you try and run, I'll use the knife.'

She was in such a state as she climbed out of the vehicle that she tripped and fell over. He was towering over her before she could get up.

'Take off all your clothes,' he said, glancing around him anxiously, 'and make it quick.'

'Please, no,' she sobbed.

'Don't worry, love,' he sneered, 'I'm not going to rape you.'

She complied hesitantly, peeling off her anorak and trousers to stand there shivering in her underclothes.

He kept his eyes on her as he bent down to pick up the garments, then snapped, 'Leave those on,' when she started to unhook her bra. 'I just want your uniform.'

She wiped the tears from her cheeks with the back of her hand, seemingly reassured by his words. 'Are you going to let me go then?' she said. 'I won't tell anyone, honest.'

He treated her to a grim smile. 'Turn around,' he said, 'and stay like that.'

Taking comfort from the instruction, no doubt thinking that he was about to drive away, she did exactly as she was told, and she wasn't aware of him moving up behind her. She didn't expect the powerful arm to suddenly encircle her neck. Her last sight was of the gently stirring trees before her spinal cord was severed by an expert double twist, and then she saw nothing.

He dumped her lifeless body behind one of the wood piles without a single regret, reasoning that a good soldier never left witnesses behind on a sortie if they were capable of scuppering the main operation later. It was likely to be days before her body was found, by which time he should be on the ferry, heading for Ireland.

But he had one problem. The uniform the dead girl was wearing. He'd managed to squeeze his broad torso into her now seriously stretched T-shirt, due to the amount of give it provided, but although her anorak was of a generous size, it had been made for a person of medium size, not someone with his muscular build. As a result, it was much too tight on him, and he was unable to do it up. As for the trousers, they were a non-starter and he had to dump them in the back of the van with the equipment. He would just have to hope any police scrutiny would be restricted to just a glance and that he wouldn't have to get out of the vehicle until he had parked up and entered the house.

His other worries were, first, that Callaghan might not let him in. He had seen her laptop, so he knew she had to have broadband installed, but it could be with another provider. On top of that, she might reject his claim as nonsense and that there was no internet problem in the area. Second, while he didn't think she would recognize him after all this time, especially as he had a full beard now and was a lot heavier than when she had last seen him, she was no fool, and there was just a chance that she might suss who he was before he could get her inside, which would bugger up everything.

Well, he would just have to take a chance on it all and improvise if that became necessary. At least he now had a motor, and he was unlikely to be stopped by the police in one dressed up like this, unless they happened to be looking for that elusive "ultra-fast broadband" promised on the side of it in big green letters.

He laughed out loud as he raided the deceased engineer's lunch box on the seat beside him to see if he fancied anything that was in there.

* * *

Kate didn't hit the motorway as she had intended. For one of the few occasions in her life, she listened to the advice she had been given — this time from big Huw Roberts — and headed back to the hotel where she had stayed the previous night. She wouldn't have admitted it to anyone else, but she was once more feeling slightly nauseous and giddy, and the numbness was creeping back into the left side of her face. She was not fully recovered from her recent ordeal, she realized that now, and she needed a full night's rest before tackling the heavy traffic on the M4.

Fortunately, her old room at the hotel was still vacant and although it was after two, the restaurant was still open, and they were willing to serve her. They would have been happy to serve Templar too, but he couldn't chance her seeing him, so he drove to a nearby pub for a takeout and returned to sit in his car, munching on a pasty, washed down with a can of coke.

The two-course meal of roast beef and Yorkshire pudding, followed by an ice-cream sundae, certainly revived Kate.

She hadn't realized how hungry she was. But what she really needed was a rest and picking up her key from Reception, she unlocked the door and threw herself on the bed with a groan of relief. Then, making herself a coffee from the makings tray, she leaned back against the headboard, turning over in her mind all that she had discovered.

She believed that the jigsaw was now almost complete. Clearly, Tamara Callaghan was the late Jack Tannahill's stepdaughter, Melanie, and she had changed her name, no doubt by deed poll, to her birth mother's name, Jennifer Sykes, and then adopted the pseudonym, Tamara Callaghan. Frank Tannahill — or Sykes, if he had chosen to do the same thing — had to be Callaghan's stalker and the ruthless killer they were hunting.

The million-dollar question hanging over it all was a very big multiple why? Why had Callaghan changed her name to Sykes and then adopted a pseudonym on top of that, apparently to conceal her identity still further? Why was brother Frank — if it was him — pursuing her so relentlessly? What had she done to him and what did he want?

Then there was the question of Jane Tannahill. She had allegedly fallen off a cliff ten years ago while out running. But *had* she fallen or was she pushed? And if her death was murder, what was the motive and who was the culprit? The obvious hypothesis was that Frank was responsible. But that once more brought everything back to that key question, why? And at that moment in time the answer could not have been more elusive.

Finishing her coffee and munching on a couple of Bourbon biscuits from a packet left with the coffee makings, she retrieved her mobile from her bag and stared at it for a moment.

The phone had been turned off since Hayden's flurry of messages on the way to Pembrokeshire, and she winced as she switched it back on and saw the pages of texts from him. Poor old Hayden, he must have been worried to death. She just hoped he had not panicked and passed on his concerns to anyone else — like Percival or Diedre Hennessey, for instance.

Scanning the messages and finding that they were all indignant demands for her to turn around and "come home", she dialled Hayden's private mobile and waited for him to pick up. When he did, a matter of seconds later, his tone was rushed and anxious.

'Kate? Where the devil are you? I've been out of my mind with worry.'

Feeling a complete heel, she sighed and told him.

'Staying another night? Whatever for? Are you all right?'

'I'm fine, Hayd, but I'm a bit tired.'

'Then you stay there tonight, old thing,' he said hastily, his tone changing dramatically. 'Get a good night's sleep and then come home.'

'Any luck with our fugitive yet?' she asked wearily.

'Not in the physical sense, no. As you know, we found the Land Rover burned out in a wood, but he seems to have disappeared off the face of the earth.' He cleared his throat. 'But I have some good news to relate.'

'So have I—'

'Yes, yes,' he cut in and she picked up on the rising excitement in his tone. 'But hear me out first. It's, er, about your cuffs. We've got a result. SOCO found several partial prints as well as some smudged marks on the moulded grip, many of them overlapping. Obviously, some will be yours, which will have to go through the elimination process, and others will probably have been left by your rescuer, Ed Templar, when he released you. But SOCO also found a good thumb print on one cuff, which was different from the rest. We believe it could belong to our killer and that, while your assailant probably wore gloves for much of the time when he was handling the cuffs, hence the smudged marks, maybe he made a mistake or there was a hole in one of the gloves.'

His excitement was practically boiling over now, and she listened expectantly, making no attempt to interrupt.

'Furthermore, although none of the partials have produced any hits, probably because they're not good enough, the thumb print has been run through the PNC database and has come up with a match.'

Kate couldn't resist spoiling his big moment. 'Frank Tannahill?' she said quietly, 'or maybe Sykes.'

His astonished gasp was like a pistol shot. 'Gordon Bennett, but yes. Right on the nail. Frank Tannahill. A CRO with a string of convictions, who is wanted for GBH and is currently on his toes after skipping bail.'

'Last known address Puffins View, Marloes, Pembrokeshire?'

'Good Lord, you must be clairvoyant.'

'No, Hayd, just a good detective,' she replied, tongue in cheek. 'For your information, I've just spent an interesting couple of hours in that very village, talking to the retired local bobby.'

'The devil you have.'

'And he was a mine of information.'

He listened intently to her as she gave him a concise account of all that she had discovered, including her visit to the Pembrokeshire Coastal Path, but omitting any reference to the near-fainting attack she had suffered.

'So, we're on the home straight then?' he exclaimed. 'All we've got to do is to feel Tannahill's collar.'

'A bit more than that,' she said. 'We still don't know what's behind all this business and what Callaghan — as she now calls herself — is hiding. And talking of Callaghan, it would be a good idea to beef up her protection until our man is caught. A bloody PCSO is hardly adequate, and her brother will be desperate by now.'

'Already done,' he said. 'They've got a dog unit at the house now, so there's no need for you to worry. Just get some sleep and we'll see you tomorrow.'

She was conscious of her eyes starting to close involuntarily and she was only vaguely aware of mumbling a similar response to his 'Love you, old thing'. Then the Sandman claimed her as his own.

In the car park, Templar irritably closed his car windows to shut out the cooking smells originating from the adjacent kitchen and gulped the last of his can of coke to wash away the taste of stale pasty.

CHAPTER 26

Tamara Callaghan felt like nothing on earth. She looked at the empty bottle of vodka lying on the floor and fell back against the cushions piled up on the settee behind her, trying not to vomit. The room was spinning, and her head felt about ready to burst.

What the hell was the matter with her? She had always liked a drink — a bit too much really — but she wasn't normally prone to going on binges like this. She vaguely remembered the police coming the day before — or was it the day before that or the day before that? It was, she thought, after she had finished that last bottle, and they had told her something about her stalker being on the loose and likely to pay her a visit. She could see the police helmet bobbing about in the driveway through a chink in the curtains and thought she must have agreed to an officer being stationed outside too, no doubt for her protection. But everything else was a blur of voices, flashing colours and day merging into night and back again.

She formed the impression that Spencer Little had been in the house at one time. Was that before the police came or afterwards? And had he stayed? If so, where was he now? Oh, and the bloody manuscript, had he sneaked a look at it again?

If he had, he would have seen she'd done nothing with it for days. That wouldn't have pleased him. But she couldn't help it. She had lost the incentive to progress it, lost her sense of purpose. But why? The sodding stalker, dear, that's why, she told herself. Something to do with that vengeful arsehole who, despite all her efforts to shake off her original identity and disappear, had finally found her. And now he wanted his pound of flesh, just like old Shylock. Well, he wasn't going to get it. She was made of sterner stuff than he may have thought. And then there was the Glock pistol. It was back under her pillow in the bedroom, all ready for him if he came.

She eased herself up on the edge of the settee and sat there for a moment while the room swam in front of her, and a firework display opened up inside her head. It was quite a while before she was able to drag herself to her feet, but then it was essential because she was on the verge of throwing up.

She got to the downstairs toilet just in time and spent the next half-hour there until her stomach felt as if it had been sucked right up against her backbone, and she was reduced to unproductive retching.

The sound of the front doorbell was the last thing she wanted to hear, and she was tempted to ignore it, but when the ring became more insistent, she dragged herself from the toilet and went to answer it.

Spencer Little looked taken aback. 'Good heavens! You look dreadful.'

Nodding to the uniformed policeman standing a short distance away, she threw the door wide and reluctantly waved him in.

He walked straight past her to the living room as if it was part of a pre-determined plan. She found him bending down to pick up the empty vodka bottle and she held up one hand when she read the look on his face.

'Don't say a thing,' she said wearily. 'I'm not in the mood.'

'Coffee,' he said, 'that's what you need, buckets of it. Why don't you take a shower and get dressed? Then we need to talk.'

She wasn't used to this new authoritative Spencer Little, but she felt too rotten to argue and simply walked away from him in the direction of the stairs. He waited until he heard the pipes begin to hammer, which told him she had taken his advice, then he went straight to the study.

The computer was off, but that didn't deter him. He knew her password and firing up the laptop, he went straight to her word files. His mouth tightened when he saw that nothing had been added to the manuscript since he had last checked it.

'Damn it!' he muttered, scowling. He thought of the email that had been sent to him from her publisher just that morning, querying the continued delay and drawing his attention as her agent to her "contractual obligations", and the substantial advance she had already received.

He was so preoccupied with his thoughts as he headed back to the living room that he didn't hear the doorbell at first and it only dawned on him that there was someone at the front door when there was a sharp double tap on the knocker. Muttering in irritation, he headed back down the hallway and pulled the door open.

A large, bearded man bursting out of a blue uniform-type anorak and baseball cap and carrying a black satchel over one shoulder on a long strap was standing on the doorstep. Little glimpsed a white van parked outside with a green banner on the side advertising broadband.

'Internet problem, mate,' the man said. 'Need to check your modem connections.'

Little hesitated for a moment. After all, this wasn't his house. But then, weighed down with other worries, he shrugged.

'Then you'd better come in,' he said.

* * *

Ted Mullins had worked for the conservation group for around fifteen years and their purchase of the four-acre patch of woodland on the Somerset Levels meant that at least his future was secure for the immediate term, though he was aware that the company was in a bit of financial trouble and his long-term prospects didn't look rosy. Nevertheless, Ted always gave of his best and as an experienced woodsman, he enjoyed doing his bit for the planet, cutting out the conifers and the dead wood, ready for the planting of new deciduous trees.

Parking his van in the clearing he had created over the past few weeks, he climbed out and lit his pipe while he surveyed with pride the neatly stacked piles of logs destined for eventual collection by a local timber company. His old collie dog, Jasper, certainly seemed appreciative too, and the forester chuckled as he watched the dog inspect one pile after another before cocking his leg on each. Then the elderly man frowned.

'What you doin' in there?' he called after the dog disappeared behind one of the log piles and began to bark furiously.

'Found a rat or a dead pheasant, have you, son?' Ted said, walking slowly over to the spot and thinking Jasper might end up with something extra special for his dinner.

But Jasper was destined to be deprived of any such treat, and Ted nearly dropped his pipe when he got to the back of the pile. It wasn't a rat or a pheasant lying there in the undergrowth but a half-naked young woman, and she was just as dead.

* * *

Tamara Callaghan swayed a little as she stepped into the shower, and she had to grab the stainless-steel handrail fixed to the wall to steady herself. She stood there for a good few minutes before turning on the tap, then winced at the first rush of ice-cold water. But within seconds the heat came, and she felt her tense muscles start to relax under the caress of the powerful jets.

She had been a fool, she realized that now. She had everything — a lovely house, a successful writing career and the prospect of even better times ahead, but she had allowed herself to be seduced by the temptations of alcohol and she was on the verge of committing a sort of hara-kiri with her life and throwing everything away. She may have chosen to blame her downward spiral on the stalker, but she knew deep down that it was a lot more than that. His emergence had simply resurrected the guilt that, despite her denials, had been lurking near the surface of her subconscious for a long time. But it was all going to stop. She was determined about that. She was going to bury the past, re-start her novel and give up the alcohol altogether — at least, until she needed another drink.

Turning off the tap, she slid open the cubicle door and reached for the fluffy, white towelling robe hanging on the wall beside it. She had only just slipped it on and started drying herself when she sensed movement behind her and whirled around. Someone was sitting cross-legged on the bed with their head and shoulders resting against the padded headboard, and it wasn't Spencer Little.

'Hello, Sis,' the bearded man said quietly. 'Long time no see, eh?'

* * *

Callaghan said nothing at first but stared at her visitor narrowly for a few tense seconds. Then, conscious of the fact that she had let her robe fall open, she recovered her composure and quickly drew it around herself.

'Hello, Frank. I'm afraid you've picked the wrong time to call.'

'Oh, I don't know,' he said, swinging his legs over the edge of the bed and half turning towards her with one knee bent under him. 'Any time is the right time to drop in and see my beloved sister.'

She frowned as a thought occurred to her. 'Where's my friend Spencer?'

'Oh, the chap downstairs, you mean? Asleep in a cupboard, dear — permanently.'

Callaghan went cold as it dawned on her what her brother had done. But the horrible realization sharpened her mind, clearing away the alcoholic fuzz, and focusing on the Glock pistol hidden under her pillow. If only she could get to it . . .

She dried herself slowly inside her robe as he sat there watching her with a cold smile on his face.

'Where have you been all these years, Frank?' she asked, playing for time. 'I heard you'd left the country.'

'No choice, Sis,' he replied. 'After I chivved that kid with the Stanley knife, I knew I'd go down if it went to court, and when our dear old father refused to alibi me, I decided to skip bail and disappear for a while until everything blew over.'

Callaghan crossed the room to the bedside cabinet on the other side of the bed, picked up a packet of cigarettes lying beside an ornamental vase and shook out a filter-tip.

'So where have you been?' she said again. 'I never heard from you again after you left, following that row with father.'

'All over the place. Dublin, London, Amsterdam, Brussels. Then I met this guy in a backstreet café in Paris and he offered me a military contract and some training in Slovenia. After that, I did a sort of tour. West Africa, Libya, Iraq, Sudan. Finished up in Lebanon.'

'Mercenary,' she breathed, tossing the cigarettes across to him.

He shrugged. 'Well, I had to do something, and killing is what I proved to be good at.'

He selected a cigarette from the packet and moistened the tip as she lit her own with trembling fingers. Then she tossed her silver lighter in his direction. It fell short, just as she had intended. She quickly knelt on the bed as if to throw it again, but instead, thrust a hand beneath the pillow behind him. There was nothing there.

'Looking for this?' he asked and held up the Glock, which was almost buried in his huge hand, his icy smile broadening. 'Loaded too, I see.'

Slipping the gun back in his pocket, he reached for the lighter and lit up, blowing smoke rings at the ceiling before turning right round to face her, while still sitting cross-legged on the bed. 'Do you know, I remember you smuggling that thing in from Belgium when we were younger. To think you kept it all this time.'

He tutted theatrically. 'Wouldn't have been very nice for a sister to use it on her loving brother, though, would it?'

'What do you want, Frank?' she said wearily, sinking onto the edge of the bed opposite him.

His false smile disappeared altogether. 'You know what I want,' he said softly. 'We had a deal, you and me, remember? But you went ahead without me and now I want my cut. Fifty percent I think we agreed before my rapid departure.'

'I've already spent that money. Invested it in this place. There's nothing left.'

He swung away from her, stood up and stretched. Then he strolled slowly around to where she was sitting. Reaching down, he cupped her chin in one big hand and stared into her face.

'That's crap, sweetness, and you know it,' he said softly. 'Dear old Daddy was an art dealer and a thief, remember? So, what happened to all that lovely art he had acquired illicitly and hidden away in his strongroom?'

'I don't have it anymore. It was too hot, so I dumped it in a quarry.'

She cried out as his hand tightened its grip.

'Don't lie to me,' he grated. 'You forget, I know you too well. You wouldn't dump merchandise like that in a hole in the ground. Either you still have it, or, more likely, you fenced it through one of good old Daddy's contacts for a nice slab of dosh. In that case, I very much doubt that you would have risked banking such a large amount because it could have raised awkward questions, so you'll have stashed it away somewhere secure for a rainy day. But either way, I want what you owe me.'

'I've told you, it was too hot to move, so I got rid of it. I earn enough as a novelist now, so I didn't need it.'

He sighed. 'When I slipped in here last time and wrote that poetic piece on your mirror, I had a good look around and guess what? I came across this nice big wall safe in the basement. All you have to do is give me the combination and we'll take a look together.'

'Go to hell,' she said, stubbing her cigarette out in an ashtray.

He twisted her head sharply to one side, so that she cried out. 'The combination, dear sister, or I get really nasty.'

She gritted her teeth against the pain. 'I only have to scream and there'll be police everywhere.'

'Be my guest. Then they'll find out all about the real you, won't they? I don't think you'd like a six by eight cell in Holloway for the rest of your life.'

'I haven't got the stuff anymore, I've told you that.'

He shook his head in mock regret. 'What a pity,' he murmured and suddenly pulling a wad of cloth out of his pocket, he stuffed it into her mouth as a gag and despite her struggles, secured it in place with duct tape wound around her face and neck.

'Then, I'm afraid we'll have to play it the hard way, Sister, dear. Raise your hand when you want me to stop.'

Then he dragged her out of the room and along the corridor into the guest bathroom.

* * *

Kate awoke suddenly. Her mobile was buzzing. Shaking off the lethargy which had overcome her for what seemed from her wristwatch to have been over two hours ago, she hunted for the device among the rumpled bed clothes. She finally found it trapped underneath her pillow. The caller was Hayden.

'Kate,' he shouted excitedly. 'I'm in the Control Room. Thought I'd let you know. A half-naked woman has been found dead with a broken neck in a wood near Meare.'

Kate was wide awake now. 'What?'

'Turns out she was a broadband engineer working for a private company in Taunton.'

Kate hauled herself upright in the bed. 'It's got to be our man,' she exclaimed. 'But why—?'

'Looks like he wanted the company Transit she was driving.'

'Bloody hell, then he's going to use that to try and get past the plods at Scribbler's Halt.'

'He has already. The vehicle drove in there earlier today and the lads thought the driver was a pukka engineer calling to fix Callaghan's broadband.'

Kate groaned. 'And where is the wagon now?'

'They reckon it left about an hour ago.'

There was a heavy pause, and she sensed his reluctance to continue.

'Go on, Hayden, there's more, isn't there? Tell me, man.'

He sighed. 'The troops checked the house as soon as the possible implications behind the engineer's death were realized.'

'And?'

'Callaghan's in intensive care with just a fifty-fifty chance of making it. She was horribly tortured, stabbed and left for dead. Cigarette burns and other knife cuts all over her by the sound of it. They also found Spencer Little's dead body in a broom cupboard in the hall, with his neck broken.'

Kate closed her eyes tightly for a second. 'Good grief. It never ends.'

'And that's still not all.'

'What else could there possibly be?'

'The lads found a big wall safe in the basement of the house.'

'A safe.'

'Yes, with its door left wide open. It looks very much like our man was not there just to kill Callaghan. He also came for something she had locked away in her safe—'

He broke off with a sharp exclamation. 'Wait a minute, info's just coming through . . .' His voice rose several octaves. 'Kate! The Transit was picked up on camera just over half an hour ago joining the M4 westbound.'

Kate felt a shiver run down her spine. 'Hayd,' she breathed, 'he's heading for Pembroke Dock. Don't you see? It was on the Irish ferry coming into the country that that passenger, Tony Cameron, had his bag stolen from, closely followed by his car. The bastard's going to try to get back to Ireland.'

'Well, he won't get far. The Transit is very distinctive apparently — white, with big, green broadband advertisements and slogans all over it. It'll stand out a mile. An alert is being put out as we speak.'

Kate hissed her exasperation. 'Hayd, he's not going to hang onto the bloody thing. He'll dump it first chance he gets. They've got to pull him before he can grab another motor at one of the service areas.'

There was no answer. Hayden seemed to be listening to the police radio broadcast and she could hear the familiar metallic chatter in the background. 'Great!' he suddenly came back to her, obviously relaying what he had heard. 'Not to worry, old girl. They're also sending up the chopper and setting up roadblocks at some place called Pont Abraham at the end of the motorway as well as the roundabout at St Clears on the A477. So, unless he decides to take a diversion across country, they should nail him.'

'That's not enough. They need to have a crew at Pembroke Dock. That's where he'll turn up.'

'I'll pass it on.'

But she could tell he was distracted and not really listening to her. 'I have to be there,' she insisted. 'I know what he looks like.'

There was panic in his tone when he realized what she had said. 'Absolutely not, Kate. You're to leave it to uniform. And you're to come back home now before you do something stupid.'

'Is that what Percival says?'

'No, I'm saying it. I haven't told him or anyone else you're there.'

'Good on you, Hayd,' she said and promptly cut him off.

CHAPTER 27

The news media had got hold of the story. Kate saw that there was a live commentary on the television in Reception as she checked out. She paused a moment to watch it. They were displaying a photograph, superimposed on a corner of the main screen, of what they claimed to be an identical vehicle to the one the killer was driving, and a reporter was standing outside Scribbler's Halt, speaking excitedly into his microphone. Kate caught the drift of what he was saying. '*Murder . . . Home of well-known author . . . Police hunting ruthless killer . . . Stolen Transit believed on M4 Motorway, heading west . . . Public warned not to approach . . .*'

She swore. Bloody press! Public broadcasts were the last thing they needed right now. There was bound to be a radio in the Transit and even if the killer didn't have the news on, there was every chance he would pick it up from a television broadcast in one of the public areas of whichever motorway service station he chose to pull into. Forewarned about the hunt, it was likely that he would take a diversionary route at the first opportunity.

Studying the road atlas in her car a few minutes later, she saw that, although his options would be limited, if he knew the area well enough, as was likely, it was still feasible for him to be able to avoid the two roadblocks that were being set up, depending on where he left the motorway.

Dumping the atlas on the front passenger seat, she roared out of the hotel car park, heading for Pembroke Dock, her excitement shared by Ed Templar who, having heard a similar news flash on his car radio, felt a thrill of anticipation as he went after her.

* * *

Frank Tannahill was cock-a-hoop. He had achieved all he'd set out to do. He had not only "punished" his bitch sister but recovered what was rightfully his. Now, all he had to do was dump the Transit at one of the motorway service areas and nick another car for the last bit of his journey to Pembroke Dock. No one was likely to find the bodies in the house or the dead girl behind the woodpile for a while yet, and by the time they did, he would be in Ireland. Couldn't have worked out better.

His confidence took an abrupt nose-dive, however, when the music on the Transit's radio was interrupted by the news flash. He swerved slightly as he listened to the broadcaster, his eyes widening.

'Shit!' he snarled. They had the description of the vehicle, its registration number and the direction in which it was heading. How the hell could they have got onto him so soon? Now every cop car, every camera, every motorist who had heard the broadcast would be on the lookout for him and there were bound to be roadblocks set up somewhere ahead. He had to get rid of the van, like yesterday.

It was then that he saw the blue-and-white sign telling him Cardiff Gate Services were up ahead and he put his foot down.

He nearly turned the vehicle over as he pulled out onto the roundabout at the top of the motorway exit lane and he forced himself to slow down before taking the appropriate turn-off. There was another, smaller roundabout at the end of the road and the direction sign told him to turn left into the car park, but he ignored it. He had seen the industrial estate on the other side and made straight for it, turning in and pulling up near a block of what looked like offices. Cutting the engine, he quickly stripped off the uniform cap, anorak and uncomfortably tight T-shirt and wrapped them up inside the camouflage jacket, knotting the sleeves together to form a bundle. Then, donning a sweater from his haversack, he forced the bundle into it and quit the vehicle, taking with him both the haversack and a canvas bag containing the contents of his sister's safe.

It was a short walk back across the roundabout to the services, but he felt more than a little conspicuous carrying the two bulky bags and he couldn't wait to get rid of the bundle of clothes at the first opportunity. As with most services, there were trees and bushes enclosing the car park and he walked right towards the end, intending to dump the bundle in a suitable spot behind some of them. But he didn't have to. He spotted the parked and unattended drop-side truck on the way. It was filled with rubble, bits of fencing and twisted wire — obviously from a demolition site of some sort. It was ideal and after a quick look around, he forced the bundle into a large hole in the rubble.

Minutes later, he was walking through the public concourse, with its restaurant and shops, and into the gents toilet at the end. He needed to change his appearance before he did anything else, and certainly well before a visiting police patrol car spotted the abandoned Transit and called in reinforcements to turn the services over.

It was cramped in the cubicle, but with the aid of a small mirror and a large pair of scissors from the toilet bag he carried in his haversack, he managed to trim his beard right down and cut back his long, black hair to the nape of his neck, dropping the lot in the toilet bowl and just leaving it there when it would not flush away.

He felt as if everyone were looking at him as he left the toilet, but a quick glance in a shop window as he walked past satisfied him that he looked okay, and he walked as casually as he could manage back out into the car park.

He needed wheels, and his narrowed gaze studied the lines of parked cars and vans carefully. There was no point in nicking one, as he had originally intended. The crime would be reported to the police as soon as the driver returned and saw the vehicle gone, and that would result in instant circulation, especially in view of the hunt that was now on. Instead, he was looking for a car with a driver who might be happy to have company for a few miles.

He spotted the blue Volvo V40 almost immediately. The driver was already behind the wheel and about to pull away. Tannahill quickly stepped in front of the vehicle, forcing him to brake. His prospective "lift" was an elderly, overweight man, dressed in a fawn anorak and black shirt, and sporting a distinctive white dog-collar. A priest. Brilliant!

He greeted him through the open side window. 'Excuse me, Father, could you possibly give me a lift? Unfortunately, my car's broken down here and I need to get to Pembroke Dock to catch the ferry to Ireland.'

The clergyman looked at him over the top of his rimless spectacles and smiled benignly. 'But of course, my son,' he said in a soft Welsh lilt. 'I'm only going as far as Carmarthen, but you should be able to get a lift to the Dock from there — or you could always take the train.'

Tannahill didn't need any second bidding and dumping his bags on the back seat, climbed into the front beside him.

'This is very good of you,' he said.

'Not at all,' the man of God replied. 'Always pleased to help a fellow traveller.'

He held out his hand. 'Dai's my name, Dai Jones. What's yours?'

'Jim,' Tannahill said, shaking the warm hand. 'Jim Prentice.'

'Glad of your company, Jim,' Dai said. 'It's quite a way to Carmarthen.'

Sadly for Dai, what he didn't know was that he was never going to get there himself.

* * *

The ferry was gone. It had left a couple of hours before. Kate stared towards the empty berth and scowled.

'When's the next one?' she asked the young policeman standing beside her.

'Tomorrow morning, 0245 I believe,' he replied.

She nodded, feeling stupid. She should have checked the times before going into a panic. There was no way Tannahill could have got to Pembroke Dock before her unless he'd flown there. So, he would be looking to board the next available ferry, and she had plenty of time to arrange a nice reception committee for him with the local force.

Then a worrying thought occurred to her. She had assumed he was heading back to Ireland via the Pembroke–Rosslare route, the same way he had come in. But what if he was heading for the ferry port at Fishguard? She hadn't even considered that. Still, there was plenty of time to put out an alert there as well, but first, she needed to make another more important call.

She telephoned Hayden on his personal mobile straightaway, moving away from the policeman when he answered.

'You're *where?*' Hayden exclaimed and groaned. 'I just give up with you.'

'Well, you don't have to worry,' she said. 'Ferry's gone and there's not another one until the early hours of the morning, but I've been thinking. Maybe you should alert security at Fishguard too just in case I've made a booboo and he's heading there instead.'

'*You,* make a booboo?' he echoed with heavy sarcasm. 'That's not possible, is it?'

She ignored the comment. 'I was just ringing to touch base with you. Anything happening where you are?'

'Well, the powers that be know you're up there now,' he said. 'Percival cottoned on after my last call and he nearly blew a gasket.'

Kate smiled faintly. 'Ordered me back, did he?'

'No, he just said something like "that woman is a total liability", and stormed off.' He hesitated. 'Kate, I know you won't listen, but don't overreach yourself up there. If you spot that swine, use the local plods. Don't try and tackle him on your own. You know what happened last time.'

She stared past the young policeman across the empty car park without seeing him. 'It's not something I'll ever forget,' she said and shivered.

* * *

The V40 was quite a natty hatchback to drive, and Tannahill would have liked to have hung onto it. But he knew that was out of the question. At least he had plenty of time to get to Pembroke Dock for the ferry.

He had dumped the good Father in a ditch after killing him. He'd got him to pull off the A48 just beyond Cross Hands, allegedly to "take a leak", then lured him out of his car to look at one of the rear tyres, which he claimed was looking a bit flat. The old boy's neck had snapped like a chicken's, and the ditch beside the lane had been conveniently close to the car. The lane itself was bounded by fields and hedgerows stretching into the distance, so he reckoned the corpse wouldn't be found for a long time. That was provided his luck didn't desert him again, as it had with Sis and the broadband engineer. But at least he was ahead in the game now.

He glanced in the mirror as he drove and smiled. The dog-collar, black T-shirt and anorak the old boy had been wearing were all a bit tight, but not as bad as the woman's kit had been, and he was happy to put up with the slight discomfort. He reckoned he looked quite good as a priest too, especially with the silver crucifix around his neck. Just so long as no one asked him to take their confession.

But he soon had a lot more to worry about than confessions, and the flashing blue lights in the distance as he approached St Clears alerted him to the fact that he wasn't out of the woods yet. Then he saw the blue-and-white police signs on the side of the road, telling him to slow down. Bugger it! A police roadblock. There was a queue of vehicles building up in front of him too. He felt his stomach muscles tighten and he took several deep breaths to calm himself down. He couldn't afford to appear nervous when his turn came.

But he need not have worried. The copper who finally approached his side window just before the junction nodded when he saw the clerical collar, and only gave him a casual glance.

'Could do with you, Father,' he said. 'We need a bit of divine intervention today. Going far?'

'Just to Pembroke, my son.'

'Not hiding anyone in the boot, are you?'

Tannahill felt his heart lurch. He would have a bit of explaining to do if they decided to give his haversack and the bag containing the stuff from his sister's safe the once-over.

'Only the church silver, my son,' he joked, chancing his arm.

The policeman laughed and waved him on. 'Mind you get a good price for it then, Father,' he called after him as he pulled away, 'but don't tell the Pope.'

Tannahill chuckled as he took the Pembroke Dock road off the roundabout, knowing only too well that what he had in the canvas bag was worth a whole lot more than any church silver.

* * *

If there is one thing about Sod's Law, it is its unpredictability. Tannahill found that out the hard way when he finally reached Pembroke Dock on the London Road and pulled out onto the roundabout, intending to head down Western Way towards the ferry terminal. He had planned parking up somewhere discreet, getting a bite to eat and finding out the time of the next ferry to Rosslare. But fate had other ideas.

Jimmy Tallow was twenty-two and blessed with the abandonment of youth and the adolescent conviction that he was indestructible. He had bought the souped-up Subaru, with its extra-wide wheels, twin sports-exhausts and "go-fast" stripes, six months ago off a friend and since then had acquired two speeding tickets and a summons for having no insurance. Egged on now by his red-haired girlfriend, he approached the same roundabout from the opposite direction in Pier Road at a speed that assumed no one else would be entering it from the London Road to cross his path as he screeched round the big circular island to head up Water Street towards the town.

The collision with Tannahill was inevitable. The ironic thing was that, just for once, Tannahill was the innocent party. The Volvo V40 is quite a robust car, but the force of the collision slammed it into the nearside kerb, with the front passenger side of the Subaru partially embedded in its off-side rear wing. Tallow had little recollection of the accident afterwards, as he was unconscious. His girlfriend would not have remembered anything anyway as she was dead, crushed within the buckled steel frame of the car.

Tannahill had smashed his head on the windscreen, despite the seatbelt, and the car's door pillar had crumpled against his right arm, drawing blood, and knocking out all feeling. But self-preservation is a wonderful thing, and he had the presence of mind to force open the driver's door and clamber out onto the road.

A middle-aged man dressed in overalls ran over to him. 'You okay, Father?' he exclaimed, seeing the other's clerical garb.

Tannahill stood a short distance away from the car, swaying unsteadily and staring in an apparent daze at the speaker and then at some other people rushing across the roundabout towards them.

'I think the girl is seriously injured,' someone shouted from the other side of the car.

'Call an ambulance and the police,' someone else joined in.

The word "police" acted like a trigger, cutting through the fuzz in Tannahill's head and hauling him back to reality with a jolt.

'You should talk to the girl, Father,' the man in the overalls said. 'Looks like she's hurt pretty bad.'

But Tannahill hardly heard him. Instead, to the astonishment of the onlookers, he barged him aside and took to his heels, stumbling awkwardly across the roundabout towards a road on the other side. By the time the police and ambulance arrived, he had disappeared behind some buildings and was long gone.

CHAPTER 28

The policeman with Kate received the message on his radio around fifteen minutes after Tannahill's road collision and panicky departure.

'Got to go, skipper,' he said urgently. 'Looks like a nasty RTA at the main roundabout just up the road from here. Could be a fatal. One of the drivers has run off. A bloody priest too.'

'A priest?' she echoed.

'Well, he was dressed like one apparently,' he replied, flinging his car door open and scrambling behind the wheel. 'Just goes to show, doesn't it?'

As he drove away with his strobe lights flashing, she stared after him in astonishment. A man of God crashing a car, then taking to his heels? She had heard everything now. Maybe he'd had too much confessional wine.

But then, as she walked back to her car, something the policeman had said about the priest suddenly shouted out from inside her head: "*Well, he was dressed like one.*" With her hand on the door handle, she froze. Surely not? Tannahill dressed as a cleric? That really took some imagination. But he had masqueraded as a broadband engineer before, hadn't he? So why not a priest? She jumped in her car and sped up the road.

The police and ambulance crews had managed to get the unconscious driver and his deceased passenger out of the wrecked Subaru and into the waiting ambulance when she pulled up close to the scene.

The roundabout had been cordoned off by uniformed police officers and vehicles were being diverted. There were glass and fragments of rubber and torn metal all over the road and a crowd of onlookers lined the nearby pavement.

Kate produced her warrant card and received a quizzical look from a uniformed Traffic sergeant.

'What you doing in this neck of the woods then?' he asked gruffly, plainly having not heard of the surveillance set up at the ferry terminal.

Before she could answer, the constable who had been with her at the terminal appeared at his elbow.

'Here on another job, skipper,' he said, and briefly explained.

The Traffic man grunted. 'And you think this RTA is connected?' he said.

Kate nodded grimly. 'Very possibly our man. He's assumed another ID once before. Any witnesses who may be able to describe him?'

The sergeant nodded towards a parked patrol car. 'Over there, waiting to make a written statement.'

Kate strode across to the police car, and a constable standing talking to a man in overalls glanced up. Kate flashed her warrant card again and at the sergeant's shout the patrol-man stepped back slightly.

'Detective Sergeant Kate Lewis, Mr, er . . .'

'Morgan,' the witness replied promptly. 'Evan Morgan.'

'Did you get a good look at the driver who ran off, Mr Morgan?'

The other nodded vigorously, excitement still burning in his eyes.

'A priest,' he said. 'Dog-collar and everything. Couldn't believe it. He just upped and scarpered.'

'What did he look like?' Kate continued. 'Apart from being a priest.'

Morgan thought a second, then blurted, 'Big guy. Not fat, see, but big — you know, loads of muscle — and about six foot tall, with really ragged, black hair—'

'Ragged?'

'Aye, as if he'd cut it himself,' he qualified. 'Proper mess. I thought it was funny for a priest. Oh, and he had a bit of a beard.'

'A bit of one?'

Morgan shrugged. 'Sort of rough stubble — again, as if he'd just shaved it himself.'

'Anything else?'

Morgan frowned. 'One other thing. He was wearing a smart, fawn coloured anorak with really grubby, blue jeans, which didn't look quite right, and the anorak looked too small for him and all.' He seemed to swell with pride. 'Noticed that, I did.'

Thank the gods for a good, sharp-eyed witness, Kate thought. She was convinced from his description that the man was Tannahill. It was too much of a coincidence to be otherwise.

'Thank you, Mr Morgan,' she said. 'You've been most helpful. Did you see which way he ran off?'

Morgan turned and waved towards the far side of the roundabout.

'Took off across there and vanished up Pier Road. Don't know where he went after that. But for a priest to run off, leaving injured folk like that behind, beggars belief.'

'We've circulated a description of the priest to all patrols,' the sergeant said to her when she returned to him. 'But he could be anywhere by now. Pier Road itself is a dead end, but there are other turn-offs he could have taken and plenty of rough ground where he could hide.'

She grimaced. 'If my guess is right, he won't be wearing the dog-collar anymore,' she said, 'and he'll be looking to nick a car. Anything on the reg of the Volvo he was driving?'

'Belongs to a Rev Dai Jones from Carmarthen, according to PNC.' the constable from the ferry terminal said behind her. 'Not reported as stolen, though, and the key's still in the ignition.'

'Yet . . .' Kate breathed. 'Can I take a look inside?'

The sergeant shrugged. 'Be my guest.'

The driver's door of the car had been left wide open by the ambulance crew, and it didn't take long for Kate to learn what she had already suspected anyway.

The plastic driving licence card had been left in the glove compartment and there were several letters there too, stuffed under the car's manual, all on church matters and addressed to the Rev Dai Jones at an address near Carmarthen.

Kate showed them to the sergeant and young constable. 'The photo on the licence is of a very elderly man with white hair and specs. Hardly a match for the description of the driver your witness just gave. And there's an address here just outside Carmarthen.'

The sergeant nodded. 'We'll get it checked straightaway.'

Kate thanked him. 'I wouldn't be surprised if you found the real Rev Dai Jones lying in a ditch somewhere,' she said, then added with a grimace, 'or maybe even stuffed in the boot.'

'Then we'd better have a look,' the sergeant suggested, leading the way.

The tailgate had been buckled inwards as a result of the collision and the lock was twisted and jammed. But a crowbar from the Traffic car soon solved that problem, and a canvas bag and a haversack were immediately revealed. Heart thumping yet again, Kate carefully unfastened the haversack and tipped the contents out into the boot.

Bundles of clothes fell out, many of the garments rolled up together, seemingly to save space. Trainers, a selection of underclothes, socks, T-shirts, a pair of casual trousers, plus a small, leather bag containing a razor, scissors, flannel and all the other requisites a man's toilet bag would normally hold. There were also a couple of small, plastic bottles of water, some half-eaten sandwiches in a carton, a mobile phone, a compass and a pair of infra-red binoculars.

'Somehow, I hardly think this lot would have belonged to the Rev Jones,' Kate said drily, unzipping an inner compartment and rummaging through it, 'unless, that is, he had a really wild side and was into long-distance hiking or wild camping.'

The next instant she tugged out a passport with a plastic DVLA driving licence tucked inside, both bearing the name James Ryan, but clearly displaying the brutish face of Frank Tannahill. Even as she turned triumphantly to show the documents to her two colleagues, she was interrupted by a sharp exclamation from the constable who had lifted the canvas bag out of the boot.

'And I don't think this was the good Father's either,' he said, 'not unless someone in his parish was feeling particularly generous.'

Staring into the open mouth of the bag, both Kate and the sergeant gaped. It was literally crammed full of paper money, all of it stacked in neat bundles enclosed within thick rubber bands. Recovering from her initial shock, Kate lifted the heavy bag back into the boot and briefly flicked through the bundles of fifty, twenty and ten-pound notes.

'Hell's bells,' she breathed. 'There has to be several thousand here.'

'Several thousand?' the sergeant echoed in a shocked voice. 'More like a million.'

'It's what he must have been after all along,' she reflected, staring past him across the roundabout towards Pier Road. 'This is what this whole business has been about.'

'I wouldn't know anything about that,' the sergeant said with wry humour, 'but it looks like he's lost any chance of early retirement.'

Among the crowd of onlookers, Ed Templar watched the activities of Kate and the uniformed police officers with keen interest while at the same time listening intently to the gossip about the incident from those around him. 'A priest fleeing the scene of a serious accident?' he murmured grimly when he finally returned to his parked car. 'Not like any priest I've ever known.'

* * *

Tannahill was feeling sick and there was constant pain in his right shoulder now. Crouched among some trees inside a broken-down fence, he leaned back against a convenient trunk and carefully undid his shirt, peeling it back with a series of groans. His shoulder was inflamed and already showing signs of bad bruising, and he could hardly move it. Maybe the force of the collision had fractured something or torn a muscle. He could have done with some painkillers, but he had left his tablets, together with everything else, in his haversack, which was still in the boot of the car. What a bloody fool! The "burner" mobile he had bought for emergencies, plus the forged passport and driving licence he had kept solely for use as ID between the UK and Ireland had all been hidden away in that haversack too. Worse still, all the dosh he had lifted from the safe at Scribbler's Halt had been stashed in the canvas bag. The police were bound to find it all when they checked over the car, so he could say goodbye to the lot, without a doubt.

Everything had gone wrong. He'd lost all that he had worked for over the past months — his whole future. He had nothing left now, save what he stood up in, his wallet, and ironically, the Glock 26 pistol he had taken from good old Sis — which would be a fat lot of use in a confrontation with a police unit armed with Heckler and Koch sub-machine guns. Overall, things looked bleak.

Eight murders, including that of his sister and that bloody CID cow, all for nothing, and not even the chance of quitting the country to lick his wounds in his hideaway across the water. There was no way he could risk trying to get to Ireland now with the hunt that would be on for him, particularly in his injured condition, and in a couple of months Brexit would mean he would need another passport not only to get out of the country, but to go anywhere in Europe. He had paid a fortune for the last one as well as the GB driving licence to equip him with the new identity which had been sorted in Paris with the help of the recruiting officer of the mercenary force he had joined. Without that contact he was totally buggered and even if he had still got his mobile and been able to get hold of the guy again, it wouldn't have been advisable anyway, after the way he had had later sold his unit down the river to save his own skin.

He needed time to think and to plan what to do next, but first he needed to shut down the pain in his arm before it drove him crazy. That meant he needed some strong pain-killers, and the best place to get them, apart from a chemist, was a supermarket. He had seen two of them near the roundabout where he'd crashed, but that meant going back perilously close to the scene and in broad daylight, which was too big a risk.

No, he would have to wait until dark, which was not far off now, and slip into one of them when fewer people would be about. He brightened for a second. He might even be able to nick another motor from the car park. Then he swore to himself. Yeah, and how was he going to drive the thing with one arm? The only way he was going to go anywhere now was by hitching a lift, smuggling himself into the back of a lorry or forcing someone to drive him.

Tossing those possibilities around in his mind, he lit his last cigarette, closed his eyes, and waited for dusk.

CHAPTER 29

Hayden sounded as weary as Kate felt when she rang him again to keep him in the picture. But he quickly perked up when he learned about the latest developments.

'A million quid?' he exclaimed. 'No wonder Tannahill was so determined. That's a devil of a lot to play for.'

'I didn't actually count it, Hayd,' she said, 'but it looked to be around that figure.'

'So, where's our retirement nest-egg now?' he queried with a chuckle. 'In your boot?'

'I wish,' she replied. 'But sadly, no. It's on its way in a Traffic car to a safe in a secure police property store. I saw it leave.'

She eased herself into a more comfortable position in the driving seat of the Mazda. It was now dark, and she had chosen to park her car in an end bay of the supermarket car park, away from the pools of light cast by the rows of tall security lights, while she satisfied her hunger with a large pork pie and a can of lemonade. At least this meant she could see the comings and goings of the shoppers without being immediately obvious to anyone herself. She didn't expect Tannahill to suddenly materialize in front of her, especially as it was just a few hundred yards from the scene of the accident, but you

could never be sure about anything. He would be desperate, no doubt hungry and possibly even injured after the collision, so it was as well to be on the alert.

'At least you're safe anyway,' Hayden continued, breaking into the reverie which she had inadvertently drifted into. 'And if, as you just said, you have the passport and driving licence he was going to use, he ain't going nowhere, miss. Which means you can now leave the hunt to the Taffy mob and come home.'

'You know I can't do that. I've stirred up a hornet's nest here and I can't just up sticks and leave — especially when we're so close to nabbing Tannahill. By the way, talking of him, how's our famous crime writer?'

He sniffed, plainly annoyed by her response. 'Holding her own, I gather.'

'Be interesting to find out how she managed to amass the amount of dough we found in the car, if and when she recovers. It was obviously what was in the wall safe at Scribbler's Halt.'

'Well, you said her old man was an art dealer. Maybe it came from the proceeds of art dealings and was left to her when he popped his clogs?'

'That would certainly explain her various visits to Pembrokeshire, yes, but I doubt that he would have left her a million quid in notes. More likely, he had illicitly acquired some valuable pieces which were too hot to disclose under probate — you know what some of these art dealers are like — so she got rid of them through a fence.'

'Cutting poor old Frank out of the deal?'

'Exactly, and she could hardly bank the proceeds, could she? She would have aroused too much interest. Hence the wall safe.'

'No wonder Frank was a trifle miffed when he sneaked back home after all these years expecting to inherit a tidy little sum.'

'Which he has now lost.'

Kate sighed. 'Life can certainly be full of disappointments. Speak to you later.'

She ended the call and carefully unwrapping her pork pie, stared into the lamplit gloom on the other side of the road.

'Where the hell are you, Frank Tannahill?' she murmured, blissfully unaware of the fact that she was very soon going to find out.

* * *

He had got his painkillers, plus a couple of packets of sandwiches and a small bottle of water. He had thought about investing in a half-bottle of whisky too, but common sense had prevailed. He couldn't afford to lose what edge he had left, so he put the bottle back on the supermarket shelf.

The store was practically empty — just half a dozen customers wandering about. He kept out of the way as much as he could, but fancied people were staring at him as he passed them in the aisles. He realized it was his imagination — it was the sort of thing that afflicted every fugitive — but the feeling still bothered him, and he couldn't wait to get out of the place.

But a very real shock awaited him when he got to the checkout. He had never believed in ghosts before, but there was one walking right past the window outside, carrying a plastic bag. He dropped the note he was handing to the assistant and had to bend down to pick it up off the floor.

'Throwing it about today, aren't we, sir?' she joked with a smile.

For a moment he stared at her blankly, then caught on and forced a return smile as she handed him his change.

Outside in the car park his gaze swept the black tarmacked surface, probing in between the rows of parked cars. He could have sworn he had seen the woman. He might be injured, maybe even a bit delirious, but there was no way he could have imagined that. It had been *her* — the interfering cop he had left shut in the car boot at the scrapyard, the one who should have long since gone to the crusher.

Shivering slightly in the cold air, even though he felt strangely hot, he stumbled a few feet across the car park, away from the supermarket's lighted windows, and it was then that he saw her again. She was walking towards a familiar sports car — a dark-coloured Mazda — which was parked in the far corner, facing out towards the exit, and as he stared, he saw the courtesy light briefly illuminate on the driver's side as she climbed in behind the wheel. The bitch had survived! Somehow, she had either managed to free herself from the boot in time or someone else had released her.

For a moment he just stood there, staring at the Mazda with his mouth gaping open like that of a halfwit. Then, conscious of the strange looks he was getting from passers-by, he got a grip on himself and moved off again, heading along the perimeter of the car park in a roundabout route, so that he could approach the Mazda from the rear, on the passenger side.

So, the little cow was still alive, was she? And she had pursued him all this way from Somerset. How she had managed to do it, he had no idea, but he never looked a gift horse in the mouth. He had been desperate to get hold of a car, complete with a driver, and she was the perfect choice. Time to say "hello".

Kate had the can of lemonade tipped to her lips when Tannahill jerked the passenger door open and dropped into the seat beside her. The can flew from her grasp and hit the floor with an explosive hiss, and she found herself staring down the wicked black barrel of a small pistol.

'Hi, occifer,' he said softly. 'Looking for me?'

* * *

It took Kate a few seconds to recover from the initial shock of her quarry's sudden appearance, and her immediate reaction was to freeze in her seat as she stared at him with a mixture of shock and disbelief.

But before she could find the words to say anything, the gun was pressing hard into her cheek. 'Drive,' he ordered, 'and I mean now!'

'Okay, okay,' she replied, sensing the panic in his tone. 'But where to?'

'I'll tell you where. Just go!'

She didn't argue but snatched at the ignition key and sent the car screeching out of the parking bay like a rocket. She nearly hit the dark figure that seemed to deliberately run into her path as she headed for the exit, swerving away from him at the last moment, but she heard his fist slam into her door as she sped away.

'Friend of yours?' Tannahill asked, bending his head slightly to peer into the nearside wing mirror, then turning the interior mirror towards him in an effort to catch sight of the man.

'I don't know who he was,' Kate said, pulling out onto the main road and making a left at his barked instruction. 'But I could have killed him.'

'Tough,' he mocked. 'Keep straight ahead.'

He stared past her out of her window as they drove over the roundabout, glaring almost insanely at the two wrecked cars and the Volvo now being loaded on to a breakdown truck. It didn't take much of a guess to know what he was thinking, and she gritted her teeth as she felt the gun touch her cheek again, quivering unsteadily against her skin.

She took a chance. 'If that thing goes off, we're both dead,' she said, and to her relief, felt his hand relax. Moments later the gun was withdrawn.

'Straight,' he rapped at the next roundabout, 'and follow the London Road.'

Glancing quickly in his direction as they negotiated the roundabout, she realized that he was grasping the gun in his left hand and holding his shoulder in an awkward position.

'You're injured,' she said.

'How very observant of you,' he sneered. 'Yeah, injured and broke, but I'm not done yet, and remember, this pistol may be small, but it is quite capable of blowing your head off.'

'You need a doctor,' she continued.

'I need a lot of things,' he snarled back, 'but advice from a treacherous little bitch like you, I do not. So, just drive while you still can.'

* * *

Ed Templar was furious with himself. He had gone to all the trouble of bugging Kate's car and had managed to keep tabs on her ever since arriving in Pembroke and then, at the most crucial moment, when his days of surveillance had finally paid off with the appearance of Frank Tannahill in the car park, he had missed his chance.

Tiredness had been responsible. He hadn't slept properly for almost thirty-six hours, except in fits and starts, and sitting in his car in the comforting darkness after Kate had gone into the supermarket had been all the inducement he'd needed to close his eyes for "just a couple of minutes".

He had woken with a start around fifteen minutes later, perhaps alerted by some kind of sixth sense, just in time to see the distinctive, heavy-set figure creeping up behind the Mazda. Even then, he had been slow to react, and the killer was in the car before he recovered from his shock.

With the benefit of hindsight, he should have anticipated the immediate departure of the sports car and driven out in front of it to block its exit, but instead, he had run across the car park in a futile bid to get to it before that happened. Kate had nearly knocked him down — not intentionally, he was sure — and he realized the panic she must have been in with Tannahill in the seat beside her calling the shots. But by the time he got back to his own car, the Mazda had turned out onto the main road and disappeared.

In ordinary circumstances his frustration would have boiled over, but not this time. He had an ally — a little magnetic box attached to the underside of the Mazda. As long as that kept sending its GPS signal to the mobile device attached to his dashboard, the map on the screen in front of him would ensure he was as wise to the location of the sports car as those inside it.

* * *

Kate knew her survival was dependent solely on her continued usefulness, and she guessed that the only reason she was still alive was because Tannahill was unable to drive himself. From the quick glances she had cast in his direction, she had seen that he was in pain. He had the Glock pistol in his left hand as opposed to his right, seemingly not because he was left-handed but because he had hurt his right shoulder — probably in the accident — and he was holding it close to his side in an awkward, bent position. His face had an unhealthy pallor to it as well, and he gave frequent spasms of teeth-clenching, despite the number of paracetamol tablets he had taken with his bottle of water. Furthermore, he was perspiring profusely, beads of sweat clearly visible on his forehead in the headlights of oncoming vehicles, suggesting that he was building up a temperature.

The signs were all there, but she read him as a tough, resourceful individual, and she had no doubt he could endure his suffering with a lot more fortitude than most. It would be a big mistake to underestimate him and even thinking of trying to overpower him in a moving vehicle was obviously out of the question. Her only hope was that she could somehow get away from him when they stopped somewhere, but that didn't look to be any time soon.

They had been travelling for around fifteen minutes now, and she had no idea where they were or where they were going. She had simply followed his directions after heading straight over the big roundabout on leaving Pembroke Dock.

'You can't keep running,' she blurted finally, breaking the silence that had prevailed between them since they had left Pembroke Dock behind.

267

'Wanna bet?' he muttered. 'I've been running all my life.'

'But half the police force will be out looking for you.'

'Maybe they are. But don't get any ideas. I'm still with it and although this pistol is only small, it has a 9 mm Parabellum punch and would easily blow your head off.'

'As I said before, if you used it, we would both die,' she retorted with a spark of defiance.

He squashed against her, then pulled back with a grunt of pain. 'Yeah, but I've got nothing to lose, you remember that, whereas the way you squealed last time, I don't think you're ready for the afterlife just yet — which reminds me, how did you manage to escape from that car boot?'

'Someone heard me banging on the lid and got me out.'

Out of the corner of her eye, she saw him bend his head to peer into the external nearside mirror. She'd already seen in her own mirror that there were headlights approaching from behind them, closing fast. Police, she wondered. If it was, what happened then?

'Was that the same someone who just tried to stop you driving out of the car park?' he said.

She shrugged. 'I've no idea who he was. Just some guy who wasn't looking where he was going.'

But despite her words, she suspected that there was a lot more to the incident than that. She had only caught a glimpse of the man in her headlights, but he had certainly seemed familiar. Surely it couldn't be who she thought it was? After all, how would he have known she was going to Pembrokeshire in the first place, let alone manage to follow her all the way here? And what sort of coincidence could have put him in the same car park at the exact moment of her abduction? But if it wasn't Ed Templar, why would a perfect stranger risk his life by deliberately jumping in front of her car to try to stop her driving away?

The headlights that had been coming up fast behind them died. The vehicle, whatever it was, had turned off somewhere. She saw Tannahill adjust the rear-view mirror again to study the back window as he directed them over another roundabout, and she sensed him almost immediately relax. She was both disappointed and relieved — disappointed that it wasn't the police in hot pursuit but relieved that she wasn't about to find herself in the middle of a firefight between an armed police team and a gun-toting psychopath. At least she had some breathing space in which to try to reduce the tension in the car by distracting him.

'Why did you go after your sister?' she said.

She felt him tense. Wrong question? But then he relaxed again.

'So you know we're kin then, do you?' he said, and she felt his eyes boring into her. 'She owed me.'

'How so?'

'Nosy bitch, aren't you? Well, there's no harm in you knowing now. Everything's gone to rat shit. Thing is, we had a deal.'

'A deal?'

'You a parrot or something? Yeah, a deal. See, I never got on with my old man. He was a wheeler-dealer in the art world and thought more about the artefacts he got hold of from his bent contacts than me — or Sis for that matter. Finally, about ten years ago, Sis and I decided to bump him off and make it look like natural causes. We could then get our inheritance a lot earlier than he had planned for and while we were young enough to enjoy it. But there was a hitch. I got into a bit of bother with your lot and the old bastard threw me out, saying he was going to cut me out of his will altogether. That upset the apple cart because I had to skip the country. Even so, Sis promised to stick to our original plan. She would sort everything herself, she said, and make sure I got my fair share of the inheritance after he'd snuffed it, even though he'd named her as sole beneficiary.'

He emitted a hard laugh. 'She did do the job on him too, I found out later. When the old man ended up in a hospice with terminal cancer, she stiffed him on one of her visits by suffocating him with a pillow.'

'She murdered her own father?'

'Well, I couldn't do it, could I? I was out of the country with a warrant on my head, and anyway dear old Dad was a nasty bit of work and deserved it.'

More headlights coming up fast behind after crossing yet another big roundabout, which Tannahill appeared not to have seen yet. Kate tried to keep him talking, just in case.

'And your little sister, Jane, did she deserve to die as well?'

He grunted. 'Had to. For it all to work, she had to be out of the way before the old man changed his will. With Jane dead, it was certain that Melanie would be named as sole beneficiary.'

'Is that why you made a point of pushing her off the cliff?'

He showed no emotion whatsoever at the allegation. 'Nothing to do with me. That was down to Melanie. I had quit the country by then and was enlisting as a mercenary in Paris when Jane snuffed it.'

'You're saying it was Melanie who pushed her off the cliff? That she killed her sister too?'

He grinned. 'Well, it wasn't a bloody mermaid, was it?'

'But you must have known she was going to do it.'

'Maybe I did, maybe I didn't. But who cares? Jane was a silly little cow anyway and the old man's favourite. She would never have agreed to letting me back in on the inheritance and with her out of the way, it was a much more lucrative two-way split between Melanie and me.'

'Except Melanie had a plan of her own, didn't she? She kept the lot and staged a neat disappearance.'

In the headlights of an approaching tanker she threw him a quick sideways glance. His face was contorted into a mask of total malevolence.

'Yeah, but not neat enough,' he retorted. 'She always was a greedy cow, and she must have thought I'd never come back to find her. She obviously didn't know me as well as she thought.'

'And ironically, it was all for nothing, wasn't it? As it turned out, you lost everything you took from her when you had that prang.'

'So, you know all about that as well, do you?'

The headlights she had observed belonged to a BMW, and it raced past them, making him jump. He turned the interior mirror back to face him, so he could study the road behind.

'So you must have found her body then?'

'Except she's not dead,' Kate said.

She felt him stiffen. 'You're lying. I stabbed the bitch then drowned her in her own bath.'

'Not enough apparently. She's in hospital and will soon be singing like a canary.'

'I don't believe you. You're trying to wind me up.'

'Why would I when you hold all the aces?'

He thought about that for a moment and then he swore. 'Evil little bitch. Still, after what I did to her before I stuck her in the bath, she won't like what she sees in the mirror.'

The thought seemed to give him a lift and he emitted a sneering laugh. But his humour soon died when they rounded the next bend and were greeted by the red and blue strobes of two police patrol cars drawn up at an angle across the road directly ahead, blocking the way.

CHAPTER 30

The effect on Tannahill was electric. He dug his pistol into Kate's neck with vicious force. 'Keep going! Run 'em down!'

A fusion of blinding, flashing light threatened to turn their eyes inside out — the white laser-like beams of numerous torches criss-crossing the windscreen of the car, and in the midst of it all, dark-uniformed figures diving out of the way. Then in front of them a minuscule gap between two patrol cars, and they were through and racing off down the road at breakneck speed, while, despite his injured shoulder, Tannahill was whooping in delight.

'Now left!' he shouted maybe a mile further on, and just in time she swung the steering wheel hard over under heavy braking, which seemed to lift one side of the car several inches up off the road before it skated and slithered into a narrow lane overhung by mature trees.

'Go, go, go!' he urged her. 'Put your toe down.'

Her heart doing pirouettes, her hands trembling, she hit the accelerator hard. The Mazda responded immediately, the needle on the speedometer racing up the scale. The car bounced crazily on the pitted tarmacked surface as if it might take off completely, its headlights burrowing into a narrowing tunnel through dense woodland as she tried to keep them from careering off into the hedgerow.

Then the steering wheel was momentarily wrenched from her grip, and they briefly mounted the grass verge and travelled along it for thirty or forty yards before she was able to steer them back onto the road again. 'Where does this lead?' she shouted.

'Just drive,' he snarled back, between cries of pain as he hung on to his seat.

Used to the military way, where everything was planned and every exigency catered for, he seemed to be well out of his comfort zone in this sort of confused, reactionary situation, with no clear objective in mind other than flight. He appeared to be having difficulty handling it — she had heard the panic in his tone — so she made a point of keeping quiet. The tension in the car was rising and the last thing she wanted to do was wind him up still further. But she didn't have to. Circumstances did that for her.

Headlights appeared again behind them and this time a pulsing strobe splashed the gloom with red and blue light as the warbling note of a siren chased down the lane after them.

'They're on to us!' he shouted. 'Left, left, left.'

Kate caught a brief glimpse of a broken fingerpost and then they were heading into another tunnel of overhanging trees, bouncing up and down in even deeper potholes.

The police were still behind them, just visible on the other side of a sharp bend they had just negotiated, the strobe of the patrol car washing ahead of it over the undergrowth in flashes of vibrant colour as the siren screamed its fury.

They came to a crossroads.

'Left again,' he yelled. The road dipped steeply, then climbed to the brow of a hill where it divided into a "Y".

The lights were still behind them and seemed to be gaining ground, though the siren had ceased.

'Left fork,' he shouted, 'and hit the bloody gas!'

After that, a whole labyrinth of narrow lanes opened up before them. The lights continued in pursuit, regardless of which direction they took — until without warning near disaster hit them.

Taking another left in response to Tannahill's yells and powering down a steep hill, Kate felt the little car start to lose traction and before she knew it, she'd lost control of the steering altogether. At once, they went into a four-wheel skid on what was no doubt a carpet of farm slurry, slamming backwards and forwards between steep banks as Tannahill roared in pain.

Then, thankfully, around a hundred yards further on, the wheels bit again, and she was back in control. At the same moment, Tannahill spotted an open gateway, bearing a sign reading, "*Fulton House. Demolition Site. Keep Out.*"

'Left,' he barked, and Kate swerved in through the entrance just in time, clipping a gatepost with a sickening crunch.

A rough track burrowed through more dense woodland. Gravel rattled against the bodywork of the car, and then they were out the other end like a cork exploding from a bottle, emerging in brilliant moonlight.

Directly in front of them, on the far side of a wide, paved hardstanding sprouting a forest of weeds, a ruined mansion reared up, ghost-like, against the night sky. Largely roofless, with nests of tall chimneys at each end, its walls were festooned with creepers and other parasitic growths. Rows of long, narrow windows peered down at them with a cold hostility that carried an underlying sense of despair. The once imposing front entrance, flanked by white stone pillars, was now just a grim, rectangular gash which, to Kate's disordered mind resembled the awful, gaping mouth of Edvard Munch's famous painting, *The Scream*.

It was patently obvious that the property had long since been abandoned, a relic of a once affluent age now just a shell of bricks and mortar, empty of everything save forgotten memories. To emphasize the point, a large sign was fixed to a post by the twin stone entrance columns warning, "*Danger. Unsafe Building. Keep Out.*"

'Don't stop!' Tannahill shouted as Kate started to brake. Panic was still evident in his tone, and his gaze flicked briefly to the rear-view mirror before he pointed to an arched opening on the right-hand side of the building.

'Down there. Park around the back.'

It was a tight squeeze, but Kate managed it and they ended up in a square courtyard formed by what had obviously once been stables, which were attached to the rear wall of the main house in an inverted L-shaped configuration. She switched off the engine and sat, still trembling from the chase, waiting for instructions.

'Give me your mobile,' he said.

She tugged it out of her pocket and handed it to him.

'Is there a torch in here?' he added.

'Glove compartment.'

He found it, tested it, then nodded towards her door.

'Out, and remember, any tricks and I'll put a bloody big hole in you.'

There was a small door to the house a few feet from the car and she waited by it while he got out and stumbled awkwardly round to join her, the gun gripped in his left hand and the torch held just about horizontal in his weakened right. The door had been padlocked, but someone — most likely kids — had been there before them and the hasp was hanging off.

'Inside,' he rapped and pushed the door open.

The room they stepped into had obviously once been some sort of washroom or scullery. A broken Belfast sink, and the brackets for a draining board were clearly visible in the moonlight streaming in through the broken window, but there was very little else. Anything worth taking had long since been stripped out.

They followed the moonlight through a large but equally spartan kitchen into a corridor. Broken glass crunched underfoot and something — no doubt a rat — scurried away ahead of them.

Several doorways materialized to their left, but Tannahill ignored them all and continued on, his pistol pressed hard in her back, until they reached an expansive square hallway with an impressive wooden staircase to their right and the front entrance, minus its door, to their left.

Moonlight poured down the stairs like a river from a gap which had once been a window high up on the first-floor landing, revealing elaborately decorated floor tiles under their feet.

It was evident that he was looking for something specific. He found it a few moments later — a small door in the panelling under the stairs.

'Through there,' he said and nudged her none too gently towards it.

The door accessed what at first looked like a cupboard, but when he turned on the torch, Kate saw a wooden staircase inside, dropping away into blackness.

'You've been here before, haven't you?' she said.

He gave a sneering laugh. 'Dead right, super dick. I dossed here for a bit when I was on the run from your pals ten years ago. I thought the place might have been pulled down by now, but I took a chance. So here we are. Now go for it.'

She turned slightly as she ducked her head to get through the door, wondering, as he was still directing the beam of the torch past her, whether he was holding it in his left hand and had had to pocket his pistol. But she was out of luck. Somehow, he was managing to hold the torch in his right hand, despite his injured shoulder, and the Glock was still firmly grasped in his left.

'Disappointed?' he sneered.

The stairs were shaky all the way down and Kate expected them to give way at any second but they didn't. At the bottom, she found herself in a large oblong room with naked pipes sticking out of the far wall which had no doubt once been connected to a water tank. The place was littered with broken furniture, bits of rolled up carpet and piles of old books, and in the torchlight innumerable shards of broken glass and bits of metal glittered coldly on the rough-brick floor.

The torch also revealed some picks, shovels and a hefty sledgehammer in a corner, together with a couple of paraffin lamps. It seemed that someone was either preparing to do some work in the cellar or had completed stripping out any valuable lead and copper fittings and had not yet retrieved their tools. She wondered if there was a chance that they might return for them soon, but even if they did, it was unlikely to be at night and by tomorrow it could be too late for her.

'See if there's any fuel in those lamps,' he snapped at Kate.

She bent down and shook both of them in turn. 'Seem to be about half full.'

He handed her his lighter. 'Light 'em up.'

She did so after several attempts.

He flashed his torch around the room and trained the beam on a pair of heavy-duty wall brackets, positioned maybe three to four feet apart and some five feet off the ground close to a couple of metal pipes projecting from the wall. The brackets looked as though they may have once supported a boiler or water tank of some description.

'Hang them on those,' he ordered and waited while she strained to reach the brackets and slip the metal hooks of the lamps over them.

He shone the torch slowly around the room, then homed in on a metal bed frame dumped in a corner a few feet away. 'Sit on that,' he directed, adding as she complied, 'Now give me your cuffs.'

'You're out of luck there,' she said almost triumphantly. 'They're still with Forensics.'

'They're what?'

'Yes, and we got a nice thumbprint of yours off them too. That's how we were able to ID you from our database.'

For a moment she thought he was going to hit her, but instead, the torch beam suddenly wavered in his hand and issuing a sharp exclamation, he gripped his injured arm with his gun hand, swaying slightly. It was obvious that his shoulder was not just badly bruised but had suffered a more significant injury. She wondered how much longer he could keep going.

She got her answer even as the thought occurred to her.

'No, I'm not going to fold, if that's what you were thinking,' he grated. 'And if it ever came to that, I'd make sure I put a couple of slugs in you first. Now, take off your shoes and socks.'

'My what?'

'Do it!'

She complied and tossed them over to him, shivering as the cold from the gritty floor bit into the soles of her bare feet.

Carefully placing the Glock pistol and the torch on the floor beside him, he stripped the long laces from the trainers with his left hand, then bent over her. 'Place your hands flat on the edges of the bed frame,' he ordered, and when she did so, he looped a lace around each wrist in turn, then tied it tightly to the metal frame, grunting and hissing at the pain in his injured shoulder.

'That should hold you for a bit while I make a phone call,' he said, and stuffing her socks into one of her trainers, he hurled them both across the room into a pile of rubbish. 'If you do manage to get free, I wouldn't advise walking through all this broken glass and other debris to try and retrieve those, unless you don't mind cutting your feet to pieces — and by the way, there's an open well over there. Be a shame if you fell down it.'

Then he was gone, a thin beam of light disappearing up the stairs to the hall, leaving her alone with just the rats for company. She shuddered at the thought and tried unsuccessfully to draw her legs up onto the bed frame.

* * *

Templar followed the police Traffic car for a couple of miles down the narrow lane. Where they were going he had no idea, but their flashing strobe was beginning to hurt his eyes and the wail of the siren was deafening. He was glad when they went straight on at a minor crossroads, leaving him to turn left to follow the GPS signal. He got a bit too close to Kate's Mazda shortly afterwards and nearly overshot it, but he managed to slow in time when he glimpsed a tail light a hundred yards ahead. He dropped right back then, keeping his speed down. After all, he had no need to keep them in sight when he had the GPS. Because of his caution he didn't suffer Kate's loss of control in the thick patch of slurry.

He did, however, miss the gateway of the ruined mansion and travelled a further two miles before the GPS alerted him to his mistake. It was a further mile or so before he could find somewhere to turn around and then the GPS signal was not precise enough to pinpoint exactly where they had gone. In the end, he had to put his trust in his own instinct to locate it and even then, he initially thought it had played him false when he crept down the track to the house with his lights out and saw no sign of the Mazda.

Only after he had parked up among the trees and cautiously gone forward on foot, following the woodland around to the right to avoid stepping out into the full glare of the moonlight, did he finally find the car, minus its occupants, tucked away at the back of the house. He saw the small half-open door adjacent to the car at the same time and he was just about to investigate further when Tannahill suddenly burst through it.

CHAPTER 31

By rights Tannahill should not have missed seeing Templar. They were just feet apart. But the killer was too preoccupied with the conversation he was holding with someone on the mobile phone, and Templar's reactions were so quick that in a split second he had ducked down out of sight behind the Mazda, sliding a wicked looking 9 mm Walther automatic out of his pocket at the same moment.

It was a golden opportunity. There, just on the other side of the car, was the man he had been pursuing halfway across Europe. He could take him so easily and right the wrongs he had come all this way to redress. Yet he stayed his hand. And it was all because of that damned detective woman, who seemed to make a habit of getting in the way. He had to find her first. She could be injured and in need of urgent medical assistance, and Tannahill was the only one who would know where she was in this great big ruin of a mansion. So, he remained where he was, crouched down behind the wing of the Mazda, listening carefully to what Tannahill was saying.

'Hear me better now? Yeah, I'm outside . . . But don't worry. I'll take care of her when you get here. Then we can torch the car . . . No, I'm not doing it until you get here, just in case you decide to renege on the deal, which would leave me high and dry — I've done my arm in, see, and can't drive the bloody thing — and as for the bitch, I might need her as a hostage if the cops turn up before you . . .' A hard chuckle. 'Don't worry, you won't have to watch. There's a well in the cellar. I'll just put a bullet in her head and dump her body down that. No one will ever find her . . .' There was a long pause as Tannahill evidently listened to some queries from the person at the other end, and when he spoke again, there was naked menace in his tone. 'Listen, mister, you owe me, and this is payback time . . . If you let me down, you know I'll come looking for you, don't you? Okay, good, then I'll expect you within the hour.'

Then there was the sound of the door scraping open and Tannahill was back inside the house.

Very carefully, Templar raised his head and stared at the closed door. So his quarry was also armed, and injured too, it seemed. That was certainly worth knowing, but not really a surprise. As for Kate Lewis, it appeared she was in the cellar, wherever that was. He would have to try to find the entrance somehow. Okay, so he hadn't come all this way to rescue her yet again — he had much bigger fish to fry — but he couldn't just leave her to her fate, and there was no telling when Tannahill would decide to kill her, despite what he had said on the phone. In the end, it was possible he wouldn't wait for his mystery friend to arrive but would do the business as the mood took him.

Plainly, everything was in the balance for the plucky, but recklessly impulsive redhead, so something had to be done fast — and before Tannahill was attended to or she could be hurt in the process. But to achieve that, first she had to be found . . .

* * *

Kate could no longer feel her fingers. Her bonds were so tight that much of the circulation had been cut off and each time she tried to pull her hands free, the laces seemed to tighten still further. Tannahill certainly knew his business.

Her feet were giving her gyp too. She could hardly feel them either, because of the cold, despite wriggling her toes in an effort to restore the circulation. Then there was the inherent dread she shared with most of her sex. Rats. She had heard quite a bit of movement around her in the shadows — creepy shuffling, scampering sounds — and once she felt sure something had brushed against her bare foot, though she'd tried to tell herself it had only been her imagination.

How long she had been trussed up like this she had no idea. It was impossible to even see her wristwatch. She couldn't imagine where Tannahill had gone and why he had felt it necessary to leave her in the cellar just so he could make a phone call on her mobile. It couldn't be because he didn't want her to hear what he had to say, because she was quite sure he intended killing her at the first convenient opportunity. She could only think that he needed to be outside to get a signal.

She hoped that was all, for it had crossed her mind that he might have just dumped her here as a cruel punishment, leaving her to die of thirst and hunger or to provide a mammoth feast for the rats, while he swanned off in another car with some criminal associate he had called up.

In fact, she was proven wrong on that account and in a strange, ironic way she felt relieved when she finally heard footsteps on the stairs and glimpsed the strengthening beam of the torch coming down. When he once more returned to the cellar his body was bent over more noticeably than before, and his right arm was pressed even more tightly into his side as if it were held in an imaginary sling. But her relief that he had at least come back was short-lived when she saw the baleful look on his drawn, pale face.

'Success,' he sneered. 'I've now got someone who owes me a favour coming to pick me up. So, you see, that means I don't need you anymore.'

At the same moment, the Glock pistol reappeared in his hand.

* * *

Kate stared at her captor and the gun he held with as much defiance as she could muster, though her insides were turning to water.

'Seen the well have you?' he said and waved the Glock across the room towards a low circular wall in the opposite corner.

In fact, Kate had already pinpointed the yawning black hole when he had mentioned the danger of falling into it. She had found her gaze constantly wandering back to it with a sort of morbid fascination ever since.

'How deep do you think it is?' he went on.

He moved away from her and bent awkwardly over the wall to peer into the depths. She shuddered. Ever since she had been a child and a woman in her street had fallen down the old well in her garden never to be recovered, she had nursed a secret phobia about these deep, dark excavations. The thought of pitching into one and never being able to get out again had haunted her dreams ever since.

'Would you like to take a look?'

She knew he was deliberately taunting her. While most people suffering from the degree of physical pain he was obviously experiencing would be unlikely to even think about tormenting another human being — they would be too wrapped up in their own misery — it appeared to be this vicious psycho's warped coping mechanism. A case of "feel pain? Then hurt someone else even more."

'Let's check the depth, shall we?'

He picked up a brick from the floor nearby and staring at her briefly, dropped it over the edge, then held a hand up to his ear in a theatrical gesture.

There was nothing for several seconds and then Kate heard a faint splash.

At the same moment she saw him jerk suddenly and clutch at his injured arm with his gun hand, uttering a sharp intake of breath. Then he recovered, straightened a little and turned back towards her.

'No one will ever find you down there,' he gloated, further stimulated by his own injury. 'Though I suspect the rats will.'

He racked the slide of the little automatic. 'What do you think would be best?' he said, trying to smile even though she could see that his jaws were clenched, and perspiration was running down his face in rivulets. 'A head shot or one between those lovely tits of yours?'

Whether he would have pulled the trigger there and then instead of waiting for his lift to arrive first is unclear, but the decision was suddenly taken out of his hands. At that precise moment a loud crash, like breaking glass, from somewhere in the house above dramatically changed the dynamics.

Jerking round and almost overbalancing, Tannahill stood there for several seconds staring at the ceiling, as if trying to see through it into the hallway. He was plainly unnerved and unsure as to how to respond. Finally, snarling a curse, he lumbered across the cellar to the stairs, stopping briefly at the bottom before disappearing into the void above.

Kate was conscious of the fact that she was beginning to hyperventilate, her whole body shaking in irregular spasms as it had after her near-death experience at the scrapyard. She forced herself to calm down, taking deep breaths and trying to concentrate again on her bonds, heedless of the thin laces biting into her now bleeding wrists, in a last-ditch desperate effort to free herself. She had only been granted a temporary stay of execution — Tannahill could be back within minutes, but the laces wouldn't budge, no matter how much she strained and twisted against them.

Above her head she heard the sound of footsteps heading from right to left — towards the cupboard under the main staircase. He was coming back. 'Get out!' an unreasoning voice in her head shouted.

In total panic, she found the strength to wrench even more forcefully at the thin leather strands, moaning and sobbing as the blood dribbled down her hands onto the floor. It felt as if her wrists were on fire, and she felt sure she was on the way to cutting through an artery. But she had to take the risk. Death awaited her anyway.

Then it happened. Part of the lace securing her left wrist must have already been frayed or weakened in some way and the constant rubbing against the rusted bed frame was just too much for it to withstand. All at once it simply snapped.

With a gasp of relief, she turned to the other lace. The knot had been tightened too much from her struggles. She couldn't undo it.

Heavy feet on the creaking risers of the staircase. He was nearly here!

She finally managed to pull the knot partially open, ripping off part of one of her nails in the process. She continued to tug at it. The first strand loosened, then the next. At last, she felt the lace unravelling completely and yanked her hand free. Both her wrists were cut and bleeding and as with the handcuffs before, the circulation surged back with a painful vengeance. She tried to stand up but felt the lamplit room swaying in front of her, forcing her to fall back onto the bedstead.

The warning voice in her head reached fever pitch, screaming futilely, "Run! Hide!"

It was all too late. The shadowy figure was there at the bottom of the staircase and coming straight for her. She shrank back as he towered over her and desperately tried to pull away from the strong hands reaching out to grip her by the shoulders. But then the familiar voice cut through her panic, calling her name as he hauled her roughly to her feet.

'I'm getting fed up with rescuing you!' Ed Templar said hoarsely. 'Now, let's get you out of this place.'

* * *

For a moment Kate simply gaped at the man standing there, gripping one arm to stop her falling back again.

'What the hell are *you* doing here?' she gasped, staring at his face and then at the automatic pistol in his other hand. 'And what are you doing with a . . . a gun?'

'Never mind all that,' he snapped, glancing down at her bare feet. 'Where are your shoes?'

She waved an arm towards the pile of rubbish beside the well. 'He threw them over there.'

With a muffled curse, he pocketed the pistol and darted across the intervening space, producing a torch and probing the pile of discarded sacks, broken furniture and other detritus. His sharp exclamation indicated that he had found her trainers, and the next instant he threw them across to her.

'Never mind the laces, just put them on,' he said. 'And make it snappy. I created a bit of a diversion up there just now with a house brick, but it won't keep him occupied for long.'

Dropping back onto the bedstead, she quickly pulled the trainers on.

'So, who the bloody hell are you?' she asked, grabbing his arm again to pull herself upright.

He grinned. 'Captain Douglas Endersby at your service. Previously Coldstream Guards, lately "Focus Forty."'

'Who?'

'They're a mercenary group.'

'You were a mercenary?' she exclaimed incredulously.

'Yes, and so was Tannahill. Now come on, let's get you to safety.' He pulled his pistol out of his pocket again.

'Too late for that!' The voice came from the stairs.

Kate looked up past Endersby, and her heart sank. Despite his shoulder injury, Tannahill had managed to creep back down the stairs with the stealth of a cat and he was now standing there with the Glock almost buried in one hand but plainly levelled at them.

CHAPTER 32

Endersby, who had had his back to the stairs, froze with a grimace, his grip instinctively tightening on the pistol in his hand.

'Lose the piece, Captain,' Tannahill warned, 'or you both get it.'

Endersby's gaze met Kate's, seeking information, and she flashed him a warning with her eyes. Taking a deep breath, he bent down and laid the Walther carefully on the ground, then turned to face the man he had spent so long hunting.

Tannahill nodded. 'Thank you, Captain. Now, if you'll be so good as to sit there next to her, we can have a little chat.'

Templar complied and the killer advanced towards them and bending down, pocketed Templar's pistol.

'So, to what do I owe this pleasure, Captain?' he sneered, then turned towards Kate. 'Captain Endersby and me, we served together in a mercenary unit in the Middle East, you know,' he said. 'Killed plenty of Arabs too. Great fun.'

'They were terrorists,' Endersby corrected coldly, 'just like you became.'

Tannahill backed away slightly and deposited himself on an upturned crate a few feet away.

'Well, the money was there, Captain,' he said, 'so, why not? Focus Forty were contracted to do some dirty mopping up work for the British Army, but Al-Qaeda paid more, so it was a no-brainer for me.'

Endersby's voice dropped to just above a whisper, one that shook with emotion. 'You sold your own unit down the river. Thirty men under my command, including my brother, all massacred by the scum you allied yourself with. Jock McKitterick and I were the only ones to survive and that was solely because the filth you supplied with information thought we were dead.'

'Is that right, Captain? So, where's old Jock now? I always liked him.'

'He died later from his wounds in a military hospital.'

Tannahill eased himself into a more comfortable position, still with his right hand pressed into his side. At the same moment Kate saw his jaw clench and his injured shoulder seemed to jerk a couple of times as it went into a brief spasm. Endersby seemed not to notice.

'So, you're the only one left then, Captain,' Tannahill continued tightly. 'Apart from me, that is. Which means that when you've gone, no one will ever know what happened in Iraq, will they?'

Endersby studied him with undisguised contempt. 'The people who matter know. The company command had you tried as a traitor *in absentia*, and you were found guilty and sentenced to death. I was assigned to find you and carry out that sentence.'

Tannahill climbed slowly to his feet again. 'So, how do you reckon you're going to do that, Captain?' he said. Before Kate realized what he intended, he shot Endersby twice in the chest, the roar of the gun in the confined space bringing down a mini avalanche of dust and plaster from the ceiling.

When the dust cleared, Kate saw that Endersby had been propelled backwards by the force of the discharge and lay in an inert heap beside the bedstead.

'Good little piece, this,' Tannahill commented with a twisted, humourless grin. 'Stole it from Sis, you know. I don't think it's ever been fired before, just loaded and stuck under her pillow. What a waste.'

Kate couldn't speak. She just stared at him, numbed by the horror of what she had just witnessed.

'Nothing to say for a change, occifer?' he mocked. 'Never mind. Just get him across there to the well.'

She swallowed hard. 'I can't. He's too heavy for me.'

He moved closer, the gun pointing straight at her. 'Then you'd better find some extra muscle, unless you want to join him. So, do it right now.'

Kate was left with no choice. Tannahill held all the aces and as Endersby was already dead, stopping a bullet herself by refusing to comply would have been pointless. Dropping to her knees beside Endersby's body, she managed to turn him over onto his back. Then, slipping her hands under his shoulders, she squatted on her haunches and leaned back slightly, gritting her teeth as she attempted to pull him backwards across the detritus-littered floor. At first nothing happened, except that the cuts on her wrists from the laces opened up again and she felt her head begin to spin from the exertion. Finally, after drawing on a reserve of strength she didn't think she had, she managed to slide him backwards, past the heap of rubbish in the middle of the cellar to a point a couple of feet from the well.

'Bravo,' Tannahill mocked and walked over to her. 'Now heave him up over the edge.'

Kate could smell the foul essence rising from the well even from where she crouched, a poisonous miasma, a dank, cloying stench that reminded her of a newly exhumed grave she had once stood beside.

'No,' she surprised herself by saying. 'I'm not doing that.'

He said nothing for a few seconds, then deliberately raised the pistol to level, his expression bleak.

'Stand up,' he ordered. She climbed slowly to her feet, staring at the gun in his hand with a kind of weary resignation and wondering in a detached sort of way if the shells would plough into her chest or whether it would be a head shot, blowing her brain apart. It was then that she spotted out of the corner of her eye the length of broken chain lying on the floor by the well. It would make a reasonable weapon. Dare she go for it and launch an unexpected attack on him? After all, he was going to kill her anyway. What had she got to lose? She tensed her thigh muscles and dug her toes into the soft inner soles of the trainers, waiting for the right moment.

He came closer and stood a few feet from her to peer over the edge of the well, then abruptly turned to face her, the Glock outstretched in his hand and once more raised.

'I'll count to three,' he said. 'One . . . two . . .'

In one swift movement, she dropped to the floor, snatched up the chain and lashed out at him from a semi-crouched position with every ounce of her being — only to find herself wide of target as he lurched backwards just in time, aiming the gun again.

'Three!' he shouted and pulled the trigger.

An even more deafening explosion than before, more lumps of plaster cascading from the ceiling amid clouds of choking dust, and sharp, needle-like slivers peppering Kate's face and body like hornet stings. Simultaneously, a succession of crazed, agonized screams echoing off the walls of the cellar. For a fraction of a second Kate thought the screams were hers, but it dawned on her that they weren't. The incredible realization hit her that she was still alive. Even though Tannahill had shot her at point-blank range, she was still alive!

Then the dust clouds began to clear, and she saw him again. He was no longer clutching the pistol, and where his gun hand had been was a gory, dripping mess. Part of his lower face seemed to have gone and a single eye glared at her through a bloodied mask, which sent red rivulets streaming down his neck and into his collar.

Transfixed by the horror of it, she watched him blunder blindly into the low wall of the well. He swayed there drunkenly for a couple of seconds, desperately trying to recover his balance, then he lost it altogether and pitched over the edge. His gurgling scream quickly faded away into the depths of the black pit, culminating in a loud splash. For a few seconds after that there was the sound of more frantic splashing, then nothing. Just a heavy, sepulchral silence.

* * *

Kate was hardly aware of anything for a while. Sinking onto a pile of rubble, she sat there, staring at the mouth of the well in a kind of stupor, the multitude of shocks she had experienced over the last few days resulting in an almost complete shutdown of her senses.

She didn't hear the groaning at first and only surfaced from her trance-like state when she caught a glimpse of something moving beside the well. Then, as she climbed slowly to her feet, Captain Endersby grabbed the edge of the wall encircling the well and tried to hoist himself up off the floor. She rushed over to help him. He looked grey and in a lot of pain, and there were two ragged holes in his coat, but to her amazement, no sign of blood.

'How on earth . . . ?' she began, and he emitted a harsh laugh.

'Nine lives,' he said weakly and propped himself on the edge of the wall.

'But he shot you twice,' she said.

He nodded, undid his coat and pulled it open, revealing what looked like a black waistcoat with broad side straps underneath. Kate knew exactly what it was. She had worn similar things herself on police operations.

'A protective vest!' she exclaimed.

He nodded. 'Made from good old Kevlar. These things have saved my life several times in the Middle East and this one certainly did the job tonight.' He made a rueful grimace. 'But it's an old vest and I think one of the shells cracked a rib.'

291

Kate shook her head in disbelief. 'I thought you were dead.'

'So did he, thankfully. I hit my head on the floor when the impact threw me back and I must have knocked myself out. Seems like I missed all the fun.'

He glanced around the room. 'Where the hell is he?'

She nodded towards the well. 'He took a dive.'

She explained what had happened, and he climbed carefully to his feet and went round to the point in front of the well that Kate indicated.

Bending down, he picked up something which he brought back to her. It appeared to be part of the carcass of Tannahill's firearm.

'Squib load, I would think,' he said. 'There'll be other bits everywhere.'

'What did you call it?'

'Squib load. It's a firearm malfunction where a live round gets stuck in the barrel. When the shooter fires another shot, it piles into the round already there — then "kaboom". He must have gone for the usual double tap — or double shot — with you, hence the second round piling into the first.' He frowned. 'It's often caused by poor loading or neglected maintenance and I'm surprised Tannahill allowed that to happen. He was an experienced shooter.'

Kate nodded. 'It wasn't his weapon. He stole it from his sister, and he told me he didn't think it had ever been fired.'

He grunted. 'Yeah, it's what they call a handbag gun, but it's just as lethal as any other automatic. He was lucky to get even the first two shots off at me before it happened. Not so lucky with the second two though.'

'No, but lucky for us.' She glanced at the stairs, adding, 'Until Tannahill's lift turns up and we've got another armed heavy to deal with.'

He shook his head. 'I've a funny feeling he's not going to arrive.'

He didn't either. Instead, just half an hour later when they got back up to the main hallway and Kate's car, they were greeted by a multitude of flashing blue beacons and red and blue strobes as at least half a dozen police cars swept onto the forecourt.

The sergeant who had dealt with the accident at Pembroke Dock was first out of his car and he stopped short when Kate emerged from the arched passageway at the side of the house.

'Thank goodness you're okay,' he exclaimed as several of his colleagues raced into the house through the front door. 'We got an anonymous telephone call from an unregistered mobile telling us the fugitive was here.'

Kate nodded. 'Sounds like his lift had second thoughts.' She turned to Endersby. 'You were right, Captain,' she said. 'The guy never was coming.'

But Endersby was no longer standing behind her. He had disappeared.

The sergeant frowned. 'Captain?'

Kate heard a car start up among the trees on the other side of the hardstanding and gave a tight smile.

'No one,' she said. 'No one at all.'

AFTER THE FACT

The sun was shining when Kate left the sprawling town of Haverfordwest. She had spent the night in the main hospital, where the casualty staff had extracted five tiny pieces of shrapnel embedded in her face and neck from the catastrophic malfunction of Tannahill's pistol and had also expertly cleaned and bandaged the deep cuts on her wrists, one of which was showing signs of infection.

Then it had been a visit to the main police station for a final washup on the case via a conference call between the local crime team and the senior major incident team at the Highbridge incident room. During the joint discussions, Kate learned that while the body of the hapless priest whose car had been involved in the accident at Pembroke Dock had been found in a ditch near Carmarthen, his killer's own remains had still not been recovered from the bottom of the well, due to its depth and the dangerous state of the brickwork of the shaft. It seemed that a protracted operation was likely to be required, and one of the senior police officers attending the scene even hinted that Tannahill's corpse might never be recovered because of the difficulties involved.

There was dramatic news from Highbridge too. Tamara Callaghan, as she had called herself, had failed to recover from the severe injuries inflicted on her by brother Frank and she had died the previous night. True to the crime novelist's craft, it seemed she had kept everything to herself to the bitter end and the final chapter in her life was unlikely ever to be written.

As for Captain Douglas Endersby, it seemed that he had disappeared off the face of the earth, and Kate's one regret was that she had never got to thank him properly for twice saving her life. She said nothing about him to Hayden when she phoned her other half later, however, for fear of winding him up. She was in no mood right then to answer awkward questions about the risks she had faced and the injuries she had suffered, which would have led to yet another lecture on maverick behaviour. So, she kept things as vague as she could, and fortunately that seemed to work.

'You were lucky you weren't hurt in some way,' was all he said. 'Let that be a lesson to you about going off at half-cock.'

She smiled ruefully as she glanced at her bandaged wrists and ran a hand over the scabs that were forming on her already battered face. Did poor old Hayden have a big shock coming when she got home or what? But then, as the proverb from Shakespeare's *A Midsummer Night's Dream* declared, "*The course of true love never runs smooth.*"

* * *

The sun was less bright when she stopped briefly at Pembroke Dock to call at a florist, and then a mobile phone shop, where she purchased a cheap, temporary, replacement mobile. It was rapidly clouding over by the time she left again, this time heading through the narrow lanes to the Marloes for her last visit of the day.

Huw Roberts answered the door of his cottage almost immediately, his rugged face unnaturally pale and a haunted look in his eyes. He nodded in welcome but didn't offer a smile this time, raising his eyebrows when he saw the wreath in her hand.

'Saw you drive up,' he said. 'Going to a funeral then?'

Kate grimaced. 'Not quite, but there's something I wanted to do, and I thought you might like to be with me when I do it.'

'You're going to tell me Jane Tannahill was murdered, aren't you?' he said soberly.

She nodded and told him what she had uncovered.

'Are we going to the coastal path now then?' he said.

'I thought it would be right,' she said. 'A sort of final mark of respect to Jane Tannahill.'

They didn't speak at all on the way, and he seemed busy with his own thoughts. This time she didn't pull into the National Trust car park but drove straight down the lane they had walked along before and parked at the end.

Kate could smell the sea as they opened the gate off the lane and followed the track across the fields and down the steps onto the coastal footpath.

The scene itself was unchanged since their last visit. The white-crested breakers rolling into the shore in never-ending succession and the gulls wheeling directly overhead issuing their harsh, almost hostile cries, as if resenting their presence. There was a sense of permanence here, yet the atmosphere had changed. The sun had now disappeared behind a bank of dark clouds and the air was suddenly cold, with hints of a white sea mist creeping through the undergrowth cloaking the sloping cliffs. It was as if their arrival and what they had come here to do had changed the mood of this wild, primaeval place and the ghosts of the past were watching them with bated breath, waiting for the ritual that needed to be performed.

They made no attempt at conversation as they made their way along the path to the critical point where the cliffs became sheer and the footpath narrowed, then stood staring down at the white foam breaking on the rocks far below, where Jane Tannahill had met her death.

'An innocent young woman with her whole life ahead of her,' Kate murmured suddenly, 'brutally murdered by her own sister simply for gain.'

Roberts didn't answer for a moment, then nodded. 'That day has stayed with me ever since it happened,' he said in just above a whisper. 'It will never leave me. It's indelibly etched on my memory.'

Kate nodded. 'As it should be, Huw,' she said grimly, then turned to look at him. 'Did Melanie pay you well to keep your mouth shut after she pushed Jane off the cliff?'

He didn't deny the accusation, didn't even look back at her, but she could see the same haunted look in his eyes she had noticed before. 'How did you know?'

Kate sighed. 'Call it women's intuition.'

He released a long, trembling breath. 'I had a dog then,' he said, his confession suddenly pouring out, 'and I happened to be off duty and out dog walking on the coastal path when I saw Jane arrive for her usual run. She waved at me as she set off. I was going in the same direction and just as I reached a bend in the path, I heard a woman screaming. A few seconds later a figure in a hoodie and running kit appeared in front of me, coming from the opposite direction. They had their head down but saw me and were obviously startled enough to look up. I recognized Melanie immediately. I thought she was living in London, so I was surprised to see her there. Then I got to this spot and saw Jane's body on the rocks. I knew the sisters had never got on and as Melanie was supposed to be living away and had certainly never shown any inclination to go running, I was suspicious about what she was doing on the path. I thought about it for a while afterwards, then put two and two together and—'

'Put the squeeze on her?'

He nodded. 'Well, there was nothing I could do for Jane. She was already dead—'

'And you saw it as an opportunity?'

He flinched. 'It wasn't like that. Thing was, my divorce that year had cost me plenty and I was already in hock up to the eyeballs — a gambling addiction, which is why my wife left me — so I saw this as a way out of the mess. In a sense, I saw it as punishment for Melanie too, as it hit her hard financially.'

297

'How much?'

'Melanie gave me twenty grand to keep my mouth shut.'

'Covering up one murder and enabling her to commit another when she later killed her father on a visit to the hospice.'

'I knew nothing about that second one — how would I? But I'm not proud of what I did, and it has haunted me for a decade. I have developed a drink problem as a result, trying to erase the memories of it all, but it's always with me, every hour of every day. I can find no peace at any time.'

'Don't expect me to feel sorry for you,' Kate said, the contempt in her tone evident. 'You were a policeman. You took an oath and you betrayed everything you should have stood for — not to mention debasing every aspect of human decency.'

He flinched. 'You don't need to tell me that. I'm under no illusions as to what I have done. The thing is, what are you going to do about it?'

She shrugged. 'Nothing much I can do is there? Despite your confession, it's my word against yours, and as I heard from my own nick this morning that Melanie never recovered from the injuries inflicted on her by Frank and died last night, I have no way of proving anything against you.'

She handed him the wreath. 'All I can do is leave this with you and hope that there is some semblance of human decency left in you to do the right thing by Jane and whatever god you have the gall to worship.'

Then she turned on her heel and left him there. Back in her car, she sat behind the wheel, staring through the windscreen for several minutes, her eyes glazed in thought. She was sorry about Huw Roberts — sorry *about*, not sorry *for* him. She had liked the big, affable ex-copper and it had come as a shock when it dawned on her what he had done. There was no excuse for his actions. He was a disgrace to humanity and the force he had once served. He had stepped over the line and become one of the very criminals he had been appointed to put behind bars. She only hoped he would now have the courage to do the right thing.

Then, abruptly, she surfaced from the dark place into which she had drifted and picked up her new mobile to phone Hayden. She received a recorded message and smiled as she left a short reply.

'On my way home, Hayd,' she said. 'Take the top off a really special bottle of red. I'll need it, believe me.'

Then, turning the car, she drove away without a single glance back.

It wasn't until the following morning that a couple of twitchers on the coastal footpath saw the broken body clutching a wreath in one hand lying at the bottom of the cliff, and the local newspaper later ran the headline: "*Death of Much-Loved Local Policeman In Cliff Accident.*"

In the end, Huw Roberts had done the right thing by everyone.

THE END

ALSO BY DAVID HODGES

DETECTIVE KATE HAMBLIN MYSTERY SERIES
Book 1: MURDER ON THE LEVELS
Book 2: REVENGE ON THE LEVELS
Book 3: FEAR ON THE LEVELS
Book 4: KILLER ON THE LEVELS
Book 5: SECRETS ON THE LEVELS
Book 6: DEATH ON THE LEVELS
Book 7: POISON ON THE LEVELS
Book 8: WITCH FIRE ON THE LEVELS
Book 9: STALKER ON THE LEVELS

Thank you for reading this book.

If you enjoyed it please leave feedback on Amazon or Goodreads, and if there is anything we missed or you have a question about, then please get in touch. We appreciate you choosing our book.

Founded in 2014 in Shoreditch, London, we at Joffe Books pride ourselves on our history of innovative publishing. We were thrilled to be shortlisted for Independent Publisher of the Year at the British Book Awards.

www.joffebooks.com

We're very grateful to eagle-eyed readers who take the time to contact us. Please send any errors you find to corrections@joffebooks.com. We'll get them fixed ASAP.

Printed in Poland
by Amazon Fulfillment
Poland Sp. z o.o., Wrocław

86327587R00183